More than a Spirit

BAKER CITY: HEARTS & HAUNTS 2

JOSIE MALONE

MORE THAN A SPIRIT
Copyright © 2019 by Josie Malone

ISBN: 978-1-68046-855-7

Published by Satin Romance
An Imprint of Melange Books, LLC
White Bear Lake, MN 55110
www.satinromance.com

Published in the United States of America.

Cover Design by Lynsee Lauritsen

CHAPTER ONE

Ann Barrett scooped up the hoof pick she kept in the soap dish whenever she showered. Designed to clean horse hooves, the small steel hook on a poly handle could do serious damage to an attacker's face. Now that she was back home in Washington State, she knew she ought to feel safe, but she didn't. The survival lessons learned during three tours in the Middle East remained with her. She had to stay vigilant if she didn't want to be assaulted at best, raped at worst.

During her first and second combat tours in Iraq, she'd carried a pocketknife everywhere, but things were different when she went to Afghanistan on this last tour. The Command Sergeant Major told the women they couldn't keep their knives in the latrines with them, so the company First Sergeant sent home for an order of hoof picks and taught the female personnel in the battalion how to use them. When they didn't have enough, Ann asked her father who raised Morgan horses to send more.

Pulling off the plastic shower cap, she shook out her shoulder-length brown hair. She wrapped a skimpy brown towel around her, holding it with her left hand while she kept the hoof pick in her right. She headed down the short hall to the main part of the latrine where she'd left the clean set of fatigues.

She froze in the doorway.

A man stood at the sink washing his hands. He stared at *her* in the mirror.

"What are you doing here?" She snugged the towel around her, wishing the material touched her knees or her shoulders, but it didn't. "Who the hell are you?"

"Harry Colter." The dark-haired man finally responded. He swung around to face her. His piercing bright blue gaze locked onto the tops of her breasts. "This is the men's latrine. Are you lost?"

"I know it's the men's room." Ann gripped the hoof pick more tightly. She reminded herself not to allow her temper to take over the confrontation. "I posted a sign."

"Did you really?" His gaze moved onto her legs.

She raked him with a scathing glare. His white shirt emphasized broad shoulders and muscular arms. She told herself that she only looked at the service ribbons and decorations, not the wide chest that tapered down to narrow hips. She lifted her gaze, glimpsed the Ranger tab and parachute decal that signified he'd qualified as one of the Airborne elite.

His dark green dress slacks ended in jump boots. She took a second look at the black epaulets on his shoulders and recognized the three rockers that showed he was a Master Sergeant, outranking her. *Be careful*, she told herself. Even in this situation military courtesy counted and could be held against her.

She lifted her chin and met his amused gaze. She adopted the tone of sweet reason that she used to win with stubborn teens. "I'll say it slowly this time. Get out!"

He shook his head. "I didn't see a sign."

"Then, you must be blind." Ann tossed her head. She always used the men's latrine to shower after her lunchtime run; everybody in her unit did. The Army Reserve base hadn't been in the best of repair before the battalion shipped out on this latest tour to Afghanistan. During the almost two years overseas, the pipes in the women's bathroom burst. The toilets and sinks still worked, but the four showers didn't.

Of course, the request for repairs had to go through a million hoops before maintenance resolved the plumbing issue. As always, it was a case of 'hurry up and wait' in the Army. Probably the unit would be shipped out to another hotspot, the World War Two barracks would collapse while they were gone, and the women's bathroom would still be defunct.

"What's it going to take for you to leave? I want to get dressed."

"It's okay if I'm here. I'm a man. You're not. You go."

"In a towel?" Ann gave an exaggerated gasp of shock. She'd learned how to be a drama queen from the best teachers in the world, high school girls. "You're no gentleman."

He leaned against the sink, quirking a brow. "Don't have to be one. I'm a sergeant, not an officer." A slow smile tugged at his mouth. "Are you acting like a lady?"

Ann glowered. Despite the smart-ass attitude, she felt as if he'd caressed her with that warm sapphire gaze. How ridiculous could she be? Yes, he was the first man to catch her attention in a long time, but she'd absolutely refused to get involved with any of the men at the base in Afghanistan. Even if her husband, Will *had* filed for divorce while she was gone, she still felt married.

She took a deep breath. She wasn't innocent by any stretch of the imagination. She was a thirty-one-year-old divorcee with a six-year-old daughter to support. She checked her towel, shifted the hoof pick to her left hand, then bypassed him to pull open the door, remove her cardboard sign and waved it in front of her where he couldn't ignore it.

"This says W.O.M.E.N. Women! You'd never pass the physical, Colter. Now haul it out of here." In a perverse way, she enjoyed the flirtation too, but she wouldn't admit it. She jerked her head toward the door. "I'm waiting, Sergeant."

He bunched the paper towel in his hand and tossed it into the garbage. Then he started toward her. "What would you do if I kissed you?"

Heat scorched into Ann's cheeks. She gauged the sincerity on his tough-looking features. She'd taken one look at him and felt as if her knees had rapidly turned to mush. She drew in a ragged breath. The last thing she needed was to get emotionally involved with any man. She'd learned that lesson all too well.

"What's wrong?" Harry asked. "The question too hard for you?"

"I figured you had a death wish." When he got closer, she took a step back, wondering if she'd have to use the hoof pick to defend herself. She tensed and lowered her voice. "Back off, Colter. This has gone on long enough. I don't want you to kiss me. I don't want you to touch me. All I want is for you to get out of here so I can get dressed."

He came to a stop in front of her and studied her mouth for a long moment. Then he strode through the open door. "Oh, well. I can wait."

"You'll wait till *hell* freezes over!" What a cliché. She used to be a secondary school teacher, here in the so-called 'real' world. Couldn't she have done better than that? Ann caught her breath when he swung around.

"No, I won't." Harry's smile widened into an easy grin. "I'm going to marry you." He jerked his head toward her stack of clothes. "So, get dressed."

"Are you freakin' nuts?" Ann's voice rose and she struggled to control it. "You don't even know my name."

"It doesn't matter," Harry said. "The last one will be Colter soon enough."

"I wouldn't have you if you were the last man on earth!"

"Yes, you would." Harry chuckled. "But you'd stand in line. It'd be good for that temper of yours." He paused and glanced at the hoof pick in her hand. "I'd have to take a knife away from you, but a gal who can improvise and knows how to use a hoof pick, well that's the kind a man needs to marry."

The door began to swing closed. Without a moment's hesitation, she slammed it behind him and heard the roar of his laughter from the hall. She'd see to it he paid for every wisecrack. To do that meant she had to get dressed, and Ann hurried toward her uniform.

Dropping her towel on the floor, she put the hoof pick next to her uniform. She reached for the yellow silk panties neatly hidden under her fatigue pants. He was a hunk and he certainly knew it. Even now, she could recall the chiseled planes and angles of his handsome features. The harsh line of his jaw and the faint scar on his right cheek, plus the fact that his nose had been broken at one time, all showed he was more than just another pretty face.

Ann put on the matching lacy yellow bra and picked up her desert tan t-shirt which she privately thought of as baby poop brown. Another wave of heat swept into her face as she realized just how much of her body Colter had seen. She pulled on her camouflage pants, buttoning them around her waist, and adjusted the black web belt. The pants were a little baggy, but she knew she'd gain weight now that she was a civilian again, so she'd hold off on buying a smaller size. Why wasn't she more embarrassed about being caught in a towel?

Perhaps Colter's flirtation had been meant to insure just that result. If so, it increased her interest in him. Coming from the small logging town of Baker City, she preferred what she considered real men, the strong, silent ones she had to kick to see if they were still alive.

Leaning against the wall outside the men's latrine, Zeke Garvey whistled softly in admiration. Nobody saw him anymore. Hell, they didn't realize he was still here, not after that I.E.D. took him out six months ago. It'd taken all his energy to remove the sign with its red letters and then replace it. He'd done it to get Colter's attention. Yes, his childhood buddy had returned to Washington State, but he hadn't made a commitment to stay, at least not yet. A woman, the right woman would make a difference and this one had spunk. Colter couldn't leave.

He needed to stay here, so Zeke could watch over his own family. Not for the first time, he wished he could tell Twila what he felt. She'd followed him from Army base to Army base for so long and waited so patiently with their sons every time he shipped out for one more combat tour. All she'd ever asked for was a little girl, but five boys later, he'd failed there too. *I'm so sorry, baby. I'm so sorry.*

Harry scanned the downstairs of the two-story building. The center of the long room was a hallway with clusters of desks and chairs sectioned off in different areas. Portable bulletin boards served as partitions. He frowned and glanced over his shoulder at the main door and the men's latrine on the right side of the entrance.

The sign with its red letters was back in place on the door. The sign he should have noticed when he came back from the Monday morning meeting with the General, but he didn't. The truth sounded weak. He simply hadn't paid attention to the sign. Over the drill weekend the women used the upstairs bathroom, and nobody said there was a problem with the plumbing. So why had he found this gal in the men's latrine?

If he'd known she was showering, he never would have interrupted. Of course, if he'd stayed out of the bathroom, he'd have missed the most enticing sight in the world. She was a beautiful woman especially wearing a towel, so many curves in such a small package.

He noticed the green, brown and black fatigue shirt tossed casually over a chair on the other side of the office and crossed the room. Picking up the camouflage blouse, he noted the limp creases that once were part of a military press job, but no starch. It degraded the anti-infrared qualities of the fabric. His gaze focused on the small black tab fastened to the front of the shirt. His surprise guest was a Sergeant First Class. That made things easier and harder at the same time.

He outranked her by one grade, but she wouldn't be as susceptible to that as a more junior soldier. Privates thought their superiors could see through walls and scale tall buildings as easily as comic-book heroes. He frowned. This woman wouldn't be that gullible, not since she was a manager too. There was nothing like being totally in the wrong to impress a woman, he thought with sudden humor.

Recalling the triumph in her green eyes, the desire to apologize for the mistake died the next time he saw her. Her hair. It was the color of a sunrise, gold, red and bronze waves that nearly touched her breasts. Some of the strands were wet and had clung to her damp skin. He'd proven himself a gentleman and left the bathroom without touching her. That should give him points, but somehow, he doubted it would, not with a woman who didn't hesitate to order him around the first time they met, even when he outranked her.

Combing her hair, Ann wished she could leave it down, but military regulations said that female soldiers needed to keep their hair above the bottom of their shirt collars. She twisted her hair into a loose knot and pinned it into place, allowing a few tendrils to escape. It wasn't as tight as the bun she used overseas, but as the girls in her Senior English class said, there were times when a woman needed to look hot and the presence of a new guy required it.

Questions about Colter raced through her mind. When did he join the company? How old was he? What were his personal details? Surely, he was married. No way was he gay. The only logical reason for him to be in the building was that he was newly assigned to the Army Reserve, her unit in particular. Ann would have to do his paperwork for in-processing, but as an E8, he'd know which questions were too personal. At least, he should know about personnel management to be in this battalion.

She focused on the face reflected in the mirror. High cheekbones didn't make up for the cheery roundness of her features or the dash of freckles sprinkled on a small nose. Her green eyes weren't out of the ordinary either. She was just an average woman.

She straightened her bangs, allowing a few strands to flip over her right eyebrow. This was a Monday. None of her superiors would be in after they'd worked all weekend. Like most of the male sergeants, Harry undoubtedly wouldn't know all the rules about female soldiers, or that the regulations guided how she was supposed to wear her bangs too. Then again if he did, maybe he wouldn't notice or comment on it.

How tall was Colter? He'd towered almost a foot above her own five feet, five inches. She grabbed her dog tags and dropped the chain around her neck. The small metal identification plates immediately drew attention to the curve of her breasts, so she tucked the tags under her shirt.

She took one more look in the mirror, adjusted the camouflage pants so they bloused over her suede combat boots and then headed for the door and the main room.

He stood at her desk and turned at the sound of her footsteps. "Playing detective?" Ann teased with a smile. "Why bother? I'll talk."

Harry didn't hide his own amusement as he laid her shirt across the chair. "Would you tell me everything, Sergeant First Class? Or just what you want me to know?"

Ann inclined her head in mocking salute. "Smarter than you look, Master Sergeant Colter."

"Thanks." Harry headed for the coffee pot. "Would you like something to drink before we get started?"

"That's why I made it," Ann agreed, trying to control her quick sarcasm. However, he caused a nervous reaction she was unaccustomed to feeling. She followed him to the corner of the room where they kept the always brewing coffee.

"I'm curious," Harry said. "Why were you in the men's room?"

"Because the female shower doesn't work. That's why I hung the sign."

"I guess I wasn't paying attention." Harry filled a foam cup with coffee, passed it to her and then poured a cup for himself. "I just walked in. I don't know what I was thinking."

"Is that an apology?" Ann tilted her head, allowing her curiosity to show.

"That's one of the things I don't do." Harry smiled but there was no humor in his eyes. "I'll fix the female latrine though. How's that?"

"Sounds wonderful to me." Ann studied the dark depths of her coffee and tried for a more casual subject. "I should have put a note on the front door. Then you'd have known Margo and I went running at lunchtime. We used to go every day before our units shipped out to the '*box*,' and thought we'd start back up again."

"I wouldn't have seen your note." Harry's smile broadened into a more genuine one. "I came in the back way from the supply room."

"Well, that could cause a problem all right." Ann controlled the urge to giggle. "Have you been in the battalion very long?"

Harry smiled down at her. "A week. It's one reason why I'm so glad the Sergeant Major got me somebody to do word processing. Granted the computers haven't gotten back here yet, but the adjutant at HQ promised we'd have them in a few days. I can set them up, but I'm all thumbs at typing."

Ann stared up at him. *Typing?* The word ricocheted in her head. Her stomach clenched. "Who are you, Colter? What are you doing here?"

"I'm the new company technician."

"What?" Ann almost choked on the question.

When the battalion finally got the word they were coming home, she applied for a job as an Active/Guard Reserve office worker here at Fort Bronson. She'd do paperwork and basically run this company by herself on weekdays. She'd attended a course to update her skills in military payroll instead of training in California with the rest of her unit during the past three months as they transitioned from active duty to civilian life, finally returning to Washington State two weeks ago.

Her head buzzed and it was hard to hear, much less understand what he said as he continued about something. She forced herself to listen.

"We've got a lot of work to do to help the battalion finish the transition from combat to peace time. Sergeant Major said he'd get somebody to handle the paperwork while I catch up supply and the motor pool."

She lifted the cup to her lips, but doubted she'd be able to swallow. The lump of tears in her throat grew. "You've got your work cut out for you, Sergeant."

Harry nodded. "You've got that right. I thought I'd seen sloppy units when I was active duty, but if we get hit with a surprise inspection, the C.O. will be in trouble. That stuff still runs downhill, and HQ won't cut the battalion any slack for only being in Seattle less than a month or morale being in the swirly."

She struggled to control the urge to break down. Her knees shook. She wished Harry would simply talk straight. Had she been passed over for the office job with the unit? Colonel Stewart, the battalion commander said they needed two more full-time people, one to handle supply, weapons, and vehicles, while the other dealt with correspondence, payroll, and filing.

She took a deep breath. After all, Colonel Stewart had said that nobody else could be as motivated or hardworking as she was. He'd practically guaranteed her the new job before she left California for the payroll school back East. She'd flown in last Saturday night, but the CO ordered her to take three days off to reunite with her family.

She relaxed, drank coffee and then asked, "How long were you active duty, Colter? Did you just transfer to the reserves?"

Harry glanced at her, obviously measuring her sincerity. "I got in my twenty, but I'm not ready to retire, so I came here from my last tour. I was in the Rangers most of the time."

"Then you must have seen a lot of combat." Ann frowned at the epaulets on Harry's shoulders. He had a great deal more time in the Army than her fourteen years in the reserve. "How many times have you been in the *Sandbox*?"

Harry frowned at the reference to Iraq and Afghanistan. "Six. Seven, if you include the first Gulf War. How about you?"

"Three." Ann sipped her coffee. "This one was the longest."

"I know your rank, but I don't know your name."

"Ann Barrett."

Taking another sip of her coffee, Ann stared at Harry as the warmth faded from his face. "What is it, Colter? What's wrong?"

He moved to stand between her and the front door. "I suppose the Colonel didn't call you?"

Ann shook her head. "Why?"

Pity seeped into his face, and his voice softened. "Did the Command Sergeant Major?"

"Last week while I was still back east at payroll school. He didn't tell me you were here." Dread trickled into her soul, but she had to make one last ditch try. "The C.O. wants two more full-timers anyway."

"The unit only gets one more full-time technician, Barrett." Harry shook his head, regret on his face. "And that's me."

CHAPTER TWO

Ann felt the blow as if she'd been punched in the stomach. "What?" She struggled to breathe, and then raised her voice above a whisper. "They hired some damned man to take my job?"

"Not your company commander," Harry said, his tone overly patient. "Captain Meade went to the wall for you. She demanded they give her both of us, but the battalion is only entitled to three technicians. They already had two before I got here."

"But the officer cadre promised." Ann's voice faded. Tears stung her eyes, and she struggled to hold them back.

"Your battalion made its recommendation, but the Army Reserve headquarters back in St. Louis chose me to fill the slot."

"Is the lecture on military procedure supposed to make me feel better?" Her rage grew from a small blaze to a forest fire.

"I know you're upset." His voice softened. "There are other jobs. I'm sure you'll get one soon."

"You dumb son-of-a—!" Ann clenched her fist on the cup, acrylic nails biting into the foam container. Coffee splattered all over the tile floor. What a mess! It only added to her fury. "I was promised this job when I found out my civilian employer replaced me and there aren't any full-time openings at my old district. I've got a kid to support. Sure, I have the money I saved while I was overseas, but I wasn't planning to spend it while I looked for work. And all you can say is that there might be other jobs?"

She stormed across the room and grabbed her shirt. "You idiot!" She jerked open the desk drawer and yanked out her purse. "I ought to feed you to the pigs, but it'd probably kill them."

Harry stared at her, then obviously choked back a burst of laughter, but couldn't hide his smile. "Pigs? I didn't know anybody raised them in Seattle." He strode to his own desk and found the request the battalion commander had signed the day before. "This will get you orders for ninety days until the middle of June. The Colonel called in some favors, and we got approval to pay you from today, but he told me you were off till Wednesday."

"Would you like me to tell you what to do with that piece of paper?" When he didn't answer immediately, she headed for the door.

"Come on, Barrett." Harry tried again. "You'll be paid, and this will give you a stop-gap to find another job. While you're here, we can arrange for the Army lawyers to deal with your previous employers. They're required to keep your position open for you or offer you an equivalent one when you return from a war."

Ann planted her fists on her hips. "Look, you stupid Ranger, since I've got to find a job, I'd better start looking right away. If *your* predecessor sat on her buns instead of doing the job, *you've* got a problem. I sure as hell don't!"

Harry leaned against the wall and waited. "Reservists can go on active duty stateside for six months per year which means we can employ you until September, and the Army's new year starts the first of October."

Ann gritted her teeth. He was right and she hated when that happened. It was already the beginning of March and she wouldn't get anything except a few days substitute teaching for the next three months until school got out for the summer. It sounded like she had a possible six months to work and then the new fiscal year began so she could be employed until next spring, but it wasn't what she wanted. She couldn't move off the family farm with a temporary position and her stepmother was already asking when Ann expected to leave.

She tossed her head. "How am I supposed to feed my kid on a promise of a job? You can't guarantee me regular work."

"Maybe your husband could help. He owes you that much."

"My ex-husband just lost another job. He left for a new one in Texas, but it'll be a couple weeks before he has a paycheck." Ann flung the words at Harry, wishing they were bricks. "It'd be great if you went too."

"Then I couldn't have taken your job," Harry agreed. "Cut me some slack, Sergeant. I didn't know you'd applied. There's a shortage of qualified people, and we'll keep you on the payroll till you have another position."

"I don't care." Ann stalked toward the door, pausing as she came closer to him.

Her breath caught in her throat as he leaned forward to touch her shoulder. She jerked away and stepped back. It was as if his fingers had started a fire in her veins, one that promised sensual delights, not one of anger. She lifted her chin. "I'm going to find a full-time job where I won't get jacked around."

"Calm down," Harry said in a soft voice. "I'll take care of you. You've got orders for the next ninety days and we'll have them extended afterwards through the end of the summer. I'll keep you working till a real position comes through."

"I don't need your charity." Ann flashed, trying to keep back her tears.

"Your orders are being cut today." Harry's tone was velvet edged with steel. "You'll be here at seven tomorrow morning."

"No, I won't," Ann spat. "I'm never coming back here, and you can't make me. So put that in your pipe and smoke it."

"You heard me." Harry didn't raise his voice. Instead he lowered it, but the bass rumble sounded even more menacing. "The battalion needs your help and so do I."

Ann put her two little fingers together and made a sawing motion. "Know what this is? A tiny violin playing '*My Heart Bleeds*'. If the battalion needed me, they shouldn't have screwed me."

Harry stepped in front of her. "Now it's my turn to say something."

"Say whatever you please. It won't make any difference."

"How old are you, Ann? You should be able to handle this more maturely."

"I suppose you were a saint at thirty-one," Ann gibed. "How old are you, Colter? Fifty?"

"Thirty-eight." Harry rubbed his jaw ruefully. "I don't know what to tell you, Ann. I know you're disappointed because you didn't get the job. But this is the Army, and most of the time we don't have the opportunity to make our own choices. Nobody made you volunteer."

The sincerity in his low tones brought tears to her eyes. "I hate your guts." Ann choked.

"I got that, Sarge." Harry folded his arms and leaned against the wall. "Why don't you take the rest of the day off? Just be on time in the morning."

"I can't get here at seven-thirty." Ann snapped. Rush hour traffic was terrible, but that wasn't her only problem. She wanted to get her daughter dressed and turned over to her grandparents for the day before driving to work. They delivered Devon to school most of the time and spoiled her rotten afterwards.

What did it matter, Ann thought? She wasn't coming back here! If she was at her parents' house, she'd take care of her daughter.

"Then come in at eight. We have a lot of work to do. You catch up the office stuff, and I'll hit the supply room."

"You really are a macho chauvinist." She wondered what it took to make this man angry. Nothing she said or did seemed to have any effect on Colter. "All of the complaints and problems come over the phone or by e-mail when we have computers. When the battalion headquarters staff comes to visit, Master Sergeant Waller is a total pain in the backside. I'll be stuck dealing with all the hassle while you're hiding in the motor pool or the supply room."

She headed for the door and pushed it open, giving him a backwards glance. "I'm getting those damned orders revoked and finding a new unit."

"You're being rated on your job performance." He didn't move. "You have to be here for me to do that."

"Would you like me to give you something to rate?" Tears burned behind her eyes, but she refused to let them fall. Instead she lifted her chin high. He didn't answer and she nodded in quick satisfaction. "I didn't think so, Colter."

Harry straightened. "Just a moment, Sergeant!" His voice was stern with no empathy in its depths. "Get rid of the camo nail polish. It's against the regs. You know that."

Ann's rage almost choked her. Even if he was right about her nail polish, now was no time to correct her. "Anything else?"

"Either put all of your hair up or else get it cut," Harry ordered. "You can do it tonight or I'll take you to the barbershop. You may have brought the war home with you, but don't bring it to work with you in the morning. My office runs by the book, Sergeant. One fit's enough. Don't push me."

"And you can just kiss it, Colter." She shoved open the door. "It's a total *Charlie Foxtrot*, but it's all yours!"

Slamming out of the building, she ran to her Ford Taurus. Yanking open the driver's door, she fell into the seat, more enraged when tears poured down her cheeks. She ignored them and stabbed the key at the ignition. She'd never been so humiliated in all her life. She'd believed that the orders to attend the Army finance school were just a stop-gap until the battalion received confirmation of her new status.

Why hadn't anybody told her the truth? Ann pondered the question dully but didn't care about the answer. She had to find a safe shelter from this emotional storm. Like an injured animal, she needed to lick her wounds and give them time to heal. She turned the key and waited for the engine to come to life. She twisted the key again. Nothing happened. No sound, no soft mechanical hum.

She pumped the gas pedal and tried once more. A muted click came to her ears. Now what? How would she get home now? And how on earth would she get her car fixed? Leaning her head on the steering wheel, she allowed her emotions full rein, crying, sobbing out all her anguish. The worst day of her life had dwindled into pure misery. She didn't have the money to have the car repaired, regardless of what was wrong with it. Losing this job meant that even making the payment this month to the dealership might not be possible unless she tapped into her emergency fund and she was still waiting for her Army pay. The former unit clerk had left everything in disarray when she quit.

It wasn't as if she had anyone who'd help. She certainly couldn't depend on her ex-husband Will to pick up the financial slack. They weren't married anymore, and he complained nonstop about the amount of child support the judge ordered. They'd stopped talking before her unit shipped out to Afghanistan and she hadn't realized how angry he was about her re-enlisting in the Army Reserve until he divorced her for going to war.

Her stepmother still demanded payment for babysitting Devon while Ann finished her master's in teaching degree. There was no way Ginger would let her father loan Ann money for the car repairs. Her dad had changed the oil, put on new tires and charged up the battery when she called to tell the family she'd be home soon. According to him, the Ford ran like the proverbial song. Ann cried harder. Damn this car. Damn Colter and damn her own stupidity for daring to dream. Every time she tried to make her life better, she made it worse instead. She just wasn't good enough. Through her sobs, she barely heard the car door open.

"What's wrong?" Harry asked. "Is it just the job?"

"My car won't start!"

"Will crying help? If I were you, I'd open the hood and deal with whatever's wrong."

Ann wiped away the last of the tears with the back of her hand. Other than the basics, she didn't know how to repair the car, but she wouldn't tell him that. Instead, she pulled the lever that released the hood latch. "Then get out of my way."

Harry obediently backed up a step. "Come on, Barrett. We don't have all day."

Ann climbed out of the Taurus and stomped toward the front of the car. "Why don't you go back inside and pretend to do your job?"

"I am doing it." Harry followed her. "I'm keeping my subordinate from making a fool of herself."

"Go to hell!" Ann said, fury making her voice shake. "I hate your guts. You stole my job. You're damned lucky I don't do your payroll. I'd see to it you never got paid."

Harry chuckled. "Well, I admire your guts, Barrett. Grown men are afraid to fight with me."

Ann shrugged. "I don't see why." She suddenly realized she told the truth. Colter didn't yell the way Will did, and she couldn't imagine Harry getting drunk and fighting in the alleys or in the bars, despite his words. He seemed to have too much self-control to behave that way.

She stared at the car engine. It looked like one gigantic mess to her.

Why hadn't she studied auto mechanics in school instead of opting for a college degree in education? "What do I fix first?"

Harry lifted one broad shoulder. "If it was my truck, I'd check out the battery. Usually, that's why my rig won't start. The terminals get dirty."

"The whole thing looks pretty dirty to me." Ann muttered.

"Giving up?" Harry drawled. "You don't have to worry your pretty little head about it, Barrett. I'm sure if you go into Battalion Headquarters and cry, Derek Waller will come to your rescue. Of course, he's the same guy who will laugh about it later with the Colonel, or one of the reserve General's full-time staff when they're playing golf on Friday."

Ann drew a deep, ragged breath. She wouldn't swear at him, no matter how much he deserved it. She'd take control of the situation. She knew where the battery was. Will had shown it to her, right after she got the car. "You're making my ex-husband look better and better. He might drink too much and get into too many barroom brawls when he's between jobs, but at least he fixes my car without dumping it on me."

"Then he's a fool. A sergeant must be able to lead the troops. She can't be a wimp."

"I'm not a wimp even if I don't know how to repair a vehicle!" Ann reached out and touched one of the cables that went from the battery to the motor. Nothing happened. She tried a gentle tug on the cable. She gasped when it came loose from the battery. "That's not supposed to happen."

"Nope. I'd bet they've both worked loose. Got a wrench?"

Ann shook her head. "No. I've never needed one. Dad or my ex always took care of the car." She paused and reached in her pocket. "I've got a hoof pick. It usually works when I need a wrench or screwdriver."

This time it didn't. The blunt tip was too thick and there was no way to tighten the nut on the clamp. "Well, that's freaking great." She glanced up at Harry. "Can I borrow a wrench?"

"On one condition." Harry met her gaze evenly. "The unit hasn't done anything wrong, Barrett. You do the payroll for the troops before you leave, and I'll loan you that wrench."

"Okay, it's a deal." She paused. "But I'm fixing this car myself, Colter."

"You got that right," Harry said. "You've got to look out for yourself. Nobody else will." He hesitated, then added. "Just a suggestion, Barrett. This battery looks shot at and half dead. It will probably hold a charge to get you home, but I'd plan on stopping at a tire store and have them replace it before you try driving any distance."

"Well, that doesn't make any sense." Ann studied the battery again. It did look old and she wondered why. She'd bought the used car three years ago and Will kept it in top shape because she not only needed it to drive to the high school where she taught, but also to go to the university four nights a week for graduate studies. "I know Will put in a new battery before the unit shipped out this last time. Could it have worn out while the car sat in the garage?"

"Not likely, Barrett. I'd say you got ripped off. I'd check out the garage. The owner should be able to tell you what happened to your rig."

Ann nodded, but didn't mention the garage had been her father's, not a commercial establishment. She'd bring up the problem when she arrived home. At the present time, she stayed in the guest room at her parents' house, but she planned to change that by the weekend when she checked out some rentals. Her dad said she could stay forever if she wanted, but Ann saw the censure on his wife, her stepmother's face. A week would stretch the bounds of hospitality.

While she processed the payroll over the next three hours, she pondered Harry's accusation that she couldn't look after herself. It didn't make sense. She'd been in control of her life since she was five years old. She had a hard time believing she'd so totally lost control and yelled at the poor man. It wasn't Colter's fault the Army had screwed her.

And it really wasn't her style. Life was often a crapfest and she'd dealt with her share of bull when she was a teacher. Even in the reserves, there was an olive-drab ceiling and although women went to war with men, they were still second-class citizens when it came to promotions and competition for jobs.

Who could have vandalized her car? Will wouldn't take the battery. Stealing from her was beneath him. Ann shuddered. She didn't want to remember the disaster that her marriage turned into, much less her divorce. She didn't want to think about her family.

No matter how hard she tried to win her stepmother's affection, she felt as if she'd treaded in oatmeal. She kept sinking instead of gaining ground. The woman still preferred her son to Ann or her sisters. Maybe if she was a better person. If she quit making mistakes, then her life wouldn't be in the dumpster. Just like the horse in *Animal Farm*, she'd have to try harder.

The sound of footsteps caught her attention and Ann looked at the front door. Instead of Harry Colter, an older man entered the building. Although he wore jeans and a t-shirt, Ann had no trouble recognizing the sandy-haired visitor as the most influential non-com in the battalion.

She took a deep breath, grateful she'd cleaned up after the car repairs. Her hair was neatly confined in the bun she customarily wore, and she'd glued back her bangs with a heavy-duty application of mousse. "Can I help you, Command Sergeant Major Jenkins?"

Relief began to ease the strain written on Jenkins' face. "No thanks, Sergeant Barrett. I hoped to explain the situation in person, but the Colonel told me you wouldn't be in before Wednesday. Colter called and told me you were here now."

Ann reached for her fatigue shirt and pulled it on, trying to maintain control of her emotions. She couldn't allow her feelings to take charge. If she blew it with the Sergeant Major, he'd see to it she never got a full-time job at the base. "What situation?"

"The one that got Sergeant Colter your job," Jenkins said bluntly, eyeing her curiously. "I'm glad you're being so professional about this."

Ann inclined her head in acceptance of the compliment. "Of course, I am. I wish you'd told me when we spoke on the phone last week. I know you and the rest of the cadre must have had some warning. It couldn't have come as a total surprise to you the way it did to me."

A guilty flush edged along Jenkins' cheeks. "We couldn't decide how best to handle the problem. I didn't want to ruin your chances of making top student at the school."

"Well, I made it." Ann stood up and came around to lean against the front of the desk. "Of course, I also made a fool of myself when

Colter told me who he was. I chewed him out thoroughly. I figured he had to be joking because I didn't have any notice."

That should take care of anything that Harry said to the officers or the top non-coms about her meltdown. She'd admitted to losing her temper, but in such a way that she didn't sound like a wimp. Luckily the Command Sergeant Major hadn't come along when she was bawling like a baby. Even if he was married with four daughters, he probably wouldn't understand about women crying when they were angry. He'd view it as some sort of hysterical weakness.

"I hope that doesn't cause problems for you two during the next few months. Colter was the one who told us that we couldn't just cancel your orders. We had to give you enough time to find another job."

"I see. Were you told why I was passed over for the position when I had so many recommendations?"

"He's more qualified. Twenty years active service and Waller going to bat for Colter pretty much guaranteed he'd get whatever slot he wanted here at Fort Bronson." Jenkins shrugged. "You'll be employed soon. It shouldn't take you too long. You have a teaching certificate and your master's degree."

"Yes," Ann agreed. "That and five bucks should get me a beer in Ballard, especially with the economic downturn. Nobody hires teachers at this time of the year." There was also no way that she was going back to teaching in a large city for a living. While she could handle the drugs, the gangs, and the guns, she wasn't about to suck up to the administrators or the department chairs who couldn't find their butts with two hands and a roadmap.

"Don't worry, Sergeant Major. Pop's Café is hiring up in Baker City, and my daughter would love it if I went to work at her favorite restaurant. I appreciate all your efforts on my behalf. I'll find something."

Harry heard the last taunting statement and a heavy frown twisted his mouth. It'd been bad enough when she was fighting with him. *He* could handle it. However, sniping at the Command Sergeant Major was professional suicide. Harry strode around the partitions into the main part of the room. "Did you get that payroll done, Barrett?"

"Almost." She must have seen the annoyance on his face, because she added, "Come on, Colter. There's been a ton of pay problems ever since our last full-time person got pregnant so she wouldn't have to stay in the 'box.' This is a mess and it'll take me almost a week if not more to get everybody paid."

"Almost only counts in hand grenades and horseshoes." Harry poured himself another cup of coffee. "Sergeant Major, I want to show you the gas masks. I had a call from the armory, and they said we're supposed to have a detail laid on for weapons cleaning tomorrow. What's the rotation for that? Have you already arranged for it, or should I?"

"Actually, Sergeant Colter, you do the same thing I always do in this situation." Sergeant Major Jenkins glanced at Ann. "I turn it over to the acting First Shirt for the company. Organize a detail to clean weapons, Barrett. Okay, Colter. Let's go inspect those gas masks."

Harry saw quickly suppressed irritation on Ann's face before she stood and went to a file cabinet. She pulled out a file, returned to her desk and reached for the phone. It looked as if he'd have the help he needed, but the Command Sergeant Major just showed he preferred Ann for the full-time job.

Harry started for the door. He'd figured being stateside in a reserve unit meant he'd be safer and, in less trouble, since he didn't have Zeke Garvey around to watch his back. *I should have known better.*

Man, oh man. What a cluster f- - k, a real Charlie Foxtrot!

Not for the first time since that last patrol six months ago, Zeke wished he was alive. Of course, if he was, he and Colter wouldn't be here. They'd be finishing up their last tour and he'd be going back to his family, ready to put in his retirement papers so they could move home to Baker City and both of them could work here at Fort Bronson with their old buddy, Derek Waller. Zeke longed to tell Ann Barrett that Harry was one of the best guys he knew, except she'd never hear him. Would anyone?

CHAPTER THREE

She left the base at 4:30, but the dashboard clock read 6:30 as she pulled into the farm outside of Baker City. White board fences and green pastures lined the first gravel driveway that wound past the huge indoor riding arena and horse barns to the three-story house where her stepmother and father lived. A second driveway further east led to the modular home Ann and Will rented from her folks shortly after their marriage when the local paper folded, and Will was one of the casualties in the economic disaster, losing his long-time job as a delivery driver.

While she was in Afghanistan, Will moved out of the second house on the farm after filing for divorce. Jack moved in and he was still there. Ann grimaced at the sight of her younger brother's Jeep parked in front of the turn-of-the-19th-century house. Jack would be the center of attention as usual and she should be grateful for the distraction he'd provide his mom and their dad. But she wasn't.

Ann sighed. Yesterday, her stepmother and father had hosted a big party at the family ranch. Her brother came with his current girlfriend and her sisters showed up with their husbands and kids. Then, what seemed like half the town arrived carrying food, beverages, presents and plenty of good wishes.

So did her ex-husband, Will with his latest flavor of the month, a skinny, scrawny blonde bimbo in fashionably ripped jeans and a tight tank top showing she thought bras were unnecessary. Ann had succeeded in keeping her mouth shut and combat boots firmly planted on the floor. She hadn't disgraced herself by kicking him and the slut to the curb, or off the Madison property.

Six-year-old Devon spent all her time playing with the other children and Ann barely saw her daughter except as one of the screaming monkeys that raced all over the yard, corrals and pastures. Escaping to the solitude of historical Fort Bronson this morning felt like paradise after she took Devon to school and her daughter sulked during the thirty-minute drive to Lake Maynard.

The Majestyk Morgan Farm was supposed to be home, but it hadn't seemed like it in a very long time. She felt like a visitor here and not a very welcome one. According to her dad and stepmom, Devon was their princess and it was one more problem Ann needed to resolve. She sighed again. She'd arrived barely in time for dinner and there wasn't time to change out of her fatigues before they ate.

That would mean one of her stepmother's eye-rolling looks. Ann grabbed her purse and headed for the back door. From there, she entered the long, narrow mudroom where she heard the buzz of conversation in the adjoining room. Ginger had insisted on having the kitchen remodeled two years ago, updating it to something that would be more suitable in a newly built structure. Golden brown wood cabinets, light granite countertops as well as a matching center island and smooth stainless-steel appliances had turned the old-fashioned room with its refinished hardwood floor into a gourmet chef's delight.

Ann sighed. Like most horse-people she believed the barns came first and if the house was functional, it would do. She'd preferred it the way it'd been when her own mother had lived in it until she abandoned her husband and three daughters for what she considered a better man and life in New York City.

However, Ann knew better than to express that opinion. Strolling into the kitchen, she forced a smile. "Hi there."

"You're just in time." Her stepmother, Ginger Madison carried a plate of fried chicken over to the table. At 57, she was still slender in ironed jeans, a crisp western blouse and laced-up cowgirl boots. Her blonde hair came from the bottle now and didn't dare show a hint of gray. She pasted on a professionally friendly smile that didn't touch her hazel eyes. "How was your day, Angelique?"

"Interesting." Ann didn't bother to correct her stepmother. After twenty-six plus years, it wouldn't do any good to remind the woman that her name was Angelica, not Angelique. She glanced around the kitchen but didn't see her daughter yet. She smiled at her father. Frank Madison was in his mid-sixties but didn't look it. Like his wife he wore blue jeans and cowboy boots. His green checked shirt with the pearl snaps was fresh from the closet and he must have shaved when he cleaned up after working on the farm all day. "Where's Devon?"

"Getting cleaned up for dinner," Ginger said. "It's just leftovers from yesterday's party, so you have time to change if you like."

"I'm fine and I don't want to keep you waiting for me."

"Oh, we wouldn't, Sis. When Mom puts a meal on the table, everyone knows to show up or go hungry." In a flannel shirt, hacked-off, ankle-length jeans and thick wool socks, Jack, tall and muscled from years of logging waved at her. Undoubtedly, he'd left his corked boots with their spiked soles on the porch. Of course, even if he wore them inside on the hardwood floors, Ginger wouldn't correct her baby. He pulled out his chair at the table and sat down. He had sunshine gold hair like his mother, but his eyes were spring green like their dad's and Ann's. "Did you kick butt and take names today?"

"Always," Ann said, feeling a genuine smile come to life. Jack might still be a pest at twenty-four going on sixteen, but he could charm a saint. "What about you? Clear a forest?"

"Nope, it was my day off." He laughed and shook his head. "I came to help Dad and Bob with their new fence line and make a few extra bucks."

Meanwhile, their father forked baked potatoes out of the oven. He grinned over his shoulder at her. "Bob and I got two rolls of fence wire up on the boundary line. Your mom and Devon worked on the garden after school."

"Terrific." The idea of her daughter helping with work instead of watching TV in the afternoon was a definite pleaser. Ann heard footsteps and turned to see the little girl come from the bathroom down the hall. She looked so sweet in her t-shirt and jeans, but the hazel eyes held a sparkle of mischief. "All washed up?" Ann asked.

Devon nodded and chewed on the end of the long braid of her black curly hair. "I thought you'd be late."

Her daughter had finally taken the first step toward a connection. Joy washed through Ann. "Rush hour can be a pain with all the traffic," she agreed, "but I'm glad to be here." She glanced at Ginger. "How can I help?"

"Grab some of the salads from the fridge. Would you get the stuff for the baked spuds too?"

"Sure." Ann opened the refrigerator and carried over a bowl of coleslaw to the table.

Jack poured soda into his glass and filled a tumbler for Devon.

"What's this?" Ann demanded, trying to keep a civil tone. "*Coca-Cola* with dinner? I don't think so. Milk."

"No way!" Devon wrinkled her nose in disgust. "Milk's for babies and I don't like it. I'm not drinking it."

"Come on, Sis. It's no big deal. Let her have what she wants."

"No big deal?" Ann put the bowl of salad on the table and picked up the glass in front of Devon's plate. "Kind of like taking the battery out of my car, Jack?" It was a guess, but by the sudden flash of guilt in his green eyes, she knew she'd scored the truth. "Why did you take it?"

"Oh, come on, Annie. My battery was going out and I thought I'd just borrow yours for a while. How was I supposed to know that you'd be driving your car?"

"Gee, how about the fact that I have a job in Seattle and needed a way to get there?" Ann took the cola over to the counter, then opened the cupboard and took out a fresh glass. "Or that the battery was mine, not yours."

"Could we please have peace at dinner time?" Ginger demanded. "There's no reason to argue."

Ann counted silently to ten while she filled the glass with milk and put it at her daughter's place. Devon scowled at her as she stomped over and sat at the table. So, they were on the outs again, Ann thought, but she wouldn't let the child ruin her health with too much junk food or soda.

Returning to the fridge she pulled out more salads—three-bean, jello, ambrosia, and fresh fruit. Her dad helped her carry the bowls to the table. Once the salads were on the table, he sauntered to the counter. He passed her the glass of Coke that she'd taken away from Devon and she smelled the whisky he'd added to it. "Strictly medicinal." He winked at her and gave her a quick hug. "I'll help you change out the batteries after we eat. Jack, buy yourself a new battery and quit helping yourself to your sister's stuff. You're too old to act that way."

"Batteries are expensive, and I don't get paid for another two weeks," Jack complained. "Do you have one I can borrow, Dad?"

"Not now. Not after what you did to Ann. Her rig could have broken down in Seattle and left her stranded."

"It did, but I fixed it at the fort," Ann said.

"That's my girl." Her father wasn't much taller than she was, but he carried himself as if he were ten feet tall. Silver streaked his bronze hair, but once it was the same shade as her hair.

She smiled into the green eyes so like her own; pleased he was finally standing up to her brother. "Thanks, Dad."

"No *problemo*." He put a hand on her shoulder. "Have I told you lately how glad I am that you're home safe and sound?"

Ann swallowed the lump in her throat. She wanted to cling to him as if she was a little girl again, but she couldn't. He was the only one in the family to express the sentiment and that cut to her heart. She bit her lip and then forced a smile. "You said it at breakfast, Dad."

"Okay, I'm saying it at dinner now." He turned toward the table. "Jack, you can help us with the rigs after supper. Devon, quit kicking your chair."

"I want my pop, not icky milk." Her lower lip stuck out and she glared at Ann. "She's not the boss of me."

Ann stiffened, hurt and furious, more than ready to argue with the six-year-old, but to her amazement, Ginger intervened.

"Devon, respect your mom or leave the table."

<hr />

Ann tapped her camo-colored acrylic nails impatiently on the steering wheel. She had too much pride to demand Will support her and Devon, so it was time to suck it up and go to Fort Bronson. She'd had to force herself to stay on the road when the other cars crowded around her. The heavy flow of rush-hour traffic sent shivers down her spine, especially when she saw trash on the shoulder of the freeway. It was just garbage, she told herself, not cover for a bomb.

The disc jockey on the radio interrupted her thoughts with the eight-o-clock broadcast. She really was late now. There was no way she'd make it to the fort by the time Harry stated. Did she care? No. She struggled to ignore her guilt.

She had never been late to a job, not since she started working at Pop's Café when she was sixteen. She couldn't even lie and say something about car trouble. The Ford had never sounded better, especially now that she had the original battery back where it belonged.

Her dad and Jack had helped install the battery, then her younger brother charmed their folks into letting him put a new one on their account at Summer's Feed Store for his Jeep. Ann didn't point out that if she'd been in the same situation, she'd have had to wait until payday to get a battery. If she ever needed a ride to work, as Ginger said, that was why God made busses.

The two of them should get along better, but her stepmother had irritated Ann from the time she was five years old and didn't show any signs of stopping. No, that wasn't fair. Ginger had taken Ann's side last night at supper and that was a first.

She tossed her head. Her hair was neatly pinned above her collar and stayed glued in place, but today she'd opted for hoop earrings instead of her usual gold posts. She studied her fingernails where they rested on the steering wheel. The glittering polish shone back at her. Too bad, too sad. That was tough. She would drive Master Sergeant Harry Colter nuts. From now on, she wouldn't make any decisions or suggestions at all. She'd sabotage all his efforts to improve the unit. She'd send him back to the Rangers as a total failure, and she didn't care if he gave her a bad performance review. *Like hell, she didn't!* Okay, maybe she wouldn't go that far.

Ann found a parking space and turned off the motor. She picked up the box of doughnuts and sack lunch as well as the book she was currently reading. She'd almost finished this novel and she promised herself she'd stop by her favorite bookstore on the way home tonight. She strolled down the sidewalk, recognizing Harry's blue pickup as she passed it.

The rows of two-story white buildings seemed brand new in the cool March morning. Even the peeling paint wasn't that obvious. There was moisture on the grass, and Ann stayed on the sidewalk instead of cutting across the lawn to her unit. She didn't want the water or the grass to stain her suede combat boots. Besides, she was already late. It wouldn't save any time.

Pushing the swinging door open, Ann stepped into the empty office. She frowned as she placed the box of doughnuts beside the still-brewing coffee. How long had Harry been here? Was he serious when he wanted to start at seven? She crossed to the small refrigerator and put away her lunch.

Moving to her desk, Ann looked distractedly for a note. There wasn't one. No message. Nothing. She glanced across the room. His fatigue shirt hung on a chair behind the desk across from hers. She went over and looked. Nope, he hadn't left a note there either. Well, if Harry Colter hadn't left her anything to do, then she could make a case that she was waiting for him to give her orders.

Granted, she had a ton of payroll forms to fill out for the soldiers in the unit, so they'd get paid for drill last weekend, but Harry hadn't told her to complete the payroll this morning. Well, she'd try to finish them before she went home tonight, even if she didn't tell her supposed boss about it. She wouldn't screw over her fellow reservists although losing the job as unit tech totally pissed her off. She tucked away her purse, but deliberately left the book on the desk. Then, she opened the file of forms and got started on the next soldier's payroll.

Harry frowned as he strode toward the office from the supply room. Where was she? The car had been running well enough when Ann left. If she had a problem, she would have called him, wouldn't she? It was proper military procedure, not to mention the only courteous thing to do. He glanced at his watch, *oh-nine-hundred hours*. Where was she? Harry jerked the back door to the office open and saw her sitting at a desk. "Where have you been?"

Ann slowly came out of the book, her gaze lingering on the page. "Right here, Sergeant Colter. Is there a problem?"

Harry knew better than to trust the wide-eyed innocent look, but he wouldn't let a woman push him over the edge either. She was angry with him, but he'd hoped the two of them wouldn't be at loggerheads immediately. He decided not to answer the question and asked one of his own. "What time did I tell you to be here?"

Ann shrugged, and stared at him from under her lashes. "I don't remember. I'm here now. I've been ready to work, but you didn't leave me a list. What do you want me to do?"

Harry deliberately looked at the insignia on her shirt. After a long moment, he drawled. "How many leadership courses have you taken, Barrett? What is the first rule for a non-commissioned officer?"

Ann glared up at him. "Which rule?" She heaved a sigh. "There are so many of them."

Harry inclined his head in acceptance of the challenge. This battle obviously was going to take longer than he'd expected. He didn't underestimate his opponent. He reached for the paperback Ann still held and took the book from her grasp. Closing it, he placed the novel on the desk. "What do you usually do when you arrive, Barrett?"

"I make the coffee." Ann propped her chin on her fist and studied him with cool defiance. "But it seems you already have. What should I do, Master Sergeant Colter?"

Harry folded his arms and leaned against the partition. "You aren't going to make this easy for me, are you, Sarge?" His tone was deceptively soft. "Am I supposed to entertain you and the kids that have come to clean weapons?"

Ann lifted one shoulder. "Whatever." She glanced around the office curiously. "We're the only people in here and there's nobody upstairs. Where's your detail?"

"Squaring away their uniforms," Harry said. "Then I'm taking them to the barber shop. I can't take them down the hill to the armory until they look like soldiers."

"Are you for real?" Ann asked. "Come on, Colter. How bad can it be? These are good kids. We haven't been home long enough for them to be total party animals."

"They're still out of uniform." Harry's voice deepened to a rumble. "Well, I can't send you out in public with them either when you are too, especially since you're determined to piss me off. No wonder they don't have any respect for themselves."

He stalked over to the switches and turned on the brilliant ceiling lights. "While I'm gone, Barrett, you can clean up this dump. I want the windows washed, the floors waxed, and buffed. Throw away those civilian posters on the walls and scrub them too."

Ann jumped to her feet. "What the hell do you think I am? The maid?"

"Nope," Harry said. "If you were, I'd fire you. You're a soldier, just like I am. And I gave you a legal order, Barrett."

"You're joking. I'm a reservist again, now that the unit's home. I don't do windows."

"No joke. You're a soldier, and you're out of uniform. The military has regulations about hair, earrings and nail polish. You came in here looking for trouble, Barrett. You found it." Harry glanced at his watch. "It's nine-fifteen. You have until *Twelve-Hundred* hours to get this place shaped up. In case you've forgotten, that's noon."

Ann lifted her chin. "What if I don't?"

Harry's voice became even more menacing. "Then I'll have to give you every dirty job I can find for the next three months till your time is up."

Ann planted her fists on her hips. "I can take whatever you dish out, Colter."

Harry chuckled. "Don't push me, Barrett. I only need to give you time off to sleep. The other twenty hours a day, you're mine."

Ann obviously couldn't believe he was serious, judging by the stunned look on her face. "You sure try to run a *'strack'* outfit, Colter. You're wasted here. Take your wife and life and go back to the Rangers."

Harry laughed, and turned toward the coffee pot. "I'm not married. Not yet. I'll wait till you're over your snit, then I'll marry you."

Ann tossed her head. "In your dreams, Colter. I've been married. Never again."

"Don't bet on it." Harry strolled to the coffee pot, stopping as he saw the box of doughnuts. "Did you bring these? Can I take them out to the kids who came to clean rifles?"

Ann smiled. "Sure. They'd love it."

"I'll tell them you brought the goodies." Harry collected a cup of coffee, and the box of doughnuts. Then he headed for the back door. "Otherwise, they'll think I'm a nice guy."

"That won't last long." Ann sounded sweet, too sweet. "I'm sure a big, tough Ranger can set them straight. Of course, you know that I forgot all about the troops, Colter. I just stopped at the new bakery in Baker City because I was late."

"And you guessed chocolate doughnuts would mellow me out." Harry turned back to face her. "Good thinking, Barrett."

"It works for my daughter. I've always figured men had the same intelligence level as most six-year-olds."

Harry grinned. She tried to goad him, but it took more than a woman's insults to anger him. "It won't work. You can't scare me off but go ahead and try. We'll both enjoy the fireworks for a while."

Ann glared at him. She gestured toward the door. "Go away, Colter. I'm sure the kids need a babysitter and you're elected."

"Afraid?" Harry teased.

"Not of you. We're never getting together. You're not my type."

"Want to bet? Sooner or later, I'll catch you. You can run, but you can't hide, not from me."

Ann raised her chin in defiance. "Get out. I've got work to do. I don't have any more time to waste on you. I need to pay those kids you've got waiting around for you."

"You can do that this afternoon." Harry pushed open the back door. "You've got your orders for this morning. *G.I.* this place."

CHAPTER FOUR

Ann stripped off her fatigue shirt and went in search of the mop. She'd clean this place all right. She'd wax the floors till they were as slippery as a skating rink. She'd wash the windows till the glass seemed invisible. By the time she was finished with the walls, Colter would think she'd painted them while he was gone. And somehow, she'd beat him. She'd get her job back and send him crawling to the Rangers, begging for his old position.

She hated housework and usually avoided it whenever possible. Now, she'd been given an order that meant she had to do a job she abhorred. She could leave, but if she did, she'd be the loser in this war with Harry Colter. She'd be the one who was A.W.O.L., because the unit had arranged for ninety days of active duty with more work to follow.

The Colonel and the rest of the officers would think she was a quitter. That meant she'd never get a full-time job, so as the saying went, she had to suck it up and follow orders even if she didn't like them. Secretly, she admired the way Colter played the game. He was good, but she'd beat him.

Where had the *Super-Soldier* come from? She'd known a lot of active-duty types during training and overseas, but none of them carried themselves the way that Colter did. No wonder Margo referred to some of the headquarters staff as *lifers*; like them, Harry acted as if he could run the Army single-handed.

He didn't know that he'd met his match. She'd graduated with honors in all her military classes, including the arduous courses for first-line supervisors. The same went for her college level classes. She kept the 'honor cords' for her master's degree in the same drawer with her graduation robe. Back in real life, she'd been a high school teacher. She learned more mind games from her teenage students than Harry Colter would expect.

Even if she liked the good humor and warmth in his bright blue eyes, he didn't have a need to know that. She wanted him to think she despised him, and she had to make sure he didn't see beyond her sharp tongue to the way he turned her knees to mush. This attraction was stupid. Yes, she liked the guy, but that didn't matter. She had to win the A.G.R. job and he had to go.

Secretly she was a little amazed that he didn't plan to take the credit for thinking of the doughnuts. Will never tried to explain anything. He shrugged and told people to think whatever they pleased. If it meant he took credit for another person's work, that was okay with him and he didn't see it as being immoral. Ann told him *'what goes around, comes around,'* but he couldn't see the connection between the life choices he made and consistently losing each new job when other employees and supervisors got tired of the way he acted.

At one time this had been an active post to protect the early settlers in Seattle from hostile Indians, and frankly Ann knew she'd dealt better in a warzone than with an angry first-grader or with the upcoming Memorial Day celebration in her hometown where she was expected to be the token guest of honor. She filled the mop bucket with hot water and headed for the main room. She had a lot of work to do, and it was time to get started.

Her legs ached. Her lungs burned. Every labored breath knifed through her. Sweat trickled down her spine under the thin, clinging fabric of her t-shirt as she ran. Her black poly-nylon shorts swished. She hated that sound. Think of Devon. Her daughter deserved a good life and the

Army would provide that for them. They wouldn't be rich, Ann thought, but at least she could pay her own bills and she wouldn't have to worry about being rifted every May.

The desire was enough to make her keep going. She felt the spring sun beating down on her, and she concentrated on running each step of the way. The disc jockeys on the radio promised rain to break this heat wave but so far nothing had happened. It hadn't been this warm back east when she attended the finance school. She'd been the most serious student in the class, but no one realized she worked so hard to make the time pass more quickly.

She'd missed Devon more with each day. Talking to the six-year-old on the telephone hadn't been easy, especially when her daughter insisted that she was busy and didn't have time to waste on the phone. Ann fought for another breath as she reached the fence that was the halfway point of her daily run. Margo was already there, half collapsed against the cyclone wire mesh. The fact that her best friend looked as limp as Ann felt was consoling.

"Let's go back through the obstacle course to cool out," Margo suggested. She pushed at a damp strand of strawberry blonde hair. "It has all those shade trees."

Ann managed to nod. "Okay." She took a few deep breaths and then was ready to continue the run. The two of them jogged side by side for a short distance and turned onto the path that curved into the trees. She caught a glimpse of the white rows of headstones in the post graveyard and tried not to shudder. Three of the soldiers from their unit died in the 'box' during this last tour and she hadn't made herself visit their graves yet. It'd been hard enough to try to render psychological first aid to Sullivan Barlow and the other survivors of the I.E.D. blast.

Margo followed her gaze. "It's tough, but it gets easier, Ann. Let the wounds heal. First Sergeant Raven Driscoll would be the first to say so."

Ann nodded. "Come on, Margo." She began to jog again. "Get the lead out."

Margo heaved a sigh and fell into step beside her. "I hate jogging. Exercise stinks. I want a piece of banana cream pie for a reward. My job's the pits. I should pitch a fit until I get my room back at Miner's Creek Elementary in Lake Maynard. Why did I ever agree to work down the hill at HQ?"

Ann panted for breath. "Because-you-wanted-food, and-a-place-to live? And didn't want to put up with Janet Gundersen, the principal from Hell?"

"I still can't believe it. We go to war and they shift the principals around in our district like it's a square dance." Narrowing sky-blue eyes, Margo frowned at Ann. "Put your hands on top of your head. Then you'll be able to breathe, and we can talk."

Ann obeyed the order and felt the air ease her aching lungs. They continued to jog up the road. The pavement divided, and Ann slowed as a truck came down the hill. With a sinking sensation, she recognized Harry as the driver.

He braked the truck, and Margo waved her thanks as they trotted across the road and into the tree-lined path that led to the obstacle course.

Behind her, Ann heard Harry's shout and humiliation sent a burning blush up her cheeks.

"Hey, Barrett. We don't take prisoners."

"Cute." Margo laughed. She slowed into a walk again. "Who is that jerk?"

Ann dropped her hands and sighed. "The buzzard who stole my A.G.R. job."

"What?" Margo grabbed her arm. "Say that one more time, Ann. Who could take your job? Your battalion C.O. wrote a letter of recommendation. My boss said you were perfect for the job and he doesn't praise reservists lightly."

"I know. He makes a point of telling everyone at Fort Bronson what he thinks of us." Ann felt the sting of tears at the corner of her eyes and blinked them back. "All I know is I finished up that stint at the finance school and got back to the office here yesterday. I met Colter then and he surprised me with the news that he has my job. Would you believe he walked in on me while I was showering?"

"That's it!" Margo stopped and pulled Ann to a halt as well. "I'll tell Colonel Williams; the senior JAG lawyer and he'll get rid of him. The Army makes a big deal that they don't tolerate sexual harassment. We know it's *bs*, but we can always use it to get your job back."

For a few minutes, Ann contemplated the idea. It was a sure-fire way to get rid of Colter. He'd probably get reprimanded and either return to active duty or be demoted or even be immediately discharged. Command Sergeant Major Jenkins was death on harassment, maybe because he had four daughters at home, and he was looking for an excuse to dump Harry. Then again, it might cause him to lose his retirement, and the guy was a war hero. Seven tours in the '*box*' had to be worth something. Did she want to hurt him that badly? *No!*

"Margo, the whole thing was a stupid mistake. I can't take advantage of that and destroy his career. I want to get rid of him, but I have to be able to look myself in the face when I put on my makeup." She pulled free and began to walk up the cement path. "Did I tell you he left almost immediately? Or he made the unit give me a ninety-day tour? He helped me fix my car when it broke down yesterday. He let me come in late today, and he's working really hard on the weapons and the other equipment."

"He swiped your job," Margo reminded her. "The least he can do is work. I'm still going to talk to Williams about this. He ought to be good for something more than brushing the dirt off the suede on his combat boots."

"I don't think he can help us out on this one," Ann said. "You told me Colonel Williams started out in combat. Harry has twenty years in the Army, most of them in the Airborne Rangers. The two of them will have more in common than you think."

"You may be right, but we've got to do something." Margo rubbed her forehead. "I just think you've had enough problems these past two years. What with losing your teaching position, and your marriage—well, you've had a tough row to hoe. You didn't need to be dumped one more time. And Will certainly didn't help matters when he got laid off and took that job in California while we were overseas. I couldn't do anything to help you."

"You were the one who came up with the idea to call Will's parents and ask them to pick up the slack with Devon when she was being passed around between his sisters and mine while he was out of state. Because they did, my dad could get Ginger to step up," Ann reminded her friend. "If it hadn't been for them, I'd have had no choice except to pay my older sisters to take care of Devon and both their husbands make me puke. Coming home early from Afghanistan wasn't an option. Then, you suggested I go for a full-time position here at the base and helped me get into the school back east. Knowing all that information about finance is going to make it easier to find another position."

"I suppose this means you aren't even considering taking this job away from Harry Colter?"

"I didn't say that." Ann replied. "If we can think of a way to get rid of him that doesn't make me feel like dirt, I'm all for it." She drew a deep breath, as she suddenly realized that Harry had no more choice than she did. He hadn't intended to take away her livelihood. In fact, he'd tried to make life easier for her, but he'd treated her like a person, a peer. Harry hadn't patronized her the way that Will would have in the same situation.

She shook her head. She wouldn't win anything by being nice. Hadn't she learned that lesson a long time ago? Nice, good and polite were synonyms for weak, gutless and being a doormat. Hadn't she spent enough years being walked on? It was past time to demand respect, dignity and courtesy. She had to look out for herself and Devon. Nobody else would, not without wanting her soul in exchange.

"I've got to go." Ann started up the path that led to her company's building. "I'll call you. Devon is going with my folks to the Grange Supper, so I don't have to hurry home tonight."

"Great!" Margo said. "Come to my place tonight and we'll brainstorm. Between the two of us, we'll come up with a plan."

"Okay." Ann paused. "Do you want to check out that new Mexican restaurant in Lake Maynard? You said you wanted to try it."

Margo grimaced. "I already did. Colonel Williams took me there after the admin drill last week. He was a total jerk."

Ann frowned. "About what? He couldn't have griped about your appearance. You may call the career soldiers *lifers* but you're never out of uniform, and you're always polite, not like me. When I see a jerk, I say so."

Margo shrugged. "Remember slimy Major Fisher? The one that makes like a frog and tries to jump every sweet, young thing in the unit?"

Ann shuddered. "He's a creep and a half. He came onto me once, back when I was still married. I told Will. He confronted Fisher and the slimeball left me alone after that."

"Yeah, but you left the reserve command HQ anyway and

transferred to the personnel management battalion," Margo said. "You didn't trust any of the officers to step up, not even the lawyers in the JAG section. Well, Fisher went after my new assistant, a nice, little eighteen-year-old ROTC candidate who comes in two days a week. She's a replacement for Lieutenant Powell who I lost in the *Sandbox*. And you know that black belt I've got, Ann, the one that doesn't go with any of my uniforms. I lost my temper—"

Ann gaped at her friend. "You hit him? Margo, what if he brings you up on charges? You could lose your commission not just your position at HQ."

Margo grimaced again. "Believe me, Ann. I would rather be unemployed for the rest of my life than listen to one more of Williams' lectures. He chewed me up one side and down the other. He says I may still face discipline and if I'm reprimanded, it'll end up in my file which will slow down my next promotion, but at least it'll be in-house, and I won't be court-martialed."

"Why didn't you tell Williams the reason you hit Fisher?" Ann asked. "If you did, wouldn't Fisher be out of the Army?"

"The Colonel already knew. He listens to the rumor mill and he had plans to force Fisher out the door, but I overstepped when I kicked butt. Like Williams says, this little gal that works for me would look like pond scum by the time she finished testifying. She's an innocent and I won't let her ruin her life for garbage like Fisher. As it stands, the official line is I decked Fisher because he made a pass at me." Margo hesitated. "And you're undoubtedly right about not yelling harassment. Williams would be bound to think I put you up to it."

Ann nodded. "Let's just leave him out of it. I'm going to apply for other openings on the base."

"Does it have to be one with the Active Guard/Reserve Program?" Margo asked. "There are some openings in civil service. They don't pay as much, but the benefits are pretty equal."

"I'll think about it," Ann said. "Of course, I'd have to stay with my unit. I won't work in the same building with Fisher."

"I don't blame you." Margo began to smile. "But you're too old for him now."

"True," Ann agreed. "And he may slow down since you've decked him. Was he badly hurt?"

"Nope. The hospital didn't even keep him overnight. He wound up with a couple cracked ribs, some bruises, a bloody nose, and a mild concussion when he hit his head on the floor." Margo shrugged. "He freaked when Williams offered to call the police and have me arrested."

"He was afraid you'd tell the cops why you assaulted him." Ann pointed out. "Attempted rape is against the law and we're stateside now. He can't get away with it in Seattle. He'd end up in jail after he got out of the hospital. Just be careful, Margo. He'll be out to get you after this."

"I've got it covered." Margo glanced at her watch. "I've got to go. I'll see you tonight."

Ann nodded, and took the upper path that led back to her own office building. "I'll meet you at four-thirty. Let's go to Pop's Café. We haven't been there since we got home."

"Sounds good." Margo turned and began to jog down the other path that led to the headquarters building. "I'll call if I come up with a brilliant plan in the meantime."

Ann couldn't help smiling at the sarcasm in her friend's tone. She wasn't as dumb as Margo thought. It wasn't a sign of weakness to refuse to destroy Harry Colter's career. If he'd been a moral degenerate like Ed Fisher, she never would have hesitated, but there was a big difference between a man who played tease and tickle with innocent girls, and Harry, who flirted in an almost old-fashioned way. He made her feel like a woman, not a piece of meat. And she wouldn't ruin him, not when she had to live with herself afterwards.

Cutting around the fence, Ann hurried into her unit's building. She heard banging on the pipes and paused. The door to the women's restroom at the top of the stairs was open. Ann stepped inside the latrine. "Is anybody in here?"

"Me." Harry grumbled from the shower room. "If you lock me in here, I'll wring your neck."

Ann restrained a smile as she caught a glimpse of him. Harry's black hair was wet and rumpled. Grease streaked one lean cheek, and his fatigues were soaked. "I thought the water was off in here. What happened, Colter?"

Harry put down his wrench and strolled toward her. "I was trying to get this done so you could shower up here today. I fixed the pipes, tightened the joints, and then turned on the water."

"What happened?" Ann gestured toward his wet uniform. She couldn't help but be touched by his thoughtfulness.

"One of the pipes burst." Harry glared back at the shower-room. "But I'll fix it!" He waved his wrench for emphasis.

"I bet you will." Ann smiled at him. "However, today I'll use the men's latrine. No interruptions, Colter."

"I don't repeat myself, especially when I've made a mistake."

"Really? I'll hold you to that." Ann headed out of the room and down the stairs. She hung her uniform on the back of the door and dropped her combat boots to the floor beside the bench. She stripped off her pink t-shirt, then she reached for the fastener to her bra. Before she could unhook it, there was a rap on the door.

Ann glanced at it suspiciously. Did Harry Colter have a fetish for showering women? She crossed to the door and called through it. "What?"

"I bought something for you."

Ann pulled the door open a scant two inches and peered around the edge of it. "What?"

"Check it out," Harry passed her a small paper sack. "Take your time, Angel. I'll run interference."

Ann continued to look around the edge of the door, watching him stride away. Then she turned her attention to the paper sack. What was he up to now? Bribery? Could she use this to get rid of him? She closed the door, wishing it had a lock, and then opened the sack to find a bottle of nail polish remover, and a card of hairpins.

"In your dreams, Colter!"

With an angry swoop, Ann threw the sack into the garbage. Her hair and fingernails had become a point of honor. She might have to take care of both things eventually, before the next unit drill, but she wouldn't do it a moment sooner. She still remembered the way Will called her, *G.I. Jill*. He said the military made her lose all semblance of femininity, although he was willing to admit that she needed to be in the reserve to pay her student loans from college.

Determined to be considered a woman, not just a soldier, Ann made a point of always wearing cosmetics and perfume regardless of her uniform and Army regulations. She finished taking off her clothes and headed for the shower. She still had time to get cleaned up, and enjoy not only her lunch, but also a chapter of her book.

In less than fifteen minutes, she was at her desk. Harry was still upstairs, working on the female bathroom. She could tell by the banging on the pipes. Ann located her lunch and her book. At long last, she would finally discover what had happened to the hero.

In the latrine, Harry squinted at the package of caulking material. Damn it, he thought as he dropped the wrench on the concrete floor. Immediately he cursed his own behavior. He had enough work to do. He didn't need to make the job harder on himself. Leaving the bathroom, he went downstairs to the first floor and down the short hall that opened into the main room that served as the office. He spotted her sitting at her desk. "Angel? Have you got a minute?"

Ann sighed. She carefully put her spoon in the container of yogurt. "I happen to be on my lunch break. What is it?"

"I left my glasses at home." Harry handed her the tube of glue. "Come read the directions to me so I can finish this and get out to the supply room."

"All right." Ann marked her place in the book and placed the paperback novel on the desk. "But I want to finish this chapter as soon as we get done."

"I'm sorry about the interruption." Harry struggled to control the bitterness that laced his words. "I'll bring my glasses from now on."

Ann stared at him. "Harry, it's not just my lunch." She jumped to her feet and hurried toward him. "Will always said books meant as much to me as football did to him. And I'm afraid he's right. Once I start reading, I can't stop. It frustrates me when I can't find out how the story ends. I shouldn't have been so nasty."

Harry gazed down at her. "I shouldn't be so ornery either. I just get frustrated when I have to stop in the middle of a project."

Ann began to smile. "Maybe we have more in common than we think."

"Does this mean my job is safe? And you're not out to get me?"

She shook her head, but her voice was a bare whisper. "I'm still sending you back where you came from."

"Georgia? I served enough time there." He framed her face with his calloused hands, raising her chin so he saw the emotions in her green eyes. "I'm not going back, honey." He slowly feathered his thumb over her lips. "I told you I'm marrying you and staying right here."

All right, boys and girls. That's more like it!

Zeke applauded, grateful for the first time that they didn't know he was here, cheering them on as they found a new future together. Well, at least he hoped they were. Now, all he had to do was get Harry to go back to Baker City with Barrett. What would that take? A miracle or two? Or just another few moments of privacy?

CHAPTER FIVE

"Never again, Colter." Ann pulled away, looking up at him. "I'm never marrying again. I've been that route and it hurts too much when the whole thing blows up in your face."

Harry eyed her. "If he meant that much to you, why did you divorce him?"

She stared past him, into the darkness of the hall. It was like the long darkness of the past eighteen months that left an aching void in her soul. "I didn't," she said softly. "He found someone else, several someone elses. He divorced me when I was at Bagram." She felt tears stab her eyes and wished they helped, but nothing did. "I wasn't good enough, Colter. Not for him...." And not for herself either.

"Maybe we've got more in common than we think," Harry said, repeating her words. "We're both walking wounded, Barrett. I got my guts ripped out in this last tour—"

"You were injured?" Ann demanded.

"Not physically," Harry said. "My best friend died. Small arms fire..." Those words were too simple for what Zeke Garvey meant to him. The two of them met in grade school, played sports together all through middle and high school, enlisted at the same time, did boot camp together, wound up in the Rangers and watched each other's backs in more than one combat zone. They were friends, closer than most brothers. They'd done too many things together, living, fighting, and then falling in love with the same woman, but Zeke won Twila Desmond, and kept her even after his death.

Coulda, woulda, shoulda. Colter, get off the cross. Somebody else needs the wood. Zeke glared at the door to the latrine, amazed when it swung closed. *It's not your fault we ran into that ambush or that I died. Now, drive on and get busy living. There's been enough dying.*

Ann stared up into his face and realized Harry had gone through the same emotional minefield she had. Some people faced hell and emerged stronger than before. Her life dissolved into fragments she barely held together, and his had too.

She touched his arm. "It's going to be okay, Harry." Her voice held the same comfort, and warmth it did when she reassured her daughter after a bad dream. "Everything will be okay. You'll see."

"Thanks, Angel." He took her hand and led her to the bathroom. "So, what's your book about? Life and death?"

She relaxed and felt a ready smile come to her face. "It's a murder mystery. I'm trying to figure out *'whodunnit'* before the detective does. Right now, I'm betting on the doctor."

"It can't be." He released her and picked up his wrench, heading for the shower. "The butler did it."

"How do you know that? Have you read this book?"

When he laughed, she realized he teased her. "Just for that, I'll make you read the part where the butler has an ironclad alibi. You'll learn not to give me a hard time about my books." She studied him curiously. "What do you like to read?"

The screwdriver clattered to the floor and Harry bent to pick it up. He flicked a sideways glance at her and then shrugged. "I usually have too many projects to read, Angel. I like Westerns and some modern stuff."

"Who's your favorite author?" Ann questioned. "I started reading westerns when I was a kid. My grandfather left me his whole collection of L'Amours and I've read all of them." She crossed the room and sank down on the bench to watch Harry adjust one of the pipes.

"Right now, I'd like to hear what the directions are for applying that caulk," Harry growled. "If it isn't too much trouble, Barrett."

She sighed and turned the tube over. "You don't have to give me a hard time when I'm trying to be polite." She read the directions in a cold, hard voice. Harry Colter was an arrogant, muscle-bound creep. Maybe, he deserved to lose his job. She might let Margo set him up. It'd serve him right for pissing her off.

Her frustration faded by the middle of the afternoon. Ann found herself wondering what kind of glasses Harry wore. Why was reading such a chore for him? She was supposed to wear her own glasses whenever she opened a book, but she seldom did. She used them when she graded papers to help decipher teenage hieroglyphics. She was in the middle of the necessary paperwork to pay the soldiers in the unit when Harry returned to the office building.

He scanned the large open area filled with rows of desks, and chairs before glancing at her. His voice was softer than usual, but she still heard the almost lazy menace. "I thought I told you to clean up this place. When do you plan to get started, Barrett?"

Ann stared at him. "Are you serious, Colter? What do you think I spent the morning doing? I took down Raven Driscoll's motivational posters like you said and put them in the office she used. I washed the walls. I even mopped the floor, but nobody had a buffer they could loan me. And I couldn't find any wax either, so the floor is as good as it's going to get. As for the windows, I did the ones I could reach since I didn't have a ladder or stepstool. I wasn't about to break my neck climbing on a chair."

Harry sized up the room again. "It's still not *clean* in here. And it won't do, Barrett. The weapon detail is back. Now, you'll have help." He gestured to the clock over the main door. "Before you go home tonight, this entire building will be *G.I. 'd.*"

"I'm not staying late." Ann rose to her feet. "And you can't make me." But she was afraid he could.

Harry chuckled. "Go ahead and go. You'll be *Absent With Out Leave* and you know what that will do to your career."

Ann glared at him. "Why are you doing this, Colter? I do my job."

"Because you don't look like a soldier, Barrett. You look like an actress playing the part." Harry eyed her narrowly. "If you want to go home on time, then obey the regs. Don't start a fight with me."

Ann rested her hands on the desk and continued to glower at him. "I can take whatever you dish out, Colter."

"Good." Harry strode across to the shelves that held the notebooks of regulations. "Then come over here."

Reluctantly, Ann obeyed. "Now, what?"

"Pull the A.R. that deals with uniforms." Harry stood like a rock and waited while she found the appropriate binder and then the correct page. "Okay, Barrett. Read it to me. What does the Army say about haircuts, and nail-polish?"

An hour later, Ann was still fuming. She hadn't pinned up her hair or cleaned off her polish, but there was nothing like being totally in the wrong to make her mad. Harry organized the cleaning this time. He sent one of the boys to purchase supplies at the Post Exchange, a small general store.

Another boy went down to the headquarters company where Margo worked to borrow the buffer. Meanwhile, Ann and the other three soldiers moved all the furniture out of the way and scrubbed the walls again.

While the younger soldiers finished washing down the last wall, Ann stalked into Harry's small office. "All of the desks are out of the way so we can do the floor when the buffer arrives. The walls are scrubbed again."

Harry slowly lifted his gaze from the stack of paperwork on his desk. "Including the hallway? And female latrine? What about the upstairs, Barrett? Is that ready to be mopped, waxed and buffed? Have you got two people on the windows yet?"

Ann gasped. "We aren't staying till midnight, Colter."

"You are if this building isn't clean." Harry stood and towered over her.

Despite the distance between them, Ann still felt angry and intimidated. How dare he order her around? She ignored the guilt that trickled through her. If she hadn't refused to clean up her act, then he wouldn't have thrown his weight around, and now all of them were being punished, not just her. Deliberately, she closed the door and advanced on him. "It's not their fault, Colter. You can't keep the detail late because of something I've done."

"Yes, I can." Harry said. "It won't be the first time a group of soldiers was punished because their sergeant acts like she's incompetent. And we both know it's better if you learn to follow my orders now, not when everyone's lives are at stake during a war."

Ann raised her chin in defiance, matching him glare for glare. Damn, she hated it when a man was right. If they'd been back East or overseas, she knew she would act differently, but they were in Seattle, not Afghanistan. The hell with Harry Colter! "What if I send them home at the regular time?"

"Then you'll stay by yourself until the job is done." A faint smile creased his face, and Harry added. "And I'll wait right here till I think the place *is* clean and you've finished."

"I suppose you'd still expect me at eight tomorrow morning, too." Ann snapped.

Harry's smile broadened. "No, Angel. I'd want you here at seven, the same time I get here."

"But you said I could come in at eight—"

"That was before you were late this morning." Harry's low drawl didn't fool her this time.

Ann knew he was as angry as she was. He just handled his emotions better than she did or Will did for that matter. Harry Colter didn't shout or punch people or things. He just turned the tables on his adversaries. She wondered if the Rangers coined the phrase, "Don't get mad, get even," or if that was simply Harry's personal creed? "You're a—"

"Soldier," Harry interrupted. His deep tones softened even more. "Just like you are, Barrett. And soldiers fight wars, or they train to fight, or they prepare for training or fighting. Cleaning is part of preparing. You've got a lot of work to do, and it won't get done while you're in here."

"You're right." Ann spun around and stormed from the small room. Somehow, she'd show him. The entire building would be clean, and she'd still get her troops out of here on time, and she wouldn't stay a minute past four-thirty either!

It was shortly after five when the last of the cleaning was finished.

Ann looked at the weary soldiers who had insisted on staying till the end. Her resentment and anger toward Harry doubled. "It looks great in here. Go home."

Phil Smith, a stocky former high-school quarterback who had earned a recent promotion to Private First Class shook his head. "You'd better ask *him* first, Sarge. We aren't going till you do."

"That's right," Juan Rodriguez said. "If you stay late, we do too."

Ann glanced at the other four soldiers. Dani Chang sat on the edge of one desk, swinging a booted foot and didn't move, her jaw set. Beside her, Lafayette Jones leaned against the wall and waited. Even the two slackers in the company, brother and sister, Ronnie and Tina Marvin didn't head for the door.

Ann almost surrendered, then changed her mind. The youngsters were loyal to her and their unit, not to Harry who was still an outsider. He wasn't part of their team yet and *she'd* kept them alive in Afghanistan.

"No." She gestured toward the door. "It's my fault this whole mess got started, and it's over. I'm giving you a direct order. Go home. You've worked hard today, and I appreciate it."

"All right." Phil picked up the buffer and headed for the stairs. He waved to the rest of the young reservists. "Let's go."

Ann waited until they had left the building before she went downstairs and toward Harry's office which was in one of the four small rooms. Because the base was so old-fashioned, there were few private areas in the two-story building, and only six tiny offices. Since he had status as a full-time unit technician, Harry got a room to himself.

Ann knew she looked like crap and didn't care. Stains and dirt covered her fatigue pants. Her t-shirt clung damply to her skin. There were cobwebs in her brown hair, and she suspected she wore more than one layer of dirt over her makeup, but she was too worn out and angry to refresh the cosmetics. She threw open the office door, not caring when it banged against the wall. "It's done, and I'm leaving."

"Are you asking or telling me?" Harry sounded more dangerous than ever. "After we get done with the lessons on military appearance, then we'll get started on courtesy, Barrett."

Ann raised her chin. "Go to hell, Colter!" She swung around and stalked toward her belongings. Grabbing her fatigue shirt and purse, she stomped toward the door. She was going home and if Harry wanted to have her declared A.W.O.L., he could. She didn't give a damn!

"Barrett!" Harry's voice cracked like a whip, and she paused. "Oh-seven-hundred hours. Not one minute later."

Ann counted silently to ten, but she still lost her temper. She opted for the worst thing she could say to another Army non-commissioned officer. Without breaking stride, she yelled. "Yes, sir!"

When she pulled into the parking lot at the headquarters building, she spotted Margo exiting the red-brick building. Ann parked next to her friend's car, pushed the button to lower the driver's window and waited. She glowered at the ruined polish and two broken acrylic nails. Damn, now she had to get them redone tonight. She always went to a salon in Lake Maynard, but she didn't know if she could make it there before closing.

"Hey, what happened to you?" Margo asked, stopping next to Ann's car. "You're late." After a sweeping glance, she added. "And you're filthy."

"Harry Colter." Ann glared through the open window. "He decided he wanted our building mucked out. Now, it's cleaner than one of my dad's barns and you know how fussy he is about his purebred Morgan horses. I'll need a shower before we go for dinner. Even Pop would kick me to the curb."

"No worries since we're headed home. We can swing by my place anyway. We're pretty much the same size and you can wear my civvies since you haven't been home long enough to go shopping to get your own." Margo pushed a button on the key fob. "I'll see you there."

Rush hour traffic filled the north-bound freeway and it took almost two hours to reach the exit for the highway to Lake Maynard and Baker City. Ann saw fewer cars as they left Lake Maynard behind and headed further east toward the snow-capped mountains. She wondered what was going on when Margo slowed before they reached town. The right-turn indicator flashed several times, and her car swung onto a gravel drive.

In the next moment, Ann saw the brightly colored sign that read, Cedar Creek Guest Ranch. What was going on? Why had Margo decided to visit these people now? Ann grimaced. She looked like a total slob and her friend was an idiot. The other car came to a stop in front of a row of small cabins with lawns that sloped down to the creek, running deep with snow melt.

Ann parked her vehicle, frowning when Margo waved at her and then walked toward one of the small buildings. Taking a deep breath, Ann followed her. "Why are we here?"

"Remember I gave up my apartment and put my stuff in storage when we got ready to ship out?" Margo bypassed the two Adirondack chairs on the deck to unlock the front door. "I still haven't found anywhere I want to live so I rented this place from Cat McTavish while I look for a house to buy."

Ann grimaced, remembering the voluptuous redhead who'd apprenticed with her at a training stable. "O.M.G., I always hoped she'd grow a brain and dump her loser husband. I guess she didn't. How did she end up living here?"

"The Williams family hosted an essay contest and she won it and this place. I don't know why you're calling him a loser. Rob helped clean up the mess when the hot water tank sprang a leak and told Cat to give me a break on the rent because it saturated my area carpet in the kitchen. I said it'd be fine, but he helped me hang the rug out to dry and then take it back inside later as well as changing out the tank. He even apologized because they hadn't realized it was defunct."

"He told Cat?" Ann followed her friend inside. "And he's still alive? She never backed down from a fight in her life. Maybe she divorced the guy I remember and remarried. He sounds different."

"I don't know about that. They seem to be on the same page most of the time and the twins call him, Daddy."

"Well, I hope for her sake that everything works out okay." Ann glanced around the bare-bones kitchen. The left-hand wall held a short counter with a double sink, a coffee maker, tiny microwave and electric range. The adjacent small living room had a couch, one chair, bookcase and TV. An open staircase led to a loft bedroom. To the right, she saw a door which turned out to be the bathroom. "This is actually very cute."

"And livable." Margo gestured to the bath. "There's fresh towels in the vanity. I'll bring you down some clothes. Jeans, t-shirt, sweatshirt and undies? Or did you want to dress up tonight?"

"Are you serious? We'll get kicked out of Pop's Café and I'm starving."

"Get cleaned up so I can take you out in public."

Laughing, Ann followed orders. As they headed into the town a short time later, she spotted the large barn on the right-hand side of the street. A sign painted on the building proclaimed, "Summer's Feed and Tack." On the left, was another large structure, the Baker City Mercantile. *Home*, Ann thought, *I'm finally home!*

The café was further down the street, so she parked behind Margo's Jeep Cherokee. They walked toward the restaurant in yet another cedar shake building. A tall, muscular blond man in his late thirties who was leaving held the door for them. Ann paused as she recognized her cousin, Heather McElroy's fiancé. "Hey, Durango. How are you?"

"Doing good." He leaned down to brush a kiss over her cheek, warmth filling his rugged features and cobalt blue eyes. "I flew in last night. Sorry to miss your party. Did Heather call to talk to you?"

"Very nice." Ann laughed, shaking her head. "No, she didn't, but if she had I couldn't tell you. I've been sworn to secrecy until I can tell her that Nighthawke Security is out of the mercenary business and you're no longer a sniper."

"Wow, the Empress certainly holds a grudge, and somebody has to take out the bad actors." He grimaced. "When you talk to her again, tell her I said that a five-year, foot-stomping, snot-slinging, head-tossing hissy fit is over the top even for her."

"No way. I've got too much sense to get in a catfight with her. You're on your own." She followed Margo into the restaurant, smiling when a spry balding man holding a stack of menus came to greet them. "Hey, Pop. How are you?"

He froze for a moment, then hurried forward. "Annie, I heard you were back, but I didn't expect to see you before the weekend, not when your dad said you were still working at the Army base."

"Only for a few more months, possibly through the summer." She hugged him.

His smile widened, his face crinkling like a brown paper sack and he teased, "Does that mean I get one of my best waitresses back?"

"I'll think about it since I don't have a teaching job yet."

"Your dad bought the school in town when it came up for sale and he's been putting together a board to reopen it. Folks aren't happy about sending their little ones and middle-schoolers all the way to Lake

Maynard especially since the buses are mainly for the high school crowd. The little kids end up sitting in the gym waiting a couple hours for their classes to start. Now, what can I get you?"

Ann shared a look with Margo. "Let's start with two glasses of Chardonnay. If that doesn't convince the citizenry they want different teachers, I don't know what will."

"They know their kids and if they had to teach them, they'd be drinking stronger stuff than that silly wine." Pop showed them to a booth and handed over the menus. "Find what you want. It's on the house."

"We'll buy our meals."

"Not here you won't and since I have the only restaurant in town, it's my way and I'll stop you before you get to the highway."

"It's easy to see you're one of his favorite people." Margo opened her menu. "I wish I'd grown up here. Nobody ever offered me a free meal."

"Really?" Ann tilted her head to one side, eyeing her friend. "You mean to tell me that Colonel Williams split the check when the two of you went to dinner last week?"

"Shut up, Ann." A blush crept along Margo's high cheekbones. "I don't want to talk about it."

"Really?" Ann glanced over her own menu. "Tell me more. Don't leave out a single, sexy detail."

CHAPTER SIX

While they ate dinner, Linda MacGillicudy, Pop's daughter stopped by the booth and told them all the news about what was happening in Baker City, including the fact that a new hair salon had just opened. Quinn Murphy had two nail technicians on staff, and at least one worked until nine most nights. That meant Ann could have her acrylic fingernails fixed after they ate.

In the salon, Margo kept her company, flipping through the fashion magazines and debating about whether she wanted to have her hair dyed a different color. She decided to stay with her natural strawberry blonde. On the way back to the dude ranch, they stopped at the mercantile and bought two more bottles of Chardonnay. Neither of them slept much anymore so they sat on the porch, watched the clouds roll across the night sky and wiped out the wine, but they still hadn't come up with a plan to get rid of Harry Colter.

The next morning Ann arrived early at the base. She parked her car and headed down the cracked sidewalk to the office. Sunlight sparkled off the recently washed windows, and she felt a new pride at how clean the office building looked in comparison to the others around it. She wondered if Derek Waller, the lead technician for the battalion would follow the example set by their structure. Since she had enough work to do for her company, she usually didn't visit the other building, unlike their former clerk.

Ann shrugged. She still hadn't done anything about her hair, but she'd had the nail polish changed to a more natural, clear color that adhered to regulations. While she was dressing this morning, Devon came into the guestroom and chose her earrings, complaining she was afraid her mother had gone away to war again because no one had seen her the previous night. Normally, the little girl made a big deal of watching cartoons before breakfast, but today was different since she'd been asleep when Ann tiptoed into the princess bedroom to tuck in her baby girl again.

Smiling, Ann strolled to the office. Yes, she still planned to sabotage all of Harry Colter's efforts. Just because she didn't plan to actively take away his job didn't mean she had to do one iota more than any other reservist would. And there wasn't anything that Harry could do to turn her into a *lifer* like him. One sergeant that changed his uniform in a phone booth was enough. She would style her hair, wear earrings, put on new nail polish and just go on being herself. She'd also try to find another full-time position on the base, one where she didn't have to work with Harry Colter or Major Fisher.

With those decisions firmly in mind, Ann walked up the steps and into the office exactly at oh-seven-hundred. She poured herself a cup of coffee, and then headed toward her own desk.

"No chocolate doughnuts today?" Harry asked, as he strolled out of his own office looking more attractive than ever in camouflage fatigues. "Aren't you going to try and get on my good side anymore?"

Remembering what he'd said the day before, Ann raised her mug to her lips and tried a sip of the strong coffee. "I never make the same mistake twice."

Harry chuckled and crossed to her. He held out his hand. "I came on too strong yesterday, Barrett. I'm sorry. Shall we start over?"

Ann hesitated. Then she put the mug on her desk. "I don't usually bear a grudge." She placed her hand in his. "No more lectures?"

Harry gripped her fingers gently for a moment. "I don't like repeating myself, but I'll admit you try my patience, Angel."

"I didn't know you had any." Ann said in her sweetest tone.

Harry chuckled. "Not much. Let's make a deal. You get rid of the earrings and I won't say anything else about your hair."

Ann stepped away and removed the dangling green and gold shamrock earrings, placing them in her purse. "I can live with that."

"Let's grab some breakfast." Harry suggested. "My treat, but you pick the place. I don't know my way around the area yet."

Ann paused. Was he serious? She risked a glance at his good-humored smile and decided he was. "What kind of food do you like?"

"Home cooking. The more the better."

"Let's go to *Beth's*. They serve a great omelet, and their coffee is better than yours."

"Thanks a lot." He followed her to the door.

Beth's Café was near Green Lake, and not far from the base. To Ann's amazement they arrived early enough to avoid the customary wait outside the restaurant. The cafe was small, and Ann hurried to grab a booth before another desperate customer did. The restaurant was decorated in what she considered an early "homey" style with mismatched silverware, and glasses. Despite the effort to make the café appear like what her father had always called, "a greasy spoon," and her stepmother stated, "a real dive," the restaurant was clean and the coffee wonderful.

Harry eased into the other side of the booth. "What are you going to have?"

Ann tilted her head to one side. "I'd love an omelet, but I can never finish one by myself. If you order one, I'll split it with you."

Harry laughed. "What if we each have one? I'll finish yours if you can't."

"I'll bet you can't eat a whole one. I've never seen anybody finish one, not even my younger brother and he devours everything."

"What do I get if I win?"

"You won't. But, when you lose, you must bring me back. I love breakfast here."

"It's a date."

Ann felt a blush heat her cheeks. "Not when I'm in uniform. That's harassment."

"Angel, you haven't been in uniform since we met. I'll wait till we're both in civvies. Deal?"

Ann held out her hand. "Deal."

When they walked out of the restaurant almost an hour later, she scanned Harry's lean figure again. "I can't believe you ate an entire twelve-egg omelet by yourself. Where do you put it? You don't look fat."

"I skipped lunch and dinner yesterday." Harry cocked an eyebrow at her. "I've been eating in mess halls for the past twenty years. When I don't, it's either sandwiches or a restaurant."

"Remind me to buy you a cookbook." Ann slid into his pickup and waited for him to close the door. "Why don't you just get those meals that can be nuked in a microwave?"

"No flavor in those things." Harry grinned at her. "So, when do I collect my winnings? Tomorrow night, Friday? We'll go to dinner and a movie."

Ann considered the idea. A date with Harry Colter might be fun. "Can I pick the movie?"

"Only if you promise not to choose one of those stupid, action-adventure things." Harry groaned. "I hate it when Hollywood goes to war and fakes what I spent most of my life doing."

"They're doing a film festival of Shakespeare's plays in the University district. I can't stand going to movies by myself. It'll be fun."

"It sounds like school again. Shakespeare, Ann? You're joking, right?"

"No." Ann sighed and stared out the window of the pickup. "Never mind, Colter. I'll convince Margo to come with me. If I promise to go watch one of those awful karate movies with her, she'll watch Shakespeare with me."

Harry stopped for a red light. "I never understood Shakespeare."

"There's not that much to it," Ann said. "You probably just had crummy teachers that had to make his plays harder than they actually are. And it's almost impossible to read and understand a play. They're meant to be seen on stage."

"All right, Angel. We'll check it out, but you can't laugh at me if I'm too dumb to get it."

Ann gasped. "Do you mean it, Harry? You'll really go? I could never get Will to…" Her voice trailed away. It was rude to compare her ex-husband to Harry, but Will's refusal to attend plays or consider new ideas or visit other teachers always made her feel stupid for wanting to expand her horizons. "Just wait, Harry. You'll love the plays once you really see them and you'll forget everything you've read or heard about Shakespeare."

She paused as the truck came to a stop and he switched off the engine. She glanced at the row of shops, realizing they were a few blocks from Fort Bronson. "Why are we here?" she asked. "Do we need to pick up something?"

Harry gestured to the shop with the distinctive red and white barber pole. "It's your choice, Angel. Either your hair gets pinned above your collar or you get a haircut. Now, what's it going to be?"

Three hours later, anger still simmered. Granted, he was right about regulation hairstyles and what was allowed in the Army, but he'd told her earlier that if she gave up the shamrock earrings, he wouldn't bitch about her hair at the office. How dare he renege on his word? What kind of man was he?

She finished the payroll form and added it to the stack for Harry to sign. To think she'd had her nails trimmed down and the color changed. Once she'd had the broken ones replaced, the rest of the artificial nails could have waited at least another two weeks for a fill, but she'd decided to try to follow the rules at least a little bit. She should have known it'd recoil on her.

The ring of the phone on her desk interrupted and she picked it up, rattling off the standard military greeting. There was a pause, then a tentative female voice asked, "Is this Angelique Barrett?"

"This is Sergeant First Class Angelica Barrett," Ann said. "How can I help you?"

"Are you Devon Sweeney-Barrett's mother?"

"Yes, I am. Is she all right?"

"Yes, ma'am. She's fine. I'm Lynette Porter, Principal Gundersen's secretary here at Miner's Creek Elementary. I'm calling because Devon has been suspended for fighting and we need you to pick her up."

"I'm on my way." Ann froze for a moment, not believing what she heard, then common sense took control. "I want the nurse to see my daughter immediately and tell her to call me back on my cell phone."

"That's not necessary."

"It is to me. Tell the nurse to call me about Devon within the next ten minutes." Ann stood, snagging her purse and keys. "Do it now."

"Yes, ma'am."

Ann replaced the receiver, then recalled that Harry had gone to Army headquarters at the base of the hill. She didn't have time to track him down and explain the situation, not when her baby needed her. It only took a few minutes to call Margo and ask her to find Harry and tell him there'd been a family emergency.

"I'm on it," Margo said. "Keep me posted. Call and tell me how the little chickee is when you pick her up."

"I will." Ann hung up and hustled out the door, pausing long enough to answer her cell phone and hear the report from the school nurse that Devon was fine, only requiring an icepack for bruised knuckles.

Since it was the middle of the day, Ann didn't have to battle heavy traffic on the freeway and could treat speed limits as a suggestion, not the law. She reached Miner's Creek Elementary in Lake Maynard in slightly more than an hour. She locked the car and hurried into the office. She glanced around the entry but didn't see her daughter anywhere nearby. A blonde woman sitting at a desk behind the counter glanced up with a professional smile.

Ann nodded politely. "I'm Sergeant Barrett. I had a call about my daughter, Devon Sweeney-Barrett."

"Yes, ma'am."

"No, it's not ma'am. It's Sergeant First Class Barrett. You can call me, Sergeant or Sarge, but don't ever call me, ma'am. I work for a living."

"Yes, ma—" The younger woman gulped, stood. "I'll tell Principal Gundersen you're here."

"Thank you." Ann took a deep breath, struggling to wait patiently.

At the sound of heels clicking on the tile floor, she glanced toward the hallway and frowned when she saw her older sister, Barbara accompanied by her husband, Reid Kramer returning from one of the classroom wings. Like their mother, Barbara was a tall, statuesque redhead with a penchant for designer clothes. She'd never been one to enjoy the farm and at forty-three, she still avoided the barns and the horses, opting to manage their father's other business endeavors. Sandy-haired, more bulk than muscle in his dark suit, Reid operated a car dealership in Lake Maynard.

"Your daughter is a demon." Barbara announced, planting her hands on her hips. "She deserves a good whipping."

"Since I don't know what happened yet and I don't believe in hitting children, you'd better know that's not going to happen." Ann lifted her chin. "Why are you here?"

"Principal Gundersen called us when Devon attacked our poor little Bobby for no reason at recess. I want to take him to the doctor, but he refused to go."

"He's nine, isn't he?" Ann arched an eyebrow, curious. "Is he really the boss of you?"

"He's okay." Reid chuckled and hastily suppressed it at his wife's icy blue glare. "Got a couple bruises, but he's tough. He knows better than to put his hands on a girl, so he says he didn't touch Devon."

"That's because the little witch is Dad's favorite and Bobby is smart enough to understand I'll lose my job if it comes to a choice between us and Princess Devon."

Ann counted silently to ten, determined not to start an argument in public, grateful when the secretary returned. Without speaking, she followed the woman down a short hallway to an office. A dark-haired woman in her mid-forties sat behind a large wooden desk and Ann recognized Margo's arch-rival and enemy, Janet Gundersen. On the other side of the small room, Devon huddled in a chair.

Sweeping the child with her gaze, Ann noticed the torn white tights, scraped knees and the bruise forming on Devon's cheek. Drying mud on the short red skirt and grass stains on the cream sweater revealed she'd hit the ground at some point. Ann crossed the room and held out her hand for the plastic baggie containing melting ice. "Put this on your face."

"I want Gramma Ginger, not you."

"I know." Ann smoothed the little girl's black curls. "We'll go see her as soon as we're done here."

"That's going to take some time." Janet Gundersen frowned fiercely. "We have a zero-tolerance policy here for fighting."

Ann drew up a chair and adopted the teacher tone guaranteed to irritate any teenager or unreasonable adult within her sphere. "Zero-tolerance means her cousin Bobby Kramer will be suspended too since he was involved in the fight as well."

That evening after supper, she carried a bottle of wine out to the back deck and settled on the porch swing to watch the sunset. She filled a glass with golden Chardonnay, flicking a glance at the back door when it opened. Carrying a goblet of her own, Ginger Madison came to join her. Ann nodded a greeting but didn't speak to her stepmother first.

"I'm sorry the school called you away from work. I'll remind the secretary to call me or your father when I'm in Lake Maynard next week, not to bother you." Ginger picked up the bottle and topped her own glass. "I hope it didn't make problems at the Army base when you left before lunch."

"Devon's my daughter and I'm not imposing any further on you, Ginger." Ann shrugged and sipped the alcohol, allowing the wine to warm her. "I'm home now and it's my responsibility to step up."

"Did she say why she and Bobby fought?"

"No. She was pretty upset by the way the principal acted, so I took her out for ice cream after we went to the emergency clinic. I wanted a 'real' doctor to look at her. She has too many bumps and bruises for it to be a case of him not fighting back, but the other kids claim that was the case and there weren't any playground supervisors close enough to see what started the scuffle."

"Unfortunately, that seems to be a common occurrence at the elementary. They need to provide more supervision on the playground, but I doubt it's going to happen with the current administration." Ginger sighed and raised her glass. "The secretary never calls Will even when he's in town because he always claims to be too busy with work whether he has a job or not."

"I know." Ann leaned back in the swing. "He's still pissed because I stayed in the Reserves for the benefits and then went to war with my unit."

"I don't think you had much choice in the matter. Soldiers follow orders."

"True, but that doesn't mean he's going to 'daddy-up' for his kid."

"I'm glad you realize that, but your father and I are always here for Devon and for you."

Ann focused on the wine glass in her hand and didn't say she doubted her stepmother's words. The next morning, she rose early and fixed pancakes, eggs and bacon for breakfast. Her dad sipped coffee and glanced through the morning paper. Ginger set the table. Ann poured four glasses of orange juice and passed them around.

"I have a Baker City Auxiliary lunch meeting today," Ginger said. "We're finalizing the arrangements for the town memorial at the end of the month. Frank, can you come down early from the fence and take care of Devon? Should I call a sitter or Vanessa and see if she can look after her for a couple hours?"

Ann frowned as Devon came into the room, still wearing her pink pony pajamas. "What will she do today if she's with you or her Grandmother Vanessa?"

"Hang out and play computer games or watch TV," Frank said. "If she's in the barn, and sasses the barn workers, I send her to the farm office, and she uses the computer there for games."

Ann eyed the defiance on her daughter's face when she plopped into a chair at the table. "Devon, do you understand that if I take today off work, I'll get in trouble with the Army?"

Devon kicked the table leg. "Yeah, the Army comes first. I wish you'd just stayed in Afghan—"

"If I had, I wouldn't have enjoyed the pleasure of having your principal yell at me about your execrable manners."

The sarcasm went over her daughter's head, but the adults got it.

"Ann, I hope you don't think we encourage rudeness, or hitting other kids," Ginger said.

"I know you don't, Ginger." Ann crossed to the counter and refilled her cup of coffee. "You helped Dad raise me from the time I was younger than Devon. I'm very familiar with your rules." Sipping the coffee, she eyeballed her father. "And I'm sorry that my daughter feels the need to make trouble for you and your staff. You can't afford that with the economic slump and thirty-seven horses to feed. So, I think the best place for her is with me the next three school days."

"Oh, my!" Ginger gaped at her while Frank hid his amusement behind the paper and Devon cut loose with wails of protest.

"Eat your breakfast, Devon Joyce Sweeney-Barrett." Ann's voice slashed across the room in the same tone she used for recalcitrant troops. "And other than eating, your mouth had better be shut."

Sudden silence ensued. Devon hastily picked up her fork and dug into the scrambled eggs. Ann drank her coffee while the rest of the family ate. The caffeine did wonders for her headache and she promised herself she'd cut back on the booze. She usually didn't drink that much, but she'd hit the sauce for the last three nights. It was time to end that practice before the habit became an addiction. *Nope, not going there!*

Once her daughter finished eating and went to dress, Ann went through the child's backpack and organized schoolwork for the day. The PSP and IPOD were turned over to her grandfather and he promised to lock them up in his desk while she was suspended from school. Ann added a box of crayons and a coloring book of puppies, as well as a bedraggled copy of the first Harry Potter novel.

They were on the road in the next half-hour. Ann glanced in the rear-view mirror, surprised at Devon's continued silence. Did her daughter plan to sulk all the way to Fort Bronson? No, the child was sound asleep. Black curls tumbling to her waist, in blue jeans, a pink Disney princess sweatshirt and paddock boots, she looked like the little angel she wasn't. A smile tugged at Ann's mouth.

Parking in the main lot, she looked for Harry's truck. It wasn't there. Maybe he was late today. She checked her watch. They were. She gathered up her purse, their sack lunches and pushed the button that unlocked the doors "We're here. Let's go inside."

"What building is yours?" Devon demanded, climbing out of the back seat. "They all look really old."

"Because they are." Ann glanced around but didn't see Harry Colter. It meant she could take time for a history lesson with her daughter. "This Army base was originally built more than a hundred years ago to defend Seattle from the Indians and later from naval attack."

"What does that mean?"

"What's a navy?"

Devon tilted her head, considering the question. "Ships and stuff."

"Exactly." Ann smiled at her daughter. "You're super smart. Now, where would ships and stuff come from to start a fight with people who lived in a city?"

"The ocean."

"Precisely." Ann glanced around at the rows of white buildings, rolling lawns and budding trees. "Eventually, there would be several wars and that meant more soldiers needed to be trained, so they lived here until they went off to fight in World War Two and then in Korea."

"I didn't know any of that," a deep voice rumbled behind them.

The world seemed to stop for a split second as she saw Harry coming from the parking lot. She met his teasing blue gaze. "Good morning."

"You're exactly fifteen minutes late. I hope you have a good reason." Harry grinned mischievously. "Is it the same as mine? Derek and I were in Ballard for breakfast and the bridge was up quite a while for a boat."

"I came the other way, so we missed that." Ann took a deep breath. Somehow, she had to explain that her child needed her today. No matter what, her daughter came first.

Devon tipped back her head, eyeing him. "Hi. Who are you?"

"Master Sergeant Harry Colter. I didn't know it was 'bring your kid to work' day. What's going on, Barrett?"

"I got kicked out of school," Devon informed him. "So, my mama is stuck with me today 'cuz my grandma has a meeting and my grandpa has too much to do at his barn to look after me."

"I'm not stuck," Ann protested. "You're my baby and I love you."

"She has to say that." Devon tossed her head. "It's a 'mama' rule."

"Got it." Harry grinned down at her. "Why did you get kicked out?"

"Fighting. I kicked my cousin's butt."

"That doesn't surprise me at all. You must be a lot like your mom. She's a fighter too."

CHAPTER SEVEN

Still holding his set of keys, Harry followed the pair toward the building wondering about the bruise on Devon's cheek. She'd claimed to be in a fight, but who would hit a little girl? There had to be more to the story. This explained the message he'd received the day before about Ann leaving early because of an emergency. It sounded as if their plans for a date tonight would change. Shakespeare wouldn't be suitable for a child regardless of how smart she was. "How long will we have the pleasure of Devon's company?"

"At least three days." Ann waited while he unlocked the main doors. "If the teacher doesn't impress me with her skill set, I'll look into home school."

"Does that mean I'd be with Gramma Ginger and Grampa Frank all the time?"

Ann shook her head. "No, you'd be with me unless I find a decent tutor."

"That'd suck."

"And so, does your language. If you want to return to your classroom and friends, you'd better start trying to impress me."

Harry suppressed the urge to laugh. It sounded like the apple didn't fall far from the tree as his grandmother often said. He held the door and let them enter the building ahead of him. "What's the plan for today?"

"I need to finish the unit payroll and take it down to headquarters this afternoon, so it gets off to Division HQ by close of business today. Otherwise, you'll be hearing from the Inspector General office and one of their officers."

"Is that bad?" Devon asked.

"Yes." Harry put down his newspaper and sack lunch on an empty desk and crossed to the file cabinet where he'd set up the coffee station. He'd start the first pot of the day brewing before going to his office. "Folks need their wages. Second, nobody wants to deal with complaints, especially me."

"Okay." Devon eyed her mother. "What am I supposed to do?"

Ann tucked her purse into a drawer. She walked over to a tall metal closet, opening it to reveal cleaning supplies. "Master Sergeant Colter likes everything neat and tidy, so you can wipe down all the desks and chairs."

"Why me?"

"Because I said so." Ann eyed her daughter. "Getting kicked out of school doesn't mean you receive rewards."

"You yelled at Principal Gundersen for not treating girls and boys the same and that was pretty awesome, plus we got to go for ice cream."

Harry remained quiet, keeping his attention on the coffeepot as he scooped grounds into the basket, wondering how Ann would get out of that conundrum.

"The ice cream was because you behaved at the emergency clinic during all the tests when we saw the doctor, not a reward for fighting with your cousin and you still haven't shared what prompted that behavior."

"You didn't ask the right questions and I'm not a snitch." Grabbing the dust cloth and polish, Devon stomped to the far side of the room. "This sucks."

"Good." Ann sat down at her desk, opening a file folder.

Amused, Harry left the two silently working, pausing to turn on a radio on the way to his office. Classic country music filled the air.

He'd admired Ann's looks, intelligence and kick-butt attitude from the moment they met on Tuesday afternoon, two and a half days before.

She made him laugh even when he wanted her to 'soldier' up. Now, it became clearer that if he played his cards right, he'd have a family of his own soon. Granted, he didn't know her daughter that well yet, but he liked the girl. She had guts.

Obviously, Ann was a good mother, one who stood up to her kid, but didn't abuse the child. To win the pair, all he had to do was share their interests. If they felt important to him, he'd earn their love, care and affection. Ann would marry him in the next few months because he'd give her everything she'd ever wanted.

Zeke didn't follow his friend right away. Instead, he leaned against the wall and watched the little girl storm from one desk to the next. Would the daughter Twila always wanted have been that feisty? He hoped so. Of course, he'd have taught his sons to look after her, not bully her if he'd had the chance. Twila didn't take any crap, not from him or their kids but he probably wouldn't have had the opportunity. She never hesitated to step up when he was home.

Some of the guys complained about how bossy their wives were when they returned from the *Sandpit*, but he didn't. Like Harry's grandfather used to tell them, 'the strongest structure is an A-frame and the two of you need to lean on each other.' Twila had to run the entire family when he was gone, and she couldn't if he'd sabotaged her when he was around. Besides, she was super sexy when she planted her hands on her hips and started hollering about the messes the boys made. He should have told her that more often.

Too bad Colter couldn't hear him, or he'd be able to pass on the message.

Ann glanced after Harry. He looked nearly as good in his fatigues as he did in his Class B office attire. She couldn't help smiling as she filled in the sections on the paperwork, one letter or number to each box on the form. It seemed that Harry had won over her daughter as easily as he had her. She shook her head and forced away that thought. She wasn't interested in anything about Colter except her job.

When the coffeepot gave its last gurgle and the aroma of dark roast took over the room, Ann rose to her feet. Devon sulkily continued the task of wiping down the furniture. Ann left her daughter to the chore and went to fill two cups. She carried one back to Harry's office. "Here you go. Thanks for not busting a gut about the kid."

"It isn't a big deal." He frowned at the gas mask in front of him and then fitted in a new filter. "What did the doctor say about Devon's injuries?"

"Scrapes and bruises, sore muscles from falling or being knocked down on the pavement and a possible concussion. I checked on her several times last night, but she always knew her name, age and what she wanted for her birthday."

"What's that?"

"Either a puppy or a pony of her own. My dad will lose it if I bring a dog around his purebred Morgan horses so once I find a place for us to live, we'll go to the shelter and adopt one."

"My grandmother's collie had pups last month by the neighbor's cattle dog. By the time you find a place, move in and get settled, they'll be at least eight weeks old and ready for homes."

"Are you serious or just messing with me?"

"Puppies are too important to fool around." He fitted the next filter into place. "Don't fret about inconsequential things, Barrett. This unit and the battalion have enough monumental problems to keep both of us busy."

That seemed to be his attitude to life, Ann thought later that afternoon. Everything would be dealt with and Harry never lost control. Even the knowledge she was after his job didn't upset him. Could anything? When Devon had a tantrum and threw the incoming mail on the floor, Harry hadn't been angry. She glanced at him curiously. If he hadn't stolen her job, she would have liked him. She was starting to anyway. Ann paused to check on Devon napping on the couch outside Harry's office. She straightened the beloved patchwork quilt she'd made with her mother-in-law when she was expecting Devon, pleased the little girl still took it everywhere.

"You're staring." Harry kept his back to her and continued to rewire an old electrical connection.

Ann picked up a small screwdriver and passed it to Harry. "I don't see why you're bothering, Colter. Fixing up this old place won't make a difference. The unit is moving to a new building in Bellevue in the fall."

"I'll believe that when it happens," Harry grunted. "The commander said the move has been in the works for the past two years, Angel, even before the battalion shipped out to the *Sandbox* the last time. Besides, you'll need more power when the desktop computers arrive next week." He took the screwdriver from her. "If you don't take care of what you have, you'll never own anything."

"So, that's Colter's rule of life. Pardon me if I'm not impressed." She couldn't help but respect the man and she'd never admit it, not to him. "When I arrived here after my transfer back in the day, all we had were old manual typewriters. First Sergeant Raven Driscoll raised hell and got us laptops. I don't have a problem working with what's available."

"What's your rule of life, Barrett?"

"My rule?" Ann laughed bitterly. "I've learned everybody is out to take advantage and hurt you. So, my rule is to do onto others before they get the chance to do you in. What are you after, Colter?"

He shrugged one broad shoulder. "Nothing much, Angel. I've got a good job, my grandpa's farm and you to marry. What more could any man ask?"

"I've been married, Colter." She stared at the close-cropped black hair on his head speckled with a few dots of gray. "I'll never put my trust in another person again, just in my job."

"Do you think I'm like him?"

"Not yet. You're the typical street gentleman and house dog. Men are all the same. Crude, disgusting, immoral, unfaithful swine. And that's an insult to the pigs."

"You're a prejudiced little twit, aren't you?" He began to fasten down the plate that covered the plug-in. "Do you ever think you have a lousy attitude?"

"All the time. I'm not a positive person at the best of times and I'm probably doing what you said. I brought the war home with me and I shouldn't be taking my gender bias out on you."

"A bad attitude doesn't scare me."

She watched him stand up. He was so big and muscular. She longed to run her hands over his body and see if his wide chest was the same bronzed color as his tanned arms. She couldn't tell with the tan t-shirt he wore. He stopped in front of her. "Harry?"

She moistened suddenly dry lips. His gaze had taken on the blue of a stormy sky and her pulses thudded in anticipation. She took a step back, her voice a husky whisper. "No."

"Do you ever wear a skirt, Angel?" Harry's hands closed over her elbows. "I'll bet you have the sexiest legs in the battalion."

Slowly sanity came back to her. What was she doing? Anyone could come in and Devon might wake up at any moment. Ann wrenched free. "No, Harry. Not here."

"Then where, sweetheart?" He eased his hold and she stepped free.

She scanned the worry and concern etched around his eyes and mouth. Ann reached up to touch his cheek with a gentle finger. "Don't hate yourself. It was my fault."

What kind of a woman was she? Hadn't she outgrown her past even now? She'd tried so hard to shed her party girl image from high school. Yet, no other woman would have taken one look at Harry Colter today and fallen into his strong arms. She turned away, sickened by her behavior.

He strode after her and his hands closed over her shoulders. "I'm an adult, Angel. Don't make excuses for me. You're right, though. This isn't the time or the place, but I don't have a lot of willpower where you're concerned."

She trembled. She ought to pull loose, not want to melt against him. She shouldn't long to feel his mouth on hers. All she really wanted from Master Sergeant Harry Colter was *her* job, nothing more. Even if he did accept responsibility for his actions, that didn't make him perfect.

The telephone rang and she welcomed the diversion, grateful when Harry went to answer it. Her voice would have shaken, revealing her unsteady emotions. She had to have her control firmly in place when he looked at her. Otherwise, she'd melt in the heat of his gaze.

He replaced the receiver and swung back around. "That was the commander. He wants a detailed report on the status of the rifles and pistols. When can you do it?"

She stared at him for an instant, reading the seriousness on his features. "Colter, I thought you were doing the supply room while I took care of things in here. I'm handling my job. Why should I do yours?"

"Because I don't type. You do. The C.O.'s not going to be able to read my crummy handwriting."

"Nobody could. I've seen your signature. How did you make it through high school?"

"Barely. I joined the Army and was in basic training right after graduation." His features hardened into a fierce mask of planes and angles. "The next year I was in Kosovo."

She cursed her bitter tongue. Why hadn't she thought before she spoke? She watched him start toward the back door and hurried after him, tears stinging behind her eyes. "Harry, I'm sorry. I shouldn't have said that."

His back stiffened and his tone grew tighter. "Now, you know all about me..."

She heard the self-disgust in his voice, and she castigated herself again. "That you enlisted when you were a senior? I don't think most of the guys in my class bothered to finish high school and they didn't join the military. I never intended to insult you."

"Yes, you did, but I'll cut you some slack on this one, Sarge. I'll believe you never intended to hurt me. You probably didn't think it was possible."

She choked, feeling a lump rise in her throat. "I said I was sorry, Harry. I'll do the damned report."

"You're right about that." He stalked to the back door. "And you can take care of the rest of the supply paperwork as well. Maybe if I find you enough things to do, you'll quit hassling me."

"The hell I will!" She tossed her head. "I apologized. As far as I'm concerned, that's the end of it."

"Wrong." He uttered the word softly, too softly. "Clerks type reports and that's your job."

"Wow, we should call you, Sergeant Chauvinist."

"Are you two going to keep fighting?" Devon yawned. "You woke me up."

"Sorry about that." Ann went to her daughter. "Are you ready to get up?"

"Not really." Devon heaved a sigh, then closed her eyes. "I'm super tired after you kept waking me up last night. Uncle Reid said you should spank me. I'm glad you didn't."

"I don't believe in hitting kids." Ann smoothed the dark curls. "When did you hear him say that? He wasn't in the office when I was, so I didn't hear him."

"Before you got there." Devon slid further under her quilt. "He told Mrs. Gundersen that he spanked me lots of times when I stayed with them, but it wasn't enough for me to learn how to be good and mind him and my boy cousins."

Fury rose and Ann clenched her fists, nails biting into her palms. She struggled to keep her voice even. "Why didn't you tell me before?"

"You'd gone 'way, and Daddy took me there. When Aunt Barb and Uncle Reid went to the store, they left us with a babysitter. I told her I wanted Grampa Phil, and his last name was Sweeney. She found my cousin Jassy in the phone book. The sitter called her, and she told Grampa. He came and got me. He and Gramma Nessie said you had enough to worry about in the war, not to scare you and they'd keep me safe until you came home."

"I'm glad they took good care of you." Ann kissed her daughter's forehead. "Now, finish your nap, sweetness."

"You and Mass-Sarge Harry won't fight no more?"

"Not when you can hear." Ann glanced over her shoulder at him, surprised at the rising anger on his face. Now, what was his problem? "I promise."

"Good. When Daddy phoned from Idaho, Gramma said for him never to take me there again or else he'd be in big trouble. She told him they were taking me to Disneyland too and they did. It was the best time ever. I got pictures taken with Mickey Mouse and all the princesses. Gramma told Daddy to send them to you."

"He didn't, but I'll get copies from her. I'm glad you had fun." Ann adjusted the quilt. "Finish your nap, sweetheart."

Harry took a step forward and gripped her arm. "Let's go out on the stoop." He didn't give her time to answer but escorted her from the office.

"What is it, Colter? You decided to get mad because my ex-husband is a louse? I could have told you that."

He shook his head and glared at the building opposite. "No. It's what Devon said. She's only six now. How could you allow someone to put their hands on her when she was even younger?"

"Are you assuming my brother-in-law had my permission for what he did to my child? Or I agreed my ex-husband could take her to my sister's house? I wasn't consulted. I was in combat, for God's sake and as you heard my in-laws opted to keep it a deep, dark secret." She jerked away from him. "I'm going to the P.X., Colter, and as far as I'm concerned, you can go to hell!" She started down the sidewalk. "And if my abused kid wakes up, send her to the bathroom."

It was only a couple of blocks to the little building that served as the Fort Bronson Post Exchange. Ann nodded at the two saleswomen and hurried to the cooler that held the soda. She selected a cola for herself and after a long moment, picked out one for Harry. He'd defended her daughter. That took some effort on his part and he'd been sincere. She was still amazed by his behavior. Would any other man have stood up to her because he felt Devon might be in jeopardy? Her father would and so would Phillip, but they were in the minority.

Obviously Will hadn't even cared enough to set guidelines about appropriate discipline when he dropped their daughter off at her various aunts and uncles. Ann wandered back up to the candy bars and gathered up three. Crossing to the check-out stand, she glimpsed the toys and turned back to study the limited assortment. She picked up a medium-sized, stuffed teddy bear.

"That's adorable. Are you getting it for Devon?"

Ann turned with a smile. Margo's strawberry-blonde hair was twisted into an exquisite knot on top of her head. Her blue eyes had a purplish cast today. She must have changed her contacts again. Her fatigues were as immaculate as always. "I couldn't get down to headquarters last night, not after the call from the school."

"I don't blame you," Margo replied instantly. "Devon would be my top priority too. How is she?"

"In major trouble with that witch, Gundersen. She suspended Devon for fighting with her cousin and Bobby didn't even get in-school detention."

"What's new about that? Janet's always cut boys more slack than she ever does girls. Isn't Bobby older than Devon?"

"He's in third grade and I'd bet he did something to her when Will dropped her off to stay with Barbara. Devon just told me that Reid spanked her when she was there and as soon as she got the chance, she ratted him out to her grandparents."

"Well, he's a 'dead man walking.' Which of us gets to kick his backside first? You or me?"

"Don't do it in uniform, or you'll never hear the end of it."

"Got that right. Which grandparents?"

"Phillip and Vanessa. They took her to Disneyland. She loved it. She got her picture taken with Mickey Mouse. Will was supposed to send me copies of the photos, but he didn't because then he'd have to explain why they went there. I need to call Vanessa and take her to lunch this weekend."

Ann tucked the teddy bear under her arm and headed for the cart of marked down items. There were usually a few toys and Devon could always use more crayons. "I'm so glad Phil and Vanessa stepped up and took care of her when Will and Reid started trying to outperform each other."

Margo began to pick through the assortment of dolls on sale until she found a pretty redhead. "What do you think? She drinks, wets and cries."

"And she has your hair and eyes. She's perfect." Ann held out her hand. "Give me the doll."

Margo shook her head. "No. Devon's my favorite kid. I want to give her something."

"Forget it!" Ann grabbed the package. "Every time you see her, you spoil her rotten. When you got home, you bought her more stuff than her grandparents gave her for Christmas. I'm trying to raise a decent kid, not a spoiled brat. Her birthday's coming up and I know you'll do it again. No way, Margo."

Tears welled up in Margo's eyes. "You hate me."

"No, I don't," Ann protested. Even if she knew Margo could shed tears like someone turning on a water faucet, it was still an effective weapon. Ann felt her guilt growing. Margo really did love Devon.

"What's the matter here?" a deep voice boomed. A tall man built like a truck driver glared at them.

Ann glowered back. "She's performing, Colonel Williams. I don't care if she runs Personnel at HQ and is my best friend. It won't work. I'm giving the doll to my daughter." The best defense was a good offense and she demanded. "What are you both doing up here? Who's running the headquarters?"

Margo sniffled. "You never let me give her anything and she is my only godchild."

"Don't cry," Colonel Williams interceded, winking at Ann. "I'm sure Sergeant Barrett will let you buy her something, Captain Endicott, especially if she wants my help in getting that A.G. R. job." He raked a hand through his prematurely white hair.

Margo's smile could have melted a stone, Ann thought, and Williams was obviously prejudiced in her favor. Shaking her head, Ann swung around and stalked to the checkout counter. "I guess I'd better pay for these."

"All that talent." The cashier, an older woman leaned toward her and glanced at Margo. "She's wasted in the military. She should be in the movies."

Ann choked back an appreciative grin. "Just don't tell him." She jerked her head to where Colonel Williams was helping her friend find a suitable toy for Devon. "You'll break his heart."

"I used to think he was a smart man. I suppose even they fall as hard as the rest."

CHAPTER EIGHT

The words remained in Ann's mind as Margo came toward her. Was that the truth? Was the Colonel attracted to Margo? If he was, it certainly explained why he spent so much time teasing her.

Ann waited until they were walking back to her office. Williams had purchased a can of chewing tobacco and returned to the headquarters. "What's the Colonel's first name? And how long has he been chasing you?"

"He's not," Margo put on her most plastic smile. "He claims he cares about me and yes, we're sleeping together. If you say a word, I'll rip out your tongue."

"No wonder you said he'd help me, but you didn't tell me his first name. Why aren't you two getting hitched now that we're home?"

"Because he thinks I'm just grateful he helped me when I lost it with Fisher and all I want is an affair." Margo stared blindly at the cracked pavement. "You have enough problems, Ann. Why the hell am I sharing mine?"

"Because I'm your best friend and you know I won't do anything to jeopardize your career or his. The ship would hit the proverbial sand around here if anyone else found out, especially one of those PC people who'd start screaming 'sexual harassment,' even if he's not your direct supervisor. Anyway, I brought Devon to work with me since my folks were too busy to look after her today and that will make waves."

"What about the Ranger? What did he say? If Jared—I mean Colonel Williams. If he finds out, he'll rip you apart. We aren't supposed to have dependents on post."

"What about you?" Ann inquired. "Are you going to tell him? You're in love with him."

Margo blinked. "You're a witch, Ann. Of course, I'm not gonna tattle. How did you know what I felt?"

"Because you're sleeping with him. As for Harry, he likes Devon. He's not saying a word except he yelled at me for letting Reid touch her."

"What a nice guy. We'll have to let him have a turn when we kick Reid's butt."

"Not happening. It's a girl thing. You and I have it covered."

"Then, you should let me babysit Devon tonight so I can take her to the dojo with me."

"Why would I do that when she already got in trouble for fighting?"

"Because karate would teach her discipline and self-control as well as how to defend herself. Think about it. If she's with me there, I won't buy her a ton of toys."

"That's worth considering." Ann pulled open the swinging door and led the way into the main room. It was automatic to check on her daughter before she did anything else. Devon sat in a chair reading her book. "What are you doing, honey?"

"Would you believe Mass-Sarge Harry doesn't know anything about *Harry Potter* or *Hogwarts*? So, I'm teaching him."

"Okay." Ann glanced at Harry who was shifting some of the desks around and he grinned at her. She crossed to him and offered a cold soda while they listened to the little girl read, occasionally stumbling over a word. He earned points when he didn't try to help with the vocabulary issues, but let Devon resolve them on her own.

When she reached the end of the chapter a few minutes later, Ann said, "Aunt Margo's here."

"I know. I saw her." Devon put the book on the desk, jumped down and ran to hug the other woman. "Did Mama tell you I'm in big trouble for kicking Bobby's butt?"

"She told me." Margo tipped Devon's face to the light streaming in the windows. "Hmm, you didn't do a very good job if he nailed you, honey. When you stomp somebody who needs it, you have to block their punches."

"I didn't know that."

"It's why I need to take you with me to my dojo and have *Sensei* teach you how to really fight."

"Wow." Devon glanced over her shoulder. "Mama, can I go?"

"I'm thinking about it." Ann twisted the cap off her cola and took a sip of the icy drink. "Your Grandma Ginger will have a stroke. She likes you to be a dainty princess."

"Grampa Frank always wants her to have what she wants. He says it makes the house more peaceful, 'cause a 'happy wife means a happy life' and that means I can't do it."

"*I* didn't say that." Ann eyed the well-loved book on the desk. "I'm your mom and I make the rules for you. How many times have you read this book?"

"I don't know. Tons since Aunt Margo gave it to me when she got home 'fore you did."

"Be specific."

Devon heaved a dramatic sigh and counted silently on her fingers. "Eight. Today doesn't count 'cuz I just started again."

"I see." Ann studied the pair, the red-haired woman with an arm around the dark-haired child. "I have conditions if you two are having a date night. Devon, you have to mind Aunt Margo and be polite."

"I will. I promise I will."

"I'm not done. You have to try your best and listen to the karate teacher."

"The one Aunt Margo calls, '*Sensei*'?"

"Precisely. Margo, you have to stop at the mall in Lynnwood and get her the next book in the *Hogwarts* series." Ann barely managed to put down the soda bottle before Devon reached her and grabbed her in a fierce hug. "What's this about?"

"You're the best mama ever."

"Cupboard love, but I'll take it." Ann hugged her daughter tight. "Why didn't you look at the school library for the next *Harry Potter* book?"

"I did, but Mrs. Small said I could only check out first grade chapter books and she wouldn't listen when I said I'd read them years ago."

Ann exchanged a look with Margo who smiled smugly. "I don't want to hear it."

"Too bad, too sad. I'm gonna say it anyway. I told you teaching the kid to read when she was three would come back to bite you in the butt. Felice Small has no imagination or creativity. Of course, she can't handle a smarty-pants like your daughter."

Devon turned her head. "I wish you were my teacher, Aunt Margo."

"Me too, honey, but your principal won't give me a classroom because I told her she was a major twit back in the day when we were in college together."

"Well, thank you for cleaning that up."

"Didn't she actually say it, Mama?"

"She said worse. She's sugar-coating it because I don't like it when she swears in front of you."

Devon nodded. "I remember. You both got in trouble with Mrs. O'Connell for teaching me to say 'bad' words when I was in preschool. Uncle Jack still says them."

Harry chuckled. "It's hard not to say them sometimes."

"Uncle Jack uses 'em in the barn. He called Mama's horse, a 'f-ing' monster and Grampa sent Sky away to live with Mrs. Cat."

"Not forever. He's at Cedar Creek Guest Ranch to be trained. Your grandfather says Cat McTavish is doing a good job with him. I'll have to stop and see him this weekend."

"Easy enough to do," Margo said. "If you and Devon stay over with me tonight, you only have to walk up the driveway to the barn. I have carrots in the fridge. Cat lets me ride her horse with the twins most Saturdays."

"That works. Thanks, Margo."

"No worries." Her cell phone buzzed, and Margo pulled it out of her pocket, grimacing at the screen. "I've got to go. Fisher just entered Reserve Command HQ and my ROTC candidate is alone in Personnel today. Give me your finance forms for the unit and I'll drop those off for you. I'll be back at the end of the day for Devon."

Organizing the downstairs took most of the afternoon. Devon spent her time completing math worksheets occasionally asking her mother for help, reading to him from the Harry Potter story and finally carefully using her new crayons to color puppies in the new book Margo had brought.

Harry deliberately didn't mention that Ann should be more professional with her friend and maintain the respectful distance the military expected between a non-com and commissioned officer. First, it wasn't a topic he felt comfortable bringing up in front of a child and second it was clear that the women were close friends. They were smart and undoubtedly put up more of a front when others were around.

When Devon went off to the bathroom, he strolled over to Ann's desk. "Are we still on for dinner and that Shakespeare festival tonight?"

She frowned thoughtfully, then nodded after a moment. "Sure. I just need to call and let my stepmother know that we're staying over at Margo's."

"I heard you mention Cedar Creek Guest Ranch. Are you talking about the one near Baker City?"

"I don't think there's a different place with that name on this side of the Cascade mountains. My dad has Majestyk Morgan Farm on the far side of town. Why?"

"It's a small world. My family comes from there and my grandmother still runs the local preschool."

"Oh, my Gawd. You mean Janine O'Connell is your grandmother? She threatened to make me hunt snipe in her parking lot if I didn't stop cussing in front of Devon back in the day."

"I won't tell you how many times Zeke and I had to do that when we were home on leave. I didn't think there was a single cigarette butt in a twenty-mile radius when we finished."

"Well, maybe she collected them from the local bars and salted her parking lot, but I didn't want to push the woman not when she wasn't going to let me go to kindergarten because I was so naughty when I attended her school."

"What did you do?" He hitched a hip on the corner of her desk. "Beat up the boys like Devon?"

Ann grinned appreciatively. "No. During cut and paste time, I created packs of cigarettes and sold them to the other kids. When I got in trouble for that, she sent me off to play with blocks. So, I set up a bar and hired some of the girls and boys to be servers. Everyone else got to be customers."

Harry laughed, imagining how hard it must have been for his grandmother to maintain discipline. Even if she hadn't said so, she'd have enjoyed the creativity a young Ann displayed. "Where did you learn how to do that?"

"My McElroy grandparents owned the Baker City Saloon before they sold it to Steve Garvey and retired. Much to Ginger's disgust, they used to let me play there when I visited most weekends. I loved wiping down the booths, doing jigsaw puzzles—"

"That was the place where the old man glued the completed ones together and decorated all of the walls with them."

"Yes, and he taught me to play pool with him." Ann leaned back in her chair. "Your grandma got all excited when I used her decks of cards to teach the rest of the kids to play poker."

"Mama, you were bad." Devon gaped at her mother, obviously amazed. "Nobody ever told me that stuff."

"Yes, I was, but I never kicked my cousin's butt or even my older sisters' tails." Ann drew her daughter close. "I'll bet your grandpa kept all of my hijinks to himself because your grandma certainly wouldn't be happy if he shared my dark secrets."

"It's not very princessey and that's how she thinks little girls should behave." Devon pressed close. "Was that what your real mama thought too?"

"I barely remember Lucy, so I don't know what she liked, honey. She left when I was three. Your grandpa started dating your Grandma Ginger when I was five and they married a short time later."

"Didn't she want you to call her, Mama?"

"Afraid not." No emotion showed on Ann's face. "She made it very plain to me and my older sisters that we were 'passing through' and not her kids."

"That's sad." Devon turned her attention to Harry. "Mass-Sarge Harry, were you always good when you were a kid?"

"Nope, but my grandma always claimed I was and made me lots of my favorite chocolate chip cookies." Harry glanced at the clock. "It's almost four-thirty. Let's finish up so you're ready when Captain

Endicott arrives. You don't want to be late for your first karate class."

The sun teetered on the horizon, barely beginning to rise when he parked next to her car. Ann leaned back in the seat. "So, what did you think of the plays?"

"You'll never let me hear the end of it when I say I actually enjoyed them, will you?"

She laughed. "No, but only because I know how annoying it is when someone says, 'I told you so' repeatedly. What was the best part?"

"The fact that people don't change." He switched off the truck motor. "They get bored, make trouble for each other and fall in love."

"Wow, Harry. I think you just rolled up an entire semester's worth of classes in one sentence." She watched a smile ease across his face.

She'd thought he looked amazing in uniform but seeing him in jeans and a blue-checked flannel shirt added even more appeal. She glanced at her watch. "I need to get on the road home before Margo thinks she has Devon for the whole day."

He nodded. "We'll have to do it again, but next time I pick the activity, Angel, one suitable for Devon to join us."

"That means it can't be an all-nighter. She goes to bed at eight, so it should be closer to home."

"No worries. I'll think of something special." He opened his door.

"Sounds good." While she waited for him to come around to her side of the pickup, she slid out of the vehicle. He still towered above her and she tipped back her head to meet his gaze. "What happens now?"

He feathered a thumb over her lips. "Neither of us are in uniform."

"Got that right." She was grateful she'd still had the jeans, t-shirt, sweatshirt and light denim jacket in the car after hanging out with Margo a couple days before. "Isn't this when you kiss me, Colter?"

"Definitely." He pulled her against him, and his head lowered.

His mouth descended on hers like a plummeting eagle and she met his fire with her own. It'd been too long since a man touched her, especially one who knew how to kiss her, and Harry seemed to quench the fires of suppressed passion just before he lit them.

Her fingers twisted and twined in his short dark hair. She was shocked by her own eager response to the touch of his lips, but it didn't stop her from opening her mouth beneath the fierce pressure of his. She welcomed the invasion of his tongue with her own. How could she have forgotten what this was like? Then she realized that nothing had prepared her for the sensual delights he promised. His mouth trailed a series of kisses over her throat and she moaned softly.

When he lifted his head, she swayed against him, struggling to catch her breath. "Wow, I didn't expect that."

"I did." He framed her face with his hands. "Will I see you this weekend?"

She shook her head. "I have to find a place for us to live so Devon can have that puppy. I need to call your grandmother about it. Do you want to give her a 'heads-up', so it doesn't come as a total surprise?"

"I'll do that tomorrow when I join her for Sunday dinner."

"If you go to church with her in Baker City, I may see you there."

"I'll look forward to it."

"Me too." She tiptoed up to brush her mouth over his. "If not, Devon and I will see you Monday."

"Eight-o-clock, Barrett. Not one minute later. And I'll bring the doughnuts."

"That's do-able." Smiling, she stepped out of his hold and headed to her own car. He didn't have far to go since he'd told her he lived in the Bachelor Enlisted Quarters on base, but she had a long drive to the guest ranch outside Baker City.

He drove past the office buildings, cemetery and chapel to the building that served as a barracks for Fort Bronson. Most of the time, he and two or three other non-coms were the only ones who stayed in the two-story structure. When he parked, he spotted Master Sergeant Derek Waller, smoking on the porch. While they were the same rank, the other man had a dozen years on him.

Harry crossed to the stairs. "Morning, Derek."

"Morning, Harry. Joining us for breakfast?"

"I already ate. I'm hitting the sack."

"Sounds fair. I dropped off those lightbulbs you wanted by your door. It's a puzzle. Why do you think your bulbs keep burning out?"

"No idea. I've checked the wiring and it's fine."

"Hmm, it's still interesting." Waller pulled out a second cigarette and lit it from the first, dark eyes narrowing. "How was your date?"

"Good and that's all I'm saying." Harry stepped around the solid, muscular man whose worn features looked as if he'd won more fights than he'd lost in his thirty-plus years of military service.

A few minutes later, he opened the door to his room. A narrow twin bed, dresser, wall-locker, portable TV, and a desk with a single chair was the extent of the furnishings. He'd added a small refrigerator in the corner, but it didn't take up much power. He flicked on the light switch and nothing happened. He debated changing the overhead bulb and decided against it. Enough sunlight came through the two windows.

He unbuttoned his shirt, shrugging out of it and put it on the chair. A chill breeze blew through the room and he glanced at the closed windows, then at the door he'd locked behind him. The fort might be on its last legs, but he'd survived worse. For now, he'd distract himself by thinking where he could take Ann and Devon next weekend.

Zeke aimed a kick at the wastepaper basket. It barely rattled and remained near the desk, not rolling across the room. He glared at the radio on the dresser, but it didn't come on and play Colter's favorite country music. After that steamy kiss, his buddy should have taken the woman home. There was bound to be a motel close enough to Baker City that Zeke could have seen Twila while Colter took Barrett to bed. *Instead, you acted like a leg and sent her off by herself. Colter, quit being such a numb-nuts. I want to go home.*

CHAPTER NINE

Ann arrived at Margo's in time to join her and Devon for breakfast, then headed up to the loft bedroom to catch a nap. When she woke a few hours later, she found a fresh pot of coffee in the small kitchen along with a note on the table inviting her to join the other two at the barn where they'd gone to visit the horses. It sounded like a great idea. She hadn't seen Skyrocket in almost two years except in occasional videos.

Two young collies came to greet her, a tri-color male toting a tennis ball which he dropped at her feet. Ann carefully tossed it across the lawn in the opposite direction from the corral where she spotted her daughter riding with two other girls, obviously sisters. The dogs tore off in pursuit of the toy and Ann kept walking. When she arrived, Devon reined the small black pony with white spots toward the fence.

"Mama, this is Rainy Night. Isn't he beautiful?"

"He's lovely." Thankfully, he was only about forty inches at the withers, short enough for her daughter to be in proportion to him, but Ann didn't say that or ask who loaned the child an equestrian helmet. Instead, she admired the gelding's white socks and blaze that offset the speckled, Appaloosa snowflake pattern of his dark coat. "Is he named after the song?"

"I didn't know there was a song about him. What is it?"

"Oh, it's an oldie, but a goodie." Ann leaned her elbows on the top rail of the fence. "I'll find it for you on my computer and you can sing it to him next time you visit."

Devon petted the pony's neck. "Samantha says he was a rescue and her mom wants to find a good home for him. I really, really want my own pony."

"I know you do and I'm thinking about it." Ann glanced toward the stable when she heard hoofbeats and voices. She saw Margo leading out a palomino Quarter-horse followed by Cat McTavish, a tall redhead with hip-length copper hair. Today, she wore a blue tank top under a flannel shirt and loose, faded jeans. Pausing to close the barn door, Cat glanced toward the ring, a smile warming her face and emerald green eyes.

"Well, hello there. Welcome home, stranger." Cat came through a gate and hurried forward to greet Ann with a hug. "I heard you were here. I'm glad you made it back safe and sound."

"Thanks." Ann swept her gaze over the other woman, noticing the weight gain and swelling of her stomach under the checked, blue-flannel man's shirt. "You're pregnant."

"Yup." Cat grinned. "Thank goodness, it's one baby, not two. Rob's over the moon. You'd think we'd never had a kid before."

"Rob?" Ann eyed her one-time friend. They'd met and bonded when Cat came to intern with the same natural horse trainer who'd hired Ann eleven years before. "I thought your husband's name was Frazer."

"It was, but when we reconciled after we almost divorced last fall, he decided he wanted to go by his middle name instead. Fresh start, fresh name."

"Why do I feel there's more to it than that?"

"Because you've always been smart. Come see Sky. He's in his stall finishing lunch. Rob was tacking him up so he could join the girls on a trail ride, but now you can take them with Margo instead."

Ann nearly said from what she remembered of the wanna-be-professional gambler that she wouldn't trust him as far as she could throw him uphill in a snow storm, much less around the horse she rescued when he was almost killed in a stock trailer on the way to a rodeo. She opted to remain quiet long enough to check out the situation. Perhaps, she could arrange for her dad to find a stall for the

Morab gelding now that she was home, although it'd totally tick off Ginger who'd already hinted more than once it was time for Ann to move on to greener pastures.

They entered the barn with large box stalls on either side of a wide aisle. Ann spotted the flashy bay nosing a dark-haired guy in cowboy garb. Six-foot-six, short thick black hair that was almost a military high and tight cut, narrow-hipped, he glanced toward them with the kind of smile she didn't remember seeing on Frazer's face before.

He scratched the horse's golden-brown neck, nodding at her before he turned his gaze on Cat. "I thought you were going to the house to rest."

"Get over yourself, Rob. I'm pregnant, not helpless." Cat slung an arm around Ann's shoulders. "This is Ann Barrett, Sky's owner. She wants to ride him."

"Good. If she goes with Margo and the kids, then you can take a nap while I clean the barn."

Ann stepped up to the front of the stall to stroke her horse's blaze wishing she'd remembered to bring carrots. "Is that why Margo is riding your horse, Cat? Because you're preggers?"

"Yes. Ever since Doctor MacGillicudy confirmed it, Rob's been a major pain in my backside. He thinks he can tell me what to do." Cat tossed her head, narrowing her eyes. "If it's not hassling me when the deliveries come, it's ordering me to leave the cat box for him to clean and freaking out when I carry a bag of groceries into the house, or muck stalls or drag around the hose to water the horses. When he heard I planned to continue riding and training until my seventh or eighth month, he went ballistic even though Doc said I'd be safe enough as long as I didn't take a fall."

"Are you serious?" Ann shook her head. "Remember what Mario told us back in the day? Good riders always keep half their weight in their seats and half in their feet. Even if your doctor doesn't get it, you know that constant downward pressure of your body when you're in the saddle might cause a miscarriage."

"Shut up, Ann. Rob doesn't need any encouragement to be an arrogant know-it-all who tries to boss me around."

"I tell my wife what to do because she doesn't have the sense to figure it out on her own." Rob picked up the bridle from the outside hook and replaced Sky's halter with it, handing the reins to Ann. "Check the cinches on those ponies and Paladin before you leave the corral. Trail riding is done at a walk. Margo knows which paths I've cleared."

Ann blinked, amazed at the authoritative tone. He didn't sound at all like the man she'd met so many years ago, the one that oozed practiced charm on all occasions. "Okay, I guess. What are you doing?"

"Taking care of my wife." Rob petted the horse once more when Sky nudged him, then left the stall, advancing on Cat. She squealed and stepped back, but he snagged her wrist before he picked her up, holding her in his arms. "I told you to go rest. Now, I'll see to it that you do."

Ann watched the pair leave the barn, amused when Cat waved at her, obviously not upset by the macho posturing. "He's totally different today, not the guy with the fastest hands in the West that I remember." She straightened the horse's black forelock before pushing the door wide. "Well, let's go see what Cat taught you while I was gone."

In the corral, she led the gelding into the middle of the ring, dropping his reins so he'd stand ground-tied for a few moments while she adjusted tack on the ponies. She tightened Rainy Night's cinch first, automatically eying the length of Devon's stirrups before moving onto the light gray Arabian-Welsh. She nodded to the little redhead sitting in his saddle. "Hi, I'm Ann Barrett, Devon's mom."

"I'm Sophie and that's my sister, Samantha. We're twins. Are Mommy and Daddy off kissing again?"

"Probably." Ann secured the knot on the latigo. "He wanted her to take a break while we go riding."

"He's been looking up stuff on her computer 'bout what she should and shouldn't do, 'cuz we're having a little sister or brother soon. Mommy says he's 'gravating her."

"Aggravating her," Samantha corrected from a short distance away on a solid-looking Welsh Mountain Pony. "But, our daddy's not a bully like Bobby so Mommy doesn't have to kick his butt like Devon did her cousin."

"I didn't know Bobby was a bully." Ann slid her fingers between the string cinch and the pony's side, then snugged the straps. "Is he in your class?"

Samantha nodded; her summer-sky-blue eyes serene as she recited what she apparently thought were just the facts. "Him and his friends steal lunch money and push the little kids 'round, then they lie about it to the playground teachers and our teacher and the principal."

"They're sneaky buggers," Sophie finished. "You gotta watch out for them. Our daddy told Bobby's daddy that if he comes after us, Daddy will stop at the car lot and Mr. Kramer won't enjoy the visit."

"Okay, good to know." Ann crossed to Margo's horse. "One more cinch and we're outta here."

"Great. When we get back, let's talk to Cat about the big guest cabin near mine. If you and Devon rent it, we can ride together a lot more."

"I'll think about it."

That was rapidly becoming her answer to almost every question. She didn't want to commit, not when she remembered the way Cat's husband, Frazer Hendrickson tried jumping her in the past. Today, he'd acted as if he didn't know her, not as if he was the same guy who cornered her more than once in the training barn or the apartment she'd shared with Cat. She'd told Cat the guy was a creep, but it hadn't done any good. Eventually, she simply distanced herself from her friend, focusing on the work at hand and learning everything she could from Mario O'Rourke while she lived at his stable.

They left the corral with Margo in the lead on the Palomino and the girls strung out behind, Devon sandwiched between the twins. Ann brought up the rear on Skyrocket. The bay flicked his ears a time or two, then settled into a comfortable walk, staying approximately twelve feet behind Samantha's pony. Ann barely had to squeeze her legs to adjust his pace and when she sat back in the saddle, he slowed. He didn't fuss or chew on the bit which meant she wouldn't have to worry about him drooling, a sign of stress according to Mario. She reached down to rub his neck. He'd turned into a 'real' horse while she was gone.

Margo led the way down a fenced lane by rolling pastures to the creek that wound along the front of the place between the guest ranch and the highway. They rode by the next building, a combination dining hall and party barn. Beyond it were tennis courts and baseball diamonds. A cool, late March breeze rustled the trees when they crossed the driveway and entered the woods. Next came the bridge over a narrow stream which the twins told her their father built so the ponies wouldn't get their hooves wet.

When they circled around on a different trail that eventually would take them back home, she saw the small guest cabins again. She found herself wondering if she really could live here with Devon. They'd have to discuss the situation with Bobby. Granted people had to stand up to bullies, but it wasn't her daughter's place to take on each and every ruffian in the world.

Two hours later, they rode into the corral. The twins waved at Rob when he came out of the barn to greet them. He closed the gate behind Ann and Skyrocket.

"If you're good with it, the kids can help me with horsy chores and you ladies can go to the porch and entertain Cat. Then, she won't be out here making mischief."

"Daddy, you'll be in big trouble again," Sophie warned him. "Mommy says having babies is perfectly natural and she doesn't need to rest all the time."

Margo swung out of the saddle. "I want to talk to Cat anyway, so I don't mind missing out on shoveling horse poo for once."

"I'll come too." Ann glanced at her daughter. "Devon, if you really want that pony, you have to learn how to take care of him."

"And Mister Robbie says he'll teach me everything 'bout him." Devon leaned forward past the saddle to hug Rainy Night. "I love him so much."

Ann met Rob's amused dark gaze. "She means the pony."

"I know." He stepped up to hold the rein close to the bit. "What did you think of this guy?"

"That Cat did an amazing job with him." Ann dismounted, passing over the reins. "I couldn't have done better. I'll tell her so."

"He threw her more than once. After I saw her take a couple bad falls, I rode him first. She had a fit and fell in it, but I wasn't letting him hurt her."

"I remember you telling me there wasn't a need for horses in this world, not when people could drive cars. You thought Cat and I were insane for paying to work with Mario to learn to train them."

"Must have been when I was going through my stupid phase. When I got out of the hospital last year, it was time to grow up."

"We all get there sooner or later." Ann left the corral with Margo heading toward the three-story Victorian house. Behind them, they heard Rob direct the girls as they unsaddled their ponies. She flicked a glance at her friend. "He's changed. He didn't leer at me once. Back in the day, he used to talk to my boobs."

"I've lived here since January and he's never acted like a lech."

"Well, since they're having another kid, Cat didn't geld him."

Margo nearly choked on laughter, then elbowed Ann. "Be nice when we get there. The woman needs more friends."

"And that's different too. Frazer used to do his best to isolate her from everyone."

They climbed the steps to the wraparound porch and Ann saw Cat sitting at a table in the corner, a pot of tea in front of her along with three cups, accompanied by a plate of homemade chocolate chip cookies. "We've been sent to keep you company."

"Rob does like to think he's the man in charge. It's fun to watch." Cat gestured toward the front door. "Margo, will you show Ann where to wash up? I'm betting she doesn't want to taste horses when she has a cookie."

"Got that right." Ann lingered for a moment on the porch. "Sky is amazing. He's dead quiet. He didn't even spook when he saw rabbits scurrying around in one of the fields. You did a wonderful job training him."

"I can't take all the credit. It was a team effort."

"So, I heard."

After washing up, they rejoined Cat on the porch. Ann drew up a chair. "Okay, educate me. How did you turn your hubby, Frazer Hendrickson into a human being? Are we going to see the process on reality television?"

"I didn't do it." Cat filled three cups with raspberry tea, passing them around. "He left for a casino job on a riverboat down South and I filed for divorce. Then, I won this place in an essay contest and moved here with the girls, Lad, your horse and mine."

"What was the catch with the guest ranch?" Ann asked. "There had to be one."

"I had to restore it to its former glory and reopen it as a destination resort. After I ran it for ten years, I could sell it but only to someone who continued to operate it as a dude ranch."

"And Frazer? He said he was in the hospital. What happened?"

"After he lost everything in Louisiana, his job, his sports car and all his money, he came back and tried to reconcile with me."

"Did you take him back?" Margo sipped her tea. "Or not?"

"Not right away. He was helping us work on promoting the town for Halloween and went for supplies in my truck. We didn't know someone cut the brake lines. He's a hell of a driver, but the rig fishtailed and went over the cliff at the 'S' turns between here and Lake Maynard."

"Oh, my Gawd! Is that why he was in the hospital?" Ann stared at her friend. "He's lucky he lived."

"They lost him four times, but they managed to bring him back from the dead each time." Cat passed around the plate of cookies. "When they did, he was different. I don't know if you want to call it an epiphany or what. I just know I fell in love with the man I brought home from the hospital."

"He's lucky to have you." Ann bit into a cookie. "A lot of women wouldn't have been able to forgive him after everything he did. You told me he cheated on you several times."

"Not Rob. He has too much honor to betray my trust, but Frazer lied when the truth would serve. He did a lot of crappy things but thank heaven Rob has partial amnesia after the accident and doesn't remember any of that." Cat refilled their cups. "Frazer's gone for good, but Rob is here for the duration."

Later, while they ate dinner at Pop's Café in town, Ann contemplated her options. She could continue to overstay her welcome at her father's house, or she could go for the two-bedroom cabin at Cedar Creek Guest Ranch. She glanced across the table at Devon who happily dunked fries in ketchup since she'd finished her grilled cheese sandwich. "Did you have fun today with the twins?"

"Best day ever, Mama. Samantha said they want to be friends with me 'cause I'm brave. I didn't know that. Even Uncle Jack says I'm a brat."

Ann stirred her mocha with a straw. "I used to call him one when I was a kid."

"Really?"

"I got in trouble with your Grandma Ginger whenever I did but it was worth being grounded, doing time-outs or losing toys I loved. Thankfully, she never believed in spankings."

"Are we gonna live at Sam's and Sophie's house?"

"Not in their house, but maybe in one of the cabins. What do you think?"

"I could see Rainy Night every day after school. Sophie says I can ride in the van by her and Sam and nobody will be mean to me on the way to school or the way home. It'd be okay 'cause Bobby lives in Lake Maynard and I wouldn't be going to his house when Gramma Ginger is too busy to pick me up on time."

"I don't want you there at all."

"Me either." Another French fry swirled in the ketchup. "Mister Robbie says he'll teach me to brush Rainy Night and saddle all by myself. We'd need lots of carrots 'cause he believes in treats and so does Mrs. Cat. It'd be like having my very own pony."

"I talked to Cat about buying him for you."

"You did? Really, Mama? I'd be so good if I could have him."

"First, you have to know how to feed and water him. You must clean his stall and be able to lead him back and forth to the pasture. There's more to owning a pony than riding him."

Tears filled Devon's hazel eyes. She slid out of the booth, hustled around to Ann's side of the table and grabbed her in a hug. "You're the bestest mama ever. I will be good. I promise."

"I love you so much." Ann hugged her daughter tight. "Just do your best. That's all I want. Now, finish up your supper and we'll have ice cream sundaes for dessert. Then, you can tell me all about karate."

Devon fell asleep in the car on the short drive to the Majestyk Morgan Farm. Ann didn't wake the child. Instead, she carried her daughter into the house and to the princess-style bedroom. The little girl dozed while Ann removed her clothes, switching them for *Disney* pajamas. She tucked Devon into the canopy bed, a stuffed toy dog and teddy bear beside her.

Clicking on the nightlight, Ann closed the door partway and then headed for the living-room where she heard the television. She found her father and stepmother sitting in their matching recliners watching a crime drama and waited for the next set of commercials.

Her dad muted the sound when the advertisements started. "How did Devon do at the fort?"

"Fine." Ann leaned against the doorframe, not bothering to take a seat on the couch. "Like I told you when I called last night, Margo took her to a karate class so Devon could try it out. She really enjoyed it, so we've enrolled her in the beginning session."

"How are you going to manage that when you work in Seattle?"

"Margo and I will work it out with our bosses. When we have a late night, Cat McTavish says she or her husband will drive Devon to the *dojo* since they plan to sign up the twins for the same class."

"I don't think rewarding Devon for misbehaving at school sends the right message." Ginger shuddered. "Karate isn't very feminine. You never took it."

"I wish I had." Ann struggled to keep her voice even. "Then, I wouldn't have had to worry about being assaulted or raped at college or while I was in the *Sandbox*. Why do you think I told Dad to send me a case of hoof picks? My daughter isn't going to be a punching bag for any boy."

"Nobody wants that, Annie." Frank stirred in his chair. "Has she said what prompted the fight?"

"No, she hasn't, but I'll get it out of her sooner or later." Ann folded her arms, taking a deep breath. "I've found a place for us to live. After supper at Pop's, I called and arranged to rent a cabin at Cedar Creek Guest Ranch. We'll move tomorrow after church."

CHAPTER TEN

After parking in the lot adjacent to the church, Harry walked beside his grandmother toward the over-sized carved wooden doors where a silver-haired elderly man stood waiting. He didn't wear the traditional dark suit associated with most preachers, but a plaid, flannel shirt tucked into faded jeans.

He nodded a greeting. "Good morning, Janine. Is this - - -?"

"My grandson, Harold Colter. Say 'hello' to Reverend Thompson."

Harry winced at the sound of his full name or was it the bony elbow jabbed into his side? "Morning, Reverend Thomp—"

"Tommy. Reverend Thompson was my father."

"And I'm Harry." He shook hands with the minister ignoring the glare his grandmother shot both men. A petite gray-haired dynamo in her polyester slacks, flowered top and sandals, he was pretty sure she made the loggers quake in their corked boots if they had to pick up their children at her preschool.

"Mass-Sarge Harry! Mass-Sarge Harry!" Devon raced up the sidewalk. "Mass-Sarge Harry, guess what?" She paused long enough to hug his grandmother. "Mrs. O'Connell, I almost got a pony."

"How do you get an "almost" pony, Devon?" Reverend Tommy asked. "Is he part horse?"

"No, he's a 'real' pony." Devon hugged him too, bouncing up and down in black patent leather shoes, white tights and a frilly, red velvet dress trimmed in white lace swirling around her knees. "He lives with Mrs. Cat and I got to ride him a long time yesterday. And Mama says if I learn everything Mister Robbie teaches me about how to take care of Rainy Night, she'll get him for me. And I'm gonna learn it all and we're moving there and—"

"Take a breath, Devon." This time it was another woman that spoke when she joined them. She looked to be in her late fifties or early sixties. Her blonde hair came from the bottle now and didn't dare show a hint of gray. She pasted on a professionally friendly smile that didn't touch her hazel eyes. "Nothing's decided yet and you live with us now. Good morning, Reverend. Mrs. O'Connell, is this the hero grandson we've heard so much about?"

"It's Mass-Sarge Harry." Devon tugged on his hand. "Come talk to Mama and tell her you have your truck and you'll move my stuff to our new house. I wanta live with Rainy Night and if I'm super good I bet I get a puppy soon. Mama says so."

"Then, you'd better behave properly at school instead of getting suspended."

"Someone had to kick Bobby's butt 'cause he's a big bully, Grandma and now that I'm taking karate, Aunt Margo says I'll do a better job. Come on, Mass-Sarge Harry."

"Go along, Harold. Invite Devon's mama for Sunday dinner and then the child can visit my dog and her puppies. You told me at breakfast you thought Angelica Barrett wanted one."

"Empress had babies?" That earned Mrs. O'Connell another hug. "I bet they're bootiful 'cause she is the best dog ever. She used to give me lots of kisses."

"She's still very good with the other children who come to my school. You'll see if you come to dinner."

"I'll ask Mama too." Devon pulled on Harry's hand. "Come on. We have lots to do today, not only listening to Reverend Tommy tell everyone in town to be good, not just me."

"I think she just gave my entire sermon for me."

Amused, Harry let the little girl tow him in the direction of the parking lot where he saw Ann talking to an older man. The strong resemblance between them meant he was undoubtedly her father. Same bronze hair although his had silver threads, same leaf-green eyes and a certain set of their jaws added to the similarities. The older man must be in his mid-sixties, but he didn't look like it in a green checked western shirt, blue jeans and cowboy boots.

Meantime, Ann had opted for her Class B uniform rather than camo fatigues and black pumps instead of combat boots. He wished she'd worn the skirt instead of slacks, but he was smart enough not to say so. Her hair was pinned up above her collar and she sported a double set of service ribbons on the white shirt.

"Grandpa, this is Mass-Sarge Harry." Devon tugged him closer. "He has his truck and he's gonna help us move to our new house so I can live with Rainy Night."

"Did you even ask the man, Devon, or did you tell him?" Ann managed a smile, but tension filled her face. "Good Sunday morning, Colter."

"Morning, Angel. I figure the apple doesn't fall far from the proverbial tree. Her mama gives me lots of orders and my truck is at your disposal. I'll do whatever you want."

She heaved a huge sigh. "Next time I give you crap at the office, remind me you're a great guy. Dad, this is Master Sergeant Harry Colter, my new boss. Harry, this is my father, Frank Madison, owner of the Majestyk Morgan Farm."

Harry freed his hand from Devon's to grip the other man's. "Seems like you've had a busy day already."

"Yes, and the drama never ends." Frank stepped away after shaking hands to put an arm around Ann's waist. "Sweetheart, you only arrived home a week ago. There's no rush to find a place for you and Devon to live. You can stay with us until your brother moves into his own house and—"

"But, I wanta live with Rainy Night," Devon interrupted. "He's gonna be *my* pony. I know it."

"I'll have a trainer work with one of the older Morgans and you can ride it, Devon. One of the staff will groom and tack up for you whenever you want to ride."

"No, Grandpa." Tears filled the little girl's hazel eyes. "I wanta learn to brush and saddle and take care of Rainy Night myself. I wanta be a cowgirl like Sam and Sophie, not a princess and—"

"Enough." Ann held up her hand. "Just stop. Devon, you're not riding a full-size horse until you're much older and taller. Dad, I appreciate everything you and Ginger have done for me and Devon, but we need our own place, one where I make the rules and my kid does what I say, when I say it. Tell Ginger you tried to keep us, but I'm signing the lease today and it's a done deal."

"What about me, Angel? What do I get to do?"

"You get to be the strong back and help us move later. Right now, we'd better head into church or Reverend Tommy will call down the rain on all our heads."

A sunshine smile broke out on Devon's face and she abandoned Harry to grab her mother's hand. "Mrs. O'Connell invited us to dinner, and she says I can play with her puppies and their mama, Empress. Can we go?"

"I'll decide after church."

"Okay." Devon darted away to greet Samantha and Sophie as well as their parents when Rob parked a classic candy-apple red Mustang in the lot.

Once her father strode off toward the church, Ann heaved a sigh and glanced at Harry. "There are times when the *Sandbox* seems a lot saner than all the family theatricals here in Baker City. There it was just life and death." She shuddered. "Here, the stakes are higher. My stepmother is having kittens because I'm leaving and Dad's catching the fallout. She never considered when she treated me as if I'd overstayed my welcome as soon as I arrived that I'd take Devon with me when I left."

"Lots of fun, huh?" He took her hand, smiling down into her lovely face. "Are you happy?"

"Not yet, but I will be once Devon and I get settled."

"Then, it's all that matters."

It'd taken forever, but he was finally home. Zeke lingered by the church steps barely listening to the preacher do the 'meet and greet' routine. He wanted to see his own family. Whenever they visited, Twila rounded up the whole kit and caboodle insisting they attend Sunday services at the vintage church in Baker City. He barely glanced toward the parking lot when he spotted Barrett's dark-haired cherub coming his way accompanied by two other girls slightly older and taller, obviously twins, but found himself drifting toward the trio.

One of them stopped and looked at him. "Hi, I'm Sophie. You're new. Who are you?"

"Be polite." Her sister elbowed her. "Mommy says you have to say, 'hello and we're glad you're here' before you ask lots of questions."

"I was gonna do that, Samantha." Sophie looked him up and down. "So, we're glad you're here but you gotta follow the rules or Mommy and Daddy will send you to places you don't want to go."

"I'm Zeke Garvey." Zeke barely managed to speak, still stunned by the fact these two saw him when the other girl hadn't. She eyed the twins curiously but didn't interrupt the conversation. "What rules?"

"The mayor doesn't come to church that much. He's at Pop's Café. Go ask him 'bout the rules." Samantha gestured to the cedar-shake building down the street. "Or you can talk to Mrs. O'Sullivan at the school. She'll tell you."

"I have to stay here. I can't go anywhere until Colter does."

Sophie heaved a sigh. "You're dead, Mister Garvey."

"Sergeant First Class Garvey."

"Okay, Sergeant Garvey. You can go wherever you want, but you gotta follow the rules," Samantha said again. "The living are only tied to you if you want. Go talk to the mayor."

"I won't do it!" Ann glared at Harry. He stood like a rock and his face reflected patience. "It was bad enough typing those stupid status reports about the weapons. I won't do inventory in Supply and you can't make me."

"I'm the Non-Commissioned Officer in Charge. I make the decisions. We need to count all the organizational material in the storerooms. It'd be much faster if you helped me, Angel."

She planted her fists on her hips and tossed her head. "You said that before. I was supposed to help get the weapons ready to go for repairs. I wound up typing the forms and what about the charts on the maintenance for the gas masks? I did those too! What are you good for, Colter?"

"Oh, I'll bet we could find something, Angel."

She ignored the blush that heated her cheeks when he slowly looked her up and down. How could he make her feel like the sexiest woman alive in fatigues and combat boots? She continued to glower up at him as the door opened. Margo came in with Devon clinging to her hand. "How was lunch?"

"Great," Margo beamed. "I had one of those special kid's meals. I always wanted to try one."

"I don't like 'em," Devon announced. "They're for little kids."

Ann felt her anger sliding away. She went to hug her daughter, smiling at Margo. "Thanks. We got a lot of work done while you were gone."

"I worked here too, Mama. I washed down the desks and chairs again today."

"You did a great job." A sudden idea sprang to life. She smoothed the girl's black hair and looked at Harry. "We're gonna help Colter do inventory in the supply room. You count and we'll write."

"I don't know why Sergeant Colter lets you be the recreational director, Ann. That sounds awful." Margo glanced at the clock. "I've got to get back to my office before someone from HQ comes looking for me and finds out you have company." She winked at Ann, smiled at Harry and brushed a kiss over Devon's cheek. Then Margo was gone.

Devon rubbed her eyes. "I'm tired. Is this gonna be a lot of work?"

"I'll bring your blanket. Then if you get tired, you can sleep, D.J." He suited the action to the words. "Shall we go, ladies?"

Ann stomped toward the door, knowing he'd outfoxed her again. Why hadn't Harry worried about Devon making a mess of the supply room? Most supply sergeants would have come apart at the seams at the mere threat of a child in their sanctuaries. But, not Harry Colter. No, he always had to be different. "Somehow, some way, I'll get you, Colter. I promise you that."

"I can hardly wait," Harry retorted in good-humored tones. "I'm easy where you're concerned, Angel. You don't have to make an honest man of me first."

Ann considered all the nasty comments she could utter at a time like this and gave up. She didn't want to hurt Harry and she didn't want to think about that.

It was hard to remember her goal the next day while she typed letters. Harry was his usual saint-like self, she thought bitterly. When would he realize that she was setting him up, left, right and center? If any of the senior unit noncoms learned Devon had been here most of the week, they'd have fits. If the Command Sergeant Major discovered she and Harry were on a first name basis, he'd bust a gut.

Once again, Harry was fixing up the rattletrap structure where they worked. Today, he was replacing the tiles that had come loose from the floor. "I don't know why you're bothering, Colter. We're supposed to move before Christmas."

"We haven't moved yet." Harry wiped up the excess glue and pressed down on the old linoleum. "I'm not spending my winter freezing. Didn't you say the base was more than a hundred years old?"

"Am I supposed to give you a history lesson now? Do I look like a teacher in my combat boots?"

"You look like an angel." Harry glanced over his broad shoulder. "But I'd never put you on top of a Christmas tree."

"I'm being good," Devon chimed in. "I want Santa to bring me stuff for Rainy Night and my new puppy."

Ann frowned at her daughter, determined not to be cheered up. "Sweetheart, I'm arguing with Harry. Don't interrupt. Just color in your book."

Devon put down her crayon on the desk and slid off the chair, obviously eying the pair of them. "Stop fighting, Mama. His grandma said I could call him just Harry when we were at dinner. I love him." She climbed up on Ann's lap and nestled close. "I love you."

Ann ruffled her daughter's dark hair. "I love you too, baby."

"I'm not a baby." Devon argued. "I'm in first grade. I grew up while you were gone."

"You certainly did." Harry chuckled as he bent and swooped her up in a warm hug. "How about if you make me a picture?" He carried her back to the desk where she'd been coloring. "I love you too, Devon Joyce. But right now, your mama wants to talk to me."

"Don't fight, Harry," Devon said firmly.

"We won't." He brushed a kiss over her hair. "I love your mom."

"You don't know her mom." Ann glared at him as he passed her. Today he wore fatigues, but the camouflage shirt hung on the back of a chair. Every muscle rippled under his t-shirt, cotton clinging damply to his supple, lean frame.

"You're disgusting," Ann threw the words at him, wishing they'd have some effect on him.

"And you're frustrated," Harry returned in a lazy voice. "Either you're horny or else you skipped breakfast again."

Ann gasped. She felt the stinging, burning blush flow into her cheeks and grabbed for her paperback dictionary.

"Don't you dare!" He swung and paced toward her. "I always thought books were supposed to be respected and cherished. You throw that at me, and I'll treat you as if you're Devon's age again."

The heat increased in her cheeks and she raised her chin defiantly. "What does that mean?"

He leaned forward and gripped the arms of her chair, neatly trapping her in the seat. "What do you think, Angel? I figure if I make you stand in a corner, you'll grow up. Particularly if I'm there with you." His sensual tones left no doubts in her mind what exactly they'd do.

"I think you're the most loathsome, filthy, macho slug that ever slimed his way across the face of the earth."

He bent closer, fierce desire in his blue eyes. "Why don't you say what you really mean, honey?"

Ann trembled. Her insides had turned to liquid fire and the rest of her was melting in his gaze. "Harry, don't."

He leaned closer; his breath warm on her lips. "Then behave, Angel. Watch that sharp tongue."

"What if I don't?" She demanded in a whisper. Somehow her anger was escaping in leaps and bounds. "What will you do?"

"I'll forget the fact that you don't want to get involved." Harry threaded his hand in her hair and brushed her lips with his. "And I'll make sure you like it, my darling."

She shivered with wanting and pressed forward to touch his hard mouth with her own. The fierce kiss sent flames licking through her and she wound her arms around his neck. "Oh, Harry." His name was a moan.

Harry's tongue claimed the dark area behind her teeth, forcing the surrender she longed to give. He drew her up into his arms, bringing her so tightly against him she thought her bones would melt into his.

How could she stop him? And why should she want to? She tangled her fingers in the night darkness of his hair, trying to hold his mouth on hers. Remembering Devon's presence slowly seeped into her mind. Before Ann broke free of the embrace, the raucous honking of a horn came to her ears. He lifted his head and gently maneuvered her back into the chair. He straightened and strode toward the front door.

"Where are you going?" She heard herself ask. Why did she care?

His slow smile was an assault on her senses. "The roach coach is here, honey. Figured I'd satisfy that other hunger of yours." He glanced quickly at Devon. "Ready to go get a doughnut, D.J.?"

"Yes!" Devon carefully laid her crayon aside and ran to grab Harry's hand. "Is it okay, Mama?"

"Of course, sweetie." Ann forced a smile. "Come right back. I'll miss you." She drew a deep breath. She had to remember the end goal. It wasn't to fall in love with Harry Colter. It didn't matter if he had a sexy smile, if his touch was magic or even that he was so good to her kid.

She rose to her feet and went in search of the newspaper. It'd become a habit to read it at this time of the morning while they were taking a break. She had to get some dirt on Harry in order to take his job. But what could she use? And why did she feel like such a bitch?

She opened the paper and lifted out the comics, spreading them on the desk Devon used. Her daughter could read them while the rest of the news would be devoured by Harry with equal intensity.

Harry and Devon came back in with the pastries and a carton of milk for the little girl and Ann accepted the maple bar with a smile. Devon hurried to her part of the paper. Ann waited until Harry had filled both of their coffee cups and sat down before she began to read the headline story.

The spring sun beat down that afternoon and Ann sighed. Even with the windows open to provide a cross-breeze, it was unseasonably warm. Devon napped on the couch; her quilt clutched in her hand rather than covering her.

Ann blew at the damp hair that fell across her brow and studied the letter in front of her. The Command Sergeant Major had left the correspondence and the last sentence simply didn't sound right. She knew what he meant but the words didn't make sense. Of course, every time she fixed the grammar, the punctuation, the language and corrected the spelling, it caused friction between her and the senior noncom. She was more tactful than Derek Waller who didn't hesitate to tell Jenkins he sounded like an illiterate hillbilly which was why she ended up doing the letters instead of the clerks at battalion HQ.

She looked at the back door as it opened. Harry came toward her, holding out an ice cream bar. "Colter, I'm going to weigh five hundred pounds and the Army will throw me out."

"No, they won't." Harry grinned at her. "I figure I'm losing pounds in this heat snap and you must be too. I got Devon one. Should I wake her up?"

Ann unwrapped the ice cream as she considered. Her daughter should have a nap, but it was just too hot. Devon wasn't a light sleeper normally, but she was so restless today. Ann nodded. "Go ahead. I'll put her to bed early tonight, as soon as it cools off."

She leaned back in her chair and took the first bite of her own treat as she watched him. He was so big he ought to be clumsy. Instead he moved with all the grace of a jungle animal, lethal and deadly. She grimaced as she recalled just where he'd learned those skills. Colter had the soul of a poet. What on earth had made him decide to become a professional soldier and make a career out of the military?

He bent over Devon and touched her shoulder gently. "Time to wake up, sweetheart. It's too hot to sleep. I got you a popsicle."

Devon immediately opened her eyes. "I'm awake, Harry." She sat up. "Ice cream?"

"It's a popsicle, Devon." Ann pushed away from her desk and went to join them. "Want a bite of my ice cream?" She hid her amusement when her daughter refused and took the half of the orange popsicle Harry offered.

"You must be around kids a lot." Ann waited while he tucked a tissue in the neck of Devon's t-shirt. "Most guys don't know how to do that."

Harry smiled. "Zeke and Twila have six kids. His brothers and younger sisters are married too. I was everybody's uncle."

"My sisters have kids too, but I barely know them," Ann

commented. "Barb and Chloe had both left home by the time I was eight and they were too busy to connect with me when I was a teenager or went to college."

"Is that why you have so many friends?" Harry inquired. "Do you mind being by yourself?"

Ann shook her head. "No, I enjoy my solitude when I have it, but my stepmother made it clear that my dad belonged to her and Jack. I liked most of the other students in my cohort when I was in grad school. Margo and I connected because we were both counting on Army benefits to help with tuition. We needed that money."

"Is everyone getting their wages? I've had calls about back pay."

"Are you asking about company policy?" She hurried on before he answered. "Harry, I correct every mistake I can but the gal we used to have made nothing but errors. I'm still fixing those. The best thing to do is get emergency pay for those folks who haven't seen any money. Then the computer techs would realize they're still on board."

"Okay." Harry gave Devon the other half of her popsicle. "Go ahead. Let's get everyone in the company paid."

Ann gaped at him. Had he been listening to anything she said? "Harry, we can't. Colonel Stewart absolutely forbade it when Captain Meade went to him. If I do the paperwork and you sign it, he'll raise hell and try to get you fired or reassigned."

"Then you'll get the full-time job as unit clerk," Harry pointed out in cool tones. "That's what you want, isn't it, Angel?"

Ann trembled. Of course, it was what she wanted. Her gaze fell on her daughter who had sticky orange remnants of popsicle written all over her face. Her child loved this man, Ann thought, and she wasn't immune to him either. Could she go against the battalion commander's orders and let Harry take the heat?

"No way, Colter. Granted I need my pay since I'm one of the people the computer lost on the way home, undoubtedly because I gave our previous clerk a hard time when she bailed out in combat. You'd be helping me, but I won't be responsible for fragging you."

Harry gripped her chin and bent to kiss her lightly. "Do it, Ann. After all my time in the active Army, I'm pretty sure I can get out of it. If I'm wrong, I'll go over Stewart's head and ask for advice from one of the head honchos at HQ. You could arrange that, couldn't you?"

Ann inclined her head. A tug of suspicion caught her mind. "Don't bamboozle me, Colter. Colonel Williams handles the complaints, but he doesn't like you either."

"Of course not, but he respects my judgement and he knows I'm a grown man. I guess I'll just have to do this myself. What's the number for the head of Army Finance? I'll see how many cages I can rattle. Then we'll get some action."

Ann glared at him. "You're a macho creep. If you start harassing the higher-ups, Stewart will really be on the warpath. All right, I'll do the finance forms." She stomped across to her desk.

"Do yours first," Harry commanded. "Then you can quit whining about money and buy that pony for D.J."

Ann stuck her tongue out at him and concentrated on the letter on the laptop screen. If they were going to annoy the commander, they might as well go root hog or die. She glanced at Harry. "How does this paragraph sound? I think it needs help."

CHAPTER ELEVEN

"It's sixteen-thirty, Angel." Harry unplugged the coffee pot. "Shall we call it a day?"

Ann stared at him for a moment and then stood. "That's fine, boss." She logged off and shut down the computer, stacking the paperwork. "Will you sign these letters tomorrow morning when I finish them?"

Harry nodded. "Works for me."

She collected her camo shirt and purse, turning her attention to Devon. "Gather up your things, honey while I get the lights." She grabbed her running clothes. "See you tomorrow, Colter."

She had to get out of here before she told Harry about the meeting tonight. This should be enough to cost him the job. When the commander and the rest of the staff arrived and neither of them were here, Colonel Stewart would totally blow his stack. She'd be covered because Harry was the boss. He'd be up a creek in a canoe without a paddle.

Harry followed them out of the building. Before he could lock the doors, the telephone rang, and he went back inside to answer the landline. Ann stared at the car after Devon climbed into the safety seat and buckled up. With their things stowed on the back seat next to her daughter, they should be on the road. Ann heaved a sigh. Unfortunately, she was having a sudden attack of the guilts.

Granted, Colter was her new supervisor. He made the decisions and he'd told her to leave. She was a soldier and she followed orders. He'd stolen her job. He walked in on her while she was showering. He made fun of her when she was jogging. He'd constantly lectured her about military bearing. He ordered her to clean their office building until it was more immaculate than her father's barn and that was nearly as sterile as an operating room. All in all, the man deserved every speck of the trouble she was giving him.

On the other hand, Harry treated her daughter so well and patiently. He let her read to him, always asking for more of the boy wizard's adventures and seeming disappointed when Devon took a break from story time. He showed her how he wired the plug-ins for the computers, encouraged her when she had trouble helping set up the new desktops and printers. He bought her treats, but always checked with Ann first.

He helped them move to the dude ranch and had consistently showed courtesy to Ginger ignoring the older woman's meltdown when she refused to let them take Devon's canopy bed or the matching furniture. He helped Ann repair the Ford last week. He tried to cover for her with the Command Sergeant Major. He fixed the women's restroom so she wouldn't have to use the men's latrine anymore.

He kisses like a dream. No, I'm not thinking about that.

She glanced at the building once more as Harry came through the front door. He waved, gesturing for her to join him. Slowly, Ann complied, walking toward him. Had he learned about the seven-o-clock briefing tonight? "What's wrong?"

"Nothing." Harry finished locking the door and checked it. "That was the elementary school secretary. She wanted to remind you about the meeting tomorrow morning with Devon's teacher and the principal. It sounds like I should expect you at lunch time tomorrow, Angel."

"That's about right. These things always take longer than a person wants." She started for the car and came to a stop as she recalled the briefing again. "Harry, there's an administrative meeting tonight at seven."

Harry shook his head. "Not anymore, Angel. We changed the schedule before you returned. The commander agreed everyone's worn out from that last tour in Afghanistan and needs time to reconnect with their families and hunt for jobs. We're going to have two weekday drills a month instead of four. It'll improve the esprit-de-corps."

"I wasn't going to tell you." Ann stared at the sidewalk, utterly ashamed of herself. "I figured you'd fall flat on your face and—"

"I'd sneak off and leave the job to you. Don't kick yourself, Ann. You're a fine, moral person. I trust you and I know you'd have told me before too much longer. I'll see you tomorrow." He glanced down at her. "I'll miss hearing the rest of Devon's book. She'll have to read it to me another time."

"Poor Harry." Ann rose on her tiptoes and brushed a kiss over his cheek. "Thanks for telling me about the meeting in the morning. I'd better go. I must try to find some civvies and I don't know where everything went during the divorce."

Two hours later, she hummed along with the radio as she drove through the suburbs of Lake Maynard toward her in-laws' home. Harry Colter was one of the strangest men she'd ever met. She had to admit he was the best looking too, but there was something different about him.

He never should have trusted *her* to do the payroll. Any time a mistake was made on the paperwork, the unit technician got in trouble with his supervisors. Since Harry had the job, he was the one who would have to take the heat. Yet he wanted her to fill out the forms, while he signed each and every one.

His signature was a mere scrawl. Ann choked back a grin. Why couldn't men write legibly? She remembered mail call back in the *Sandbox*. Her father's letters could have been used by archaeologists to decipher hieroglyphics. She always struggled with the urge to correct the spelling and grammar in Will's notes and cards when he wrote during her first two tours. It hadn't been a problem this last time since he filed for divorce nearly as soon as she left the U.S.

Her frustration with his inability to communicate should have told her their marriage was doomed to failure. Of course, she also could have had a clue when he bitched non-stop about her re-enlisting in the reserve to get that second bonus to help pay for college since her teaching salary always went on their bills.

She parked in the sweeping driveway in front of the large gold house where her ex-in-laws lived. The neighborhood was filled with expensive homes that all seemed to have been made from the same mold, as if the architect had been making building-shaped cookies. Her lips quivered at the fantasy. She straightened her uniform as soon as she got out of the car and opened the back door.

Devon yawned, slowly waking up and then grinned as soon as she recognized where they were. She hastily unbuckled her seat belt and climbed out, racing ahead of Ann up the walk to the front door. She followed her daughter. Before either of them rang the bell, the door opened to reveal a lovely, silver-haired woman in comfy lounge wear who promptly hugged Devon.

Ann smiled at the pair. "Hi, Vanessa."

"Annie, you look beautiful. Did you lose weight at your school? Come in." Vanessa held the door wide. "I'm so glad you're here. I'm sorry we missed your party last weekend, but Phil had that silly business trip and we couldn't get back in time."

Ann couldn't hide her amusement. Whoever had written the rules about mothers-in-law had obviously never met Vanessa. She was as loving to Ann as she was to her own children. Secretly, she knew she was fonder of Vanessa than she was of her own mother, Lucy Madison or Ginger, but that was something that could never be shared. Vanessa would be appalled at the idea that she might have come between Ann and her family. She stepped into Vanessa's warm hug and was grateful once again that the divorce hadn't spelled the ruin of the relationship with Will's parents.

"You're great for my ego, Vanessa, but I really enjoyed my time at the school. It allowed me to decompress and adjust to being back. The food was terrific." Ann closed the door behind the three of them. "The weather was much nicer, and I got hours of solid sleep. No wonder I gained ten pounds."

"Nobody could guess that by looking at you." Vanessa put an arm around Ann's waist. "Thank you so much for letting us share Devon with your folks while you were away. You'll be sorry. I'm afraid we barely obeyed any of your rules about bedtime or vegetables."

"Don't tell Mama that, Grandma. I'm trying really hard to be good, so she'll buy me Rainy Night. He's the bestest pony ever."

Ann smiled. Even though Vanessa and Phil spoiled Devon, Ann knew she was lucky to have them. How many other grandparents would be so willing to babysit at the drop of a hat? They weren't talking about for a day or two either, not when she was on active duty for a year and a half and in combat for most of that time. "Don't worry. I'm just happy the two of you were able to take care of her when everything went sideways for Will."

"That's our job." Vanessa drew Devon close. "Can you stay for dinner? It's a chicken, broccoli and rice casserole, one of Phil's favorites."

"We'd love to." Ann took a deep breath, glancing around the living room but she didn't see her former father-in-law. "I've rented a cabin at Cedar Creek Guest Ranch until I get a full-time job and I know where we'll be living for good. I don't have room for all my things, but I do need my small kitchen appliances, dishes, cannisters as well as my civilian clothes. Will doesn't answer when I call his cell phone. Do you know where he stored them?"

Silence fell and an odd tension seeped into the room. Vanessa heaved a sigh. "I love my son, but he can be such a disappointment sometimes. I'm sorry, Ann."

"Sorry for what?" Ann eyed the older woman. "What did he do?"

"Daddy had a garage sale."

"What?" Ann gasped, anger replacing her initial shock. "He sold my belongings?"

Vanessa glanced down at Devon. "Honey, your mama and I need to talk in the kitchen. Would you like to watch a movie?"

It was Devon's turn to sigh. "You two are gonna say bad things about Daddy and you don't want me to hear. It's okay, you know. I get mad at him sometimes too."

"Mind your grandmother." Ann felt her nails biting into her skin and forced her clenched fists open. "I'm sure she has the first *Harry Potter* movie. Do you need me to set it up for you?"

"I'm not a baby. I'm six. I can do it."

"Probably better and faster than either of us." Vanessa guided Ann toward the gourmet chef's kitchen. "I think we both need some *Irish Cream* in our coffee and I'm talking about the imported kind from Ireland."

Putting her purse on the island counter, Ann hitched up on a stool and waited for the promised drink. Once she'd taken a comforting sip of the liquor, she managed to nod at Vanessa. "Okay, tell me about this damned garage sale."

"Paul's niece, Jacinth called us and told us that Will had posted a garage sale on the Internet. She didn't think anything of it because she knew he'd lost another job. She's always on the hunt for hand tools for the Sweeney ranch so she stopped by. When she realized he was selling all the household goods along with your clothes, she confronted him and he said that if they were important to you, then you wouldn't have left them behind like you had him and Devon."

"Oh my Gawd. It wasn't like I had a choice. When the Army tells you to go, you go."

"You're preaching to the proverbial choir, honey. I married Phil after he came home from Vietnam and my dad served in World War Two. My mom was a *Rosie the Riveter* in an airplane factory." Vanessa drank more of her coffee. "Jacinth rallied the old-time families in Baker City, the Sweeneys, O'Learys, MacGillicudys, McElroys, O'Connells, Garveys, O'Neills and the O'Sullivans. They bought up what they could, but Will chose *Fourth of July* weekend since there'd be a lot of flatlanders who didn't know you and most of your things were already gone."

"What a filthy stunt." Ann caught her breath. "Oh Vanessa, I'm sorry. I shouldn't have said that."

"I said worse when I got there. I chewed his ears big time and so did his dad. It's why Will dropped Devon at Chloe's when he left town the first time and then later at Barb's and Reid's."

"I understand he was angry with me, but I'll never forgive him for taking his rage out on our daughter."

"Have some more coffee." Vanessa refilled the cup and added liquor as well. "Jacinth heard at church that you're home and now have your own place, so she's passing the word that you're out at Cedar Creek. Ginger wouldn't let us store anything at Majestyk, but you should have what we managed to save by this weekend."

"I owe you and Phil so much."

"No, you don't. It's the least we could do when you were off serving your country. We're just glad you came home alive and well this time. I saved the photo albums you made of Devon, her baby clothes and the convertible toddler bed. Her toys ended up here or in her room at Frank and Ginger's. I'm pretty sure that Will didn't send you the photos from Disneyland, so Phil made copies for you."

Ann focused on her drink. When she was back in control of her turbulent emotions, she said, "I can't wait to see them."

"I'll get them for you after dinner."

"Okay and I'd better help put it together if we want to eat soon."

Despite enjoying the meal and the conversation, anger and hurt still swept through her whenever she thought about her ex-husband's actions. She didn't share that with his parents. They'd obviously been upset by their son's behavior. When they moved to the living room, Vanessa gave Ann two small packages wrapped beautifully in gold foil paper tied with ribbon.

Phillip Sweeney sat down in his favorite recliner and studied her with pretended sternness. "Well, aren't you going to open them?"

Ann managed a shaky laugh. "Devon, do you want to help me?"

"Yes!" Devon grabbed the first present and began to tear at the paper.

"Wait till Christmas." Phillip smiled and his brown eyes twinkled. "I'll have to rent a dumpster."

Ann hurried to hug him. "Thank you. I do appreciate everything you did while I was overseas and back East. I'm so glad she could come visit you and Vanessa. Taking her with you on vacation, that was beyond the call of duty."

Phillip chuckled and rumpled his salt and pepper hair. "We were delighted when you agreed she could come with us. Without her I'm sure Disneyland wouldn't have been half as much fun." The small man's grin widened as Devon began to wave the gift in the air.

"Mama, see what we got you!"

Ann obediently returned to her daughter and helped open the flat white box. Inside wrapped in tissue paper was a silver-framed, elaborate photo of Devon cuddling with Mickey Mouse. Every inch of her daughter's sunny smile could be seen. "It's beautiful."

"It's me, Mama." Devon pointed. "With Mickey."

Ann glanced at Will's parents. "This is the copy you promised me, isn't it?"

"Yes, dear." Vanessa smiled. "There should be another present inside. Devon picked it."

Ann nodded and searched through the tissue paper. She lifted the jewelry box and slowly opened it to see a beautiful pair of diamond earrings. "They're lovely."

Where on earth would she wear them? This wasn't the first expensive gift Vanessa and Phillip had bought her. When Devon was born, they'd given Ann an artificial white fur jacket. She saved it for special occasions. Will hocked it once when he sold the other presents from his parents, but Ann had managed to get the coat back. It was probably long gone along with the rest of her clothes and she hoped whoever bought it enjoyed it.

Ann crossed to the mirror as she contemplated how to answer the question. She unfastened one of the small gold studs and replaced it with the diamond cluster. She put in the second diamond earring. "I owe you two so much."

"You don't need to worry about us." Phillip hugged Devon when she came over to lean against his chair. "Very few mothers would allow their ex-in-laws all this time with their grandchild."

"Just because Will and I are finished doesn't mean you don't care about his daughter." Ann slipped the studs into the jewelry box and proceeded to pack the small box into the larger one. "Thanks for everything. I'm going to put Devon's photo on my desk at work. Phil, could you make more copies so I can keep them in the new photo album I'm starting and at our new home?"

"I'll go through my files on the computer. You'll have fifty or hundred shots to choose from."

"I don't need to pick. I'll take as many as I can get." She closed the box. "We have to go, sweetie. You need your sleep since you have school tomorrow."

"We love her," Vanessa said, giving three albums to Devon to carry. "Phillip wants to have our attorney talk with yours and arrange for the child support to be paid. You'll accept the money, won't you, honey? We know it's in arrears and your parents wouldn't take a cent."

"Of course, I will," Ann promised as she took the last album from Vanessa. "I can't deny it'll come in handy. The military is notorious for having slow pay. I always get my wages but sometimes I have to wait for months."

"It never changes," Phillip grinned. "One day we'll have to get together and exchange war-stories, Ann." He reached in his pocket and pulled out his wallet, removing several bills. "Here. This should tide you over until my lawyer and I talk."

CHAPTER TWELVE

Ann debated about wearing her dress uniform to the meeting at the school, then opted for the fatigues and combat boots she planned to wear to the base that afternoon. She carefully pinned up her hair, making sure it adhered a hundred percent to military regulations. Master Sergeant Harry Colter would be pleased, but she wasn't doing it for him. She did it for herself.

She packed a lunch for Devon while her daughter finished eating her cereal and then the two of them headed for the Ford Taurus. She waited while Devon buckled up, eyeing the little girl's jeans, Disney princess sweatshirt and running shoes. "I thought you liked dressing up for school."

"It's what Grandma Ginger wants, but I like pants better when we have outdoor recess." Devon tilted her head to one side, black hair neatly braided. "Are you okay with it? You wear pants lots of times."

"I think you look nice." Ann slid into the driver's seat. "Let's go see what we find out. I've arranged for you to ride home with Cat McTavish's daughters and hang out at the barn with them after school."

"That means I can ride Rainy Night if I help do horsy chores tonight."

"Fair enough." Ann started the car and headed toward Lake

Maynard. "Make me proud, sweetie. Aunt Margo will pick you up and I'll be here in time for dinner."

It took slightly more than a half hour to reach the school, but the parking lot only held a few cars since classes wouldn't start for another hour and a half. Ann carried her daughter's backpack, surprised and pleased when Devon took her hand. The secretary came to open the locked door and led them toward the conference room where they found Janet Gundersen and Felice Small, a dainty blonde dressed in a navy suit waiting for them.

Ann nodded a greeting, guiding Devon to a chair. Before the meeting started, she unzipped the backpack and removed the assignments the little girl had completed during her suspension, passing them to the first-grade teacher.

Janet Gundersen frowned at them. "Well, Devon. What did you learn during the past three days?"

"A lot, ma'am. I'm not to put my hands on another person, ma'am. If I see someone being hurt, ma'am, I'm to find the person in charge, ma'am and tell them, ma'am so they can keep people safe, ma'am."

Ann stared at her daughter, stunned by the overwhelming politeness. The courtesy wasn't something she'd ever heard a six-year-old use, much less her own child. She cleared her throat. "I think it'd be better if the first graders went to recess with the kindergarteners and not with the older students. Is that a possibility?"

"We'd have to restructure too many classes, Mrs. Barrett."

"Sergeant First Class Barrett," Ann corrected. "Why is it too much? They'd be closer to the same ages and same sizes. Isn't sending six and nine-year-olds out together just asking for problems?"

"We haven't had issues before last week," Janet said. "We'll consider bringing it up at the next staff meeting."

"All right." Ann folded her hands on the table, studying the other women. "How many adults supervise the children at recess?"

She arrived at Fort Bronson shortly after lunch. When she walked into the building, she found Harry in his office reading the paper while he ate a sandwich. She lingered in the doorway, watching him for a moment. "It's been a crazy morning, but Devon is back in school."

He stopped eating; his attention totally focused on her. "Is she happy?"

"I'm not sure." Ann drew up a chair and sat down. "When did you teach her to play, *'Last Word'* and call adults 'sir' or 'ma'am'? I never heard that conversation."

"When you and Captain Endicott were out for your daily run. We practiced so Devon would be ready to win the battle. She kept giggling when I pretended to be the principal. Did she manage to keep a straight face this morning?"

"Oh yeah." Ann laughed. "But I almost lost it when she went after her teacher and explained about me teaching her to read when she was three and she didn't want to be limited to little kid books."

"Did she get what she wanted?"

"For the moment." Ann leaned back in the chair. "I'm not holding my breath, Colter. There's a lot going on at that school and I have a feeling my daughter's education doesn't come first. I talked to the playground supervisor and explained my child's safety had better be a priority."

"Will it?"

"Supposedly. We'll see what happens the rest of this week. Next week is spring break and I have to set up places for Devon to go and things for her to do."

"Well, if you get stuck, it's no problem having her here."

"Thanks. I'll keep it in mind."

Surprisingly rush hour traffic wasn't as heavy as she'd expected that afternoon and the drive to the dude ranch didn't take as long. She parked in front of the cabin taking an extra moment to gaze at what her grandmother would have called a 'pay-day' house and her grandfather would have said was built in 'shotgun' style. It was approximately sixteen feet wide by forty-eight feet long with a deck on one side and an emergency exit by her bedroom at the far end.

She carried the sack of groceries to the porch closest to the living room. She stopped when she saw two cardboard cartons by the main door. She unlocked the door, walked through the living room to put the food on the breakfast bar in the kitchen, then returned to pick up the boxes.

When she opened the first one, she found the set of stoneware she used for every day. She'd searched for hours online to find the brightly colored turquoise, red and gold dishes with the herd of galloping horses. She carefully unpacked the plates, saucers, bowls and cups, delighted when she found the 'completer' set of a sugar bowl, gravy boat, meat platter and serving bowls wrapped in newspaper and kitchen towels. The second box held the matching cannisters, tablecloths and flatware.

She heard a knock on the door and turned to see Cat McTavish carrying a full laundry basket. "What do you have?"

"Curtains. Jassy Sweeney brought them by and I wanted to wash them again." Cat closed the door behind her. "I thought Frazer had a monopoly on rotten stunts back in the day, but he never held a garage sale to get rid of my treasures."

"Will was totally pissed off when I didn't leave the Army for him, but how could I? Every cent I made went toward rent, utilities and our other monthly bills."

"You mean your dad charged you to live at Majestyk Morgan Farm? I thought mine was a jerk, but it sounds like Frank was too."

"He's a 'go-along to get along' guy who has crappy taste in women." Ann put the basket on the table and gestured for Cat to sit in the empty chair. "He won't fight with Ginger. Whatever she wants, she gets. I think he probably did the same thing with my mother. They must have had serious problems, or she wouldn't have left when I was three."

"Well, he brought me horses to train last fall, two Morgan geldings we'd almost finished when Doc confirmed I was p.g. They need miles put on them, but Jacinth said she'd ride them for me. Rob's too tall and looks out of proportion although he's not too heavy. You're gone almost twelve hours a day at the fort in Seattle so I figured you wouldn't have time to help with them. What's the plan for spring break?"

"I was going to talk to you about that. What are the twins doing?"

"Virginia Thompson and Janine O'Connell are doing a church

camp in the mornings and the twins loved the holiday one, so we signed them up this time too. They'll be going until lunchtime every day. Do you want me to ask if they have room for Devon?"

"That'd be wonderful. My boss said I could bring her back to the base, but the Army Reserve really isn't fond of 'bring your kid to work' days. We were lucky none of the higher-ups popped in and noticed she was there during her suspension."

"Okay, then she can come here after lunch and hang out with my two. Jacinth is going to work in the afternoons with the horses your dad brought in. He spends a lot of money with me, but I'm not going to suck up to the guy."

"Which is why he respects you." Ann shook out the first curtain with a pony print. She laid it across the back of the other chair and continued searching for the ones she'd used in her kitchen before. "He's glad I'm home and so am I."

An hour later, Cat left, strolling to her own house and Ann headed over to Margo's to join her friend and Devon for dinner. When she knocked on the door and walked inside, she found her daughter setting the table in the small kitchen.

"How was your day, dear?" Margo glanced over her shoulder before returning her attention to the green pepper she was chopping. "Ready for a drink?"

"Definitely." Ann crossed to the counter and took a glass out of the cupboard. "What are we having?"

Margo gestured to the almost empty glass beside her. "Peppermint schnapps. The bottle is in the lower drawer where I keep the potatoes."

"Works for me." Ann found the bottle and filled the small glasses.

"Now, tell me all the dirt about the meeting at school today." Margo finished with the pepper and moved onto a tomato. "What's the good word? How is Devon doing? Do you like the school?"

"Don't be silly." Ann suddenly realized her daughter was listening eagerly to every word. "You know I'd rather have her in your room, but beggars can't be choosers. Maybe, you'll have a classroom by next fall."

"I'm applying everywhere I can think of," Margo said. "Working at Fort Bronson HQ is just a stopgap. I love kids and I miss being with them."

"Me too." Ann heaved a sigh. She longed for the security of a full-time job. If it couldn't be in a middle or high school, then it would have to be something else. She wasn't about to settle for anything less.

———

Since Margo had a date with Jared Williams, Ann found herself at home with only Devon for company on Friday evening. Her daughter sat at the breakfast bar finishing her math homework while Ann prepared supper. "What was the best part of school?"

"It was a half day and I'm out for a whole week." Devon stared at the worksheet in front of her. "Gramma Ginger came to get me, but Mrs. Tommy said I had to ride with her 'cause you hadn't said different and you're my mama."

"That's right." Ann grated a carrot into the shredded cabbage in the large salad bowl. "I'll check in with your grandmother over the weekend and we'll get a schedule worked out for you to spend time with her and Grandpa Frank during spring break."

Silence permeated the air for a moment then Devon lowered her pencil. "Grandma told Mrs. Tommy that she'd be taking care of me again when you left. I didn't know you were going anywhere."

"I'm not. I'm staying home with you, well except when I go to work. Usually, you'll be at school then."

"She said the Army would take you 'way again and you'd be gone a long time."

Ann stiffened, fury swamping reason for a moment. Damn Ginger. Why did her stepmother have to be such a witch? "I just got home and I'm in the reserve, honey. With any luck at all, I won't be going anytime soon."

"I don't want you to go again."

Ann forced herself to take one deep breath, then a second before she turned her attention back to the coleslaw. "Me either."

"Okay." Devon propped her chin on her fist. "Do you love Harry?"

Ann felt a blush burning its way up her neck and into her face. "Devon Joyce!"

"I saw you two kissing."

Ann turned away from the salad to the hamburger patties in the frying pan and refused to comment. The heat in her face had increased until she didn't dare look at anyone, much less her sharp-eyed daughter. "We're not talking about that."

"Just checking. I like him."

Me too, Ann thought, *but I'm not saying so!*

A knock on the front door interrupted them. Ann turned down the heat on the stove and went to answer it. She froze when she recognized Harry. "What are you doing here, Colter?"

"You forgot your jogging stuff, so I thought I'd bring it over on my way to my grandmother's house. She's not home anyway. She's off playing bingo at the senior center in Lake Maynard."

"Come in," Devon invited. "Mama's making dinner. Want some?"

Ann couldn't help laughing as she went forward and took her small duffel from him. "Are you staying for supper? It's not a ritzy meal, hamburger patties, baked potatoes, coleslaw and cornbread with peach cobbler for dessert."

Harry smiled and closed the door behind him. "Anything's better than a microwave dinner, Angel. I was supposed to cook for myself tonight and after all those years on active duty and depending on mess halls, I'm not much of a chef."

Ann stared at him. "You're staying with your grandma this weekend?"

"I don't have much choice. She called and told me she expected me to come for the town memorial this weekend because she needed help setting up tables for the street fair."

Ann watched red creep along his cheekbones. She never would have believed that a man could be so sentimental. Of course, this was Master Sergeant Harry Colter and he seemed to have the monopoly on caring about others. "You're a very nice person, Harry."

Harry rumpled his dark hair, his blue eyes smiling down at her. "Does this mean you're falling in love with me?"

"No." Ann took his arm and guided him toward the kitchen. "It means I like you."

"I love you, Harry." Devon hugged him.

Dinner turned into an enjoyable meal with Harry to entertain them. He didn't complain about the bill-of-fare, Ann noticed. Instead, he accepted second helpings of the salad and meat. She was grateful she'd bought a peach cobbler at the new bakery. Otherwise, dessert would have been impossible.

After the dishes were washed, Harry glanced at the clock. "What about a movie? There's a Disney film festival in Lake Maynard that starts in an hour. We could all go."

Ann frowned. It was one thing to eat supper in her fatigues. It was another to go to a show in them. Devon would need to change too. "I don't know. We really should make an early night of it. Attendance is mandatory for us at the town memorial tomorrow too."

"I see." The amusement faded out of Harry's eyes. He turned toward the front door. "Well, maybe another time."

"Oh, Mama. Let's go. It'd be so fun."

"All right, but I don't want to hear any complaints when we're up and going bright and early tomorrow. Harry, there's coffee in the pot. Help yourself."

"Sounds good. I'll wait here with the coffee."

"We'll only be a few minutes." Ann smiled over her shoulder. "We have to hurry so we don't miss the cartoons."

"Cartoons?" Devon demanded. "Do you think we'll see Mickey?"

It took a moment for Ann to understand what her daughter was asking. "Maybe, honey. I don't know. We'll find out. What are the movies, Harry?"

"The first set is the *Lady and The Tramp* series."

"We'd better get a jump on," Ann urged Devon down the hallway toward the bedrooms. "We'll be right back."

When they returned a few minutes later, she saw him finishing the cup of coffee. He swung around at the sound of their footsteps. She didn't have much choice in civvies, except the clothes she'd borrowed from Margo. He'd seen the blue jeans that outlined every curve, a red Washington State University sweatshirt and a light denim jacket trimmed in white embroidery last week when they went to the Shakespeare festival.

"You look beautiful."

Ann smiled and felt a pleasant new warmth course through her, then remembered she wasn't getting involved with Colter regardless of how nice he was. She glanced at her daughter.

Devon had insisted on purple overalls and a matching t-shirt. Rather than argue about it, Ann had selected a purple ribbon to twine around her daughter's ponytail.

"Let's go now," Devon ordered. "I haven't been to the movies in forever."

"Has it really been that long?" Ann asked. "Okay, we're going. I don't want to be late."

"Nobody does, Angel."

Locking the door after them, she strolled beside Harry toward his pickup. She stared at him in growing wonder. She barely recalled 'date nights' with Will, much less the times boys asked her out when she was in college. Her father was always busy on the ranch and didn't have much time for her or her sisters. Was that part of the reason her insecurity always multiplied instead of dividing? Did she really believe she was destined for failure? None of her relationships ever worked and for the first time in years, Ann wondered if it really wasn't her fault. That was too painful to consider now.

Despite her determination not to think about those strange questions, Ann found the thoughts returning later that evening. She might not be as desperate to get Harry's job as she'd always believed. She deliberately blocked that idea from her troubled mind and glanced across the cafe table to where Devon sat. "Did you like the movies, sweetie?"

Devon dug a spoon into the scoop of chocolate ice cream. "They didn't have any *Mickey Mouse* cartoons, Mama."

Harry chuckled and slid an arm around Ann. "I'll find some old *Mickey Mouse* movies, Devon. We'll watch them tomorrow night at your house."

Devon put down her spoon and grinned, chocolate smears adding to her pleasure. "Really? Tomorrow, Harry?"

"Tomorrow night after the celebration up town." He glanced at Ann and leaned closer. "It's called chasing the calf to catch the cow, my darling. Think it'll work?"

"I happen to be a single woman." Ann glowered at him, trying to hide her amusement at the country reference. "What are people going to think when you arrive at my house with your scummy movies? Everyone will decide I'm a floozy."

"Really?" Harry beamed. "I'll let you prove it to me. That'll be lots more fun than watching TV."

CHAPTER THIRTEEN

Ready for bed, but unable to sleep, Ann roamed from room to room in the small cabin and finally settled in the living room with a cup of coffee dosed with Irish Cream. She leaned back in the rocking chair wishing she hadn't finished her last paperback. Turning on the television would wake Devon and her daughter needed sleep, not a late night when they'd be at a town celebration the next day. Perhaps, they could take a trip to the library in Lake Maynard after the event.

Ann sighed, recalling her solitary childhood. From the time she was three, she'd attended Janine O'Connell's preschool and Harry's grandmother didn't believe in limiting children. When Ann expressed an interest in learning to read, Janine taught her. The Baker City library became a second home where she'd found acceptance in the shelves. Hiding in her bedroom with a stack of books meant she avoided her stepmother's demands, escaping to one fantasy world after another. Even though Ann was in college when the library closed due to lack of funds, she'd still cried.

Tears filled her eyes when she recalled the rooms filled with books in the house she shared with Will. What had he done to her old and beloved friends? Sold them at his garage sale? Given them away? Dumped them in the trash? If he'd been in Washington State, she'd have hunted him down and ripped his ego to shreds since no judge would throw him into the proverbial hoosegow for a crime only another bibliophile would understand.

In their house, paperbacks jammed the shelves, mixed and mingled with hardcover novels and texts. Poetry was crammed in beside psychology. She'd always meant to catalog the books and put them in order. She never had, figuring it was enough if she separated her classroom library from her personal one. She glanced at the empty bookcases framing the old entertainment center with its TV, DVD player and movie collection. In the opposite corner, stood the small airtight woodstove that would heat the place during power failures.

Cat admitted it'd be too expensive to provide cable for all the cabins, so she planned to highlight the peace and tranquility at the dude ranch as the perfect place to avoid a gadget driven society. Ann decided to talk to the other woman about providing reading material for her guests and see if she wanted to hit the local thrift stores and libraries to hunt down used paperbacks.

She finished her drink and rose to her feet. Morning came early. When she put her cup in the sink, she spotted the note they'd found taped to the front door when they returned, a message to call her former department chair who later became a principal at the last high school where she taught. She grimaced. What did Smitty O'Sullivan want or need?

He was retired and the likelihood that he had a line on a job for her ranked between slim and not hardly. It'd taken longer than she'd originally expected to complete her education since she'd done a tour in Iraq, a cost of enlisting for the money to pay her way. She'd graduated from college with BA degrees in English, Math, History and an associate degree in Geology in addition to her teaching certificate. She was highly qualified to teach a variety of classes, but it didn't make it any easier to obtain a position when she didn't have seniority at any school district because of the time she'd spent in the *Sandbox*, preparing to go to war, or completing the Army training with her unit prior to transitioning back to civilian life.

She switched off the lights and headed down the hall toward the two bedrooms, pausing to look in on Devon. The little girl was a lump in the center of the twin bed and Ann adjusted the blankets over her daughter, trying not to disturb the child. She slid into the queen-size bed in her room warmed by the electric blanket. She closed her eyes, determined to sleep. She loved teaching, but it was almost impossible to find a full-time job at this time of the year and substituting was so hit and miss. The last time Smitty evaluated her performance, he'd found the students paraphrasing *Romeo And Juliet.* On his way out the door that afternoon, he'd told her she was a natural and thanked her for sharing the show with him.

There were no answers tonight and every question brought more. She struggled not to cry. How could she plaster up a confident facade when she had to face most of the people in town tomorrow? Although she'd been in a combat zone three times, she was such a coward. She didn't have the courage to call Smitty and ask if he knew about a prospective job.

All she could do was go to sleep and hope tomorrow would be better, although she knew it wouldn't be. How many of the locals would feel sorry for her? Even if they hadn't bought her belongings or participated at the garage sale, they knew what Will had done to her. She didn't dread the town celebration as much as she did the pity party and being the object of their mockery.

The good weather lasted for the town memorial. Ann and Devon arrived in town early enough for the pancake breakfast at Pop's Café, then joined others to watch the parade that wound through town and ended at the cemetery, followed by the crowd of townspeople and visitors. Surprisingly, neither her father, the president of the business association, nor the minister was the one who stood in the middle of the grandstand, prepared to make a speech. It was Cat McTavish wearing a white western style dress that barely showed her baby bump, white cowgirl boots and a white hat who stepped up to the microphone, flanked by her daughters in miniature versions of her attire.

"Good afternoon, Baker City." Cat smiled and waited for conversations to die. "For those of you who don't know me, I'm Catriona Rose O'Leary McTavish, the *O'Leary* and these are my girls, Sophia and Samantha who share my *Gift.* We're glad to be home with you and recognize all of our friends, old and new."

Silence fell upon the crowd for a moment. Cold spring breezes blew through the graveyard and then applause erupted from most of the onlookers. Ann flicked a sideways glance at her daughter, then at Harry who'd just arrived to stand beside her and his grandmother. "I don't understand. What's she talking about?"

"She's who we've been waiting for." A tear streaked down Janine O'Connell's cheek. "We've always depended on the *O'Leary* to maintain peace, order and keep everyone calm and happy here in Baker City. We didn't have one for a long time after her grandmother passed, but then Ed and Adam Williams found Cat last year when she entered their essay contest and won the dude ranch."

"I still don't understand. She's not a police officer, is she? She's not dressed like one and I'm sure she didn't take their training."

"Oh no, she's not in charge of that kind of law and order. My son, Dick is still the chief. He doesn't have the *Gift*. He can't do what the *O'Leary* does, and he wouldn't even try. Now, hush. I want to hear everything she has to say."

Ann took a deep breath, deciding to listen and interview Cat later. It seemed as if there was another story, a deeper one but she suspected her father wouldn't know the details. Granted, his parents moved here when he was a boy and he'd lived near Baker City for more than fifty years, but they would undoubtedly be considered newcomers for another fifty since they weren't members of a founding family, even if her father had married into the McElroy clan.

"Until I came back here, I didn't remember the tragedy of Baker City until Summer O'Neill shared it with me." Cat looked around, her voice softening. "More than a hundred years ago, in February 1910, it seemed like spring should be on the way, but instead it continued to snow. Drifts piled up to more than ten feet deep. The clouds couldn't get over Mount Carmody or the rest of the range. A foot of snow fell each hour and it lasted night after night. Valentine's Day, it suddenly warmed up, began to rain and the avalanches started."

"How many avalanches?" A visitor called.

"There were five," Cat said, her tone still gentle. "Today, we remember the two biggest ones that hit the town. Those wiped out the train station, the hotel, the school, three shops and five homes. Sixty people died. It took months to dig out all the bodies. The last funeral was for Mrs. Doireann O'Sullivan, the schoolteacher who'd come from Ireland. After her husband died in a farming accident, she returned to teaching and remained at the school until her death."

Another spring breeze freshened the air and Cat paused for a moment. "We're here to celebrate and honor their lives, so they know we remember and respect them. In the future, we'll erect a monument, but for today, we'll read the names."

Ann watched as her father and Reverend Tommy joined Cat at the podium. They took turns reading the names and ages of the ones lost. While the majority came from the founding families, there were others, strangers who'd been in town. Cat took the time to say where everyone died. She apparently knew all the locations, amazing after more than a hundred years.

"She must have researched for months to learn all those facts," Ann whispered.

"No, she's the *O'Leary*." Janine leaned against Harry. "All she had to do was ask and she'd be told the answers."

Ann assumed the older woman meant Cat visited the families to learn the facts needed for the memorial. As the list of names wound down, the men on the grandstand stepped back, the twins going with them and Rob joining his wife.

The two held hands, but he was the one to speak. "For those who are ready to move on, go in peace and serenity with our prayers and well wishes. For those who want to stay, know you're always welcome in Baker City. As we've said for the last hundred and fifty-plus years, 'our folks always come home regardless of where they roam.'" His deep voice took on a stern note. "Remember the rules the first *O'Leary* set forth and follow them."

Ann glanced around the crowd of people, but nobody seemed concerned by the lecture. "Who is he talking to?"

"The ghosts, Mama." Devon took her hand. "If they're bad, Mrs. Cat and Mister Robbie have to send 'em away, 'cause she's the *O'Leary* and that's her job."

"What?" Ann stared at her daughter, stunned and bewildered. "Where did you hear such nonsense? There's no such thing as ghosts."

"You shouldn't say that in Baker City. We have lots of them here. It's why we need the *O'Leary*. Everybody knows it."

"I don't." Ann turned her attention to Harry. "Do you?"

"No." He shook his head, reaching to tug gently on Devon's braid. "Folks love ghost stories especially if they're not too spooky."

"His father married a flatlander with no imagination." Janine rested a hand on Devon's shoulder. "But, you're half Sweeney, child. Your family has been here since the beginning of Baker City and you know to always respect the *O'Leary*. Then, if you ever need her help, you can call on her."

"Or Mister Robbie." Devon heaved a dramatic sigh. "Sophie and Sam talked to Mass-Sarge Harry's friend when we met him last week at church, but I couldn't."

"What friend?" Ann asked. "I didn't see the three of you with any strangers."

"They said it was Sarge Zeke. They told him to go to the café to talk to the mayor and other ghosts. I 'spect he's here with them now, but I don't know for sure."

"You'll have to ask the twins when they finish the presentation," Janine said.

Devon nodded. "I wish I could talk to my pony the way that Samantha and Sophie talk to theirs."

"Practice and you can learn."

"That's what Mister Robbie says."

After Reverend Tommy led everyone in a closing prayer, he reminded them of the rest of the day's events including the bazaar, carnival, baked salmon dinner at the café, and to cap off the evening, the street dance for young and old.

"What kind of memorial is this?" Ann inquired. "Shouldn't it be more somber?"

"It's a celebration of life." Janine took Harry's arm. "Come along, Harold. You need to help set up the rest of the tables for the fair. We don't forget our loved ones by inviting them to party with us."

This was totally strange, Ann thought. She'd have been the first to think her former pre-school teacher didn't have a touch of whimsy. Devon rushed off to greet her friends and Ann followed her daughter, coming to a stop when Smitty O'Sullivan approached her, a tall, solid looking, mixed-race man in a dark suit, his close cropped, once black hair now totally gray.

He held out his hand to her, warmth filling his dark eyes when he smiled down at her. "Did you get my message?"

"Last night." Ann shook hands with him. "I didn't have a chance to call you yet. My cell phone service is hit and miss in Baker City."

"So is everyone else's. We need more towers. I'm glad you're here." Smitty grinned at her, obviously looking her up and down in the dress blues. "You look good, Annie. In that uniform and with those combat ribbons, you might even make an impression on the kids, but I'm not guaranteeing anything."

"Not much ever impresses teenagers and I wasn't showing up in jeans and a sweatshirt today since my civvies disappeared while I was gone. I didn't want to borrow more clothes from Margo." Ann managed a smile, then forced a laugh, determined not to sound pathetic. "So, do you have a job for me?"

"In September."

"What?" She gaped at him. "Are you serious? Where? I thought you retired."

"I did and then your dad came calling. I was determined to work in my shop, clear my property and plant a new orchard in addition to my wife's vegetable garden. Come see our school."

"I can't today. I have my daughter with me, and I promised to take her to the carnival."

"We'll let Frank babysit for a little while. It won't take long." Smitty put a hand on her shoulder and propelled her toward her father. "Hey, Frank. Do me a favor and watch your grand-daughter long enough for me to take Annie to the school."

Nodding, Frank broke away from his conversation with the minister. "That'd be fine. Where shall we meet up later?"

"At the bazaar," Ann said promptly. "If you need a break, turn Devon over to Harry Colter and his grandmother."

"We won't. Ginger's there helping Vanessa set up the booth for the quilting group. She's really missed Devon this week. You'll be lucky if you get the kid back before supper."

"That's fine. I wanted to talk to the two of you about spring break and see if Ginger would like to have Devon stay overnight on Tuesday. I have to work late at the base, and it'd be a great opportunity for the two of them to have some gramma-grandkid time."

"You're a doll." Frank kissed Ann's cheek. "Thanks for thinking of us."

"Hey, I don't know what I'd have done without both of you when Will disappeared on her during my last tour."

"He undoubtedly figured the Army would give you emergency leave to come home and straighten out your family," Smitty said. "He couldn't grasp the fact that it was a war-time situation and you wouldn't be back for at least a year. Now, come on, Annie. Let's go to school."

"Okay. Okay. Where's your car?"

"Why would I need one when the school's right there?" Smitty pointed past the cemetery to the historical two-story building with the cupola on the shake roof. "We're walking and you won't even get your shoes dirty."

"Good, because I hate polishing them."

They walked side by side toward the old building, up the stone staircase to the door. Smitty reached into his pocket, removing a set of keys and unlocked the main door. "Do you remember your way around?"

Ann nodded. "Straight ahead are the stairs to the second floor and the older kids' classrooms. I graduated from eighth grade here, then went to Lake Maynard for high school. Downstairs was the elementary." She gestured to the addition at the rear of the structure. "That's where the office was, the lunchroom and the bathrooms. We didn't have a gym. We'd play games outside and the teachers would take us to run around town for exercise."

"Well, let's go upstairs and see your room."

"My room? Smitty, have you completely lost it? The school's been closed forever."

"Only for ten years. When it came up for sale, your dad bought it. He put together a board of directors and I'm the guy in charge of that. We've been approved to reopen as a kindergarten through eighth grade facility like it was before. Now, we're hiring teachers. We want you and Margo Endicott to start."

"This is nuts." Ann followed him up the stairs, wondering what her best friend would say when she heard the news. There were two large classrooms, one on each side of the hallway. There weren't any lockers, just old-style cloakrooms at the far end of the rooms. The restrooms were directly above those in the addition.

She spotted the narrow door that opened to the last staircase. She remembered studying hard to earn the privilege to ring the bell in the cupola that announced the beginning and ending of the school day. Smitty stood in the doorway of the classroom overlooking the front of the building and she went to join him.

She froze when she saw several educational posters defining the qualities of a hero. She'd found those when she was in graduate school and used them to decorate her room. She turned, spotting more that described the writing and editing process. Along another wall, she saw those with math formulas. She walked over to the windows, eyeing the low bookcases filled with textbooks, literary fiction, paperbacks in every genre. Instead of individual desks, there were several tables lined up in neat rows, each with three chairs. She had more than enough space for twenty-seven students.

"This is my library. But, how did it get here? I heard Will had a garage sale."

"He did and Jassy Sweeney called me before a single book left your house. I missed out on your computer, but I got your desk and the file cabinet with hard copies of all your lesson plans. Luckily, your classroom library was already packed."

"I didn't have time to unpack it when I took it home. We were shipping out and all I could do was collect all my belongings and take them to the house."

"Jassy, Summer O'Neill and I took boxes and went after your personal library. Will tried telling us to leave and Jassy rained all over his parade and lectured him about what a 'real' guy does and how he wasn't a patch on her man's jeans, that if he hassled her for one more minute, she'd have Laredo Hawke rearrange his face. She even told Will he was an embarrassment to the family, and he'd be lucky if the rest of the Sweeney clan didn't disown him."

"I wish I'd been there to see it."

"If I'd had a better signal on my phone, I could have filmed her grabbing Will's arm and literally throwing him out of the house. That woman may be no bigger than a flea, but she has some serious anger issues. Of course, none of the Sweeneys ever suffered fools gladly. Laredo told me once that when it comes to Jacinth, 'duck' is not a noun, but a word to the wise."

Ann laughed and walked across to stroke the spine of a copy of *To Kill A Mockingbird*. "Where is my personal library?"

"At Summer's. She had the most room plus we weren't sure where you'd end up. Your dad and I hadn't started putting the school together yet. It was still in planning stages. Jassy didn't want you to have to drive to the far end of nowhere to get the books at her grandfather's ranch and I was concerned they'd draw moisture in my shop."

"When did you set up this room?"

"Once I heard you were back in *The World* as we used to say when I was in Vietnam. Cat O'Leary McTavish's husband, Rob Hendrickson helped put it together. He wants a school here for his and Cat's kids. So do most of the folks who are driving to Lake Maynard every day."

"Are you going to have buses?"

"That's next on the list. First, we get teachers, then support staff like cooks, secretaries, drivers."

"Who's going to be the principal?"

"I don't know yet." Smitty leaned against the oak desk. "I figure you teachers will know what you want in an administrator so you should help hire one."

"That's different."

He shrugged. "Hey, we've been up the hill, over the mountain and chased the coyotes. We know what it's like to have someone in charge who isn't a team player."

"Do we ever." Ann looked around the room again. "This is a dream come true. I have to talk to Margo or did you already?"

"Not yet. I asked Cat and Rob to leave a message for her last night when they left one for you. I'll track her down."

"Where is her room?"

"Downstairs. Would you like to see it?"

"Definitely."

When they walked out of the room, Smitty locked the door, then handed her an extra pair of keys. "Here you go. You'll need to make plans for the school year. The electricity is on and we've ordered computers and printers. They should arrive in two weeks."

"Good to know." They reached the bottom of the stairs and she heard children's voices in the addition. Instead of turning toward the classrooms, she headed toward the administrative offices where she found Devon with Cat's daughters. "What are you girls doing?"

"We brought our teacher flowers." Sophie walked out of what would be the principal's office. "She likes roses best."

"But she likes tulips and daffydils too," Samantha added. "She's the best teacher ever. She could tell us apart even when we wore the same color dresses last year at the haunted town and had our hair the same and everything."

Sophie tilted her head to the side, obviously listening to someone else, someone Ann couldn't or didn't see, then giggled. "She says it's 'cause we're two different people who happen to look the same."

"That's 'cause you're 'dentical twins." Devon told her friends, glancing back at the office. "Bye, Mrs. O'Sullivan. We're going to the 'zaar now. The new baker's gonna give free cookies to all the kids."

This time it was Samantha's turn to listen intently before she heaved a sigh. "We'll tell her 'bout him, but I don't promise she'll hear us. Our daddy says some folks take a while to understand 'bout those 'uns everyone can't see and you gots to have patience till they learn better."

Ann took a deep breath, then folded her arms. "Exactly, who are you girls talking to?"

"Mrs. O'Sullivan," Sophie said. "She's glad the school will be open again, but she says she's been a teacher long enough. This is her place and she'll be the new boss."

"That's a principal." Devon beamed at her mother. "I bet she'll be better than Mrs. Gundersen."

"It wouldn't be difficult." Smitty gestured to the main doors. "Run along, kids. You don't want to lose out on Twila's cookies, and they'll go fast."

Ann waited until they were alone, or then again maybe they weren't. She looked at the mixed bouquet of tulips, daffodils and two red rosebuds in the vase on the desk. An antique wood and gold handheld teacher's bell stood beside the flowers in the otherwise empty office. "Are you going to tell me you believe in ghosts?"

"I was born and raised in Baker City. Of course, I do."

"Well, I don't."

"You will someday soon." Smitty took her arm. "Now, let's go see Margo's room."

"I'm ready." Ann walked beside him, tossing a quick glance over her shoulder. For a moment, she thought she saw an insubstantial woman in a white shirtwaist blouse and a long black skirt walking behind the desk, braided hair in a bun on top of her head.

Ann blinked hard, deciding she was just imagining it.

And the office door swung closed!

CHAPTER FOURTEEN

"What did you think of the memorial, Angel?" Harry studied the woman sitting next to him on the couch. He deliberately kept his voice low so he wouldn't awaken the little girl who'd dozed off in the middle of the last *Mickey Mouse* cartoon and slept through the *John Wayne* movie he'd brought. "Where did you disappear to after the speeches? It took a while for you to get to the street fair."

"I'm going to plead the Fifth Amendment and put Devon to bed." Ann cuddled her sleeping daughter close. "I've got some thinking to do about a possible job in the fall, but I'll keep you posted and let you know when I make a decision."

"You have orders for ninety days which will last through most of June and we were going to arrange for another ninety after that."

"I know, but if I take this job, I'll have to leave the base in early August." Ann shifted, easing to her feet. "I want to talk to Margo about it. Hopefully, she'll be around in the morning."

Harry stood, picking up Devon who snuggled deeper into his arms. "Do I want to know who she dates?"

"No, you really don't." Ann led the way down the hall to the first bedroom, gesturing for him to put the little girl on the bed. "I'll be back in a few minutes once she's settled."

"Okay, I'll go G.I. your living room."

"Wow, I want to see that so don't work too quickly. Harry Colter cleaning should be in a different sort of movie."

He chuckled but didn't bother to say that he'd done his share of cleaning in the last twenty years. The military figured every soldier should be able to do laundry, make a bunk and mop floors. Picking up three glasses, empty ice cream dishes and the large popcorn bowl only took a few minutes as did washing them. He found the broom stationed near the garbage container and swept the floor.

All that remained were three cardboard cartons stacked in a corner. He slowly studied the letters spelling out her name and oddly enough the word *keepers*. What had she brought back from the feedstore? It wasn't his business, but since he'd carried them inside for her, he knew how heavy the boxes were and he didn't want her moving them without him. He peeled back the gray duct tape on the top one and opened the flaps to find brightly colored paperbacks.

He looked over his shoulder at the sound of soft steps on the tile. "Why do you call these books, *keepers*?"

"I read a lot." Ann shrugged, wariness in the leaf-green eyes. "Most of the time, I'll donate books to the library for fundraisers or swap them for novels I haven't read at a used bookstore. These are exceptions, ones I simply can't give away, so I call them *keepers* and apparently it rubbed off on Will's cousin, Jacinth Sweeney who loves books as much as I do. Summer O'Neill stored them for me, but I have room here for some of my favorites."

"How many more do you have?"

"Probably another twenty boxes."

He blinked, amazed at the idea. "I'll help you put these away."

"Isn't your grandmother expecting you?"

"I have a key, Angel and I'm a grown man. I don't have a curfew."

She laughed. "All right. Let me get a cloth and wipe off the shelves. Then, you can pass the books to me and I'll sort them by genre and author."

"Authors I know. What do you mean by *genre*?"

"The type of story. Is it a romance? A western? A mystery?" She turned toward the kitchen. "Your English teachers should have taught you that back in the day."

"Zeke and I played a lot of sports, so we pretty much got a pass as long as the teams won."

"I hate that crapfest and it still goes on today." Ann came back from the kitchen with a dust cloth as well as a can of furniture polish. She proceeded to spray the shelves and wipe them off, the smell of lemon pervading the room. "Smitty used to throw fits whenever a coach tried to convince him that athletes didn't have to pass their core classes like Math, Science, History and English."

"We didn't have a Smitty at our school when I was there." Harry removed six books and passed them to her. "If we had, our football team might not have been state champs quite so often."

"Indubitably."

With the two of them working together, it only took slightly more than an hour to put away the books. She liked him more than ever when he didn't comment about how many romances she had or when she moved certain titles to different shelves. Instead, he just followed directions and handed her the copies. She stroked the cover of her favorite *Georgette Heyer* novel and eased it into place next to the rest of the regencies.

"Now, it feels like home. Thank you, Harry."

He smiled and trailed a callused finger over her lips. "Didn't I earn a kiss after all that hard work?"

"I never thought of putting away paperbacks as hard work. It must have been lifting the hardcovers that belong to Devon." Hiding a smile, she fell back a step as he took a step closer. "Good help is so difficult to find."

"You're telling me." He stopped in front of her, hunger written on his stern features. "Do I scare you, Angel?"

"Of course not!" She took a step forward and put her hands on his chest, feeling the pounding of his heart increase. Did she cause that reaction in him? "Colter, I'm confused enough since I got home. According to my ex, I'm not a good, decent person. He told everyone in town that I'm conniving, selfish and nasty, a real sleaze. I don't want to hurt you. So, go away."

"I've always wanted a ruthless woman who'd have her way with me despite all my pleading for mercy. You shouldn't listen to morons and if your former husband wasn't one, he'd never have let you go."

"I'll have to remember that the next time I'm in Baker City." She slowly laced her arms around his neck. "This is only a physical attraction. Will you go home?"

"In a minute." He lowered his head. "After I kiss you goodnight."

If he kissed her, she'd melt in his arms. She knew that even if he didn't. Before she could escape, he swooped her up in his arms and carried her toward the couch. "Harry, no." She wasn't frightened of him, only of herself. "Stop it! Put me down."

"I will." He dropped her on the couch and followed her into the cushions, pinning her beneath him, his mouth a mere breath away. His lips teased hers with featherlight pressure.

She gasped. Did he feel her nipples stabbing into life? Or the way her breathing was so ragged? Even she heard the pounding of her heart. He was so big, and she couldn't help pressing her fingers against the skin of his shoulders. "I've got news for you. Just because I haven't decided if I want your job or not doesn't mean I'll sleep with you to get it."

"Good. Because you aren't getting it." His soft chuckle rasped along her nerves like sandpaper. "All you're getting is me, Angel. I'm marrying you and I'll keep you busy with a houseful of kids."

"The hell you will, you chauvinist. Devon is kid enough for me."

He breathed a gentle kiss into the hollow of her throat. "I'll change your mind. I'm making love to you, tonight and every other chance I get. But I won't take you to bed until you promise to marry me."

"That isn't happening."

"I think it will." He kissed her with leisurely tenderness.

She caught her breath again. She couldn't resist him even though she knew it was the saner decision. She melted against the fierce, lean strength of his body. A fire started within her and she moaned when his lips traced a slow path along her neck. She couldn't help her low cry when he used his weight to force a new contact against her legs. How did she struggle against a spell that was as tender as it was stormy?

His tongue claimed the depths of her mouth even as his hand sought her breast.

She moaned and thrust her fingers through his dark hair. She wasn't a small woman, but he made her feel as if her well-built figure was as beautiful as a model's. When his hand slid over her sweatshirt, she trembled.

His mouth tugged at her earlobe. "When are you going to marry me? I've already told you how I feel."

"No, you haven't. You keep saying you want to marry me. You don't say what you feel."

"And if I told you how much I cared?" He pushed up the hem of the shirt, searching for the front clasp of her bra. His fingers began to explore her breast as he slowly palmed her nipple. "You've got issues and I don't think you trust me yet."

"Hey, I'm smart enough to look out for myself and my daughter. Getting a 'Dear Jane' letter during that last tour taught me a lot."

"It should have taught you that your former husband was an incredible jackass, but I'd bet you're still blaming yourself instead of letting him own what is his to own." His thumb teased her nipple into a taut peak.

She closed her eyes against the intense emotions he caused, dazed at the effect on her senses. Despite herself, her hands lifted, and she buried them in his hair again. "Harry—"

His soft groan of pleasure and hunger sent a new thrill through her. Will never made love to her with this intensity and she deliberately blocked the memory. Why think of her ex-husband at a time like this? She moaned and drew Harry even closer until their lips met in a fierce kiss. All she wanted to think about was the pleasure of his touch. Every other thought had escaped into a tangle of emotions.

"Mama? Mama, where are you?"

Ann stiffened, pushing at Harry's shoulders. "Let me up." Turning her head, she called. "I'll be right there, Devon. I'm coming."

"I'll come find you," Devon called.

Ann shook her head. What on earth could she do now? Before she was able to rise from the couch, Harry stood and moved to block her from Devon's view. "I thought you were sleeping, D.J."

Ann hastily pulled down her sweatshirt and rolled to her feet. "What's the matter, sweetie? Did you have a bad dream?"

"No." Devon came into the room. "Nobody read to me, Mama."

Harry quirked a brow and bent to pick up the child. "What does that mean, D.J.?"

"I want my story," Devon announced. "Now, Mama."

"It's too late, sweetheart." Ann stepped around Harry and reached for her daughter. "Time for you to be asleep."

"No!" Devon shrank closer to Harry and out of Ann's reach. "I want my story. Harry, read to me."

Harry stiffened. He met Ann's gaze, but didn't speak.

"Devon, it's bedtime." Ann took a deep breath. "Harry *won't* read to you tonight. You're going to bed right now."

"Honey, I don't mind. Do you want me to read to her?"

"Shut up, Colter. Or I'll throw you out on your ear." Ann marched down the hall. "Bring that brat with you."

"I'm not a brat," Devon cried. "I'm being good so I can have Rainy Night."

Ann flipped on the light switch in her daughter's room. "Get into bed and Mama will *tell* you a story, but no books tonight."

"Harry tells it," Devon demanded. "Not you."

Ann refused to meet Harry's amused gaze. Of course, he was laughing at her. Would another mother have so much difficulty controlling a six-year-old? She glanced quickly around the small bedroom to make sure Devon's clean clothes were neatly stored in the closet and dresser. Her stuffed animals shared the bed with her along with a favorite doll.

Thank heaven she didn't appear to be a total slob, Ann thought. Now, how could she tell Harry this performance was the normal bedtime routine for the past few days? She didn't get mad at Devon. But sometimes the child threw such embarrassing tantrums. Ann paused. She still did the same thing when she got angry. Why did she expect Devon to control her temper when her parent didn't?

Ann slowly swung around and eyed the dark-haired child. Devon's curls were such a contrast to the purple jammies she wore. "Put her down, Harry. She'll get under the covers."

"Okay, Angel." He dropped the girl on the bed, and she bounced gleefully up and down.

"Do it again." Devon rocked to her feet, arms extended to Harry. "Drop me."

Harry obeyed, gently dumping her on the twin bed. "Under the blankets, sweetheart."

Ann choked back an appreciative grin. His voice was so deep that the endearment sounded rough and tender at the same time. "You do realize, Colter, that you're ruining the springs on the bed. We're going to hear about it from Cat and Rob if it breaks."

Harry lifted one massive shoulder. "We'll have to buy furniture for the house on my grandpa's ranch anyway, honey."

Devon clambered under the covers. "Tell me a story, Harry."

Harry sank down on the edge of the bed. "What story should I tell?" He held out a hand to Ann. "Come sit here, Angel."

She obeyed, wishing she had more common sense when he wrapped an arm around her shoulders. Harry Colter was the kind of man that should only be taken in small doses. Large ones were addictive. "Keep it short and simple. She needs her rest."

Harry glanced around the room obviously seeking inspiration. Ann pointed to the framed silver photo of Devon with *Mickey Mouse* on the bureau. He nodded and began to tell the story of the cartoon the girl had missed.

Ann waited until her daughter was sound asleep before she led him out of the room. Switching off the overhead light, she gently closed the door partway. "I've seen you every day for the past week, Colter. I don't want to see you tomorrow. Is that clear?"

"Scared, huh?" Harry sauntered down the hallway to the living room. "I knew it."

"What does it take to get the message across, Colter? I don't want you hanging around. I absolutely refuse to marry you or date you or anything."

He swung around, tipped up her chin. "Angel, if you hate me that much, why do you kiss me back so sweetly?"

Ann felt a red-hot blush scorching its way into her face. "I don't hate you. You're a good, wonderful person, but you should be involved with somebody decent without a ton of emotional baggage. I'm no angel."

"That's a matter of opinion." He bent and his mouth teased hers.

She shuddered with waking desire. She gritted her teeth. He had to leave. Now, before she surrendered and told him whatever he wanted to hear.

He lifted his head without deepening the kiss. "I'm going home. You think about us, Angel. We make a hell of a team."

The next afternoon, the warm April sun beat down on the roof of the stable. Ann wiped the back of her sweaty hand over her forehead. Stall mucking was hard work, but when they'd run into them at church, she'd promised Rob she'd look after the horses so he and Cat could have a day away with the twins. This barn had to be cleaned and she was the only one to do the job.

A few stalls away, Devon happily brushed Rainy Night. Ann reached for the rake and began to smooth the load of cedar shavings she'd just dumped. Seven horses and three ponies lived here now, the rest of them enjoying the chance to graze in the paddocks. She'd brought in the P.O.A. for Devon, but left Skyrocket out with his horsy friends.

She took a moment to recall her dad's love of his beautiful, valuable animals. The barn at Majestyk Morgan Farm was always full. She didn't need to spend tons of money to find the perfect mount, much less ride his purebred stock. The horse she'd rescued from the rodeo trailer was more her type. She loaded her tools in the wheelbarrow and moved to the next stall. Standing her rake against the wall, she began to pitch manure. When she added the contents of the muck tub in the corner, it didn't take long to fill the barrow and she pushed the load up the barn aisle.

"Let me do that for you, Angel." Harry strode toward her.

Ann gaped at him. She wished desperately that Devon would abandon Rainy Night long enough to run interference and tossed her head. She was an adult. Surely, she could handle being alone with a man, even Harry Colter.

Today he wore a cotton shirt with ripped off sleeves, halfway open to expose the dark mat of hair on his broad, tanned chest. Faded jeans clung to his long legs. She focused on the muscular arms and felt a surge of heat flow into her cheeks as she recalled the way he'd held her.

His slow smile sent shivers down her spine. The memory of his kisses was enough to stir her even a day later. This had to stop. He was just a man. She'd been married before. She knew what all the shouting was about, as the saying went, and Colter wasn't worth the emotional gamble. She took a deep breath, angry at herself for liking him, even angrier for wanting to sleep with him. *No, I don't have sleeping in mind.* "What are you doing here, Colter?"

She lifted her chin and tried to sound as rude as possible. Maybe, he'd be offended and leave. "What the hell do you want, Soldier?"

"A rough, tough cowgirl," Harry taunted, looking her up and down in the jeans and t-shirt she'd bought at the feedstore this morning. "But I can wait, *Annie Oakley.*"

"You didn't answer my question." She stamped her foot in the new riding boot. If the wooden floor hadn't been covered with a rubber mat, it would have made a better impression. She glared at him and refused to smile when she saw laughter in his blue eyes. "You have no business here."

"Sure, I do." He gently gripped her waist and lifted her out of the way. "I said I'd dump it for you. Where does it go?"

Ann couldn't believe it when he started pushing the wheelbarrow down the main aisle of the barn toward the gate. He acted as if the load of manure weighed less than feathers. Maybe it did to him. She stalked after him. "I'm not a weak, helpless female. I can handle this job."

"You don't have to when I'm here."

Ann hurried to open the gate for him and led the way around the barn to the manure pile. Cat had told her where to dump the used bedding to keep the spring run-off from a nearby shallow creek out of the stable.

"If a guy dug that crick lower," Harry mused, "it wouldn't overflow."

Ann gasped. How had he known immediately what Cat was doing? "Who told you the plan?"

"Nobody, Angel." Harry shrugged one broad shoulder. "I was born upriver, and I lived near Cedar Creek while I was growing up. Every time the water rose, our house flooded, and we moved to my grandparents who have a place downstream from this dude ranch. My grandpa taught me how to control nature in the hopes my dad would listen to me."

"Did he?" Ann inquired, her natural curiosity taking over. She wanted to pump Harry for all the information he'd give her and learn everything she could about him.

Harry shook his head. "Gramps should have taught my older brother. My dad would have listened to him. As for me, the old man thought I was destined to be a sissy. He used to give me hell because I liked poetry." Harry grinned ruefully, laughter lines deepening around his eyes. "Guess he figured I'd never be a real man."

Ann choked on her amusement. "Poor Harry. Somebody should have told your dad that there are a lot of *male* poets. Some of them even made money. Shakespeare, Tennyson and Whitman not to mention Robert Frost were all men."

"Didn't Frost write the ones about miles to go and picking apples? I liked them."

Ann pushed a strand of hair off her face. "My favorite was *The Road Not Taken.*"

"Mine was, *The Highwayman.*" Harry turned and strolled to the creek, measuring the road that wound up the hill. "I had a coach who quoted that thing all the time. Got to where I used to say it at home."

"No wonder your dad was upset." Ann tried for a teasing tone. "He must have gotten tired of hearing it." She closed her eyes for a moment and concentrated. She remembered some of the old ballad.

"The wind was a torrent of darkness among the gusty trees,
The moon was a ghostly galleon tossed upon cloudy seas,
The road was a ribbon of moonlight over the purple moor,
And the highwayman came riding - riding - riding,
The highwayman came riding up to the old inn door."

Harry headed back to the barn with the wheelbarrow. "Most people wouldn't know that much of it. Why do you, Angel?"

"I love the English language and certain things just stick in my head. You're lucky I didn't rattle off half the sonnets or my favorite lines from the plays when we went to the Shakespeare festival."

"I can handle it."

"Is your dad still alive? If I meet him, I'd love to tell him the story of *Flanders Field* and the soldier who wrote the poem about the poppies there. He didn't survive *World War One.* Back in the day, I created entire lesson plans about it and made my kids try to write poems that were as poignant. Some were pretty good."

He stopped and stared at her. "You're a teacher?"

"Well, I was. Me and Margo, but we can't get teaching jobs now."

"Why not?"

"We're Army Reservists, Harry. Kids don't stop learning when their teachers go off to war for damn near two years and school districts don't operate without full-time instructors. You can't blame them for replacing us."

"Do you?"

"Oh, hell yes! I started applying to the local districts when I knew our return date, but the response from all of them was the same. I could substitute until next fall, but that's hit or miss. You never know if you'll be working until they call first thing in the morning and I can't afford to sit on my butt and wait."

"So, that's why you opted for the A.G.R. slot at Fort Bronson." His tone made it a statement, not a question. "I'm lucky you don't hate me for getting the job."

"What's the point?" Ann opened the barn door. "This is when I get on my soapbox and say there's too much hate in the world. I know that on an adult level even when I rant and rave. I'm sorry I was such a baby the day we met. It wasn't your fault."

"Careful." He grinned at her. "If you act like too much of a saint, I'll start looking for the real Ann Barrett who takes names and kicks butts. Find me a shovel and I'll dig down that drainage creek while you do the barn."

"Sounds good."

"Afterwards, we can have a picnic. I want to show you my place and Grandma packed us a big dinner."

CHAPTER FIFTEEN

Fenced pastures rolled lazily down to Cedar Creek. Ann glanced behind her. A large two-story log house was nestled in the shadow of the protecting ridge. Across another field was the bulk of a huge hay barn. She stretched out her long legs and allowed the sun to warm her all the way through. Before they left the dude ranch, she'd taken a quick shower at her own cabin changing to denim shorts and a sleeveless western shirt with pearl snaps, more treasures she'd found during her shopping trip at the feedstore this morning.

Devon napped on the other side of the blanket in the shade of a huge maple. Harry leaned against the trunk of the tree; his eyes closed. Despite that, Ann knew he was still awake. "So, is this your family homestead, Colter?"

"Yup." Harry didn't move. "Most people figure it's too secluded. My folks, brothers and sisters live in different towns around Washington State. When all of them agreed to sell it to the banker in Lake Maynard who wanted to buy it for the gravel, Grandma called me. My great, great, great-grandfather homesteaded the place almost a hundred and fifty years ago and she doesn't want to see it go out of the family."

Ann propped herself on one elbow and continued to study him. "When did you get it, Harry?"

"Spring, three years ago. Zeke and I were home on leave for Easter. I was staying with Gran. I've looked out for her since Gramps died."

Did Harry know how special he was? She doubted it. Warmth filled her when she looked at him again. His eyes were still closed, and he seemed totally contented. An aura of menace clung to him. It reminded her of a sleeping panther, as if he'd be alert in a split second. "What did you do in the Rangers?"

"Killed people." He opened one eye. "Mostly it was nosy females who wouldn't let me sleep off Sunday dinner." He paused and the faint amusement continued to grow as he teased. "Especially the kind of meals my granny packs—meatloaf sandwiches on her homemade bread, potato salad, real lemonade, chocolate cake and all."

Ann felt a quick smile tug at her own lips. She rose to her feet and crossed to him. Dropping to her knees beside him, she brushed her mouth over his. "Can't I keep you awake, Colter?"

"Yes." He pulled her down on his lap and his arms tightened around her as he rested his chin on her hair. "But I don't want you to."

She giggled and pressed her cheek against the material of his cotton shirt. She slid one hand inside and felt the heat of his bronzed skin against her fingers. "Isn't it my turn to seduce you, Harry? I liked the way you were kissing me last night."

"I know." He stroked her hair. "You don't get to have your wicked way with me in front of the kid. Wait till later."

Ann twined her arms around his neck and tried to reach his lips with her own. The hard line of his mouth was a temptation. She touched his lean cheek with the tip of one finger, marveling at the harsh beauty of his features. "It amazes me you're still single. You should have been roped and hog-tied years ago."

Harry's soft laugh teased tendrils of her hair and he gently kissed her forehead. "If I'd married out of high school, I'd have to find someone like Twila Desmond who never hesitated when Zeke made a career out of the military. She followed us all over the continental U.S., to Alaska and Europe."

"The new baker in town?"

"Yes. She always found a job near where we were stationed, but she and Zeke planned to move back home when he retired. But, he didn't. She brought the kids and came here to be close to his family after he died. He wanted to be buried here and so did I, but we figured it'd be years from now."

"I know." Ann heaved a sigh. "We lost three of our folks and an LT from Personnel at Army Command HQ this time. An I.E.D. when they were on patrol, taking supplies to a girl's school. We'd been lucky. We had close calls before in our last tour, serious injuries but nobody died."

He nodded. "When you go again and again—"

"Your number comes up." She pressed closer, listening to his heartbeat. "What would you have done if you hadn't volunteered for the Army?"

"I'd have been a logger or a truck driver. There aren't many job opportunities in Baker City, and I'd have missed out on a lot, Angel."

Ann sighed and pillowed her head against his chest, listening to the beating of his heart and feeling him stroke her hair. "I know, Colter. You might never have gone on night raids, commando operations or suicide missions. Just think of all the fun you'd have avoided."

"How did you learn that much? I haven't talked about it."

"You don't talk about anything, Colter." She wrinkled her nose. "Not your family—except in numbers and to introduce me to your grandmother. Not the Rangers - which is where you've spent the last twenty years, but I saw what they did when we were overseas. They're the elite and they deserve to be with the risks they take."

"I wasn't a Ranger the whole time. I was regular Army before I went to Ranger school. Zeke and I were mechanics in a motor pool, our first assignment after Advanced Individual Training. Totally boring which is why Twila told us to go for broke and apply although we didn't know if we'd be chosen. The selection process was rough. Rangers lead the way and they only accept the best candidates."

"Now, I'll know to look for you in the motor pool when you see our old trucks." Ann grinned. "But, what about the rifles, Harry? The kids told me all about the way you repaired those when they went to the armory. Where'd you learn that?"

"In the Rangers, sweetheart." Harry yawned and his eyelids drooped. "If a guy's weapon malfunctioned and he didn't fix it, he ended up dead. I wasn't trying to be a hero." His arms tightened and he drew her closer. "Now, shut up so I can sleep. Do you always talk so much?"

"Always," Ann agreed mischievously. "It drove Will crazy, especially at night. He'd want to sleep, and I'd be wide awake."

A sensual grin twisted Harry's mouth. "If I was in your bed, Angel, I wouldn't complain if you kept me awake every night. I might die of exhaustion, but I'd take you with me."

"Shut up, Harry." A scorching blush raced up Ann's neck and burned her face. "I don't want to hear one more word." At the sight of the amusement etched on his chiseled features, she wrenched free. It was time to make a discreet withdrawal before she totally lost the war with her senses and him. "I'm going up and look at the house."

Harry dug into the pocket of his jeans, managing to caress her bare leg at the same time. Ann backed away. He tossed a keyring to her. "It's the third one. There's four bedrooms upstairs and two down. No bookcases but I'll build them for you. Nobody in my family ever had your love for books."

Ann remembered his own deep feelings about the written word and decided not to mention it. Obviously, Harry was sensitive about his background. "Bookshelves, huh? Is there anything you can't do, Colter? Or are you planning to be *Superman* before you turn forty?"

He contemplated her through narrowed eyes. "If you don't scram, I'm gonna haul you back here and make love to you till you beg for mercy."

"Remember my kid. You were the one who wanted to wait until we didn't have an audience." Laughing, she backed another two steps.

Turning, she hurried for the distraction that the house offered. Climbing up the stairs to the wooden wraparound porch, she frowned. There was a legal notice on the front door. Ann stiffened as she scanned the words. The sign stated the property was due to be auctioned off— for non-payment of the property taxes.

She carefully tore it free, determined not to lose her temper when she returned to tell him the news. She'd wanted to explore the log house, but that would have to wait for a better time. She hurried back and passed him the sign. "Harry, look at this. The place is being sold for back taxes."

"I never bring my glasses on a picnic." He scanned the small print on the paper and then glanced at her again. "What does it say?"

Ann nodded and began to read the legal mumbo-jumbo in a tight voice. Tears stabbed behind her eyes. What right did anyone have to take Harry's home while he was gone on active duty? None, she thought. If they could find a military attorney, maybe they could even prove it was illegal right now. Would Margo know one that could be contacted today?

"All we can do is stop on the way to work tomorrow and pay the property taxes. Hang onto that paper, Angel. I'll put it in the truck and then we'll have it."

"We?" Ann sputtered. "What makes you think I'll ride to work with you? I've got my own car."

"It doesn't make sense." He took the notice out of her hand. "You're dropping Devon at my grandmother's house tomorrow for spring camp and I'll be there too. We're both going to Fort Bronson. We'll both be coming back to Baker City. We may as well go together."

Ann glowered up at him, admitting that logic was on his side. How could she push Colter away if she spent more time with him, not less? "I won't do it, Harry."

"Yes, you will." He bent and his mouth touched hers. "Otherwise, I'll carry you out to the truck in the morning and shock the town. Besides, I need you tomorrow, Angel. When I pay those taxes, I want a witness."

She rested her palms against his shoulders, smiling up at him. "Prove it," she purred. "Bribe me."

He tugged gently at her hair. "Behave. I'll ravish you after we get home, not when we might upset Devon."

"Not hardly, Colter. I always have a headache on Sunday nights."

"I've got a good cure for those."

His promise came back to Ann later that night. They'd had supper at Pop's Cafe in town and then he'd driven them home before he went to talk to his mother about the missing property tax payments. Devon had her bath and wore green pajamas tonight. Ann finished brushing out her daughter's curls. "Time for bed, honey."

"I want a story." Devon grabbed her robe, pulled it on and hurried into the living room, climbing into the rocking chair. "Now, Mama."

Ann sighed. "One story, Devon Joyce. No more." She gestured to the books and her daughter hustled across the room. "Find one."

Thank heaven Harry had left. Maybe Devon would willingly go to bed after her book and they wouldn't have their usual argument, but Ann doubted it. She sat down in the rocking chair and turned on the small lamp beside her. "Ready, Devon?"

Her daughter pulled out a huge hardcover *Disney* collection of children's stories. "Read to me."

"One. Only one." Ann scooped Devon up on her lap and opened the book. They were halfway through the story when there was a tap on the door. Ann looked and hastily suppressed a smile when Harry strolled inside. "I thought we'd seen the last of you for tonight."

"Hi, Harry," Devon called. "Mama's reading to me."

"Is she?" Harry sauntered across the room and dropped down on the carpet, resting his head against Ann's knee. "Go ahead and finish, Angel."

"You don't mind? It will take a while longer. Devon loves *Puss in Boots*."

"Read to me," Devon ordered. "Did you see *Puss*, Harry?"

Ann obediently showed Harry the picture of the swashbuckling cat and then returned to the story. She read every word slowly and with feeling, much to her daughter's delight. When she finished the adventure, Ann closed the book. "Time for bed, Devon."

"No," Devon pronounced adamantly. "I want a story."

Ann took a deep breath. "I already told you, Devon. Only one. I won't read another."

Devon clambered off the rocking chair and Ann's lap, the book clutched in both hands. "Read to me, Harry."

When she dropped onto his lap, he cuddled both the child and the book. "Now, sweetie, what did your mom say?"

"I want another story, Harry. You read to me. It's your turn. I read to you lots of times."

"You do and you die," Ann said sweetly.

"Now, Angel, one more won't hurt her."

"Have I ever told you about the mule my great-grandpa used to have?"

"Nope. What does that have to do with me reading Devon another story?"

"According to my grandpa, this happened when his parents married. They were coming back from the church in a fancy mule-drawn cart.

The mule stumbled and his dad said, "That's once." When they were halfway home, it happened again and his dad said, "That's twice." The third time the mule stumbled, he went down on his knees. By then they'd arrived in the front yard. His dad said, "That's three." He went in the house, got his shotgun, went out and shot the mule. According to Grandpa, his momma had a real fit, shouting and screaming about losing such a valuable animal. When she finished, her new husband said, "That's once." Do you understand what I'm driving at, Colter?"

Harry carefully laid the big book on the coffee table and rose to his feet, lifting the little girl at the same time. "I guess so, honey. It's time for Devon to go to bed."

"No." Devon tried to squirm free. "Not goin', Harry."

"Yes, you are." Harry ignored the screams as he started down the hall toward her room. "I'm not fighting with your mama. You're doing what she says."

"I'm glad you got the point of my story." Ann smiled and followed him. Her grandmother always claimed her grandfather had made up the entire thing since nobody would shoot a good, well-trained mule that obviously needed a hoof trim. Grandpa had just laughed and said, 'that's once.'"

"I'm not tired, Mama." Devon wailed. "It's spring break and there's no school tomorrow. I wanta stay up."

"Not happening, dear heart." Ann lifted the blankets so Harry could lower the child onto the bed. "Remember you're going to camp tomorrow with Samantha and Sophie? You're getting your rest, so I don't receive a bad report when I come home from work. Don't you want to see Harry's grandma or her dog's puppies again? I thought you wanted to play with the other kids."

"Okay, so I'm not going to work with you," Devon decided firmly. "I'm going to camp."

Ann tucked her under the covers and kissed her forehead. "It will be fun. You can tell me everything you've learned when I get back from work. Mrs. Cat expects you to take riding lessons in the afternoon with the twins, your Cousin Jassy and Mister Robbie."

"And I get to take care of Rainy Night again."

"That's right."

"Kiss me goodnight, Harry," Devon demanded. "It's your turn."

"She'll do anything to avoid bedtime." Ann rose to her feet. "Go ahead, Colter. Maybe she'll go to sleep then."

Harry chuckled and followed directions. He brushed a tender kiss over Devon's tiny forehead and smoothed her dark hair. "I love you, sweetie. See you tomorrow."

Ann smiled and turned on the nightlight. The small mouse figure bathed the room in a soft glow. Devon had pounced on it in the feedstore when she spotted *Mickey Mouse*. Ann led the way back to the living room. "Harry, we've got to talk."

"Are you going to read me from *The Book*, Angel? You're right. I shouldn't have knuckled under to the kid."

Ann spun to confront him, planting her hands on her hips and glaring up at him. "Damn it, Colter. I hate it when you do that. The least you could do is listen to all my arguments and then say you're wrong, not take the wind out of my sails by agreeing with me beforehand."

Harry lifted one shoulder, a wry grin playing about his stern mouth. "If we have a big bust-up fight, Angel, I can't make love to you. I've never been a parent. I wouldn't know where to start or how to do as good a job as you are."

Ann felt all her anger and frustration seeping away. "Do you really think I'm a good mother? I try so hard and sometimes I feel like such a screw-up especially when I get back from the *Sandbox*."

"I've already told you more times than I can count," Harry said as he paced toward her. "I think you're perfect." He reached out and caught her hand, pulling her down to sit on the couch with him. His lips brushed hers. "I've missed this."

"You didn't have to." Ann met his teasing kisses, determined not to surrender too quickly. She wasn't falling in love with him, regardless of the temptation. "You were the one who said we had to wait."

"Anticipating is half the enjoyment." He nibbled his way to the pulse-beat in her throat and back to the corner of her mouth.

She shuddered with the responses that wracked her body and wasn't certain if it came from her turbulent emotions or from his touch. She should put a stop to this, but she wasn't ready to call it quits yet. Besides, why should she when she enjoyed him so much? "Aren't you worried I'll insist you marry me right away?" She tried to catch her breath. "Or make you give up *my* job at the base?"

"I'd marry you in a minute." His hold tightened and her hands slipped around to the smooth muscles of his lean back as he moved, trapping her beneath him. "We can get the license tomorrow when we pay the property taxes. I'm keeping *my* job so I can support you and Devon as well as the rest of the kids and you can teach school."

Ann gasped as the light exploration of her lips gave way to the fierce hunger which seemed to be a part of him. His drugging kisses ravished the inside of her mouth, his tongue fencing with hers in a savagely tender battle that lasted forever, to her dazzled mind.

As the assault intensified, Ann found herself surrendering. He made love as well as he did everything else. He combined an innate gentleness with bold, masculine power. The impression he made was impossible to ignore and somehow it was growing harder to resist both sides of the man, her friend and this stranger who had such a devastating touch.

Who was Colter really? Was he a fierce commando or the man who tried to take such good care of her? In his arms, she experienced a new quandary. She had to decide whether to give in or be strong enough to send him away. And would surrender grant her anything? The dizzying idea mingled with the electrifying touch of his fingers on her skin.

Ann moaned softly when he unfastened the pearl snaps on her western blouse. She didn't want to stop him. Not yet. She would shortly. She attempted to block him as he found the front clasp of her bra and he gripped her fingers, moving them to his shirt.

"Take me to heaven, Angel." His husky voice teased her skin and her emotions. "Touch me."

She unbuttoned his cotton shirt, pushing the material out of the way so she could run her hands over the broad, tanned strength of his wide chest. Her breath caught as she slowly slid her trembling hands through the mat of dark hair. "Like this, Colter?" she teased. Then she brushed her mouth over his bronzed skin. "Or like this?"

His low groan of pleasure increased the urge to tease him. She felt daring and adventurous. She traced a line toward his masculine nipples. He stiffened as her lips followed the trail her fingers had started.

He finished unfastening her bra and pushed the material aside. His hands claimed her breasts and then his mouth. She couldn't help her low cry as his lips closed over one nipple, sucking gently.

Moments later, she felt him sliding lower, his hand caressing her hip as he laid a path of kisses down to her midriff. An almost combustible blaze of emotion caught her spinning mind as his tongue teased her navel. A white heat of flame arched her body as his hand began to stroke the long line of her legs, tracing a line up to the bottom of her denim shorts.

Her fingers shook as she stroked the strong width of his chest, slipping along his ribcage and exploring the lean hardness of his stomach. "Harry." His name was a moan of pleasure.

When he began a tormenting, leisured journey back up to her lips, she clung helplessly to him. She couldn't help pleading for more of his steamy kisses and intoxicating caresses. This depth of passion was brand new, one she didn't remember experiencing with her former husband. She was overwhelmed by the temptation to tame this man from a jungle cat into a house pet. Could she do it? Did she really want to? She framed his face with her hands, studying the openness of his steady blue eyes. "We barely know each other."

"I know you, Angelica Barrett." He punctuated his words with kisses. "You're passionate, lovely and sexy. You're gentle and good to children. And I love that dash of temper. Sugar needs spice to make it palatable."

She sighed and rolled on top of him, staring into his face. "Talk to me, Colter. Why did you decide to come home now?"

"I was ready to do something different." He pulled her mouth down to his and kissed her.

She tore her lips away and shook her head. "There's been enough monkey-business. We've got to know each other. Why didn't you stay in the military?"

Harry shifted beneath her and his hands slipped up to cup her breasts, thumbs rubbing her nipples. "Because I was done watching people die and it was time to restore the farm."

"You didn't have to wait, Colter. The Army would have sent you through college. Why didn't you become a doctor or a lawyer or an engineer?"

"All I ever wanted to be was a farmer and I only wanted one piece of land." He studied her, his gaze narrowing. "What's really on your mind, Angel?"

"You don't trust me enough to tell me what you learned about the tax situation. What did your mother say about the payments?"

"I'd better go home, Angel. This isn't getting us anywhere."

"Run away, Colter. That's what you want to do, isn't it?" Ann slid off the couch to her feet, bitterness swamping other emotions. She fumbled with her clothes, fastening the bra and snapping her blouse. "You won't let me get close to you or find out if there's a real man behind that facade."

Harry stood and began to tuck in his shirt. "What the hell do you want to know, Ann? I've tried to give you what you need."

"Yes, you certainly did." Ann tossed her head. "But I'd like to know the person under *Superman's* uniform. Every time I try to learn who you are, you push me away."

"What makes you think you'll like the mean side of me? I'm no saint."

"And I'm not perfect. Shall I tell you about me, Colter? I'm no angel. Not unless you're looking for the honky-tonk kind. I grew up in Baker City and my older sisters told everyone that I was the local slut. This weekend when I was at the feedstore, Summer O'Neill warned me Will didn't tell the truth. He didn't say he filed for divorce because I stayed in the Army. He told everyone I'd cheated on him more than once."

CHAPTER SIXTEEN

Ann watched him leave. He wasn't like Will who wouldn't have resisted the urge to ask the names of all the men who'd shared her bed before, not that there'd been too many, just a couple boys in college and then she met Will. She'd been faithful to him the entire time they dated, during their engagement and of course when they were married. She doubted he could say the same.

Worry mixed with anger and tormented her mind. Would she ever know the real Harry Colter? Or was she doomed to stand back like the rest of the world? He could do all sorts of things, but rewiring old electrical plug-ins, fixing broken plumbing, digging ditches—none of that told her who and what Harry Colter was. She didn't even know his middle name.

The next morning Devon set the table while Ann fixed breakfast for them. Her daughter flashed a sunshine smile over her shoulder. "I can't wait to go to camp."

"I know. It will be fun." Ann put a plate of scrambled eggs, a rasher of bacon and piece of toast in front of her daughter. "Eat up and we'll leave."

"Then I'm going to Mrs. O'Connell's school." Devon grabbed her fork. "I get to see the kids who live in Baker City and Emmy's babies again."

While she ate, Ann took a few minutes to contemplate the child's meaning. Then she recalled what Janine O'Connell had said. "They're puppies, Devon. Baby dogs are puppies."

"I still want a puppy." Devon decided between mouthfuls. "And Rainy Night."

"Let me think about that." Finishing her own breakfast, Ann lifted a cup of coffee to her lips.

Would Cat and Rob want another dog running around here? She'd have to talk to them before she got one of the O'Connell puppies for her daughter. On many farms, dogs were used for protection and to ward off coyotes. They weren't pets and while she didn't know if that was the case with Lad and Lassie, it'd take more investigation than she had time for this morning.

"Are you done thinking, Mama?"

"Not yet, sweetness. Let me think at work. Okay?"

Devon nodded agreement, scooping up the last of her eggs. "I'm ready to go now."

Ann sighed and looked at the clock. It was six-thirty, a late start for them since they were going to the county courthouse before she and Harry went to Fort Bronson. By the time she'd washed the dishes, and packed both of their lunches, it really would be time to leave. "Eat all your breakfast. Then go make your bed, tidy your room and get your backpack."

"I already told you." Devon asserted, her jaw jutting forward. "Let's go now."

"After breakfast and after we clean the house." Ann stood and carried her dishes to the sink.

Before long, they were headed for the car. Carrying her purse and beret, in camo fatigues and combat boots, Margo walked toward her S.U.V., but she stopped when Devon waved. "I'm going to camp today."

"You're kidding," Margo marveled, coming to join them. "When did that happen, Devvie?"

"Mrs. Cat invited me. So did Mrs. Tommy." Devon beamed. "Harry's gramma said it too. I'm going to have fun today with the other kids."

Ann opened the car door trying to hide her smile. This conversation had been going on since last week and she was grateful Margo had the patience to go through the topic again. "Hug your godmother goodbye, Devon."

While her daughter obeyed, Ann loaded the car. "I think it's going to work out fine. In case it doesn't, I'll leave your number and then Janine can call you or me or Cat."

Margo nodded. "I'll pick her up if there's a problem." Her arms tightened around Devon. "Go to camp, honey. Learn lots and work hard."

"I'm getting a puppy and Rainy Night." Devon happily climbed into the car and then into the booster seat in the back. "Mama's thinkin' today."

Ann proceeded to help her daughter with the seat belts and cast a quick glance at Margo who waited nearby. "I haven't made a decision yet. She's young for the responsibility and I've got to talk to Cat and Rob first. We don't want a new puppy chasing their livestock."

Margo smiled, relief coming into her eyes. "My thought exactly. It isn't fair to keep a dog on a chain. Maybe we could do it in a year or two."

"Of course, if Smitty actually reopens the school in Baker City, things could change. Did he contact you?"

"He left messages and we're playing phone tag. I'll track him down when I get to the office and let you know what I hear at lunchtime."

"Works for me." Ann looked at her watch. It was six-fifty. "We've got to scoot. I'm supposed to collect Harry in twenty minutes." She hurried around the vehicle. "I'll pick up Devon tonight at Cat's unless there's an emergency. I'll call you if I need a rescue."

"No worries. Between the two of us, we have it covered."

A short time later, she and Harry headed to work. "Harry, did you need to stop at the bank? I don't know if they'll take a personal check this close to the auction."

"It's fine. I have enough cash on hand." He met her gaze. "It'll be all right, honey. I'll protect you."

"I can take care of myself, Harry Colter. And my daughter. I don't need you interfering."

"The hell you don't. I'll make you a deal, Barrett. You watch my back and I'll watch yours. Then neither one of us will get fragged."

Ann signaled for a right turn and drove toward the courthouse. "I don't think either of us will get shot this morning, but I'm willing to look out for you."

Harry relaxed. "You're the boss."

"And if I believe that, you'll sell me a bridge over Cedar Creek." It took a few minutes to find a parking place and she switched off the motor. "Do you really want me to come along?"

"Yes. I already told you, I need a witness." He strode around the car, an imposing sight in his camouflage fatigues.

Ann climbed out of the vehicle when he pulled open the driver's door. "We'll be lucky if they don't think they're under attack since we're both in uniform."

"They should be used to seeing soldiers since we've been at war for so long." He chuckled. "If they give us a hassle, we'll have range firing here instead of at the base."

Ann hesitated. She hated fighting with him, but she had to know if he'd pulled strings to get Devon into spring break camp. "Harry, did you ask your grandmother to take Devon this week? I know Cat said she'd check and see if there was room, but I wasn't looking for special treatment."

"I never thought of it. I don't butt into my Gran's business. Shades of Winston Churchill, she can tell you to 'go to hell in such a way, you look forward to the trip.' No, if Gran didn't have room for Devon, she would have said so."

The tension slipped away, and relief took its place as they walked across the courthouse campus to the administrative building. "I was concerned because she's been treated like a princess a lot while I was gone. This class will be good for her. She'll learn to behave appropriately with other kids instead of always being with adults." Ann frowned. "You aren't worrying about this are you? The staff might be obstructive because the sales take place at the end of the month."

"Too bad, too sad." Harry pulled open the heavy glass door. "Like Gran said last night, my grandfather would want me to have the O'Connell farm. It's mine and I'm keeping it. I've already paid for it with my sweat and blood. I've fought for this country for twenty years. Now they can pay me back."

Ann stopped, freezing in her tracks. She glowered up at him, fighting back the urge to cry. "You were wounded? Harry, no! You couldn't be."

"Sorry, Angel." Harry frowned at her. "I'm not a superhero. Bullets tend to make me bleed. Now stop sniveling or I'll kiss you right here which isn't a good idea when we're both in uniform."

"At least I finally found out something about you." She struggled to smile. "How many times were you shot?"

"I spent most of my time in combat. How about if I show you my ribbons tonight and you figure it out?"

"If you'd worn all of them and your dress uniform, you could have impressed all these people."

"It wasn't worth taking my blues to the cleaners afterwards. Don't embarrass me while we're here by threatening these civilians. You be sweet and charming. Save your snarky attitude for folks who can handle it like other soldiers. I'll be a real hard-nose."

"I'll bet. I'll tell them all about military lawyers in case they haven't seen them on TV. I'll arrange for the Army to sue this county six ways from Sunday."

"Try it and you won't sit down for a month." He guided her to the rows of elevators. "What floor do we want?"

She studied the list of departments on the sign before she opted for the Assessor's office. It was on the third floor. "Honestly, Colter. You're vainer than I am. I suppose you forgot your glasses again."

"That's right." He pushed the button for the elevator and frowned at her. "If you hassle me, Sergeant Barrett, you'll be cleaning latrines with a toothbrush. Got it?"

"Stuff it." She stepped into the elevator and pressed the button for the third floor. "You can't intimidate me, Master Sergeant Colter. I know everyone at HQ including the secretary for the Reserve General's adjutant and she'd help me raise hell and put props under it."

"You are a loyal, little thing. I appreciate it, Barrett, but save the urge to take names and kick tails unless we need it."

"We will." Ann led the way toward the Assessor's office. "I've been in here more times than I care to remember during different episodes with Will and all these people are creeps of the first water."

Harry shook his head ruefully. "I shouldn't be surprised you're battling the bureaucrats instead of directing your anger at the man who deserves it. What did he do to make waves?"

"Mostly barroom brawls and I had to post bail time and again."

"No, you didn't. You chose to post it. He might have grown up if he had to face the consequences of his actions, rather than having you save the day."

She grimaced as the elevator doors opened and they headed into a large office filled with desks and people coming into work. "Damn it, Colter. I hate it when you have a point." They walked toward the long L-shaped counter and the waiting clerk. "We want to see the man in charge."

Harry smiled at the heavy-set woman. "The gal in charge will do just as well." He reached in his pocket and pulled out the deed as well as the tax papers posted on the farm. "I'd like to straighten this out immediately."

"We have this property up for sale," the middle-aged clerk promptly stated, barely glancing at the legal description. "It's on the list that Herman MacGillicudy at Lake Maynard First Federal Bank will be purchasing soon."

Ann took a step forward and rested her hands on the edge of the counter. "I wouldn't try it. Master Sergeant Colter was away in Afghanistan. He found out about the mistake yesterday and he's here to rectify it now. I suggest you deal with him or I'll have the JAG officer from Fort Bronson, Colonel Williams down on your department like ugly on an ape. Am I clear?"

"I'm here to pay all of the back taxes. Who should I talk to?" Harry pulled out his wallet and opened it, lifting the stack of bills into one big hand.

Ann gaped at the money. The pile of hundred-dollar bills must be at least two inches thick. What on earth was he trying to prove? No wonder he needed a witness, she thought and scanned the room for one of the cops who provided security. Harry would probably get mugged on the way back to the elevator.

Afterwards, the stiff silence in the car grew more tense as each mile passed on their way to Seattle a short time later. Sometimes, men were uncomfortable with a woman behind the wheel, but she wasn't letting him take over and drive the Ford. "What's wrong?"

"Could say nothing except it wouldn't be true. You embarrassed the hell out of me, Angel."

"I embarrassed you?" Ann sputtered. "What the devil do you think you did to me, flashing that bankroll around the courthouse? You scared the hell out of me."

He lifted one broad shoulder. "I always do business in cash. I don't like waiting for the check to clear. You had no business causing a scene."

"A scene?" Ann gasped. "A scene!" She forced herself to keep watching the road. "You may trust people, but I certainly do not! Not when it comes to paying four years of taxes in cash. That was a lot of money and I didn't think it was enough for them to stamp the bills paid. It certainly didn't break that woman's arm to give you a receipt."

"It wasn't necessary." Harry repeated. "The stamped bills were a receipt. I didn't need another one. I also didn't like the way you kept threatening those people with Williams. That isn't my style at all."

"Well, don't worry about that. Colonel Williams probably wouldn't do squat for you anyway. I was running a bluff and we were damned lucky that those bureau-rats didn't realize it."

"Bureaucrats," Harry corrected evenly. "It's time for you to do an attitude check, Sergeant First Class Barrett. You have an abrasive personality at times."

"Shove it!" Ann took a deep breath. "When I was in the *box*, I heard all about Herman MacGillicudy buying up local farms for the gravel. He plans to make big bucks by selling rock to the county for road improvements and housing developments. The 'fix is in', Colter. I know you won't listen, but if you want to keep your land, you'd better."

Before he responded, she turned on the radio to drown out any more conversation, hoping she wouldn't disgrace herself by crying. Maybe there were government employees who didn't think they were above the law, but she hadn't met them. The tension continued for the entire morning and into the afternoon. She found herself staring at the letters she was supposed to be typing. He'd stalked out to the supply room and not bothered returning. She didn't miss him. Deliberately, she didn't look up when the back door slammed open, banging against the wall. Instead, she gazed at the computer screen.

He came to a stop behind her. "When you finish ruining the correspondence, I want you to go through the clothing records. Make sure everybody has what they're authorized. After coming home from combat, uniforms always need replacing."

Ann swung around in her chair to glare at him. "You're a supply sergeant. I'm not. How am I supposed to know what's allowed?"

"Read the regs. You can do it at lunchtime."

"Go to hell! I'm running with Margo. Do your own paperwork for once. I'm sick of it."

Harry clamped both hands on the arms of the chair and leaned toward her. "You're always griping and whining about the job you want supporting some unit. Well, part of that job is supplying the people and the organization with what they need. You might as well know what the hell you're doing instead of screwing it up."

"I won't do supply," Ann snarled the words, hating herself for wanting him even while she was furious. "You can't make me."

"Really?" He bent closer, blue eyes narrowed in rage. "Who do you want me to call? The Command Sergeant Major? Or the Colonel?"

She tossed her head. "I don't care who you call."

"I'm sure, Angel." He eyed her, the mocking smile almost making her lose control. "Shall I call all of them? I'll give you one choice. You can do it today or tonight. Make a decision."

"I only work eight hours a day. You've got no business throwing your weight around."

"Believe me, sweetheart. Eight hours is an easy day when you're in the Army. We both know that. When you're not in combat, it's more common to be in the office twelve hours, Monday through Friday and then work weekends as well. Make your choice."

"Damn it, Colter." Ann fumed silently for a while, not wanting to agree with him. "Okay, you win. I'll do it but this is absolutely the *last* time. When Command Sergeant Major Jenkins comes in, I'm talking to him. He'll say I don't have to do supply. I'm not even M.O.S. qualified."

"So, we send you to school when everything's caught up," Harry drawled. "For now, you can have On-The-Job training." He stepped back, turned away and strode toward the rear exit. "I've got maintenance to do on the pistols. I'll come take over the phones in time for your break."

Ann frowned at the stack of records, not bothering to answer. She hated these man-woman games. He wasn't a chauvinist most of the time so why wouldn't he do his own paperwork? Tears stung her eyes. Was this part of the battle they'd fought earlier? Was he the kind of man who bore a grudge? He didn't seem to be and yet she really didn't know him all that well.

The atmosphere continued to be strained for the next two days although they carpooled to the base. It had hardened into a war, she thought glumly. He was conspicuous by his absence most of the time she was in the office and she found herself missing him, which was totally ridiculous. Wednesday night after supper and housework, Ann slumped into the rocking chair and reached for a book.

Devon looked up from the jigsaw puzzle of Dalmatian puppies spread out on the coffee table. "Mama, where's Harry?"

"At home, sweetheart. Do you want me to read to you?"

Shaking her head, Devon picked up Ann's keys. "Let's go see Harry. Now, Mama."

"No, Devon. You can see Harry tomorrow." There was a stubborn look on the child's face and Ann dreaded the forthcoming confrontation. "No tantrums, Devon Joyce."

"I wanta see Harry," Devon insisted. "I need to show him my favorite puppy at his grandma's school."

"Not tonight, honey." Ann slid out of her chair and sat down by the table, looking for the next piece of the puzzle. "We'll see Harry tomorrow. We'll leave early enough for you to show us the best puppy."

"I can go to work with you and Harry instead of going to camp."

Ann didn't answer, focusing on the puzzle instead. There was no way that her daughter was returning to the base especially with the argument she and Harry were having. Hopefully, the idea would be out of Devon's head by morning.

An hour later, Devon went to bed, still talking about Harry. Ann pulled her uniforms out of the washer and hung them to dry. Back in the day, she heard her father tell stories about ironing his fatigues, but thankfully she didn't have to spend hours doing that or shining her combat boots. She contemplated calling Harry just to tell him what she thought of his macho, chauvinistic attitude and reluctantly gave up the idea. He was acting like a complete and utter jerk. Determined to distract herself, she crossed to the bookcase and found a mystery by one of her favorite authors.

Dropping off her daughter at the preschool Thursday morning, Ann envied the way the child rushed to hug Harry. She shoved her fists in her pockets and waited.

"Where have you been?" Devon demanded. "You were gone, Harry."

He chuckled and held the little girl for a moment longer. "I wasn't gone, sweetheart. I just had things to do."

"I'll go to work with you," Devon decided. "I won't go to camp today."

"Wrong." Ann stepped forward. "You're staying here and learning stuff with the rest of the kids. Don't you want to play with the puppies?"

"I wanta see Harry."

He grinned. "Harry's flattered. Shall we have dinner tonight instead?"

"Yes! Mama too."

Ann felt the heat of a blush when Harry glanced at her and agreed. She managed to maintain her appearance of calm until they were in the car, headed for Lake Maynard. "Did it ever occur to you I might have other plans?"

"Not when you're trying out for the town's Ice Queen award." He paused and then continued deliberately. "There's no need to hurt Devon when you're sulking. You'll get over your mood sooner or later and admit I was right. Then we can get back to normal."

"You're an arrogant bastard." Ann pulled into the gas station. "Even if you haven't heard from Herman MacGillicudy yet, you will. He'll be after your place and you damn well know it."

"He won't get it so stop fussing." Harry leaned toward her and caught her chin. He brushed the softest of kisses over her lips. "You've had all the time I'm going to give you to get over your snit, Angel."

CHAPTER SEVENTEEN

Without speaking, Ann climbed out of the Taurus and washed the windshield while she waited to pump gas. Somehow, some way, she had to regain control of her emotions and she wasn't knuckling under to him. She'd done that too many times before and the pattern wasn't one she wanted to repeat.

He strode back to the car, dropping both the newspaper and a box of her favorite chocolate doughnuts on the front seat. He unlatched the hood and checked the oil and water. The water was fine, but he told her the oil was down a quart.

She headed for the store before he could stop her. Chipping in on the gas was one thing. Paying for regular maintenance was something else. She pushed open the glass door, found the automotive supplies, grabbed a quart of motor oil and then stalked toward the cashier, waiting in line behind an older man in a flannel shirt, faded jeans and boots. When the tall, solid looking, mixed-race man turned, she recognized Smitty O'Sullivan.

"Just the gal I've been trying to reach." Smitty smiled down at her, his dark gaze reflected his usual good humor. "The board is meeting tonight at seven-thirty at the school, and we'd like to have you and Margo Endicott join us so we can discuss contracts and wages. Are you up for that?"

"I am, but I'll have to check in with her when I get to the base." The town wasn't that big and everybody knew everyone else's business, so she added, "I'm on orders for another month and a half and I'll have to let the Colonel know if I'm leaving after that, so I couldn't start at the school for a while."

"That's fine. If you're there in August, we'll be good to go." He winked at her. "I'm assuming and we both know what that means, you and Margo will arrive in uniform since you won't have time to change to civvies. It'll impress the board even though I think everyone knows you two are just back from the Middle East."

Ann laughed as she was supposed to and paid for the oil. "I appreciate your wanting to hire us. I have high hopes for the school, even if the board has different ideas and chooses someone else."

"You two are perfect, Ann. You always managed to engage the students when you were in class and I've heard Margo has the same quality. You received glowing references from other teachers and previous administrators."

Ann hesitated. This was a viable alternative especially when there didn't seem to be any way she could take the promised job at the base away from Harry Colter. "I have a lot of self-doubts and I'm concerned because my father was instrumental in arranging the position."

"He had the original idea but he's also the first to admit he doesn't know anything about running a school, so he sought out those of us who do. He's made it clear that his wife and your sisters won't be involved in the day to day operations."

Ann caught her breath, amazed to hear that. Normally, Ginger had a finger in every pie and all of her father's business endeavors.

The door opened behind them and Harry strolled in, menace in every line of his body. "Is there a problem, Angel?"

Ann shook her head. "No. Smitty, this is Harry Colter. He's the active duty Master Sergeant where I'm working now. Harry, this is Smitty O'Sullivan, the head of the new Baker City school board. I don't believe you had a chance to meet at the memorial." She watched the two men shake hands, surprised that Harry seemed so much bigger than Smitty.

"I think I've heard your name before." Smitty frowned thoughtfully. "Aren't you from Baker City too?"

Harry inclined his head. "Yes. I grew up a few miles out of town, but I went to school in Lake Maynard and later in Liberty Valley. My grandmother is Janine O'Connell."

"That must be it." Smitty nodded. "My grandson attended her preschool a couple years ago, and Janine told me about you. She's very proud of you."

"The feeling's mutual." Harry glanced at the clock. "We have to leave, Barrett, or we'll be late."

Ann smiled at Smitty. "Thanks again. We'll see you tonight."

She pushed open the door, aware Harry followed her out to the car where he took the quart of oil from her. He was quiet most of the way to Seattle and she flicked a wary glance at him. What was wrong now? It couldn't be the same problem as earlier this week. Should she ask? Did she want to hear the answer? "Colter, what's the matter?"

"Nothing." Harry leaned back in the seat.

"I'm sure. You've been sulking ever since we left Lake Maynard. Don't tell me you're having conniptions about Smitty. He's the same age as my father and I think has four or five kids who are all older than I am."

"I didn't realize you were keeping secrets from me, Barrett. The two of you are planning something and I don't know what."

"It's not your business and I've told you more than once we should get to know each other. You're the one who says it isn't necessary."

"What do you want to know?" Harry inquired dangerously. "Should I tell you the real reason why I stayed in the Rangers? It was because I knew how to kill, and I was good at it—"

"I suppose you liked it too!" Ann flung the words at him, wishing she hadn't intruded on his silence.

"According to my dad, I have a talent for it. My mother almost died when I was born—"

"That wasn't your fault. If she was going to have a rough time, then he should have kept his pants zipped. If you haven't ever told him, I will when I meet him." She turned into the parking lot adjacent to the company headquarters. "Have you heard anything about what happened to the money you sent her for the property taxes on the O'Connell farm?"

"My mother hasn't returned any of my calls and I won't see the rest of my family before next Christmas. They're scattered all over the U.S. Gran's the only one left in Baker City and you're going to be polite to my folks. I always am."

"Want to bet?" Ann switched off the motor, pulled the keys out of the ignition and shoved her door open. "They say one word against you, Colter, and they'll be pushing up daisies."

A faint smile touched his lips. "I won't tell you again, Angel. You'll be decent to my family, as courteous as I am to yours."

"I'll keep that in mind when you meet my sisters and their husbands, especially Reid who needs to be educated about keeping his hands to himself and off my daughter."

Harry scowled at her and handed over the newspaper. "Here, shrew. I missed getting the news while you were having that tantrum."

"I don't have tantrums." Ann tossed her head, stomping beside him. "And I know you read it yourself when we didn't take breaks together."

"It doesn't mean I enjoyed it as much without your snarky comments."

She glanced up at him, pondering the odd stillness of his chiseled features. What wasn't he telling her? Then she knew. Part of her college training had included recognizing abused children. A man that didn't hesitate to blame a boy for his mother's health issues undoubtedly hadn't stopped there. No wonder Colter barely spoke about them and hadn't shared whatever he'd learned about what his mother did with the funds she'd misappropriated.

He claimed he focused on sports in high school, not academics. How poor of a student was he? Had his parents helped him with assignments or was that another occasion when they mistreated him? The thoughts remained in her mind for the rest of the morning. She found herself contemplating the unthinkable. How well did Harry Colter read?

The idea was implausible, she told herself repeatedly. Yet it occurred minute after minute, hour after hour. She glowered at the desktop computer. Where did the answer lie? Was it in Harry's actions? She'd been reading the paper to him for weeks while he fixed up the office. He always had a project going. Right now, he was caulking around the window frames, so they didn't rattle when the wind blew. Or he had been, Ann thought wryly.

The roach coach had arrived, and Colter went to buy her a doughnut. She was done working for the moment. She reached for the book tempting her, a brand-new western she'd bought at the P.X.

Harry stopped in front of the desk. "Have a maple bar." He lingered to watch her. "What are you reading?"

"*The Rawhide Bunch*. You gonna pitch a fit about it?"

"Is your work done?" He glanced at the empty metal file basket on the edge of the desk. "It must be. Wish I had time to read. Is that one of those shoot-em-up westerns?"

"What do you want me to do, Colter? Share my book with you instead of reading the newspaper today?"

"Yes, please. I'll fix the window by your desk now."

"You're crazy." She sighed and opened the novel to the first page. Was this a proof of her hypothesis or not? She wasn't sure and she didn't dare ask him about his reading ability and the way he avoided the written word, always claiming he didn't have his glasses. It'd be an insult of the worst kind. "Why don't I just finish it and then loan it to you? You can give it back to me when you're done."

"Because if I sit on my butt and read, we'll swelter during the summer and freeze during the winter. Eat your doughnut."

Ann laughed and picked up the freshly baked treat. The first bite led to a second and she loved the luscious, thick maple frosting that oozed down her throat. "Harry, you'd make some gal a great husband. I should let Margo have you."

"No thanks." Harry strode to the window behind her. "I'm planning to kiss you every morning for the rest of my life, as soon as I get you talked into it."

"Never happen." Ann finished the pastry and licked her fingers. "You're terrible for my diet."

"I think you're perfect in every curvaceous inch. Now quit fishing for compliments and read to me."

She shook her head. She couldn't help smiling. If it was deliberate charm to hide an impaired ability, at least he cared enough to make the effort. From now on, she'd be kinder to him. And she would find out the truth.

She opened the book and started to read. *"I stood in the dusty street, my gun still smoking. Pete Garrison lay twenty feet away, choking on his blood. I'd gut-shot him. Wasn't a fit death for a man. But then Pete never had been one. Only the worst kind of coyote tries to back-shoot a friend—"*

Her alto voice rose and fell in the office, but Harry couldn't really recall that it was Ann reading him a story. Instead he was on the dirt streets of the old west town, Rawhide, Texas in the eighteen-eighties. Dust motes danced in the aisles between the desks and he felt as though this old building was the perfect place to read a western novel. He remembered her telling Devon that the base had been built nearly a hundred years before.

The slam of the front door brought her to a halt, and he looked at the clock. It was almost lunchtime on a Thursday in mid-April. Who could be here?

Ann slowly lowered the book. A scrawny, black-haired young man in worn jeans and a torn sweatshirt entered the room. His brown eyes seemed tired and old. She looked him up and down, obviously taking in the beard stubble and dirty, shoulder-length hair streaked with gray. Then, she rose to her feet, staying behind her desk. "Hello, Will."

"Lo, Annie." Will shoved his fists in the pockets of ragged jeans. "How's Devon?"

"She's fine. It's spring break so she's in camp this week."

"Are you gonna let me see her?"

Silence fell between them and Harry watched the pair closely. Finally, Ann walked around the desk and down the narrow aisleway to stand in front of the visitor. She straightened the collar of his shirt. "You're her father. Of course, you can see her."

She eyed him as sternly as she did Devon when the child was up to mischief. "But you'd better not take her without my permission. Is that clear?" She stepped back and her voice grew severe. "Now, go upstairs and comb your hair. You look terrible. We'll get you a haircut and shave at lunch. Then I'll drive you to your folk's place after work."

"I don't want to go there. The old man will yell at me for hours and Mom will cry because I haven't stayed in touch."

"Tough. You were the one who left the state. They didn't move out of their house or change their cell phone numbers. Everyone has choices, Will Sweeney." Ann pointed to the stairs. "Move it, boyo or I'll let Harry help you after we discuss your stunt with that damned garage sale when you sold my clothes and most of my belongings. It was totally inappropriate and I'm still dealing with the pity party in Baker City."

"Angel, I'm not going to clean up your ex-husband." He strode to them and held out one massive hand. "Harry Colter."

Avoiding the opportunity to shake hands, the younger man turned to the staircase. "I'd better get started." He glanced warily over his shoulder. "Are you interested in Ann? She's a good woman but she does nag a lot and as you heard always bears a grudge."

"I can handle it." Harry slowly lowered his hand. "I don't want to see her hurt."

"Harry, stop being macho. You'll frighten Will. There's no need for that."

"You won't get any trouble from me," Will responded quickly. "And I'd appreciate all the time I get to see Devon."

"I don't want her hurt either and she doesn't stay with her aunts or uncles." Harry flexed his shoulders. "Right?"

"Right," Will agreed hastily. "Whatever you say, Harry."

"Sounds like we'll get along fine." He waited until the younger man was climbing the stairs, before he returned to placing putty along the shaking windows.

Ann hurried over and caught one muscled arm. "You don't have the right to terrorize my poor ex—"

"Yes, I do." Harry expertly wielded the putty knife and secured the window. "What a mouse. No wonder you divorced that poor kid."

"Me? He's the one who filed for a divorce when the unit went to Afghanistan." Ann gasped. "What about you? You were practically threatening him with bodily harm if he did anything to Devon."

"I didn't intend to make it less than a threat, Angel. If he hurts you or D.J., he'll answer to me. Didn't you say he left her with your sisters and your brothers-in-law? Why are you being nice to him? Don't you want to kick his butt to the moon and back?"

"Yes, but he's extremely pathetic and I always end up feeling sorry for him." Ann tossed her head. "It's my life and I'll run it as I see fit. He's weak. He depends on me to take care of him. I'll keep him from dropping Devon with people who hurt her."

"You need a man strong enough to take care of you, Angel, and I'd never jeopardize D.J.'s safety. I won't share." Harry gently put the knife on the sill and snagged her shoulders. "I already told you that."

He pulled her close. His mouth claimed hers and she clung to him, her tongue dueling with his. Her fingers twined in his hair. A lifetime later he raised his head. "Now, behave. I'll take Will to the barber. You have an appointment to go running with Margo. The two of you are supposed to talk about those teaching jobs."

Ann pressed her cheek against his chest. "I can still call and have those emergency pay forms returned. They haven't been processed yet. I don't want you getting in trouble for us."

"Don't fret, Angel." Harry stroked her hair softly. "I'll be fine. I've got heaven on my side, right?"

"Right." Rising on tiptoe, she brushed her mouth against his.

Ann waited until she and Margo were cooling out in the shade trees of the obstacle course before she brought up the subject of the new school in Baker City. "Margo, have you talked to Smitty yet?"

"Yes. I toured the place Tuesday night." Margo shot her a dark green glance. Once again, she'd changed her contacts to reflect her mood. "What are you thinking? Do you want to go for it or wait until we hear back from bigger districts that offer more benefits?"

"Well, once I heard my dad isn't involved in the day to day operations, it seemed more attractive." Ann kept her gaze on the road, seeing the white tombstones from the military cemetery in the distance. "I'd rather teach than push papers here all day. How about you?"

"It'd depend on the school." Margo pushed a hand through her hair. "They can't pay as much as we make here."

Ann frowned and scuffed the toe of her shoe against the pavement. "That's what I thought, but I still want to hear the offer from the school board tonight. Are you coming too?"

"Yes." Margo eyed the trees overhead. "It's time for me to move on."

Ann studied her friend cautiously. "What's wrong, Margo? Are you and Jared having problems?"

Margo shifted her gaze. "I've started the paperwork for a transfer to a base up north. I'm pregnant. I just found out."

"Why the hell are you out here running in the heat of the day? Do you want to lose the baby?"

"No." Tears welled in Margo's eyes. "Yes. I don't know." Sobs wracked her slender frame and Ann drew her close, murmuring low reassurances. When the storm of emotion was over, her friend continued to shake.

"From now on, we go walking at lunch. No more running until you're cleared by a doctor. Got it?"

"Got it." Margo managed a watery smile. "I'm sorry, Ann. You shouldn't have to do my emotional laundry."

"Forget it. That's what friends are for." She paused as a sudden memory pricked her. "Colter had me put half the unit in for emergency pay. We were counting on you to save his butt if the battalion commander threw a tantrum. Can you get Harry in to see Williams?"

"Of course, I will." Margo nodded and brushed away her tears. "Did he fix your pay too?"

"Mine was the first." Ann started up the path again. "Will showed up this morning. I suspect he was in a hoosegow somewhere, but he didn't say that. Harry's taken him to get a haircut and a shave."

"Don't they have to keep themselves clean in jail? He's probably been released for a while. Did you talk to him about Devon?"

"Barely. Colter did more." Ann glanced at her friend. "He threw his weight around and threatened poor Will with all kinds of mayhem if Devon or I got hurt."

Margo giggled. "He's a doll, Ann. You should go out with him. Maybe the two of you could get something going."

"We're trying, but we really strike sparks off each other. Regardless of how nice I try to be, I lose my temper and say mean things."

"And what does he do?"

"Usually he talks back, or he kisses me, or he says he's going to marry me. Margo, what if I fall in love with the guy?"

"It's one way to get paid for the A.G.R. job and not have to do it," Margo said. "He strikes me as the kind of guy who steps up and looks after his family. You never had someone like that before."

CHAPTER EIGHTEEN

That afternoon she parked the Taurus in the driveway of Vanessa and Phil's house. Will climbed out of the back seat and started up the walk looking even more pitiful in his ragged jeans and a gray sweatshirt. Ann switched off the motor. "I guess we have to go in and be sociable."

"Piece of cake." Harry opened his door and strode around the vehicle to do the same for her. "Are they going to blame you for bringing him here?"

"No, we all take care of Will." Ann switched off the motor and accepted the hand he proffered. "They're good people, Colter, and they've always been wonderful to me, but he's their son and I know they love him."

"I'll behave. I won't spit in public or cuss or scratch." He smiled down at her. "Most women wouldn't be so concerned about their ex-in-laws. You're a tough act to follow."

"I can always count on you, Colter, but I'm determined to get over the impulse."

"I'm just as determined to marry you, so I may as well meet Devon's other grandparents. We'll all have to get along with each other for years to come."

"We can't stay too long. Remember you said we'd take Devon to dinner and she loves Pop's Café. After that, I have a meeting at the old school with the board to discuss a teaching position in the fall."

"I'll take her back to Gran's with me and you can pick her up there."

Ann relaxed, tiptoeing up to kiss him. "Thanks, Harry. She could come to the meeting and read a book while she waits for me, but it's better if I don't seem distracted."

"Then, we have a plan."

Ann walked beside him toward the front door. Vanessa glanced toward them as they entered the living room and Ann directed a smile at the older woman. "Vanessa, this is Sergeant Colter, my new boss. Harry, this is Vanessa Sweeney, Devon's grandmother."

As Phil came in from his darkroom, Ann repeated the introductions. Will slumped on the couch and she crossed to sit in the matching chair. The conversation was stilted at first, but Harry seemed to have no problems in getting a good rapport established with Vanessa and Phil. By the time they stood up to leave, Ann felt a new admiration for the man.

She smiled at Will's parents. "Would you like to have Devon on Saturday? I could bring her down in the morning and pick her up Sunday morning at church. She's attending spring camp this week with her friends, and I don't want to disrupt that."

The gratitude on Will's face was echoed by Vanessa and Phil as they hastily agreed to the arrangement. Ann waited until the two of them were alone in the car before she addressed Harry. "Are you going to read me the riot act for this?"

"Nope, I think you're a very wonderful, decent person. And I'm going to marry you, Angel, sometime in the next few weeks."

"Harry, I've told you before. There's nothing that great about me. I'm just a normal person and you know about my past."

"What past?" Harry mocked. "You may have gone to a lot of parties and dated several teenage boys, but you never did anything embarrassing. I used to stay out late at night so I wouldn't have to go home. I know how that particular game is played, honey."

Her anger seeped away. Her older sisters and stepmother had judged by appearances, not looked at Ann's motivation. She wished she could tell Harry how she was beginning to feel about him, but she didn't quite dare. Would he be like Margo and think she was just after the job, only in a different way?

"Harry, maybe we shouldn't get involved. I don't have that terrific a past and neither do you—"

"What does that mean? Say it again, Sarge. I don't get it."

Ann stared at the road and bit her lip. She'd intended to keep Harry's parents out of it, but she didn't see how she could. "I had to put up with Ginger's and my sisters' abuse and you said your family had their own problems. I just think we might not provide a good environment for Devon or—"

Harry laughed shortly. "At least you're finally starting to think we might have a future, honey. Things will be fine. We both know what to watch for and we can protect each other as well as Devon."

"I haven't agreed to marry you. After Will and I divorced, I promised myself I'd never emotionally commit to a man again and you'd want more than I ever gave Will."

"You're right about that," Harry teased. "At least three more kids." He paused for a moment. "I promise you'll never have to tell me to clean up or shave or get a haircut. Okay, sweetheart?"

Ann sniffed. "I wouldn't anyway. You're a noncommissioned officer, Colter. You don't need a babysitter."

Shortly after seven that evening, she parked in front of the school. She wasn't the first to arrive. Smitty O'Sullivan waved at her from the concrete steps and she walked over to meet him. "Margo should be along soon. Who is on the school board? Who do I have to impress?"

"Folks from town already know you." Smitty unlocked the doors. "We may have some outside guests. I chose someone from each of the founding families. I'll only vote in case of a tie, but with seven other members that shouldn't happen often."

"Well, that explains why my relatives aren't on the board." Ann glanced toward the parking lot when a battered old pickup turned into the drive. She recognized Linda MacGillicudy behind the wheel. "Who else is coming?"

"Maxine Garvey from the mercantile, Summer O'Neill from the feedstore, Aidan O'Leary who has the hardware, Dwight Sweeney—"

"Oh, good heavens. I haven't taken time to drive up Mount Carmody and visit him. Is he still a cantankerous old coot?"

"Worse than ever. Nobody but Jacinth would live with him, much less take care of him and the old Sweeney homestead. He's planning on kicking Will to the moon and back as soon as he sees him, and your ex is hiding."

"Hmm, maybe I better tell Dwight that Will's back from Texas and at his parents' house. It'll save my neck. Who else is on the board, Smitty?"

"Art McElroy. Since he retired from the University of Washington, he and his wife, Liz have been traveling so he'll *Skype* in from Hawaii this time. They'll be home this summer. Janine O'Connell said she couldn't be on the board because it was a conflict of interest. She makes a living running the local preschool, so I brought in her son, Dick which gets us all kinds of police protection."

"Wow, that's an impressive list of talent."

"And you haven't even heard about the Parent Organization headed by Cat O'Leary McTavish and Twila Garvey. Janine and Liz are going to help them but I'm sure they'll round up lots of support in town. Everyone's excited about having a school here."

"So am I."

The next day she found herself remembering the meeting. She hadn't signed the contract yet. The board members suggested she take time to consider their unconventional offer to teach at the small school. They couldn't afford to pay what she'd make in Lake Maynard or a larger district like one of those in Liberty Valley, but the amenities certainly tempted her.

A sunny April afternoon was the perfect time to take a ride since Devon was off to her grandparents. Ann petted Skyrocket's neck and scanned the abandoned logging road once more before she urged the gelding to a slow jog. She ought to be able to make her way from the dude ranch to the old O'Connell farm. Both places were on the same side of Cedar Creek and she should be getting close. Ann squeezed the flashy bay's sides with her legs, and he picked up a lope.

Last night when she collected Devon, Harry had said he'd be here instead of coming over to her place and she was determined to find out why. He'd refused to add anything to the statement. She could wait till this evening when he was taking her to dinner but why should she? It'd be more fun to surprise him with the picnic lunch she'd bought at the general store, along with a box of condoms.

Ann reined her horse to a stop as she saw a sagging wooden gate with a placard that read, "O'Connell's. No trespassing. Survivors will be prosecuted." The faded red paint showed that the sign had been there a long time. She pushed open the gate and rode through it, carefully closing the barrier behind them.

A gravel truck road was rapidly being overgrown by scrub alder and underbrush. She allowed Skyrocket to pick his own route at a steady walk, occasionally encouraging the horse with her voice. The track sloped downhill to another gate. She went through it and rode toward the house. "Time to rest, Sky. You can mow the lawn while I hassle Harry and hopefully jump his bones."

Her mount snorted his approval of the plan and Ann drew him to a halt in front of the large two-story log house. "Hello, the fort!" she called. "Harry, are you home?"

No answer came for a moment, but then the front door opened, and he strode out to the wraparound porch. "I should wring your stubborn neck."

"Why?" She swung out of the western saddle, taking time to unfasten the set of saddlebags behind it. "Are you hiding another woman in there?"

"Of course not. I was making a surprise for you."

"I have one for you too." She unsnapped the reins from the bridle, petted her horse's brown neck and let him start grazing on the spring grass. "I think you'll like mine. I know I will."

"Now, I'm worried." He stepped forward to take the leather saddlebags from her. "What do you have in here? Bricks?"

"Lunch from the general store in town."

He held open the front door for her. "I hope there's enough for three of us."

Curiosity swamped her and she almost asked who the third person would be, but then she saw the big, rawboned man in fatigues standing on the far side of the living room and recognized the lead A.G.R. technician from the battalion. "Hello, Sergeant Waller."

"It's Derek today, Barrett." The older man smiled at her; dark eyes amused. "I figured Colter would have brains enough to kiss you, but I've been wrong before."

"He's a bit slow at times, but he gets the job done." Ann tucked her hand into Harry's. "And I'm Ann on the weekend. What are you guys doing?"

"I was tired of hanging out alone at the base when there weren't any unit drills, so I decided to help Colter with his next project."

"And what exactly is that, Harold?"

"You're pushing your luck, Angel." He wrapped an arm around her waist.

She pulled away from him and strolled to the pile of lumber. What was he building now? She studied the boards. Unless, she missed her guess, it was cedar shelving. "What are you doing?"

"Making bookcases." He folded his arms. "Now, do you know why you were supposed to stay home? I wanted to surprise you."

Ann shook her head. "I don't get it. If they're for me, why aren't they at my house?" She tried not to tremble at the tenderness in Harry's gaze and hoped her voice didn't reveal her emotions. She was falling in love with him, more than she'd ever thought possible. She'd dreaded this ever since she'd met him so why wasn't she scared?

"No way, Angel. You want these shelves you have to marry me first."

Ann heaved a huge sigh. "The things a woman has to do to get somewhere to keep her books and they're not even oak or mahogany."

"In a remodeled homesteader's cabin like this?" Derek queried. "All the walls have real cedar paneling. Anything else would look like—"

"Garbage," Harry smoothly interrupted. "There's a lady present. Watch your language, Waller."

"I haven't even cussed yet," Derek protested.

Ann muffled a giggle behind her hand. "It probably will shock Colter, but I know what all the words mean. I can spell them and use them in sentences. That was my dad's rule. I think I swear more than Harry does."

"Oh hell! Everybody does." Derek watched Harry start toward him and hastily added. "It slipped out. I'll behave. Ann, would you like a beer?"

"Sure." Ann glanced around the empty room. There weren't any chairs yet, so she flopped down on the lumber instead. "I'm a wild, free adult today. My kid is off visiting her dad and grandparents." She wouldn't admit how abandoned she felt without Devon. Was there any way to pick the child up early?

Derek left the room, promising to take his time searching for the cooler. Harry swung to look at Ann. "Do you need a hug, honey?"

Ann nodded and gulped back an urge to cry. She jumped to her feet and hurled herself against him. "I want my baby."

Harry pulled her close, his hold obviously intended both for comfort and protection. He gently stroked her hair. "Shall I take you down to get her?"

Ann choked on her sobs. "No. Will has a right to see her. He won't hurt our daughter when his parents are there, but I miss her so much. And she's only been gone four hours."

"The time will pass before you know it." Harry lifted her chin and brushed a kiss over her mouth. "Was there anything you wanted to do today? I can work on these shelves another time."

"I was planning to let my horse ruin your yard while I jumped your bones."

Harry chuckled and his arms tightened. "Now, I'm sorry I invited Derek to join me today, but thankfully he drove his own rig. He'll head back to the base after dinner at Pop's Café and I'll take you home. We'll have all the time we need to jump each other."

"Sounds like fun." Ann laughed weakly, wiping at her tears. "I'm sorry if I spoiled the surprise but I wanted to see you."

The pleasure that shone on Harry's features was mirrored in her own heart, but she was afraid to share this very new emotion with him. Instead she rose on her tiptoe to kiss the stern line of his mouth.

Skyrocket contentedly munched the knee-high grass and rambled all over the front yard most of the afternoon. Ann kept an eye on him through the huge front windows while she helped build the new bookcases.

Harry had his own ideas about the design. Contrary to most other men she'd known, he wasn't chauvinistic about the tools. He showed her how to operate the power sander and the skill saw. Then he backed off and let her run both tools. They did work well together, Ann thought often during the next few hours. Other men liked him if Derek was to be believed. The conversation ranged over soldiers that both men knew and their present whereabouts.

"I'd better go." Ann checked her watch. "It's almost five and I've got at least an hour's ride home."

"I'll walk you out." Harry inclined his head, brushing back a wave of dark hair. "I'll pick you up around seven-thirty."

"That sounds good." Ann led the way outside, waving a cheery farewell to Derek through the windows. "I like your friend. Where did you two meet?"

"Iraq." Harry rested one arm around her shoulders, holding the almost empty saddlebags in his free hand. "Then we ran into each other in Afghanistan." He paused in the shadows of a huge cottonwood and drew her near. He bent down and his breath teased her lips. "What's the matter, Angel?"

"I'm just trying to find the man behind Superman's cape. Did Derek know Zeke too?"

Harry nodded and kissed the corners of her mouth. "Yes. The three of us served together more than once."

She put her arms around his neck and brushed his lips with hers. "Sounds like all of you did more than your share."

"We're not the only ones." Harry tied the saddlebags in place behind the western saddle. "You've done a lot of time in the *Sandbox* too. Folks either lived or died."

"I'm glad you lived," she whispered and felt her pulses begin to hammer a new truth. She loved this man whether she should or not. He'd taken her job, but he was entitled to it. He'd paid his dues over the years and she couldn't go on fighting him. He managed the reserve unit a thousand times better than she would have.

His smile caused a fire to start within her. His mouth claimed hers in a fierce, sensual kiss that sent all her senses spinning. Her bones felt as if they melted into his and she relished every intense moment of the embrace. Her fingers tangled in the short dark hair and she brought his head closer, slanting her face so she could enjoy every inch of his mouth on hers. What on earth would she do with him? Her body screamed its own answer and she moaned when he lifted his lips from hers.

"Go home. We'll talk later."

Ann grabbed for her horse's reins, aware of Harry's heated gaze in every fiber of her being. It took three tries before she managed to get her foot in the stirrup. Mounting Skyrocket, Ann turned the Morab toward Harry. "It's my decision too."

He smiled with a steadiness that made her hands quiver on the reins. "Let me take care of you, Angel. Now, go home. I won't pull you off that horse and seduce you in an unfurnished cabin in front of my friend. Go home."

Ann tossed her head. "Well, I'm not waiting for marriage."

She rode closer and stopped the gelding in front of Harry. Then she dropped the reins and leaned down to capture his mouth with hers. Throughout the fiery kiss, the patient horse stood rock still.

A lifetime later, Ann lifted her lips from Harry's. She bent and gathered up the reins. "I can have you, Colter. Any time I want, and I will later tonight!"

CHAPTER NINETEEN

The evening passed in a haze of enjoyment. They had dinner at Pop's café followed by dancing in the lounge to the western band, made up of Dick O'Connell and his grown sons. Between sets of classic country songs, Ann talked to different people who all seemed to know she'd been offered a teaching position and wanted to know if school would start after Labor Day in September. As if it'd help her decide, she received promises of dry firewood from loggers, garden grown vegetables and fruit from various small farms, fresh eggs, and homegrown beef, pork and chicken.

"Are you taking the job here or staying at the base to work as a company clerk for one of the reserve units?" Harry eyed her over a glass of beer. "You haven't really talked about it."

"I'm cogitating as they say in those westerns you love so much." Ann swirled a straw in her rum and cola. "The pay is different than anything I've had before."

"How?"

"The wages are much less than what I'm accustomed to receiving and it's not a union job, so I'd have to pay my own dues to keep my benefits. Nothing new there since I do the same thing as a substitute. However, I'd have a basic salary."

"How would you pay your bills? Rent, utilities, food, clothes, doctors?"

"Well, that's part of the deal. The school board has arranged for me to keep the cabin at Cedar Creek Guest Ranch rent free, including utilities and garbage. I'd have a monthly credit at the mercantile for groceries and one at the feedstore for sundries and pet supplies. Aidan O'Leary will service my car. Doc MacGillicudy agreed to provide medical care for me and Devon. His granddaughter is graduating from vet school and she'd look after my horse, the pony and the puppy Devon wants."

"So, as my grandmother says, 'the living goes with the job' and your salary only needs to cover clothes, gas for your car and your cell phone."

"Pretty much. If I go for it, Cat and Rob have agreed to install a landline in the cabin because the cell service is so erratic up here as well as cable TV. They'll also board Sky and Rainy Night for the cost of feed and shavings. I'll just pay for extras."

"It sounds like you want to do it."

"In a way, I do, but as Devon says, I'm still thinking. The whole thing is unconventional, and the board is talking about an administrator to manage the cook, bus driver and paperwork, rather than a principal, so Margo and I will take turns handling discipline. We both prefer that."

"Well, keep me posted and let me know what you decide." He glanced over his shoulder as the music started again. "Ready for another dance?"

"I can't wait."

A few hours later they headed to the parking lot. Behind them, Ann heard guitars and drums as the band continued to play. She glanced toward Harry's pickup and thought she saw the silhouette of a man in fatigues leaning against the fender. As they neared, the figure faded away. She grimaced, wondering if her daughter was right about the ghosts of Baker City, then dismissed the idea, deciding there was too much alcohol in her two drinks although she hadn't thought so at the time.

When they reached the guest ranch, she deliberately waited till he'd switched off the motor and then pushed her door open. "Are you coming in for coffee?"

"Not tonight, honey. I'm pretty bushed, Angel. I think I'll head straight to Gran's."

"But I already made it." Ann gave him her best 'big-eyed', innocent look. "Am I supposed to throw it away?"

"No, of course not. I'll come in for one quick cup."

She slipped her fingers into his as they made their way to the cabin. Once inside, she closed the door and switched on the hall light. The golden glow from the bulb revealed the empty glass coffee pot.

"I lied." Ann pulled him into the living-room. "I only hauled you in here to seduce you, Harry Colter and use some of those condoms I bought." She paused, "What is your middle name?"

"David."

She laced her arms around his neck and teased his mouth with hers. "Take me to bed, Harold David Colter. I dare you."

"If I stay, I'll keep you for the rest of your life, Angel." His hands tightened on her waist and he pulled her to him. "You'll never get away from me."

"I don't want to." She nibbled at his jaw. "Are you afraid of me? I thought you were supposed to be a rough, tough Ranger, not a couch potato."

He groaned and captured her lips with his. The kiss deepened and she surrendered when he claimed the depths of her mouth. He tangled a hand in her hair, pulling her head back to trail a series of hot, fierce kisses over her throat. "Angel, I ought to go home."

"No, I won't let you." She moaned as his mouth found the pulsebeat at the base of her neck. "Harry, don't stop."

"I won't." He swung her up in his arms and headed for the bedroom, lowering her onto the queen-size bed. He turned on the lamp before he followed her down. His fingers found the snaps and he began to unfasten her blouse.

"Oh, Harry." Her hands gripped his shoulders, caressing the wide strength of him. Her nails dug in as he opened the shirt and revealed the swell of her breasts.

He located the front closure of her bra and slowly unhooked the clasp, his fingers moving over the rise of her skin. Then his lips found her nipple, drawing it into his mouth as he sucked gently. He fondled her other breast, rolling the nipple between his thumb and fingers.

She gasped and speared her fingers through his dark hair, trembling beneath the heated caresses. His touch was everything she'd dreamed of from that first day, setting her nerves on fire. When he lifted his head, she sat up long enough to free her shirt and toss it to the floor. Her bra followed. The coolness of the room teased her skin briefly until he loomed over her. His lips caught hers again. She surrendered to the claim he staked, clinging to him.

Slowly he lifted his head. "I'm going to make love to you so many times that you'll agree to marry me ASAP."

"As soon as possible?" Ann began to unsnap his shirt, pushing the material aside to reveal his tanned chest and the mat of dark hair. She brushed a kiss over one white line, the remnant of an old scar. "Not happening, Colter. I'm still coming to terms with the crapfest Will pulled. I need time before I make a commitment to someone else, especially since I don't believe in walking away a loser."

"What are you saying, Angel? You're anything but that."

"Wrong." Ann slid off his shirt. She watched the garment fall onto the carpet and tried not to grin. Her mouth touched his and she interspersed her words with light kisses. "I always figured a promise was a promise and if I marry again, he won't get out of the marriage alive. Most of the guys I know are 'passing through,' not in for the long haul."

"You've known the wrong men." His mouth claimed hers for a moment. "I'm not the walk-away kind. I'll stick, stay and make it pay as my grandfather said."

"You beat feet when I'm pissed."

"That's only because I'm smart. If I hit the door before you pitch things at my head, I'll survive longer. It doesn't mean I'm a hundred-percent gone, and I'd never steal from you."

"Is that what you think Will did?"

"He sold your belongings and he certainly didn't give you the money, put it in a bank account for you or spend it on Devon." Harry pulled free and stood to slip off his jeans and boots. He came back down beside her and began to remove the remainder of her clothes. "I'd never compromise my honor that way."

Ann shivered as he unbuckled her belt, unbuttoned her jeans and pushed them off her hips. It wasn't from the air but the rising heat within her. He bent to kiss her throat and then his lips moved to her shoulder distracting her for a moment while his fingers skimmed over her panties, cupping her through the silk. The underwear followed the jeans to the floor.

His hand sought out the curls between her legs, curving over the mound. She shuddered at the touch, anticipating what came next. She clutched at his shoulders when his fingers began an entrancing dance, one finger sliding in and out of her, joined by a second while his thumb rocked against the small bud of flesh. Her hips rose and fell, unable to resist the need to move with the pattern he'd begun. She clung to him, kissing his neck, nipping at his ear. Despite the scars on his tanned body, he was utterly beautiful.

She dug her fingers into his back. "No more lonely nights."

"All you're going to think about is our future. Aren't you?"

She trembled at the fierceness in his words and his body. She longed to tell him the things he wanted to hear but she needed more time and he didn't want to hear that. Whatever answers were given tonight would have to be with her physical response. Tonight, was no time for words.

His hardness teased her softness as he pressed against her hips. "Say it, Angel."

"I want you, Harry!"

She twisted her head on the pillow as she drew him nearer. His mouth continued to tease and torment her breasts and she struggled to keep the cries of need from escaping. She managed the impossible task until she stared into his face.

His features were a mask of planes and angles as he gazed down at her. Then, he smiled. She twisted and writhed beneath him as he continued to explore her body, first with his calloused, huge hands and then his lips. Every aching touch left her burning for the next and all the time he kept smiling. The taunting twist of his lips promised a thousand sensual delights as he eased downward.

He parted her legs and his mouth claimed her. He stroked upward with his tongue, exploring the folds of skin with soft strokes before diving deep. He kept lapping, licking and finally drew the small bud into his mouth and sucked. She fell apart, screaming his name. When she returned to herself, he was reaching into the box of condoms on the nightstand.

"I don't believe you, Colter."

"I've barely started with you." He glanced over his shoulder at her, then chuckled. "I never expected you to be a screamer."

"Nobody's done that to me." She pressed against his back and kissed his neck. "Turnabout is fair play. Wait until I return the favor."

"Later, Angel." He shifted onto the bed and drew her close. "We're just getting started."

He rested most of his weight on his elbows, looking down at her. He lowered his head, trailed kisses to her breasts, then teased a nipple with his lips. She felt him probe, then slide into her. She arched against him, meeting him kiss for kiss, thrust for thrust. Long steady strokes alternated with shorter ones, before he began the lengthy, deep ones again.

Never had a man's caress meant so much. Her hands caught his head and she pulled his mouth to hers. "Now, Harry. Please. Please, Harry."

Her moaned words stopped him for a moment. He lifted his head. "Whatever you want, Angel. All you had to do was ask." His lips took hers again as he shifted between her legs, increasing the pace.

Her hands fell away from his hair and gripped his shoulders, nails biting into his skin. When his mouth left hers, she opened her eyes. His features were harsh and tight. His gaze set her on fire. A faint smile curled his lips before he lowered his head to seize her mouth again. Ann gasped as he moved with a power that swept away all her breath.

She stared up at him, accepting his possession. It was as though he'd finally succeeded in capturing her and now, she belonged to him. She shook her head. She was still herself, wasn't she? "No."

"Yes. No more tricks, Angel. You're mine, now."

She shuddered at the quiet promise in his tones. She didn't want to be owned by anyone, not even her gentle giant. He brushed his mouth over her forehead and then bent to kiss her neck.

As his lips took hers, she surrendered. She'd argue his masculine claim at another time and place. "Harry!"

His name was a cry of passion and need as he continued propelling them into the sensual storm. Every sense seemed to come alive in that moment. As the wild hurricane swept her along, her nails dug into his back, clawing at the skin of his shoulders.

The battle raged onward, leaping to its conclusion, capturing both of them in the ultimate surrender of desire. Afterwards, they cuddled each other, lying close together, wrapped in one another's arms. They made love two more times that night. The next morning, they showered together and had breakfast before leaving for church. When she left the building with Devon, Ann saw Margo's car parked in front of the school. Accompanied by her daughter, Ann headed over to the other building.

As soon as they entered, she heard old time rock and roll music coming from one of the downstairs classrooms. She spotted Margo standing on a stepladder mounting a long banner with the alphabet in printing and cursive above the whiteboard. "Why do I think you've made a decision?"

"I was going to tell you last night, but you had company."

"Who was visiting, Mama?"

"Harry brought me home after we had dinner." Grateful she didn't blush, Ann shot a quick glare at her friend before she gestured to the boxes of books. "Why don't you put those away for Aunt Margo?"

"Okay. How do you want them, Auntie?"

"Picture books go together, honey. Then, the chapter books."

"Okay." Devon started work.

Meanwhile, Ann picked up a dust cloth and began wiping down the tables and chairs the students would use. "Are you sure about this? It's not a conventional deal."

"It's actually better than a lot of districts offer." Margo continued tacking the green and white banner into place. "I can bank most of my salary since I won't have any expenses. When I had breakfast at the café this morning, Linda MacGillicudy introduced me to several parents who will have children in my class. Twila Garvey told me that if her boys give me a hard time to have them call her and she'll rain all over their little parades. She wasn't the only one. That's more support than I've had in years. You'll be upstairs, won't you?"

"I'm still thinking, but I'm real close to agreeing."

Wearing a nightgown and fleecy purple robe, Ann curled up in her favorite rocking chair late that evening. She still hadn't decided whether she wanted to teach in Baker City or wait for a job in a bigger district. She sighed and studied the book she pretended to read. Tonight, there weren't any answers, only more and more hassles. She glanced toward the door at the soft knock. She rose and went to answer, not surprised to find Harry waiting on the porch.

When he stepped inside, the light filtered across the planes and angles of his features. "Last night was a mistake, Angel."

She gaped up into his stern gaze, her thoughts reeling from the unexpected blow. Shouldn't it have taken longer for him to realize a relationship with her would ruin both their lives? Even at the rejection, she still hungered for the pressure of his mouth on hers. "What?"

"I can't think about anything else." He kicked the door closed behind him to shut out the darkness. He swung her up in his arms and headed for the bedroom. "Damn you, Angel. I knew exactly how I was going to do things."

"How dare you?" Ann sputtered. "You can't stride in here like some conquering hero and haul me off to bed. I won't have it. Damn you, Colter. Put me down!"

"In a minute," Harry bent his head. "Now complain, you shrew but wait till I kiss you. In fact, wait until I have my mouth on you."

Waiting, Ann thought a long time later had been a mistake. She studied the sleeping man and reached to tug on his black hair. "Wake up, Colter. I want to talk about us."

Harry opened blue eyes and stared at her. "I want to sleep." He pulled her closer. "Make it quick or I'm liable to change my mind and yours."

Ann hesitated for a bare instant, then allowed her doubts about their future to fade for a moment. She let her fingers spread across his wide chest. "Change my mind, Colter. I dare you."

He chuckled, and his mouth claimed hers.

Wednesday afternoon, Ann sighed and studied the computer screen. There had to be a way to reach Harry and tell him that she suspected he was functionally illiterate. The problem wouldn't be easy to resolve. How could she leave him when there was so much paperwork to do to support the unit? Smitty wouldn't wait much longer for an answer about the teaching position in Baker City not when Margo had already signed the contract.

She glanced toward the door as Command Sergeant Major Jenkins strolled inside. "Can I help you?"

"Where's Colter these days?" Jenkins grinned. "Did you feed him to the pigs like you always threaten to do to the kids when they screw up, Barrett?"

Ann grinned appreciatively and pointed to the back door and the supply room in the adjacent building. "Out there. He and Sergeant Waller are bonding over the equipment that needs to be replaced. Why?"

Jenkins grimaced. "We've got to train for the next field exercise this summer. I have to go to a conference in California in three weeks, so I'll miss our unit drill and I need someone to take over my class on camouflage scheduled for Saturday afternoon."

"Don't look at me," Ann responded. "I heard back from HQ. I'm supposed to update the financial records when the troops are here that weekend. We have too many folks who were reported AWOL by the previous clerk and the ship is hitting the proverbial sand."

"The C.O.'s on the warpath. He says that somebody sent in for emergency pay for the troops. It was a good idea, Barrett. I'll back you to the hilt."

"It wasn't just me, Sergeant Major." Ann stared after him as he crossed to the back door. "It was Master Sergeant Colter. He believes the troops come first and we did it together."

"Either way the two of you did the right thing. Our folks have enough problems returning to civilian life. Doing it without money makes it that much harder."

The memory of Jenkins' smile kept her warm over the next two weeks. At least she didn't have to worry about the repercussions regarding payroll. The idea pleased her. Despite trying to pump Colter for information about his upcoming class, he refused to discuss it. The two of them spent their days whether they were working or not, as well as most of their nights together.

They took Devon to more children's movies, watched her ride Rainy Knight, saw her shine in karate class, visited the spring fairs, went dancing most weekend nights when Phil and Vanessa or Frank and Ginger babysat and were inseparable while they hid brightly colored plastic eggs for the Baker City Easter Egg Hunt. It was a time of sheer love and laughter and the peace was a welcome one, one that made Ann happy to finally be home.

Standing near the school, she watched her daughter hunting eggs with Cat and Rob's twins on the grassy playground along with an assortment of other children. Ann forced a smile when she saw her older sister, Barbara come toward her, accompanied by their middle sister, Chloe, another curvaceous redhead who wasn't as tall. They looked like stair-steps in the pastel blue dresses and sandals they wore. It was difficult to believe they were both in their forties, since neither had a single gray hair, but maybe they visited Ginger's stylist as often as she did.

Making herself dismiss the snarky thought, Ann nodded at the duo. "Happy Easter. How are you?"

"We're fine." Barbara looked Ann up and down, scorn apparent when she saw the comfortable denim skirt, western blouse and cowgirl boots. "Ginger says you're leaving again before the month's out, shipping out with the Army."

"Wrong." Ann shook her head. "My reserve unit's home for the duration. We just meet one weekend a month for at least the next year and for two weeks next summer."

"Well, you may want to stop sleeping around." Chloe's voice dripped saccharine sweetness. "Ginger's been talking to a lawyer. She and Dad are going for custody of your demon princess. Will is testifying on her behalf."

Ann froze, breath catching in her throat, nails biting into her clenched fists. "Thanks for the heads-up. I appreciate it even if you calling my daughter names is totally inappropriate." She lifted her chin, meeting Barbara's pale blue eyes. "Are you telling me because we're sisters and you give a rat's backside about me, or do you plan to jump in on our stepmother's side and take my baby away from me?"

CHAPTER TWENTY

With a basket full of plastic eggs, Devon dashed up to Harry. "I got lots of candy. Where's Mama? I want to show her."

"We'll find her." Harry glanced around the waiting parents but didn't see Ann waiting anywhere. He'd been distracted by his grandmother who'd called him to help shift picnic tables for the community meal and Ann had disappeared in the interim. He spotted Margo talking to an obviously pregnant woman in jeans and a man's flannel shirt, remembering she'd made a speech at the town memorial. He guided Devon in that direction. "Have you seen Ann anywhere?"

Margo shook her head, but her friend tilted her head as if she was listening to someone else. "She's upstairs in the school in what we hope will be her classroom. Devon, you probably should find the twins and show them your loot and let them show off theirs even though the three of you hunted together. Your momma needs to talk to Harry in private."

"Okay, Mrs. Cat." The little girl tugged on his hand and Harry bent to listen to her. "She's talking to the ghosts. You better find out what they got to say before you go find Mama."

"Thanks for the tip." Harry waited until the child left before he looked at the two women. "I don't believe in haunts or spooks or whatever you want to call them."

Cat ran a hand through bright strawberry-blonde hair, narrowing her green eyes. "Well, no wonder you're having so many problems with Zeke Garvey then. You're lucky he hasn't gathered up enough energy to throw things at you like some of them do."

"Zeke's dead."

"We all know that. I'm the O'Leary and it's my job to listen to those who have passed on, when others don't." Impatience filled Cat's voice and she planted her fists on jean-clad hips. "You should try figuring out what he wants from you, Harold David Colter, instead of being a stubborn jackass. Now, go comfort Ann. Mrs. O'Sullivan says she's crying because her family is trying to steal her daughter. When she's ready to fight, I have a good lawyer."

"How do you know my full name? Did Ann tell you?"

"No, your grandpa did. You're named after him, you idiot, and he's nearly as annoyed at you as Zeke." Cat pointed to the old schoolhouse. "Go, damn it. I get so tired of being nagged by a bunch of spirits."

"This is the craziest place I've ever been." Harry swung around and started toward the old building, pausing to flick a glance at Margo. "Are you coming or staying here?"

"I'll talk to Ann later. She'll need to vent about her relatives, and I've told her before that her immediate family is a bunch of morons." Margo took Cat's elbow. "I'm not a medium like you so I can't hear your dead friends, but I'm sure they'd agree you should sit down and rest a while. You're packing a load with that new baby and it makes you bitchy."

"I'm not bitchy. I love it here." However, Cat walked off with Margo, still complaining about stubborn men who never listened to people who knew more than they did. "It's the living that are a pain in my butt, not their former family members."

Harry frowned and started for the school, pausing when he saw Frank Madison talking to the man Ann had introduced him to before, Smitty O'Sullivan. He approached the pair, waiting for a break in the conversation. Frank finally nodded at him in greeting and Harry eyed the older man. "I need to make an appointment to see you and your wife. When's a good night?"

"What's on your mind?" Frank folded his arms and waited. "You're Ann's boss, aren't you?"

"Harry Colter, and that's not all." Harry looked at the smaller man.

"I don't know how much she's told you. I'm marrying her. I'd like to tell her we have your and her mother's blessing, but we don't need it."

Smitty disguised a low laugh with a quick cough. "Ginger is Ann's stepmother. You'll have to track down Ann's mother back East to get her approval."

"Not a problem, but I thought your wife raised Ann." Harry deliberately raised a brow, focusing on Frank Madison. "Or am I wrong?"

"No, you're right." Frank nodded. "We'll expect you tomorrow evening after work."

"That sounds good. I'll see you then." Harry turned away and headed up the stone staircase into the old school. He was certain the problems concerning Devon weren't finished, but perhaps worrying about the effect a new husband would have on the family might distract Ann's father and stepmother.

April sunlight streamed in the large windows revealing two flights of wide wooden stairs. He climbed up them and stalked down the hall to an open door. When he entered, he saw Ann sitting behind a large oak desk, her head buried in her arms, shoulders shaking. Fury swept through him and he strode across the room.

He pulled her up into his arms, holding her tight against him. She buried her face in his shirt and sobbed. He stroked the bronze hair. "Sweetheart, which one do you want me to take out first?"

"They hate me." She cried harder. "I've never—"

"You don't have to do anything. Some people are just mean." He dropped a kiss on top of her head. "You choose your friends. You're stuck with family."

She continued to cling to him. "My sisters—"

"Your friends are the sisters you chose for yourself, like Zeke was the brother I always wanted." Harry felt her ragged breathing begin to ease and patted her back as if she were Devon's age. "I was the middle kid, the youngest boy. I had three little sisters after me, but we weren't close. Zeke always had my six from elementary on up. If my dad wasn't pounding on me, my brothers were."

"And what did you do?"

"I went in the Army after I lost it and kicked the crap out of the oldest one. He ended up in the hospital and my dad called the cops, had me arrested. My granddad bailed me out and I stayed with him and Gran or with Zeke's family until we left for boot camp."

"And your mother stood by and let it happen." Ann pulled back, staring up at him with tear-drenched, leaf-green eyes. "What a witch."

"She had to decide if she was going to live with them or step up. It wasn't in her nature to take risks." Harry framed Ann's face with his hands. "Whose butt do I kick first?"

"I've got this, Colter. I just needed to whine and wail for a while." She wiped her eyes. "I'm okay now. Where's Devon?"

"Hanging out with her friends." Harry slowly released her and took time to gaze around the room. The windows overlooked the front of the school and the parking lot for visitors. Brightly colored posters lined the walls, not only between the ceiling and the white board. Books filled the low shelves beneath the windows. Instead of individual desks, there were several tables lined up in neat rows, each with three chairs. "So, this will be your home away from home if you decide to take the job here?"

Ann nodded. "I really love teaching, but I don't want to be driven into taking the job to keep my family in line. That's not fair to the school, the board or the kids. Besides, there's so much work on the base, Harry. Who would we get to do the paperwork if I leave?"

"You won't be going until your orders end in June. You can show Derek the ropes and we can swap things around. We'll make it work, Ann. Once the ranch is in shape, I'm planning to retire and raise beef cattle."

"Makes sense. Both of us have done enough, going back to the *Sandbox* so many times, you more than me." She glanced around the room. "I'm going to clean up a bit and then I'll be ready to go downstairs and rejoin the festivities. I needed privacy so my sisters didn't know how freaked I was when they said they and their husbands plan to testify on Ginger's behalf."

"And who is she again?"

"My stepmother. She intends to sue for custody of Devon. She's claiming I'm an unfit parent because I've shipped out with my unit twice since Devon was born." Ann slid her hands into the slash pockets of the denim skirt. "And to think I was careful to provide one night a week with my kid when we moved to Cedar Creek. That's done, through and said. Ginger will be lucky if she sees Devon at holidays."

Ann walked beside her daughter toward the tables covered with food listening to the little girl chatter about finding lots of eggs. At some point, they'd have to remove the candy and return the plastic eggs to Virginia Thompson so she could use them for the next event in town. Devon came to a stop beside Ann, eyeing her aunts, uncles and their children already waiting in line. "Do we have to eat with them?"

"With who?" Ann asked.

"Aunt Barbara, Uncle Reid, Aunt Chloe and Uncle Kurt and my cousins."

"No." Ann smoothed Devon's black hair. "We're eating with Harry, his grandma, your Aunt Margo, Cat, Rob and the twins. I don't think there will be enough room at our table for anyone else."

"Good." Devon heaved a dramatic sigh. "I don't like 'em, any better than they like me."

"Fair enough." Ann smiled at her daughter, grateful when Harry came to join them accompanied by Janine O'Connell. The older woman took Devon's hand and led her toward the table that held fried chicken, casseroles, pasta and salads.

Once the child was out of earshot, Ann gazed up at Harry, remembering the hurt she felt when her older sisters ignored birthdays, holidays, military and educational milestones. Prior to leaving for Afghanistan the last time, Ann called to tell Chloe about graduating with honors from her master's in teaching program and her sister said she was too busy to attend the university ceremony and not to contact her again until she, Ann, was dead.

She took a deep breath. "Colter, I want you to start by taking out Reid."

"No worries, Angel. Which one is he?"

Ann gestured to the sandy-haired, blocky man in a dark suit standing behind her oldest sister. "That's him and his wife, Barbara."

"I'll take care of their problem and tell them I'm arranging for you to have an Army attorney. You join Gran and Devon, so the kid isn't upset."

"Got it."

Ann nodded agreement and strolled across the lawn to stand in line behind Devon and Janine. Her daughter glanced over her shoulder. "Mama, what did you and Harry need to talk about?"

"Army business and it's strictly for grownups." Ann passed a paper plate to her daughter. "What do you want for lunch, honey?"

"But he's talking to Uncle Reid now and he's mean. He spanked me lots of times when I was at their house." Tears filled Devon's eyes and began to streak down her cheeks. "He hurt me, Mama."

"I know. You already told me." Ann wrapped an arm around her daughter's shoulders and cuddled Devon close. "He and Harry will talk and then Reid won't ever do it again."

"What about Uncle Kurt? He and Aunt Chloe don't like animals, so they made Daddy take my kitty to the pound."

Rage swept through her again. Ann glared over her daughter's head toward her family. "I'm so sorry, honey."

"When Harold gets done with them, they'll be the sorry ones," Janine said. "He loves you, Devon, and he doesn't like it when people hurt little girls."

"Harry loves me. For real? Won't he stop when he hears what they say about me?"

"Of course, Harry loves you. He never says anything he doesn't mean, and he wouldn't trust them anymore than I do." Ann watched the confrontation, puzzled by the apparent jovial conversation. She saw the tension in Harry's tall frame, but it seemed that all he had to do was talk. For once her brothers-in-law were listening and she wondered how Harry did it. Neither of the other men heard anything she'd said for years.

Reid saw her waiting. He started toward her and came to a stop when Harry called something in a low tone. After a few more minutes, the discussion ended, and he strode away from her sisters and their husbands.

When he reached her, he nodded. "Okay, Barrett. It's handled. I have names, phone numbers, addresses and all the contact information you'll give Colonel Williams tomorrow morning."

Ann blinked, staring up at him. "What did you do, Colter?"

"I told them that the Judge Advocate General, or JAG, isn't just a television show. You're still on active duty for the military and the Army takes it seriously when one of their soldiers is harassed."

"I'm female so they don't think I'm really in the service."

"Then, they're dumb, Mama. You've got uniforms and boots and everything."

"You're right, D.J." Harry rumpled her dark hair. "I bet even if they saw her in the gear she wore in Afghanistan, they wouldn't believe she had a real rifle. So, that's why I told them she's a soldier and I'd help her."

"That's 'cause you're in the Army too and a Mass-Sergeant and it's your job to take care of Mama."

"That's right." Harry grinned down at her. "Now, let's get some lunch. I'm starving and I bet you are too, D.J., after all the egg hunting."

She nodded and moved forward with him. Ann folded the paper and tucked it into her pocket before she followed, glancing at Janine. "I guess I'm pretty juvenile. I wanted Harry to pound in Reid's and Kurt's faces, especially after what they did to my daughter while I was gone."

"I understand the temptation." Janine slid an arm around Ann's shoulders. "However, you need to think about where they're coming from."

"I don't comprehend."

"Sure, you do. You've proven you're a better man than they are. Neither of them ever considered enlisting in the military to achieve their goals or went to war once, much less three times. You don't need Harry to kick their butts. You could do it yourself."

"I never thought of that." Ann studied the foursome and their children of varying sizes who'd trooped in the direction of an empty table. "I was busy blaming myself because my sisters never loved me."

"Oh, I'm sure they did before your father remarried, but Ginger Madison pushed them out of the nest before she got rid of you. Someone should point out that they didn't do right when they left a child younger than Devon to suffer under what they viewed as her reign of psychological torment."

"I hate it when you make me think about others." Ann heaved a sigh. "Now, I'm going to have to keep my hands to myself and not send my older sisters on a one-way trip to the moon."

"Get used to it, darling." Janine hugged Ann. "I'm a meddling old lady and Harold's the only grandchild I have who visits me regularly.

The others are all too busy with their own lives to call on me. I'm going to interfere in your lives for the rest of mine and I expect you and Devon to come for Sunday dinner at least twice a month."

Ann laughed and leaned close. "We'll be there. She's still talking about your puppies and now that I know what happened to her half-grown kitten, I'll bet we wind up with one of each."

"Empress has taught this batch about cats, so you won't have any problems. Talk to Linda's son if you want a kitten. Dray MacGillicudy has a knack of finding strays in need of homes."

"Good to know. I'll find him today."

Ann couldn't hide her smile as she loaded up her plate. Harry had confronted her sisters and their husbands, defusing the situation in a matter of moments. How had he done the impossible so easily? She continued to puzzle over the questions. What edge did he have? He carried himself like a soldier but there was nothing vicious about him. In fact, he'd never raised his voice during the entire scene.

That evening she sat in her favorite rocker, watching Devon trail a string for the new orange and white kitten Dray MacGillicudy provided. Long, thick fur gave the youngster a fluffy appearance and he held his tail high in the air as he pounced on the yarn. Ann laughed. Both her daughter and the large-eyed feline turned to stare at her. "What are you going to name him?"

"Aslan, after the lion in my new book." Devon gathered the kitten into her arms, snuggling him close. "He has extra hair in his ears, humongous paws and a ruff like a real lion."

"That makes perfect sense."

He saw light glimmering around the edges of the curtains as he sauntered to the porch and the front door. He knocked and waited for her to answer. Yes, he shared her bed more nights than he spent at the base, but that didn't mean he'd moved in with her yet. Footsteps inside and he knew she looked through the window before she unlocked and opened the door. He brushed her lips with his and stepped inside.

"I'm putting Devon and her kitten to bed." Ann traced a line down his cheek. "Stay here or she'll come up with a dozen excuses why she should stay up late and then it'll be impossible to get her off to school tomorrow."

"No worries. You're the boss."

"Here, but I won't hold you to it at the base." Amused, she left the room.

He crossed to the couch, eying the stack of books on the coffee table. One was a Western, complete with gunfighters on the cover. He touched it gently.

"Do you read Spanish?" Ann asked, behind him.

"No." Harry glanced over his shoulder at her. "Do you? What does it mean?"

"*Massacre at Apache Hill.*" Ann shrugged. "Margo found it for me at a thrift store, and she knew I could understand it. I must read it before I put in my classroom library at the school to be sure it isn't too violent. I like to have books in different languages for the kids who need them, and the guys love cowboy stories. For that matter, so do some of the girls."

"How many students do you have from other countries?" Harry asked.

"It varies from year to year." She tipped her head and eyed him speculatively. "My Spanish is really rusty. It'd be better if I read it aloud. Would you let me try it on you? If it bores you, just say so. You don't have to play 'Sergeant Nice-Guy' with me."

"Whatever you want, Angel. I'm like your kid. I love the way you do story times."

CHAPTER TWENTY-ONE

The next morning, she left Devon with Cat and Rob at the main house so her daughter could ride with the twins to school. When she drove past the cabin, she saw Margo coming down the stairs of her own porch. Her friend waved and Ann stopped, parking the Ford for a moment and pressing the button to lower the window. "What's going on?"

"After all the drama from your family yesterday, I didn't have time to tell you that I turned in my resignation last week. I'm going to open the school in ten days. Even if I only have a few students, it will help me get back into the habit of teaching. What about you?"

"What about me?"

"Are you coming to Baker City or staying at the base?"

"I don't know." Ann stared out the windshield at the sunny morning. "I'm scared, Margo. We've been jacked around so many times. What if I start teaching and the whole thing goes sideways, and the school fails?"

"We deal." Margo folded her arms. "Ann, we're survivors. We made it through this last tour even after losing Trish Powell and your three folks. We can make this work and if it doesn't, we'll move on like we have before."

"But, why now? Why not wait until September and the new school year?"

"Because I need space away from Jared Williams. Sleeping with him started as a distraction. I wanted to forget everything painful that happened during the tour and I never meant to fall in love. He thinks it was a mutual booty call."

"And now you're pregnant. Have you told him?"

Margo shook her head. "Not yet. I will before I leave. He may not believe it's his baby. We took precautions."

"Condoms have been known to fail. You didn't plan this and now you deal with 'what is' like you just told me we'd do with the school." Her cell phone buzzed, and Ann picked it up long enough to glance at the screen. "Colter's waiting for me to pick him up at his grandmother's. I need to go. I'll be down to see Colonel Williams later today about this custody Bravo Sierra. What are you going to do with your new assistant? You can't leave her at HQ without you when that lecher, Major Fisher is in and out all the time."

"I thought I'd arrange for her to come up to your unit and have you teach her admin procedures. As the saying goes, 'The care and training of lieutenants is Sergeant's business.' During the summer she's off to ROTC advanced training. By the time she returns in September, Jared should have Fisher either straightened out or rifted."

"That works." Ann smiled at her best friend. "I should have known you'd have a plan."

When she arrived in Baker City, she recognized Harry, a total hunk in his fatigues, coming out of the new bakery. Ann honked the horn and pulled over to the side of the street, unlocking the door so he could open it. "Wow, sugar definitely brightens up a Monday morning. What do we have?"

"Figured you might need maple bars today to go with the coffee and Twila makes the best ones." He put the bakery box in the back and eased into the passenger seat. "Did you get the information about a civilian attorney from Cat McTavish?"

Ann nodded. "Yes, I'll call Bree Hawke from the office and set up an appointment with her. If she agrees to represent me, I'll pass on her info to Colonel Williams."

"It sounds like you've been thinking." Harry fastened his seat belt. "Okay, let's hit the road, Barrett."

Halfway to Lake Maynard, he shifted in the seat. "I have a question. Not trying to offend you, but something's been bugging me."

"Well, spit it out, Colter. What's on your mind?"

"Your name. Why isn't it Madison like your father's or Sweeney like your ex-husband's?"

Ann kept her attention on the highway. "When Will filed for divorce, I was hurt and extremely pissed. I don't think it'd have affected me quite so much if we'd split when I was Stateside but doing it the way he did when I was overseas, was devastating."

"Understandable and the name?"

"When I 'Skyped' with her and my dad afterwards, Ginger took Will's side and told me that I was a crappy wife, so it was no wonder nobody loved me."

"And your dad didn't call her on it?"

"My father always 'goes along to get along' with her and my younger half-brother, Jack. She may have waited until Dad was out of the room. I don't remember all the details now, but when the Army lawyer responded to the paperwork, I told her I wanted to change my last name to my grandmother's maiden one. She made it happen and I was Angelica Barrett, although Ginger still calls me, Angelique most of the time."

"Why when it's not your name?"

Ann shrugged. "Because it's one more way to get at me. She's not going to change and like my Aunt Liz McElroy told me when I was a snarky, rebellious teenager, it's a waste of my time and energy to keep calling my stepmother on it."

"I guess that's good advice, even if I couldn't keep my mouth shut."

"That's Aunt Liz. She always has something to say. I'll be glad to see her and Uncle Art this summer. Even if I opt out of the teaching job, I'm glad he's on the school board. He won't play politics and will put the best interests of the kids first."

"It will give you an ally although you may not need one." Harry rubbed his jaw thoughtfully. "Twila says her two younger boys are starting class at Baker City School in two weeks. The older ones are griping about having to go to Lake Maynard. Have you made a decision yet?"

"No. You should probably call me Sergeant Chicken instead of Barrett. Like other teachers, I always had to wait until spring to find out if I'd have a job in the fall and I'm concerned about taking another risk. At least with the Army, there's generally some security."

"Unless an Airborne Ranger takes your position while you're away studying finance."

"Not your fault and not mine." Ann laughed and signaled for a lane change. "Are you going to share the details of the class you're teaching next weekend for the Sergeant Major? It's totally bogus since we just returned from combat."

"It's required and it will help the unit keep their skills fresh."

"I hate to ruin your weekend, Colter, but we're back to being part-time warriors. The expectation is that you'll use a classroom and present a lecture about how to use the terrain to hide and shoot the enemy. Nobody wants to get dirty in these wargames, especially not the officers. And they're not the only ones."

"I don't get it, Barrett. Crap happens and sometimes life goes from sugar to sh—" He paused and then continued, "From sugar to dung in a heartbeat. Even situational awareness doesn't always help, or we wouldn't have lost Zeke and two other Rangers in that ambush."

She nodded, taking the next exit. "Folks are still pretty disheartened after the last tour when an I.E.D. took out our own. They were just going to inspect some reports, shuffle papers and update records at a smaller unit's HQ after dropping off some supplies at a girls' school. It could have been any of us, not First Sergeant Driscoll, our troops and the LT."

"I get it but let me tell you the way it's gonna be, Angel. You'll help the enlisted and the officers get ready to come into the woods. We've got permission to use the obstacle course for this exercise. Derek and I will wait for each detail and ambush them. The lecture takes place afterwards when we start talking about the best way to survive."

"Colonel Stewart is liable to croak but I'm in. It must be my new duty assignment to watch your back and keep you from getting fragged."

"The road runs both ways, sweetheart."

She spent the morning on the phone talking to people. She began with the civilian lawyer, went onto Phil and Vanessa, then tried to contact Will. He didn't pick up and she knew he was screening calls. It didn't surprise her. The man was a total coward and his streak of yellow was undoubtedly bigger than his spine. While she longed to scream and call him names, she throttled down the temptation.

She'd arranged for Bree Hawke to meet with Devon and hear the little girl's stories about what happened during the last tour. Any judge worthy of the name would have issues with Will's irresponsible treatment of their daughter. That should discount the testimony he provided on Ginger's behalf.

She stopped by the supply room, still impressed not only by the cleanliness, but also the reorganization and reminded Harry that she had to go to Army Reserve HQ before lunch for the appointment with Colonel Williams. She found Derek Waller helping store new uniforms. "Colter told me that you're assisting him with his class this weekend."

"It'll be fun." Derek winked at her. "I watched this old *Patrick Swayze, Gene Hackman* war movie last weekend, so I'm adapting their tactics. I made a few signs for the real stupid folks to wear."

"I suppose it's useless to tell you that Colonel Stewart missed out when they issued senses of humor." Ann heaved a sigh. "He's going to pitch a fit."

"Who cares? Scuttlebutt around Reserve Command HQ is he's up for replacement after losing four good soldiers in the *Sandbox* last year, including that LT who worked for Captain Endicott." Derek frowned into the cardboard carton. "He should have sorted out the payroll problems before you and Colter did. It's lucky the folks in the unit gave you the opportunity, Barrett instead of going to the Inspector General and filing complaints."

"Sounds like you and the Command Sergeant Major talk sometimes."

"We've been known to hoist a beer or two. It's always five o'clock somewhere, as the song goes."

"Yeah, well like my grandfather used to tell me, 'your problems swim better than they sink' when it comes to booze."

"Was he a drinking man?"

"He undoubtedly hoisted a few back in the day," Ann teased, "but he owned the Baker City Saloon. He used to say that to his customers. He believed in responsible drinking before it was fashionable."

"A good man." Harry glanced at the clock. "Better hustle. Williams is a 'by the book' guy. It won't do to be late if you want him on our side."

She nodded agreement, heading for her car. When she arrived at the post headquarters building, she was five minutes early, so it meant she was the one waiting for the Army lawyer. Since it was a weekday, he didn't have a receptionist standing guard in the outer office. His door was closed, but she heard him talking and figured he either had someone inside or was on the phone. She considered sitting down and reading the latest copy of *Army Times*, but chose to stand instead, proud of herself when she didn't pace the floor.

The door opened, revealing Margo on her way out of the office.

She nodded a greeting. "Your turn. Come get me for lunch when you finish."

"I'll be there."

Taking a deep breath, Ann walked inside, closing the door behind her since she didn't want her problems broadcast all over HQ. Before she could stand at attention in front of the large oak desk, the tall, muscular man waved her to a seat in one of the comfortable chairs. "I need a lawyer, sir, and Sergeant Colter sent me to you."

"He already called me this morning and gave me a 'sit-rep' about the custody issue." Picking up a pen, he studied her with narrowed dark eyes. "Why is Captain Endicott leaving?"

"What did she tell you?"

"Something about needing a change of scenery. It doesn't make sense."

"Oh, for the love of Saint Peter." Ann shook her head. "The woman's an idiot. I can say that because she's my best friend, but you can't. Okay, there's two ways to do this. One, I mouth all the right words and baffle you with Bravo Sierra."

"What's the other way?" Faint amusement crept into his face, easing the hard line of his jaw. "You dazzle me with brilliance?"

"Actually, I threaten to blackmail you about your affair with Margo. I know that the General would fire you if he found out about it." She saw Williams stiffen and knew he was catching onto her threat. "And

I'm not a fool like Margo. I wouldn't fall in love with a man who thought I was sleeping with him as a psychologically therapeutic exercise because she blames herself for letting her assistant go with our personnel people when we had that Charlie Foxtrot."

Williams' face hardened. "Is there anything she didn't tell you?"

"Oh, I wouldn't say she told me. She cried over you after almost collapsing during one of our runs a few weeks ago and I listened. I told her she needed to visit a doctor, but as far as I know, she hasn't been to one yet. That's next on my list. On our next day off, I'm dragging her to see Doc MacGillicudy in Baker City. I went through this seven years ago when I expected my daughter and denial isn't just the proverbial river in Egypt."

"Thank you." Williams leaned back in his chair, shaking his head. "A man shouldn't do recon if he doesn't want answers even if they're unexpected."

Ann read the answer in his eyes. He wasn't stupid and he was putting things together. He was starting to understand why Margo would leave rather than jeopardize either of their careers. "You'll help me keep my daughter."

"Definitely, Sergeant Barrett. That was never in doubt." He smiled with undeniable charm. "If we invite you to the wedding, will you come? Or will you tell Margo she can do better?"

"I don't think she can, sir. And we'll be there. Margo promised my daughter that she could be a flower girl in her wedding years ago."

"She is and your daughter's welcome." Williams grinned. "Now, I just have to make sure there's a bride."

"Oh, I have faith in you." Ann glanced at the closed door. "Of course, you'll also make sure she doesn't learn I brought you up to speed."

"Since we both want to go on living, I think that's best." His smile broadened. "Now, give me copies of the paperwork you brought me and the contact info so I can touch base with your civilian attorney. We'll be kicking tails together. Tell me what you want."

Wednesday morning, she fixed pancakes for breakfast while Devon did her chores, tidying her bedroom, feeding Aslan and scooping his cat box. Ann sent the little girl to wash her hands twice before allowing her to set the table. While they ate, she explained they were going to see a lawyer. "I want you to tell Ms. Hawke what happened when I was away."

"But only the truth." Devon took a swallow of her orange juice. "What are we going to do afterwards?"

"What do you want to do? I'm taking today off work. Shall we go to a movie?"

"First, I wanta go to the library in Lake Maynard and get the next two books about *Narnia*. Then, I wanta come home and ride Rainy Night."

"Sounds good. I'll ride Skyrocket with you."

"That will be mass fun. Can we ride to Harry's new house?"

"That's a bit far and I think you need to build your riding stamina before we try it. Instead, why don't you and Rainy Night have a long session with your cousin, Jassy? Are you and Rainy up for that?"

Devon nodded, a sunshine smile spreading across her face. "Yes, we're tough."

"I knew that. I'll call Harry and ask him if he wants to meet us at his place for an early supper. We'll pack a picnic and drive over there."

"We'll have the best day ever and I won't miss school at all. Samantha and Sophie are going to Aunt Margo's class as soon as she comes to Baker City. I want to go there too. Will you sign me up? She's a real good teacher."

Ann sipped her coffee. "I'll talk to her about it tomorrow at lunchtime."

Devon pushed back from the table, came around and hugged Ann tight. "I'm so glad you're home and you want me now."

"Honey, I've always wanted you." Ann held her daughter just as snugly. "If anyone ever told you I didn't, it was a mistake. I loved you from the moment Doc MacGillicudy told me that your daddy and I were having a baby."

"Really?" Devon pulled away a little to stare at her. "You're not just saying that 'cause you're my mama and you have to."

"I'll always tell you the truth. You may not like it, but I think life is too short for lies."

Devon heaved a sigh. "Daddy said you got tired of me being bad and that's why you went away, and when I asked her, Auntie Barbara told me you didn't want me no more 'cause I'm so naughty. Gramma Nessy said you had a hard job to do and you needed me to be strong and not rat 'em out."

Tears burned and Ann closed her eyes to keep them from falling. "Your dad and your aunt were wrong. I went because I'm a soldier and it's what soldiers do. They go places when they're ordered to go even if they'd rather stay home with their little girls and boys, so I went to Afghanistan."

"And it wasn't 'cause of me?"

"No, it wasn't. I did what soldiers have been doing for a really long time. It was nice of your Grandmother Vanessa and Grandpa Phil to try not to worry me, but I'm home now and I need to know what happened to you when I was gone." Ann kissed the child's forehead. "Now, let's finish eating and hit the road so we can have a splendid day together."

It was all she could do to follow her own advice. She wanted to call her sister and scream at the woman. Ann struggled to take a deep breath. Was that what they'd have told her baby if she hadn't made it home? Would they have said she went to war to get away from her child? For the first time in years, she found herself wondering about her own mother. Had Lucy Madison really left her family or had there been extenuating circumstances? Had she ever tried to contact her children in the last twenty-eight years or was Frank Madison, right? Had she walked away and never looked back?

The visit to the lawyer went surprisingly well. A tall blonde dressed professionally in a pinstriped suit, Bree Hawke flashed a genuine smile that warmed sky-blue eyes. While the receptionist brought coffee, juice and cookies to the conference room, Bree showed Devon how to play games on her laptop which cemented their budding friendship. The little girl didn't seem to realize the interview had started, but Ann did.

Afterwards, they stopped at the library. It was past time to get home but there was a package of reserved books waiting. It would only take a few minutes to collect them and find the novels her daughter wanted.

The short time stretched into almost an hour. Devon contentedly started reading the second book in the *Narnia* series, occasionally asking

Ann for help with a difficult word. She told herself that it wasn't her fault the Friends of the Library were having their annual book sale. She wandered from table to table sorting through the stacks of paperbacks.

"I also have three boxes of hardcover teen books left," Vera Griffin, the librarian said when she came in the room. "Do you want them? You're a teacher so I'd rather give them to you instead of sending them off to the dump like the new prez of the Friends demanded."

Ann nodded. She could pass up anything but donated books for her students. "I'd love them. Why on earth would someone throw away books?"

"Don't get me started on the hyper-critical members in the group. They freaked because there's several copies of post-apocalyptic fiction, *The Giver* series, the *Hunger Games* and *Divergent* trilogies and banned books like *To Kill A Mockingbird, Native Son, Fahrenheit 451* and *Huckleberry Finn* plus a lot more. They're in good condition and you could use them for your classroom library. Smitty O'Sullivan told me he was trying to hire you for a new school, and you'd need them."

"Kids love that sort of stuff and I like to use book clubs to create critical readers."

"I remember that from when you were at the high school here. My son, Brady said you were one of his favorite teachers. He'll be glad you're home."

"Me too." Ann smiled at the older woman. "Did Brady get into the college he wanted?"

"He's been accepted at the University of Washington in Seattle and Western up in Bellingham, but he's holding out for Washington State University in Pullman." Vera propped an ample hip against one of the tables, gray eyes amused. "His older brothers are at U-Dub. They make it home for the Apple Cup each year when the Cougs and the Huskies play."

"If I remember correctly, you attended W.S.U. and your husband went to the University of Oregon." Ann grinned at the woman who topped her jeans with a favorite red sweatshirt promoting the Cougar football team. "He always said he rooted for two teams, the Ducks and anyone playing the Huskies."

Devon looked up from her book. "I thought you went to college to be a teacher, Mama."

"I did, sweetie. Watching football with my friends was just for fun."

"Does Harry like it too?"

"He played on the team at his school so he must have."

Vera tilted her head to one side, silver streaked auburn hair tumbling around her shoulders. "Do you mean Harry Colter? He and Zeke Garvey went in the Army right after graduation. Harry was a star quarterback and had offers from all the state colleges. So did Zeke. They could have gone pro, but the word around town was they preferred to serve their country instead."

"Harry's a Mass-Sarge and Mama's boss. He knows everything at the Army."

"Master Sergeant," Ann said, "and my kid is right. Colter does an amazing job at the base. Unfortunately, Zeke didn't survive their last tour in Afghanistan."

Vera nodded, sadness creeping into her face. "I remember him. He was a total book-a-holic. He used to hang out at the high school library with me when we were kids. Later, when he was home on leave, he and Twila always brought their youngsters to visit when they wanted new books to read."

"I didn't know that." Ann almost asked if Harry read too but decided against it. She wouldn't share her suspicions with Vera Griffin who was delightful but had a habit of letting everything she heard come out later at the most inauspicious times. "Harry's shared some of his adventures with Zeke, but I didn't know he was a bibliophile."

"Oh yes. He used to sit and read to his kids and any others who were here in an impromptu story hour. Twila and Harry would wait for hours until Zeke was ready to go. I hated kicking them out at closing time."

CHAPTER TWENTY-TWO

They arrived at the Cedar Creek Guest Ranch in the early afternoon which meant Devon had plenty of time to ride Rainy Night before they went to meet Harry at the old O'Connell farm. They found Rob and Jacinth Sweeney, a petite redhead in the barn grooming and saddling two of the horses for a trail ride. After they agreed to supervise Devon's attempts to prepare her beloved pony, Ann left her daughter with the pair and went off to the house to talk to Cat.

Since the other woman was doing laundry, Ann jumped in to help fold clean clothes fresh from the dryer. "Thanks for the referral to your lawyer. I've asked her to try to get the court to adjust the custody agreement so Will has more supervision when he's with Devon."

"That should make the judge think he's allying with your stepmother because it's a dispute over who has Devon's best interests at heart."

Ann nodded, adding a child's sparkly pink t-shirt to the stack of clean garments. "We're on the same page. I'm majorly pissed at him for telling her that I left because she was 'bad', and my sister reinforced the message."

"That's wicked."

"You're telling me. I still have issues about my mother actually abandoning me when I was three and never contacting me again. I certainly don't want my kid carrying the same baggage."

Cat narrowed her gaze on the socks she was matching. "How sure are you that she never tried to call or write?"

Silence fell and thickened between them until Ann finally spoke. "My dad and older sisters all said the same thing, that she'd left because she was tired of being with us and preferred her boyfriend…" Her voice trailed away. "You think they lied, don't you?"

"I don't know." Cat shrugged, her focus on the clothes she removed from the washer. "It sounds suspicious. What do you remember about her?"

"Not much." Ann picked up a small pair of blue jeans, lining up the seams as she prepared to fold them. "I was only three when she left. I think my grandmother promised my mom would be home soon."

"You must remember something."

Ann kept folding the twins' clothes while pictures of a laughing woman who doled out more hugs than scolds floated through her mind. The smell of homemade chocolate chip or peanut butter cookies constantly wafted through their house. "She turned on the radio first thing in the morning and it played country music all day. I remember my cousin Heather saying my mom gave piano and guitar lessons. My mom and I used to ride all over Majestyk Morgan Farm on her super gentle, big Quarter Horse mare. After my mom left, my dad sold her to one of my Uncle Art's 4-H kids although I cried and cried to keep Lady Jane for me and Mommy."

"Do you want me to ask around Baker City about your mom?"

"I can do that. Harry's uncle is the police chief. I'm sure he could track her down, but that doesn't mean she wants anything to do with me."

"I have different resources."

"Like what?"

"Weren't you listening at the Baker City memorial? I'm the town medium, the O'Leary." Cat cracked a grin. "As the saying from that old movie goes, 'I talk to dead people.'"

Ann froze. "Are you saying you think my mother's dead?"

"Not necessarily, but it doesn't mean the ghosts in town didn't see her leave."

"I don't believe in ghosts."

"No wonder you and Harry Colter deserve each other." Cat heaved a sigh. "Zeke Garvey has been busy following him around and you're about to start teaching in a haunted schoolhouse."

"Is that how you straightened out Frazer? You claim to have turned a ghost loose on him?"

"Not me." Laughter filled the pantry while Cat closed the lid on the washing machine. "Frazer is dead and gone. It was totally his choice to go see what comes next."

"Have you completely lost it, Cat? He's out in the barn tacking up horses with Devon and Jassy Sweeney."

"That's not Frazer. That's Rob." Cat gestured to the kitchen. "Come along, Angelica Barrett. It's time for decaf raspberry tea and cookies. I'll tell you a ghost story."

"It doesn't mean I'll believe it or that it will stop me from asking you to sign papers to keep Devon if the battalion goes back to the *Sandbox* again before my enlistment ends in two years. Her needs come first, and I can't re-up if she's in jeopardy. Obviously, I don't have any relatives who will look after her and it's unfair to expect Will's parents to raise her."

"Then we have a lot to discuss."

While she accompanied Devon, Jacinth and Rob on the trail ride a short time later, Ann found herself remembering the tale Cat spun. Frazer Hendrickson was gone, replaced by the ghost who'd taken over his body. Cat said the spirit's name had been Rob Williams. He was an Army Ranger who died in Vietnam, but he opted to haunt his family's guest ranch rather than going to Heaven. Ann wasn't sure if she believed the story or not. He looked exactly like the man she remembered from eleven years before, except he didn't wear a white shirt and a dark suit. Instead, this version of the one-time gambler and casino pit boss opted for jeans, a flannel shirt and cowboy boots.

She had to admit the man seemed totally different. His jokes weren't cruel, and he always met her gaze when he spoke, never looking at her as if she were fresh meat. He didn't act inappropriately with Jassy either. That was new. In the past, he'd have flirted outrageously with the twenty-something, charming the girl until she fell into bed with him, flaunting one more affair in Cat's face and breaking her heart one more time. In addition, he was kind to Devon, answering all her horsy questions without making the child feel stupid.

On the way back to the corral, he rode beside Ann. "When I checked with her before we left, Cat told me that you wanted us to look after Devon if your unit gets called up since you don't have any decent relatives. It's fine. Tell the lawyers we'll do it."

"It could cause you problems with my father. He may not let you keep training his horses. His wife—"

"Cat gave me a 'sit rep' after the Easter celebration up town." Rob slowed the large chestnut Arabian he rode to keep pace with Skyrocket. "If Frank decides to pull his stock out of here, I'll tell him to 'man up and grow a set' instead of letting his wife run his business and his household."

"He's a 'go along to get along guy' and he never argues with Ginger. He let her take charge of me and my sisters even before they married. He'll totally freak if you say that he isn't a 'real' man."

Rob shrugged a broad shoulder. "Like I care if a 'leg' has a tantrum. Charlie Mike, Ann."

She gaped at him for a moment stunned by the last two military references which lent credence to the story she'd heard about him, then nodded agreement. She'd continue the mission, 'drive on' as they said in the *Sandbox* and keep her child safe from all threats. "You got it. Thanks, Rob."

Once they'd taken care of Skyrocket and Rainy Night after the ride, they headed home to clean up and look after Devon's new kitten. Ann preferred the deli selections at the Baker City Mercantile, so they drove there before heading out to meet Harry at his place. Her daughter scooted off to find a new toy for Aslan while Ann waited at the counter for Maxine to box up their order.

The doorbell jangled as another customer entered the store and Ann glanced over her shoulder, nodding at the police chief. "Hello, Dick."

"Hi Ann. I saw your car and it saves me a trip out to the dude ranch." He crossed to the counter, smiling at the store owner. "How's it going, Maxine?"

Ann waited while the two exchanged courtesies, then eyed the tall, older man standing beside her. Broad shoulders filled out his blue uniform shirt tucked neatly into dark blue slacks. A belt around his waist held all the paraphernalia that an officer needed. Short black hair liberally sprinkled with white was barely visible under his western hat, modeled after the Canadian Mounties' version. She suddenly realized Harry would look like his uncle in twenty years. Wow, she could certainly live with that.

She flicked a quick look at Devon, making sure her daughter remained busy in the pet aisle. Lowering her voice, Ann asked, "Were you a cop here twenty-eight years ago when my mother disappeared?"

"No, I was an M.P. in the Army back then. After I left the military, I started as a cop in Seattle, then moved to this department ten years ago when the old police chief retired. I read the files for cold cases, not that we have many of those, but not for missing persons." Curiosity crept across his rugged features, landing in the blue eyes. "Why? What did you need to know?"

"Where she is." Ann took a deep breath. "I heard she left with her boyfriend."

"I never believed that story." Maxine put the last piece of chicken in the cardboard box and folded down the top. "Granted Lucy and Frank were having problems. She wasn't quiet about him cheating on her at every horse extravaganza across the country. When she helped at the town food bank, she complained to me and Virginia Thompson about his women calling the house all hours of the day and night. Lucy said she was afraid one of your sisters might answer the phone."

"Why did she stay?"

"She loved your daddy a lot, Ann and the McElroy women aren't the 'walk-away' kind once they make a commitment. Look at your cousin, Heather. When they paid for her to go to college, her parents insisted she study nursing, so she'd have a fallback career if her dream of becoming a country music star didn't work out. She became an RN, but instead of going to Nashville, she followed Durango Hawke to war."

"But, they fought a lot about him starting Nighthawke Security when he left the Marines. They're some of the best independent contractors in the *Sandbox*. She left him five years ago because he kept going back to the *pit* as a sniper."

"Sure, but have you noticed where he lives? On the McElroy farm. He tracked down and bought back the horse she rode as a teenager. He's worked on the place, but his sister complains that he won't let her update the house. He says it stays the way that Heather's grandmother liked and when she comes home, Heather can do whatever she wants to it. Jassy Sweeney told me he doesn't date, and Linda said he doesn't even look at the flatlander women who make offers to him at Pop's. He's waiting for Heather to come home and it's no secret he looks for her whenever he hears of somewhere, she might be living. Your daddy never loved your momma like that."

"I don't think he loves Ginger that much."

"Who would? The woman's a snotty witch who plays the 'better than you' card too much for most folks. Lucy wasn't ready to walk away from your dad even though we offered to help her. She'd go when she was ready, but it'd be on her terms and she'd take all she could get. She'd have sued for full custody of you girls and would have told her lawyer she wanted at least half his assets to make sure he lost Majestyk Morgan Farm. Frank would have freaked."

"Really?" Interest piqued, Dick reached in his pocket and pulled out a notepad. "Tell me more. Did Frank file a report when she left?"

"Why would he?" Maxine began to dish up potato salad. "He was already messing around with that flatlander slut, Ginger Nevins."

Dick made a few notes. "You never said anything about that, did you?"

"Nobody ever asked me. Lucy's parents and her brother, Art McElroy wanted an investigation, but the cops said there wasn't any point when her husband claimed she'd left with another man. Frank filed for divorce a couple months later, but Lucy didn't respond to any of the advertisements when the lawyers looked for her and the McElroys backed down when Frank threatened to keep his daughters from seeing them."

"That's even more intriguing."

"As far as I know, my mother hasn't written, called or even sent a birthday card to me or my sisters once in the past twenty-eight years." Ann smiled as her daughter approached, carrying a package of small plastic balls. "Did you find something Aslan will like?"

"I checked out everything, but finally decided he wanted these. They have bells inside them so he can hear the noises when he chases them around the house."

"That makes sense." Ann rested a hand on Devon's shoulder while they waited for Maxine to finish dishing up salads.

Dick reached in his pocket and pulled out a keyring, handing it to Ann. "Harry called my mom and asked if she'd make sure you got these so you can get in the house if you arrive at the family farm before he does. As for the other business, I'll do some snooping and get in touch with you soon."

"Thanks."

Rush hour traffic was always horrendous even in the middle of the week, so Ann wasn't surprised that she was the first person to park in front of the large two-story log house. She and Devon carried their picnic supper inside, walking through to the huge eat-in kitchen.

"It's not what Gramma Ginger calls a 'chef's kitchen' is it, Mama?"

"No." Ann slowly turned, admiring the vintage cedar cupboards, matching countertops, the hardwood floor, farmhouse sink, the antique enameled woodstove, appreciating the fact there wasn't any 'granite' in sight. The old-style white appliances, a refrigerator, upright freezer and electric range obviously worked, but she didn't see a dishwasher anywhere.

Devon crossed the large room and climbed up on one of the chairs at the long table. "I like it here. Do you, Mama?"

"Yes, but I want to see the rest of the house before Harry gets home." Ann held out her hand. "Want to come with me?"

"Yes."

They checked out the pantry with its shelves, a washer and dryer, the downstairs full bathroom, then it was onto the den, the living room with its new bookshelves, fireplace and elaborate staircase to the second floor with four large bedrooms and a shared bathroom down the main hall. Back downstairs, they continued their investigations, exploring the master bedroom, its adjoining on-suite, and finally a nearby smaller room that undoubtedly served as a nursery until the youngest child was ready to join his or her siblings upstairs.

A knock on the front door startled Ann. She glanced at her daughter and they went to answer. "It's not Harry. This is his house. He'd just come inside."

"I hope he gets here soon. I'm ready for dinner."

"Me too." Ann opened the front door and saw a stocky man in a three-piece suit standing on the wraparound porch. His silver blond hair was neatly trimmed. "Good afternoon. Can I help you?"

"Yes. I'm Herman MacGillicudy." He held out his hand, a polite smile appearing on his ruddy face, but it didn't touch pale blue eyes. "I own the Lake Maynard First Federal Bank."

"I know." Ann folded her arms. "I've heard all about your hijinks last fall, Herman, when Cat McTavish took over the Cedar Creek Guest Ranch. You didn't get her place for the gravel and you're not getting this one either."

"Somebody's been telling you stories, Mrs. O'Connell." Herman's hand dropped to his side. "Of course, I have a consortium of investors looking to develop the area, but we're not the bad guys in a vaudeville act."

"Mama's not—"

"Hush, Devon. Little girls don't interrupt when grownups talk." Ann jerked her head toward the late-model, white Cadillac parked behind her Ford Taurus. "Get in your car and go."

"Let me give you my card." He extended his hand, the white pasteboard held between his thumb and first two thick fingers. "When you change your mind—"

"I won't." Ann adopted the tone she used for reluctant soldiers who faltered when she gave an order. "Go."

"Mrs. O'Connell—"

"Go!"

He turned, started across the porch and down the wide stairs to the lawn. He came to a stop when Harry's pickup pulled in beside his car. Throwing a triumphant smile over his shoulder, Herman hustled to meet the other man.

"Crap." Ann glared at the pair, then glanced down at her daughter. "Stay here, Devon. I'm gonna go kick a civilian butt."

"It's pretty big. I don't think you can miss it."

"You've got a smart mouth." Ann laughed and ruffled the little girl's dark hair. "I love you so much, sweetie."

"I love you too, Mama." Devon beamed up at her.

Leaving the child to wait, Ann stalked to where the men stood, and Herman blathered about buying the property for a fair price. "Has he told you yet that he intends to bulldoze the buildings and turn the farm into a gravel pit?"

"Really?" Harry arched a dark eyebrow, faint amusement trickling into the blue eyes. "We hadn't gotten that far. Did he tell you?"

"He didn't need to, not after the way he harassed Cat McTavish. It was the talk of the town. They *Skyped* with me all the time when I was in the *pit*. The crowning glory was when he cut the brake line on Cat's truck and almost killed her husband and Dray MacGillicudy, his own cousin, Linda's boy."

"That wasn't me." Herman almost gasped for air. "Things got out of hand last year, but I'm not responsible for what the lesser element in Baker City does."

"You are when you pay them." Ann pointed to the Cadillac. "Go."

"I'm conducting business here."

"Go."

"Do you always let your wife speak for you?" Herman turned to Harry. "She's only a woman. She doesn't understand business. She just—"

"Do you need help finding your car?" The amusement faded, lethal interest replacing it and Harry took a step forward, all menace in camouflage fatigues and combat boots. "I'm not busy."

"I'm going." Herman swung around and stomped toward his vehicle. "When you change your mind—"

"We won't." Ann kept her gaze on the portly man. "Go."

Harry waited until Herman drove away. "You know how you said that you hate it when I admit I'm wrong before you get to gloat. Well, get ready to have the wind taken out of your sails again."

She laughed, stepped close enough to rest her hands on his broad chest, rose up to kiss him. "I love being right. This is my opportunity to say, 'I told you so.' I'm not missing out on it."

"Gloat later." He pulled her closer and bent his head. "I'll get payback when I have my mouth on you tonight."

"Harry!" Heat burned into her cheeks and she could almost feel her panties dampening at the sexy threat. "You—"

"Wait, sweetheart. I love taking an angel to bed especially when she starts screaming my name." His lips claimed hers.

Sunrise lit the snow on the mountains with streaks of red and gold as he drove into Baker City toward his grandmother's home. He'd enjoyed not only the dinner but also the evening at the family farm while they discussed the furniture the large house needed. Ann had told him that they weren't updating the kitchen. She'd refused to let him take out some counter space and add in a dishwasher saying it wasn't needful. Any of them could wash dishes by hand and it was a suitable punishment for sassy children who grew up into smart-mouthed teens.

Devon hadn't looked too impressed by that idea, but she'd laughed when he'd said Ann might change her mind when they added three or four more kids to the family, and he'd do whatever she wanted. Devon put in an order for more little sisters than brothers but demanded her favorite puppy first. Still amused, Harry parked his truck in the drive and strode to the back door.

He heard his grandmother's collie give a warning bark as he turned the key in the lock. He stepped inside, careful to close the door before any of the eight fur monsters escaped from their wading pool bed. His grandmother glanced over her shoulder, but continued pouring a cup of coffee, then filled a second mug.

"Good morning, Harold. Have you proposed to that girl yet or you still toting your great-grandma's ring around?"

He chuckled and went to drop a kiss on her cheek. "Still toting, Gran, but we're going shopping for furniture this weekend after drill. I promised Devon her very own princess bed that nobody will ever take away."

"That child needs a little spoiling, but remember she also requires rules."

"I've got it." He leaned against the counter, took a swallow of the strong brew. "When I arrived at the farm last night, Ann was running off Herman MacGillicudy. She'd told me he'd be after the gravel, but I didn't believe it."

"You should have listened. I never liked that boy. Back in the day, he and Liam O'Leary used to try to lead your Uncle Dick astray, but your grandpa was still alive, and he put his foot down. He told Dick that he'd be judged by the company he kept."

Harry eyed his grandmother. "That's the same lecture Grandpa gave me along with a few other choice talks when I got in trouble."

"It worked on a lot of boys, but not your dad, Herman, Liam O'Leary or their group of friends. I gave Herman an earful when he called me about buying the farm. He got tired of my scolding him because he stopped contacting me and went to your family."

"It didn't do him or them any good. The O'Connell farm isn't being torn into a rockpile." Harry finished his coffee. "I'll have a new family soon and I'll try to keep Ann from kicking butt on a regular basis. She doesn't suffer fools gladly and the holidays may become a drama fest."

"We can use some drama, Harold. She'll be fun to watch. You just hold her coat and keep the girl safe. She hasn't had anyone on her side in years."

CHAPTER TWENTY-THREE

She'd spent the day finishing the final preparations for the upcoming unit drill that weekend. Since she had a couple hours of free time before meeting Devon and Margo for dinner after their karate class, Ann drove to the old schoolhouse in Baker City. She and Harry had dropped the boxes of books from the library in her potential classroom this morning before going to work.

On the one hand, she longed to return to teaching more than ever, but still dreaded the possibility it might not be a long-term position. She wanted to 'stick and stay and make it pay' like Harry said, not constantly be putting her resume together and looking for one more job. She hadn't shared her concern about her lack of patience with people she considered a waste of time, space and oxygen. Fortunately, those were mostly adults and there would be a minimal number of them in her classroom.

Still, she had time to organize the teen fiction and arrange it on the shelves saved for student book clubs. In the middle of sorting the books by title, she heard boots on the staircase. Expecting to see Harry, she glanced toward the door, surprised when her younger brother entered the classroom. She added a copy of *The Giver* to the stack of novels by Lois Lowry. "Hi, Jack. What's new?"

"All hell's breaking loose at home." He scowled at her, narrowing leaf-green eyes. "Dick O'Connell came with one of his officers to interview the folks about your mother. He calls it a 'cold case' because there's no trace of her anywhere in the U.S. You have to tell him she's probably married her boyfriend and is using his name."

"I don't know that. I was only three when she disappeared. I haven't a clue who the man would be, but I'm sure Dad knows his name if there even was a guy. From the scuttlebutt I've heard around town, nobody believes my mom had a boyfriend."

Ann studied her half-brother. In a green-checked flannel shirt, blue jeans and laced-up boots, he didn't look like he'd just come from a hard day logging. He was probably headed off to one of the local bars after their chat. She decided to keep what she'd heard about their dad being a serial cheater to herself, at least for the moment. Jack adored his mother and hearing that she had critics in town or that their father might do something to hurt her feelings at the least, or break her heart at the most, would devastate her younger brother.

Ann turned her attention back to the carton and drew out five more books, frowning thoughtfully at them, wondering how suitable *Ender's Game* by Orson Scott Card would be for the eighth graders. "I loved my mother like you love yours and if it's possible, I want her in my daughter's life. What else do you need to know?"

"Why haven't you said anything about this before?"

"I've been busy. It didn't seem important until Devon shared the crap she heard, that it was her fault I left, and I wouldn't have gone away if she wasn't a brat."

It was his turn to stare. "I don't get it. Who'd be mean enough to tell the kid that? Why would she believe it?"

"For the same reason I did when I was younger than she was. I blamed myself for my mother leaving. Kids own way too much emotional baggage." Ann heaved a sigh and put the last paperback on the table. "Once I recognized the similarities between her situation and mine, I wanted to know what happened to my mother."

"Why didn't you just ask Dad or Barbara or Chloe?"

"None of them would give me a straight answer. Were you aware Barb allowed her husband to spank my kid numerous times or that Chloe sent Devon's kitten to the pound?"

"So, this is all payback?"

"Oh Jack, honey. You haven't even seen me start on payback. If they didn't like the cops, wait until the lawyers arrive."

"What lawyers?"

"Bree Hawke and Colonel Williams." Ann hitched a hip on the corner of the table, swinging a combat boot back and forth. "At Easter, Barb and Chloe shared that Dad and your mom intend to sue for custody of Devon. No one in the family may realize the U.S. Army issues my uniforms, but they're about to find out when the proverbial ship hits the sand."

"That doesn't make sense. You're home. Sure, they spoil her rotten, but why would they want her? Isn't it easier to dump the mess they've made with her on you rather than straightening her out themselves?"

"You'll have to ask them."

"This is too strange for words." Jack grimaced. "I figured I'd tell you to cut the crap, but it's worse than anything I've heard. I'm checking in on the folks tomorrow and I'm asking what's up with the kid. When I was there for dinner this week, all the talk was about you marrying again and what kind of stepfather Harry Colter would be."

"Really? Are they planning to pay for the wedding?"

"I wouldn't go that far." He laughed. "You can ask. Mom was venting about you marrying into the O'Connell clan and how she'd never see Devon again. All the kid talks about when she visits is Janine and her dog's puppies or the pony out at Cat McTavish's place."

"It's hard to compete with those." Ann smiled and opted for her sweetest tone. "Of course, since Harry promised her the entire princess suite for her bedroom and she constantly tells us about her canopy bed at Dad's and Ginger's, it could become a moot point after we go shopping tomorrow night. Harry doesn't let her overstep the boundaries I set, but he does listen to what she wants."

"I'm not passing that on." Jack chuckled and looked over his shoulder at the sound of steps in the hall. "I'm outta here. I'll leave you and your fiancé alone."

"Works for me." Ann slowly rose to her feet and followed him to the doorway. She watched her younger brother pause long enough to speak to Harry before heading downstairs. "All right, Colter. You and I are having a meeting of the minds."

"What's going on, Angel?"

She crossed to him, resting her hands on his broad chest before she rose on tiptoe to kiss him. "It's politically incorrect to ride your white horse to the rescue nowadays."

"I don't have a horse." He brushed his mouth across hers. "I depend on my truck."

"Okay, share what you told my dad and his wife. Jack seems to think we're engaged. I talked to them before Easter, but I stopped when I heard Ginger planned to sue for custody. I know you've been up to mischief."

"I wouldn't call it mischief." He feathered a thumb over her lips. "I visited and asked for their blessing. I figured if they were worrying about your new husband, it'd distract your stepmother and her *Bravo Sierra* of trying to steal your kid from us."

"You still arranged for me to see Colonel Williams."

"Of course. I figured we'd better attack on more than one front."

"Brilliant." She laced her arms around his neck. "So, when are you proposing to me?"

"I already told you I planned to settle down now that I have in my twenty years and you're the wife I want. Do I still have to ask?"

"Definitely." She kissed him. "And you have to make it good. Flowers, wine, a fancy ring, the works."

"It sounds like a lot of trouble. What if I just take you to bed and make love to you until you agree to make an honest man of me?"

"You're already honest and after everything we've done in my bed, I'd swear on a stack of Bibles that you're a man." She trailed a finger down his cheek. "Come help me get these books out of the boxes. I've only got an hour left to work on them before I have to meet Margo and hear all about Devon's karate class."

"I can do that. Should we swing through the mercantile and pick up a frozen pizza on the way home?"

"Sure." Ann led the way into the classroom and came to a stop. She'd barely finished unpacking the first box of books, but now someone or something had emptied the other two cartons. Multiple stacks of paperbacks and hardcovers were neatly organized in alphabetical order by their authors on the long table directly in front of her desk.

"You've been working hard."

"I didn't get this far, but somebody else sure did."

Ann gazed around the vacant classroom and its rows of tables, each with three chairs. She walked over to the windows, eyeing the low bookcases filled with textbooks, literary fiction, paperbacks in every genre. Nobody had come past her when she left the room, at least no one she'd seen. Pausing, she folded her arms, then turned her attention to the tall bookcases on the end wall beside her desk.

"If you didn't do all this, who did?"

"I know what Cat McTavish would say, Colter. She claims the school's haunted and your buddy Zeke Garvey has been hanging out here."

"I've heard about Zeke, but I don't believe in ghosts."

"I don't know what to believe anymore." Ann drew a deep breath. "Well, since I've had help, we can just put these away on the shelves. We'll start with the A's and see how far we get."

He'd have liked to lean against the wall near the classroom door to watch Harry and Ann put away the books, but that wasn't possible, not anymore. Instead, Zeke enjoyed the sight of his buddy and his woman laughing and talking. It looked like Harry would finally get what he said he wanted during their last tour—the opportunity to settle down. Back in the day, he'd always agreed with one of their former teammates, Tate Murphy, who claimed if the U.S. Army wanted him to have a wife, he'd be issued one. Zeke grinned. It appeared as if Colter wasn't going to requisition one after all and he'd never be the team's slut-puppy like Murphy.

"They look happy." A woman spoke behind him, a lilt in her soft voice. "You did well marrying them up."

"They're not married yet, Doireann." Zeke glanced over his shoulder at the insubstantial figure of the former schoolteacher who wore a white blouse and a long black skirt. "They're not even engaged. He's still carrying around that ring his grandmother gave him for her."

"Sure and Rome *wasna* built in days either but took close on a thousand years. We'll be hoping it doesn't take these two that long to tie the knot. Now, come along, boyo. The mayor says the O'Leary has work for us."

"What work can any of us do? We're dead."

"Stop your whinging. We won't know until the man speaks."

Early Saturday morning, Harry was strangely quiet on their way into Seattle. He'd insisted on driving his truck. Ann studied him curiously. "What's bothering you?"

He shrugged a wide shoulder. "Remember when I told you I needed your help with my class, Angel? You're still going to help the troops put on their face paint, aren't you?"

"No worries. I can do that if you tell me what's really bugging you, Colter."

"Nothing."

Copying her daughter, Ann chanted, "Liar, liar, pants on fire," as he drove onto the base and up the hill toward the building where they'd meet the rest of the unit. "Start talking, Colter. Do you honestly think I don't know when you're upset?"

Another shrug and he still didn't answer. Instead, he spotted Derek Waller standing in an empty parking spot and pulled into it. Heaving a sigh, she reached for her beret and pulled it on with a grimace adjusting it to the appropriate angle.

She frowned up at him when he opened the passenger door and caught her hand to help her out of the pickup. "Now what, Colter?"

"Just checking. No earrings or nail polish?"

She sniffed and showed him her fingertips. "Clear is authorized, so are studs and it will take forever to wash out the mousse I put in my hair to keep it in place. Quit acting like some macho jerk."

Overhearing the conversation, Derek chuckled as he approached. "What's your problem, Colter? You think this is the *real* Army? If you ask any of these folks, they'll tell you they're glad to return to 'weekend warrior' status."

Ann glared at both men. "The battalion is full of good soldiers." She jerked away from Harry and stalked away, but still heard both men laugh. "You'll see."

"I wonder if this means no more earrings, nail polish and long hair," Harry drawled behind her.

"Personally, I thought you looked cute in them," Derek said.

Ann reviewed the last finance form and placed it in the appropriate file. After she checked on the whereabouts of the soldiers who hadn't arrived for drill this morning, she'd forward the attendance to Army Reserve Command HQ on Monday morning. She hoped she didn't have to include Sullivan Barlow among the AWOL contingent. Where was the other non-com? After escorting Raven Driscoll's body home, Sullivan had been assigned to the advance party preparing for the battalion to return Stateside when they arrived in January.

Ann glanced at the clock. Almost lunchtime. What had happened to Colter? His class wasn't due to start until thirteen-thirty, military time; one-thirty in the afternoon, civilian. Ann rose to her feet and strolled toward his office. Where was he hiding now? She glanced at PFC Smith, coming in the back door of the building. "Have you seen Sergeant Colter?"

"He's in the C.O.'s office over at battalion HQ," the former high school quarterback replied. "I think you should have gotten the full-time job here, Sergeant Barrett. Everybody does."

"If I had, your pay would still be loused up and it'd take another six months before you saw a check," Ann said. "Master Sergeant Colter insisted everyone receive emergency wages until the Army sorts out the financial mess we found when we returned home." She kept a steady gaze on the young soldier. "Pass that around the grapevine while you're at lunch."

"I will."

"Nice job, Barrett." Derek Waller drawled from the cubicle in the front corner of the room where he'd obviously come to fill his coffee cup. "I like the way you step up and cover Colter's back. He's not real popular at Battalion HQ either after he asked about a memorial for our lost soldiers."

"He has the fortitude to go to bat for the troops, so he should be treated with respect. I won't have him harassed."

"Ready for lunch?" Harry questioned, behind her.

"Sure, but nobody eats at the mess hall. It takes too long to get through the lines." Ann glanced over her shoulder to greet him with a smile. "Let's go to that taco place on Fifteenth. They do a great salad. While we eat, you can tell me all about the memorial. I think it's a great idea and it'd rally our troops who really miss First Sergeant Raven Driscoll. She didn't take any crap, but they always knew she had our backs."

"Hopefully they make stuff besides rabbit food." Derek came to join them. "I prefer the Chinese buffet, but it's where the ARCOM folks go and we'd never get a table."

"We'll hit the place during the week, Waller. Mark it on your calendar, Barrett."

Amused, Ann nodded and stood. She collected her purse and hat before starting toward the door. "What else did the Colonel want to discuss with you?"

"Not much." Harry shrugged. "He has a meeting scheduled with the officers so none of them will be attending my class this afternoon."

"No surprise there." Derek followed them out the front door toward the parking lot. "The battalion C.O. seems to have forgotten he's supposed to lead by example. The new commander will have his work cut out for him trying to restore the morale around here, but you didn't hear it from me."

Ann stopped and turned to stare at the two men. "Are you serious?"

"Yup, but you're on his Sierra list, so don't expect him to put you in for the next promotion board, Barrett, even though you've been acting 'first shirt' for the company. He's choosing one of the non-coms in the battalion to take over as First Sergeant here and Captain Meade backed down when he yelled at her in front of the cadre." Harry opened the passenger door of the truck and held it for her. "I don't want to hear you whining about it either."

"I don't whine," Ann said indignantly. "I'm an adult. I look out for myself."

"That's my job from now on. Quit griping and get in the truck. I want my lunch."

Ann obeyed, wondering at the mixture of pleasure, amusement and anger she felt. She really could take care of herself and she ought to be insulted by Harry's he-man attitude. No one had tried to protect her in years. In some odd way, she liked it. Did that make her a wimp instead of a sergeant? No, she looked after him the same way. What had he said before, that Zeke Garvey always had his 'six'? Well, the other Ranger wasn't around anymore so she'd step up and watch Harry's back.

Later that afternoon she presided over the instructions and face painting for the combat class. The enlisted personnel were divided into teams and everyone knew that they were supposed to make it through the woods back to the company headquarters with zero or minimal casualties. However, after their time in 'real' combat in the *Sandbox*, it was difficult for most of the soldiers to take the wargame seriously.

Despite a stern lecture, Ann could tell that the party atmosphere was still going strong as the second detail of volunteer soldiers entered the woods. She watched them leave, wishing they'd take the course less cheerfully, but maybe that was too much to hope for on a beautiful May afternoon.

While she supervised the next group, she spotted a vehicle pulling into the adjacent parking lot and recognized Margo's economy-sized Jeep. Margo, Jared Williams and a young dark-haired woman climbed out of the rig. While the other women waited by the small SUV, he came toward them. As the Colonel neared, Ann called the soldiers to attention and saluted Williams. "Good afternoon, sir."

Williams returned the salute and smiled politely, no emotion in his eyes. "What's going on here, Sergeant Barrett? Are you using the obstacle course?"

"We've received permission to hold a training exercise. The details are supposed to try and make it through to our headquarters while the other team tries to stop them."

A genuine grin warmed Williams's rough features. "Sounds innovative and fun. Who dreamed this up?"

"Master Sergeant Colter did." Ann viewed the sudden frown with sickening dread. Williams didn't have an axe to grind against Harry, did he?

"Not very even odds," Williams commented in a voice that everyone could hear. "He did nearly twenty years in the Rangers and has more tours in the *Sandbox* than anyone else in the battalion. Isn't he too earnest for your folks?"

Ann lifted her chin defiantly. She didn't know what kind of game Williams was playing but he had no business insulting a hero like her Harry. "Our people can handle it, sir. The *ARCOM* folks would be in trouble."

Instead of getting angry, Williams laughed. "We'll see about that, Barrett. I look forward to the challenge. I have a meeting with your cadre, or I'd do it now. So, we'll be back later."

"Yes, sir." Ann raised her hand in another salute, eyeing Williams with some concern. He didn't mean for Margo to go through the course, did he? Margo was still avoiding the visit to Doctor MacGillicudy, but Ann had made an appointment for the following week and would drag her friend there if she protested.

Williams returned her salute, turned and headed toward the waiting women. Ann followed. "Sir, could I speak with you for a moment?"

Williams stopped and glanced down at her, a faint smile in his eyes. "Were you going to apologize for being rude to an officer?"

Ann tossed her head. "Not unless you did for being nasty to my troops, sir."

"I think that's more than fair. Was there anything else?"

"Yes." Ann flicked a quick glance at her friend, freezing when she spotted the engagement ring on her left hand. That was new and the two of them had to talk, hopefully tonight. "Did you mean for Captain Endicott to come through the course? Because she can't—"

"I know, Sergeant Barrett." Jared's tone reflected pure calm. "I hadn't forgotten about that. Captain Endicott and her aide have work to do in your company's headquarters. I have a question. Will your C.O. be coming down to participate in this exercise?"

"I don't know." Ann prayed her face wouldn't give her away. "There was some doubt about whether our cadre could shake loose, sir. They have a lot of responsibilities."

"No more than any other command. I'll shake them, Sergeant. Don't tell Colter about this. I don't want to warn him ahead of time and let anyone get preferential treatment."

"He wouldn't give it to you anyway. He'd just be more on his guard than ever."

"I don't want that either. Then I'll never make it through. It's been years since Ranger school."

"You're a good officer. I'll bet your enlisted are like me and would follow you anywhere. Sergeant Colter really respects you."

"You could have gone all day without saying that, Ann," Margo murmured, sun glinting off the diamond ring she wore on her left hand. "Now, his hat won't fit, and I'll have to go buy him a bigger one."

"It'll give you something to do if you run out of things to do at the company headquarters while you wait for me."

Listening to the two of them spar when they walked away toward Battalion HQ reminded Ann of her quarrels with Harry. She returned to the troop of soldiers to find they were almost ready to go into the woods. All the joking had evaporated, and she studied the tense, grim group. "I think you're ready."

CHAPTER TWENTY-FOUR

Late that afternoon, she'd finished advising the last group of enlisted soldiers about their camouflage face paint when she saw Jared Williams returning, accompanied by the young, dark-haired college student. He paused to introduce her as Lisa Jensen, then they began their preparations. Ann followed them to the table of face painting materials and asked, "What is Captain Endicott doing at our company headquarters? If she's inspecting our personnel records, I'm the one responsible for any errors. I should be there."

"No, you shouldn't. She has Captain Meade to entertain her. I'm sure your commander will be able to answer any questions that may arise."

"I'm not. I'm the expert on the 201 files and those details bore most officers."

"Exactly."

Ann almost giggled at the mockery in his deep tone, realizing again why her best friend loved him. A good sense of humor helped with a lot of day to day *Bravo Sierra* and made it possible to deal with people who were a complete waste of time, space and oxygen.

"Come on." Ready to depart, Williams picked up one of the remaining weapons and glanced at Ann. "I'll take command of your detail, Barrett. Who is cleaning up afterwards so you can play too?"

"We are, sir." PFC Phil Smith stepped forward, gesturing to Lafayette Jones and Dani Chang. "We have it covered, Sergeant Barrett. We'll meet you at HQ."

"Good. I know I can rely on all of you to do a good job." Ann looked around the area one more time before she headed across to pick up her weapon.

Williams led the way into the obstacle course. "Let's be the winners in this game and make it all the way to your unit's headquarters."

"How many have won?" Ann asked as she followed him. She admired his almost silent movements on the path and tried to copy him. He had the same lethal grace that Harry did. Of course, they'd both learned it in the Rangers and then in combat.

"Only a few have won so far like your cleanup crew," Williams whispered. "The rest got tagged. Waller watches too many movies. He and Colter obviously had too much time on their hands. The folks they captured or killed wear little signs that say things like, "*Defunct. Dead. Wiped Out,*" and lots more. Now, quiet. We all know noise carries."

Ann paused, her bewilderment growing. How had Harry made signs when he left most of the paperwork to her? How could he write clearly when he barely scrawled a signature on the forms he signed? She pondered the questions as they edged through the woods, coming to a stop when Williams did.

In a clearing ahead of them was Colonel Stewart, pure fury on his face and in every line of his stiff body. Red, yellow and orange paint splattered his camouflage fatigues. Around his neck on a thin string, he wore a cardboard sign that read, "*NOT EVEN CLOSE!*"

"How could you?" Ann closed the door as soon as the three of them were safe in Colter's office an hour later, glaring at both men. As far as the Army was concerned, they outranked her but when she saw 'stupid' she said so. "Stewart is the battalion C.O. for heaven's sake, and he has to sign off on both of your performance reviews."

"He's a lousy soldier," Derek commented cheerfully. "I could have killed him a dozen times, but I didn't have to, not when my patrol did the honors."

"That fills me with confidence." Ann glared at Harry. "It was still a politically insane stunt to pull."

"Shut up, Barrett." Harry met her gaze evenly. "At least, you know the creed. Praise in public, bitch in private. I don't want to hear it. If the Colonel and his officers required special treatment, they should have remained at HQ. He gave permission for Derek to borrow folks for our patrol from other reserve units."

"He just didn't know how many volunteers I'd get, and I didn't even have to 'spin a helmet' on the bastard." Derek sauntered across the small office to lean against the old oak desk. "This was our only chance to nail him since the change of command ceremony is tomorrow afternoon at closing formation."

"What change?" Ann demanded. "I haven't heard anything about it and these formalities always take organization. You can't pull them off at the last minute."

"The orders finally came through yesterday." Derek grinned at her. "Colonel Williams was tapped to take over the battalion. The General wants a lawyer in charge to handle the fallout from the last tour and most of the cadre will be replaced by Williams' people."

Ann gaped at him, then at Harry. "Does that mean Captain Endicott will be the commander of our company?"

"Yup, but you didn't hear it from me."

"Wow, that's a surprise." Ann frowned thoughtfully as she recalled what Derek said about volunteers to help with the training exercise. "So, who was on the patrol besides you and Harry?"

Sadness darkened Derek's eyes for a moment. "Tate Murphy, Falcon Driscoll, Bianca Powell, and two of the Barlows. Raven Driscoll married Sullivan's brother, Kord, before we left last time. He's a former Seal. He worked for Nighthawke Security after leaving the Navy and this gave him the chance to 'take out' the C.O., and Sullivan was just as eager."

Ann winced, blinking hard. "Well, that explains why Sullivan didn't show up for morning formation."

"Her transfer is waiting on the Colonel's desk because Captain Meade refused to sign the form." Derek shrugged. "I told Sully we were in transition between commanders and asked her to reconsider. She and Raven were understandably tight, so you may want to reach out to her."

"I will and I'll ask Margo to consider her for the First Sergeant slot here in the company." Ann met Harry's gaze. "If she recommends me, people will think I got the job because we're best friends and since she'll be Devon's teacher in the 'real' world, I don't want to go there."

"Nepotism is always alive and well, but that isn't who the Colonel wanted to take over." Harry kept his back to the door. "Guess it doesn't matter now."

"We have one more day of drill to get through." Ann took a deep breath. "I'm glad I've been forewarned. No surprises."

That evening she had Harry drop her at Margo's cabin when she spotted her friend sitting on the wraparound porch, grateful Devon was at a sleepover with the twins. It'd be up to Cat and Rob to keep the girls in the house instead of camping in the barn with their ponies, a task Ann was happy to delegate. Margo must be emotionally exhausted too since she hadn't bothered to change from her camos or combat boots.

Ann climbed the steps and crossed to one of the Adirondack chairs, sitting down before she picked up the glass of waiting strawberry lemonade. "We have a lot to discuss. When did Jared propose?"

"Last night at dinner." A blush brightened Margo's cheeks. "We went to Pop's after we made a few last-minute additions to my classroom. He got down on one knee in the middle of the restaurant in front of half the town."

"That took guts. You could have refused."

"Not when he arranged for Pop to serve me a huge slab of homemade cheesecake with a diamond ring in the middle."

"Is this when I ooh and aah? Cheesecake isn't even on the menu in Baker City."

"I know. Jared brought a slice of my favorite kind from the bakery."

"Sounds like Pop may have to start ordering it in from Twila Garvey."

"That's what she said."

Both of them laughed and Ann leaned back in the rocker. "I'm happy for both of you."

"Good. You should be since you arranged it." Margo narrowed her eyes. "Little Miss Fix-It."

"That's Sergeant Fix-It." Ann heaved a sigh. "Shall we talk about the unit and the change of command ceremony tomorrow afternoon?"

"Only if we have to. I'd rather talk about my wedding and the baby. Let's leave the Army stuff until we're at the base and have to 'soldier up'."

"Works for me." Ann paused long enough to sip the tangy

lemonade. "I think you should offer Sullivan Barlow the 'first shirt' slot."

"I will." Ice cubes clinked amid floating strawberry slices as Margo swirled her glass. "I asked Smitty to give her a teaching position in Baker City. In addition to another elementary teacher, we'll need someone with History and Science credentials, and she'll have both when she finishes her last internship this semester at Lake Maynard High."

"That sounds good. It's coming together. I'll bet Smitty is happy."

"He'd be even happier if you stepped up now instead of waiting until September to come to the school."

"I know, but I can't, not yet. I'm afraid to stand up one more time, to take another risk. Devon is ready to rock and roll. She was thrilled to pieces when I withdrew her from Lake Maynard last Friday and vowed to be your best student. She wants to show me she's old enough to have one of Janine O'Connell's puppies."

"Have you talked to Cat about one yet?"

"No, but I will this week. Janine is keeping Devon's favorite, a little tri-colored monster. Luckily, Harry hasn't said a word to her about it, but I can tell by the long looks, he thinks I should make it happen." Ann laughed, shaking her head, sarcasm filling her voice. "No pressure there."

"Are you going to work, Mama?" Devon chirped at the breakfast table. "I mean after you take me to school."

"No, I worked all weekend and I told Harry that I'd be back on Wednesday. I need to catch up on things around here." Ann sipped coffee while she continued packing a lunch for her daughter. "I'm picking you up after school today, but when I'm at the fort, you need to ride with the twins."

"I know. We already talked about it. I'm gonna be super good at school and Mrs. Cat's house so I get Shadow to be my dog forever and ever."

"I didn't realize you'd already named him." Ann slid the cheese sandwich into a plastic container. "Why call him, Shadow?"

"Harry's grandma and I watched the *Homeward Bound* movie again and I told her I liked the old dog the best. The other dog was a brat and she said I could call my puppy, Shadow too. He already comes when I call him. 'Course I always give him a treat."

"That makes sense."

The ring tone of her cell phone interrupted Devon's chatter about the puppy and Ann grabbed it. "Hello."

"Angel, this is Harry. You're late. I thought we were carpooling today."

"Not today, we're not. It's Devon's first day of school in Baker City. I left a note on your door yesterday after closing formation that I'd be out for the next two days and told Derek to remind you I'd be gone. Call it comp time. I didn't have time to wait around and talk to you. Margo and I were meeting Sullivan Barlow for dinner."

Utter silence before he asked cautiously. "Are you still mad about Saturday?"

"Of course not, Harry. Why would I be upset about you and Derek Waller playing games and leaving me out of the loop? I'll be okay by Wednesday morning. Right now, I need to 'mommy up' for my daughter."

"All right. Tell Devon that I hope she has a good time at school, and she learns a lot."

"I will."

Late Wednesday morning, Ann forced herself to make the trip into Seattle to Fort Bronson, timing it so she arrived just before lunch. She recognized Harry's truck in the parking lot and deliberately took several deep breaths on her way into the company headquarters. She'd figured two days of housework, grocery shopping, getting her car serviced, riding her horse and visiting with Cat McTavish would settle her nerves, but apparently that wasn't the case.

Well, it was time to 'soldier up' and 'drive on' as they said in the *Sandbox*. Derek Waller finished pouring a cup of coffee and glanced toward the door when she entered. Ann nodded at him. "Hi. How goes the war?"

"We haven't lost it yet. I popped in to check on Cadet Jensen. She's been reassigned up here. I've had her do the filing and taught her to do the finance for last weekend's drill, but there's still a lot for you to handle."

"That's true." Ann dropped her purse and beret on the top of her desk, staring at the stack of paperwork. "What's this garbage?"

"Outgoing mail from Captain Meade. Incoming mail. Finance paperwork and the list goes on and on."

"Where's Colter?" Ann inquired dangerously. "Hiding in the supply room?"

"In his office. I told him we'd go through the personnel records for the soldiers being reassigned to the company. Their paperwork arrived before they did. Here's hoping that the ones requesting transfers decide to stay with the change in command."

"From your mouth to God's ears." Ann dreaded seeing Harry after the way she'd avoided him but kept that to herself. "I'll have a cup of coffee and get to work."

"Take it easy," Derek advised, starting toward the rear of the building. "You don't look like you rested much these past two days. But, now that you're here, I'll leave you and Colter to it. Just remember not to overdo it."

"I'm all right." Ann filled her mug and returned to her desk, sinking into the office chair. She began to open the mail, sorting through the orders for individual soldiers. Suddenly her own name leaped out at her. She read the papers twice. "No, I don't believe this."

Her orders for the next two months had been revoked and she knew what would happen. The military would take all her upcoming paychecks, claiming she'd been overpaid. What was she going to do?

She jumped to her feet and hurried toward the private offices. "Colter, I want to talk to you. What have you done to my orders? I can't work without approval from Army Reserve HQ. I won't get paid and all my wages will be docked."

Glancing up from the brown folders in front of him, Harry frowned. "What are you talking about? I didn't do anything to change your authorization."

"But my orders—What am I going to do?"

"Colonel Stewart," Harry returned succinctly. "He's in a snit. He'll get over it, not that it matters all that much. Colonel Williams will sort out this mess when he arrives."

Ann looked at the papers again. "In a snit? It's all your fault." Tears burned her eyes and she refused to let them fall. "You had to make a fool of him in front of the unit. He's had my orders revoked. I'm not going to get paid for this past month. How the hell am I supposed to pay my bills?"

Harry strode to her and rested his hands on her shoulders. "You've had a rough time of it, honey. Why don't you go home till you feel better? You must feel really wrung out."

Ann glared up at him. "I've bloody well had it. I'm sick and tired of pandering to all your male, macho egos. I do the correspondence. I do the finance, so everyone gets paid not that it matters when the C.O. has a tantrum. I've got to do all the filing and supply paperwork. I request orders for the troops. I don't get credit. I don't get glory and now I'm damn well not getting paid for doing your job, Colter."

Harry's grip tightened. "Calm down, Angel. I'll take care of you. This is just temporary."

"Temporary!" Ann jerked free and shoved the orders at him. "Read this. Do these damned orders look temporary to you?" Her voice faded as she saw the red creeping along his cheekbones. Then she remembered. He could barely read. And now she wouldn't be here to help him. "Oh hell! Harry, I'm sorry."

"Sorry? Why should you be sorry? You have a justifiable gripe."

"Because it isn't your fault." She felt a horrible new emotion, pity. She'd never felt sorry for him. Today, she did. What was she going to do? She couldn't afford to stay and yet how could she leave him?

"You know. Don't you?"

"That you're alliterate?" Ann tried to keep her tone calm. "You can read, but you don't. After everything I've seen these past two months, why wouldn't I know?" She took a step toward him and rested her hands on his arms. "It doesn't matter."

"Doesn't matter?" He pushed her from him, and his gaze was deadly. "I may not have much, Barrett, but I have my pride. Don't lie to me. You're an intelligent woman. Does it give you some thrill to look down on me because I'm stupid?"

"You're not. You're the smartest man I know." She didn't hesitate. "Harry, I love you. I think I have since the first day I met you."

"Now, you love me?" His blue eyes shone with suppressed pain.

"That first day I walked in on you because I didn't even read your damned sign. Did you know then?" He paused and suddenly roared. "Did you feel sorry for me then?"

"Of course not!" Ann shouted back. His loudness, his rage might have frightened some women, but she'd been in combat too. She knew how to yell back. "Why the hell should I feel sorry for you, Harry Colter? You're doing a damned fine job by yourself. I didn't pity you when you forgot your glasses—"

"Glasses?" He rested his hands on his lean hips. "I have perfect vision. I've never needed them. I'm just so dumb that I barely learned to read when I was in school."

"Either that or when you were jumping out of airplanes, you landed on your head."

"Well, at least I can do more than one thing. You can't teach either."

Ann gaped at him, feeling like she'd been stabbed in the heart. "I thought you understood. I told you about that. I don't want to go back to school, start teaching again and not have a guaranty."

"Understand?" Harry arched an eyebrow. "What's to understand? You don't even have the guts to try. Guess what, Barrett. Life comes with risks. Like my grandpa said, it's time to either fish or cut bait. Otherwise, you're just like every other teacher. It's your fault kids like me don't read."

"My fault?" Ann repeated. "How can it be my fault you got the short end of the stick in school? I was still at the elementary."

"Bigger's dumber. You teachers are all the same. You can't do the job so why even bother?"

"I can do it, Colter and I'm damned good at it." Ann flung the words at him, hoping they'd make an impression. "This is bogus. We both know you had to pass tests to get into the military."

"They weren't timed and there was a war on, so they needed 'cannon fodder' as my grandpa said. It didn't hurt that a judge ordered me to enlist."

"And most manuals are written simply so everyone can understand the material," Ann said. "In addition, Zeke Garvey had your six. Do you want me to teach you to improve your reading skills?"

Harry looked at her, his gaze as cold as a glacier. "I don't want anything from you, Sergeant Barrett. Get out of my office."

Ann fell back a step. Then another. She wouldn't cry in front of him. Turning, she stumbled through the room for a moment before she caught herself. She ran to grab her belongings and pelted for the door. She made it to her car and shoved the key in the ignition. Damn Stewart. And damn Harry. She wasn't going to give them the last month and walk off without her money.

Tears slid down her cheeks, but she ignored them. Deliberately, she turned left at the bottom of the hill and drove toward the Army Reserve Headquarters building. She parked in a visitor's spot and stormed into the contemporary white building. She wiped at her face and hurried up the stone steps into the vestibule, then headed down the hall to the JAG office where she'd find Colonel Williams.

Ann didn't wait to see if anyone else was inside with him, twisting the knob and walked in the room. Williams was on the phone. He replaced the receiver and gazed at her with obvious concern. She lifted her chin and met his gaze. "Stewart canceled my orders."

"Colonel Stewart?" Williams asked.

Ann nodded. "Yes. I've worked hard for the last month. I want my money. I don't care about the rest of the tour. I just want to be paid for the days I've put in."

Williams leaned back in his chair. "It'll take a couple days for me to sort this out, Sergeant Barrett since I'm not at the battalion yet. What does Sergeant Colter say?"

CHAPTER TWENTY-FIVE

She called Smitty O'Sullivan on the way north and he told her he was substituting for one of the principals at the high school in Lake Maynard, the place where Ann taught before shipping out to Afghanistan the last time. She parked in front of the two-story red brick building, eying the separate wing for the junior high, remembering the contretemps it caused when the district consolidated the different buildings, closing the two middle schools in Lake Maynard, claiming it'd be easier on everyone, especially the secondary students if there was a central campus. Of course, it all came down to cost which meant retiring teachers weren't replaced and neither were the ones who went to America's longest war.

When she signed in at the office, the secretary greeted her with a hug and asked if she'd been watching the district website for employment opportunities. Ann admitted she had, but there hadn't been any openings in her field, so she was considering taking a job in Baker City. With the encouraging words that the town would be lucky to have her ringing in her ears, she headed for the English wing of the building to find Smitty.

Classes were changing and students streamed toward her. Ann paused when she heard the roar of an engine. She hurried past two laughing girls and saw a boy riding a quad coming toward her. How on earth had he managed to ride that inside, much less down the corridor? She glanced at the locked outside doors at the far end of the hall and immediately realized the truth. Some mischief making friend was undoubtedly the ally who'd allowed him in the building.

Ann scowled as the off-road vehicle approached and glanced around. Where were the authority figures? What was going on? Back in the day, she and the other teachers stood in the hall during passing periods and Smitty often patrolled different wings along with the vice principal and security guards. Where were they?

Well, she wasn't waiting for one of them. She stalked toward the boy and his ATV. The other kids fell back as she neared him, and he stopped the rig when she stood in front of it. Ann kept one eye on her audience. "What is the meaning of this?"

"I'm on my way to class," the teen hastily defended himself. "Nobody needed to call out the Army, Sarge."

"I'm sure." Ann glared at the dark-haired, brown-eyed boy. "I'm only telling you once. You turn off this machine and you push it out of here. This is a school, not a road rally."

"It's mine. I rode it in here. I'm not taking it anywhere except to Washington State History."

That brought hoots of laughter from the crowd and one brave soul called, "You tell her, Tim."

"I am." Tim shoved at his shoulder-length black hair. "You're not even a teacher here. How could you make me take it out of here?"

"It's not hard." Ann advanced on the machine and hit the kill switch, then removed the key. She spun and confronted the other students still milling around the hall. "Break is over. Get to class." Deliberately, she used her best drill instructor's bark. "Move it!"

Laughing, Dray MacGillicudy sauntered forward. "Yes, ma'am."

Ann looked him up and down. "Don't call me ma'am, Dray. I'm a sergeant. I work for a living. Now, march these troops to class if you're man enough. Any *B.S.* and I'll go for lunch at your grandfather's."

"You got it, Sergeant Barrett." The senior gestured to his friends. "Come on. Let's get out of here before she calls for support or contacts our folks up in Baker City. My mom will have me scrubbing every inch of Pop's place for the next month. You're on your own, Garvey. See you later, Sarge."

Ann tossed the key in one hand. "You got that right." She glanced at Tim. "Are you still here? I'm on my way to find Mr. O'Sullivan. When I find him, I'm phoning your dad and reading him from *The Book*."

"You can't. He's dead."

Ann saw the pain behind the defiance. "Get that monster outside before security arrives. If you're lucky, they won't nail your backside to the wall this time."

"I'm gone. Thanks, Sarge."

When he began pushing the quad toward the doors at the end of the hall, Ann stared after him. Why had she backed down? She should have raised a stink. She should have arranged for Tim to be suspended. But she couldn't. He'd been hurt enough, and she suspected he'd have been shocked to learn how much he'd given away in that flat statement about his father.

Turning, she headed toward the English wing of the building, not surprised when she spotted Smitty O'Sullivan coming toward her. "Some kid told me that we had a motorcycle out here. Did you see it?"

"It was a quad, not a motorcycle." Ann held up the key. "It's gone. I handled it. What's going to happen to the boy riding it?"

Smitty glared at her. "What do you think? The principal will want him suspended for the next week or the rest of the school year. Who was it?"

"I'll tell you his name if you agree to opt for justice instead."

Smitty gave her a solid onceover. "What do you have in mind?"

"Making him help the janitor strip, mop, wax and buff all of the school floors for the next two weeks. He needs to learn to respect this place and his education."

"That's awful," Smitty slowly began to grin. "I love it. Do you think he'll step up?"

"If it's contingent upon you going to bat for him, I'm sure he will." Ann hesitated, took a deep breath and mentally stepped up. It was past time for her to return to 'real' life and stop hiding out at Fort Bronson "My orders ran out and I'm here to talk to you about the job."

"As what? Playground supervisor," Smitty inquired mischievously, "or hall monitor?"

Ann laughed. "The district would undoubtedly hire me to do that here, but I'm talking about teaching in Baker City."

"We've been waiting for you. When do you want to start classes? Does next Monday work?"

Ann nodded. "Yes, that will give me two days to set up assignments."

"Then we have a plan." Smitty frowned as Tim Garvey sauntered toward them. "You took out the toughest kid in the seventh-grade class?"

"And no shots were fired." Ann passed him the key. "I'm headed up to Baker City and checking in with Margo. Will we see you at Pop's tonight?"

"You are never getting out of our school again. Not till after I retire, and Heaven knows when that will happen since your dad took me out of the proverbial pasture and put me back to work." Smiling, Smitty rested a hand on Tim's shoulder. "Walk with me, son. How do you feel about helping the janitor for the next month at your new school instead of listening to your momma lecture you?"

"Talk, hell. She'll skin me alive and you know it. When she gets done with me, she'll go after Uncle Harry because she told him I was too young to have my quad and he said my dad promised to get me one when they got back from their last tour. Dad wasn't here, so Colter did it."

Ann shrugged, mentally filing away the information, putting two and two together. Even if he'd been a complete jackass earlier, it sounded like Harry was more than stepping up for his best friend's kids. "If you're afraid of your mom and Master Sergeant Colter, tell Mr. O'Sullivan and he'll contact Child Protective Services for you, and they'll put you in a foster home somewhere and run an intervention. Best case scenario, you'd never see your mom, brothers and Harry again."

Tim stared at her as if she'd dropped in from outer space. "You're nuts, Sarge. I could have torn up the hall and made a real mess of it if I'd four-wheeled through it like the guys suggested. No, I've earned whatever my mom and Harry do to me when they hear about me getting suckered into a dare, but maybe they'll go easy if I'm accepting the consequences." He looked at Ed again. "What do I have to do with the janitor? Clean up the place?"

"That's about it," Smitty agreed. "Do you want to start tomorrow?"

"What about baseball practice?"

"We'll work around it. Can't have the pitcher scrubbing floors when there's a game."

"You're all right. I've got to get to class. I screwed up. I'm sorry."

Ann watched the boy stride down the hall. In sloppy jeans, a ragged t-shirt and old jump boots that must have belonged to his dad, Tim looked as though he owned the place. "I like that solution better than making a dropout of him." She giggled. "When do you think he'll realize you still have his key?"

"I'll give it to Twila tonight when I pop into the bakery to talk to her. She'll be happy to have her boys back home. They've been staying with one of Zeke's brothers in Lake Maynard, so they don't have to ride the bus for almost an hour and camp out in the gym until classes start in the middle school. She told me she was concerned about the lack of discipline in the house. They're cutting the boys too much slack because they lost their dad, but Zeke would be the first to set limits."

"What about baseball? Will we have sports up in Baker City?"

"Eventually, but for now the kids will continue to play on the Lake Maynard teams." Smitty tucked the key in his pocket. "You didn't ask about the janitor. That's me and my boy, so don't think Tim will be getting off easy."

"I never expected it, not with you on my side." Ann turned and the two of them walked toward the administrative offices. "What happens with the principal here when he learns about Tim's stunt?"

"He'll be more upset about losing twenty to thirty students now to the school in Baker City as well as the others who will finish out the year here but won't return in the fall. It means the district loses state funding and that money will come our way. Margo wants me to hire Sullivan Barlow, but her advising teacher and the principals here tell me she isn't much good. She's barely passing her last student teaching practicum."

"That's *Bravo Sierra* if I've ever heard it." Ann glared up at him. "I was in the *'box'* with her and she kicks butt. When Margo and I took her to dinner last weekend, Sully said she's having to 'keep her head down' because of the constant harassment since she has her 'emergency certification' and substituted in Liberty Valley between combat tours. Margo told her it's the same kind of crap that she went through when she finished her college degree and went for her commission. She got it, but she has a higher tolerance for excrement than I do after mucking stalls for my dad and shoveling out the pigpen whenever Ginger was pissed at me."

"I figured you'd know more of the dirt than I do." Smitty grinned at her. "I'm going to observe her Washington State history classes this afternoon and see what I can learn."

"A lot. She was upset because her supervising teacher turned down a request to take the kids on an Underground Seattle field trip to see the results of the Great Seattle Fire that destroyed the waterfront and business district in June 1889. She's set up a virtual version of it so the students can view the damage and read what witnesses said."

"I can't wait to see it. Are you planning to wear your fatigues next week?"

"Those and the combat boots make an impression." Ann laughed at his expression. "I have civvies. I'll wear those, Smitty. Don't worry."

"That's my job along with washing windows."

An hour later Ann parked behind the old school in Baker City. She walked around to the front of the building and watched as parents picked up their children. Devon spotted her and raced toward her, one of the twins trailing behind.

The little girl slowed as she neared. "Are we going somewhere, Mama?"

"No, I stopped in to check my classroom and talk to your teacher about the big kids starting class next week." Ann tucked a dark tendril back into Devon's braid. "Do you still want to go home with Samantha and Sophie, or wait for me?"

"Go with them and see Rainy Night. I saved him my apple core from lunch."

"That works for me if it works for them."

Devon's friend, a petite third grader, looked her up and down. "Aren't you in the Army no more, Mrs. Ann?"

"I'm all done for a while." Ann didn't share the details, not with a child. "So, I'll be here at your school with the big kids."

"Who's gonna help Mass Sarge Harry?" Devon asked.

"He's on his own. He's a grown man. He can handle it."

"Oh wow." Another long look from the blue-eyed twin before she heaved a sigh and shook her head. "Sergeant Garvey's going to be mad at him too. I hope he remembers the rules the mayor told him when he got here."

Ann walked with the girls toward Rob who waited with the other twin. "Baker City doesn't have a mayor. My father is probably the closest thing because he's in charge of the business association and Sergeant First Class Garvey died in the war."

"The mayor's a ghost too." Another long sigh. "Daddy, you've got to talk to Sergeant Garvey 'cuz he's gonna be mad at his friend."

"When he needs it, I will, Samantha." Rob took the *Wonder Woman* backpack she passed him slinging it on his arm, along with the *Mulan* one he already carried. "For now, don't worry about it. Your mom's waiting for us at home." He smiled at Ann. "Is Devon coming with us?"

"Yes. I need to talk to Margo, but I won't be late."

"We'll be in the barn." Rob winked at Ann. "I'm pretty sure the ponies need carrots this afternoon once the girls finish their snacks."

"Undoubtedly." Smiling, Ann headed up the stone stairs and into the school.

He'd contemplated calling Ann when she was least in sight on Thursday and Friday. Obviously, she didn't plan to return to Fort Bronson until her orders were reissued and that meant waiting until the new commander arrived and was at Battalion HQ full-time. Meanwhile, the young ROTC cadet did an exemplary job of filling in at the company. She contacted Derek Waller with questions about the correspondence and finance. He provided plenty of advice, so the company continued to operate even if it wasn't at peak efficiency.

On Friday evening after rush hour, Harry left the base for Baker City still wondering what was wrong with his room in the barracks. Nobody else had the problems he did with uniforms scattered across the floor instead of remaining on hangers in the wall locker, light bulbs constantly burning out or breaking and the windows often opening on their own whenever it rained, which meant he had to deal with pools of water on his floor and soggy blankets on the bed regardless of where he put the cot.

Derek told him to 'man up' and stop stomping around the second-floor room after twenty-two hundred hours and to be sure to turn off his TV when he left for the office in the morning. The soldiers on the first floor needed their sleep even if he didn't, plus leaving the 'talking heads' blaring the latest headlines before folks had their coffee was just plain rude. The other sergeant obviously didn't believe him when Harry proclaimed his innocence. He not only kept the volume low on the TV when he was in the room, he never turned it on in the morning, preferring to listen to the radio instead. In addition, he always removed his combat boots once he'd settled in for the night, moving around in his socks.

He wasn't the one disturbing the rest of the noncoms, but that didn't mean he knew the guilty party. For a moment, he contemplated turning off the highway to visit Cedar Creek Guest Ranch and try to patch up things with Ann. He kept the truck on the road, heading for town. He opted for the wiser choice of driving to his grandmother's house, grateful all the parents would have picked up their kids from the preschool. He wasn't ready to see Devon, or her mother, not when he'd made a jackass of himself. He'd learned a long time ago to control his temper and snarling at Ann Barrett because she was smart enough to figure out his secret had been one of the stupidest things he'd done in years.

He'd always gone by the rule it was better to ask forgiveness than permission, but he didn't know how to make amends, at least not yet. When he arrived at the house, he heard his grandmother's collie, Empress bark from the back porch and the remaining three puppies yap. He didn't go through the gate into the side yard since he'd be watching for doggie landmines and didn't need those on his combat boots. Instead, he went in the front door. He found his grandmother in the kitchen tearing up lettuce for a salad.

Janine O'Connell looked him up and down, the same way she had when he'd screwed up as a teenager. "It's good that Angelica Barrett has enough patience to suffer fools gladly or she'd kick your sorry backside to the curb."

"Grandma, I—"

"You're an idiot, Harold David Colter. What did your grandfather used to tell you?"

"I don't know. He lectured me a lot."

She reached for a serrated knife, placed a ripe tomato on the cutting board. "He also said it to you and Zeke when the two of you left for boot camp and whenever you were home on leave. Does that help your memory?"

He winced. "I remember now."

"What was it then?"

"Stay alive. Don't go stupid on me, boys."

She nodded. "If he comes back tonight to haunt this house and boot your tail, don't whine at me tomorrow. You deserve it."

"What did Ann tell you?"

"Nothing about you. When she came to look at Shadow, the puppy Devon wants, it was all about 'growing up' and 'putting away childish things.' I raised Angelica from the time she was three years old after her mother left. Do you honestly believe I can't see it when she's shattered to pieces?"

Wedges of tomato in the salad bowl, Janine O'Connell took on a green pepper, fiercely cleaning it. "If your grandfather doesn't administer some old-time justice, Zeke Garvey better or I'll pin his ears back when I'm a ghost walking the streets of Baker City."

Zeke guffawed and leaned against the back door enjoying the bewilderment on Colter's face. His buddy might refuse to admit the town was haunted, but his grandma knew better. Granted her husband wasn't one of the resident ghosts anymore. The mayor claimed old man O'Connell moved on to come around again after his visit with the local medium, the O'Leary. Zeke shrugged. He wasn't there yet. He wanted to look after Twila, his boys and the baby girl who smiled at him when he stood over her crib.

Harry snitched a piece of green pepper and neatly avoided the slap his grandma aimed at his hand. "Is that what's happening at the base? My room is haunted?"

"I'm not there so I don't know, but I wouldn't be surprised. When someone looks for trouble, he shouldn't be surprised if it comes calling."

"I'm home now. It's safe here and I'm not looking."

"Really? That's news to me. What did I always tell you?"

Harry didn't answer, so Zeke did. "Good or bad, whatever you do, take pride in it."

CHAPTER TWENTY-SIX

She'd spent the last two days helping Lynette Porter, the former secretary at Miner's Creek Elementary who'd joined them in Baker City enroll sixth to eighth graders. More would undoubtedly join her class in the next week, but with fifteen students, Ann was ready to start on Monday morning.

The tentative schedule contained daily reading, writing, math, science, history and P.E. classes. She'd teach the academics and since Lynette was certificated in physical education, she would cover that. The plan would take them until the end of the school year in June, eight weeks away. Over the summer, they'd add two more teachers and lay out the curriculum for the next year.

Saturday, she left her daughter with the twins and Rainy Knight, Rob laughing at the continued requests for the puppy. Once Cat heard it was a collie mix, she'd agreed it could come to Cedar Creek whenever Ann was ready for the addition and Rob had quoted what he claimed was his father's adage about 'a happy wife making for a happy life', the same thing Ann's own dad often said, and whatever Cat wanted was okay with Rob.

Heaving a sigh, Ann drove through town toward Majestyk Morgan Farm. Working in Baker City meant dealing with her father and stepmother. The lawyers hadn't reported back about the custody issue, but Ann wasn't waiting any longer. She spotted the distinctive carved wooden sign and turned into the long, sweeping paved driveway lined by white board fences, which also separated the pastures, paddocks, and outdoor arenas. Most farms used gravel to maintain their entrances, but not her father. He always said he had to 'spend money to make money' and he ran a high-class operation.

She parked in front of the large indoor arena, spotting a late model car in the paved lot. She obviously wasn't the only visitor. Hopefully, her dad would still have time to talk. She walked through the barn aisle with its concrete aisles, spotting various employees grooming horses, mucking stalls, watering, cleaning tack and working hard without immediate supervision. She grimaced. If they were being so industrious, it meant Dad was on one of his proverbial tears or else Chloe, the family accountant had come through on an inspection tour and was looking for people to fire to save money. She always wanted to cut staff to the point that one groom was doing the work of three which prompted stress, tension and arguments when their dad refused.

Ann found her father in the elaborately decorated office lined with cases of ribbons and trophies. A silver-haired man wearing what she disrespectfully thought of as a nineteen-piece dark suit sat in one of the leather chairs facing the large oak desk while her dad stood behind it. She nodded a greeting to the two. "Hey, Dad. I need to talk to you. Shall I hang out with the horses a while?"

"Not necessary." Frank Madison folded his arms, leaning against the desk, his gaze narrowing on the visitor. "Eli said what he needed to say. He's leaving."

"I'll repeat it for your daughter. Expect Senator Hawke to do something about that school of yours unless Dick O'Connell stops his investigation into your first wife's disappearance."

"Tell Tex Hawke there's a lot of voters in this town." Ann kept her tone even and didn't raise her voice. "They asked Dad for a school and they have relatives around the county. Dad's family still has plenty of influence in Liberty Valley. They didn't all move to the Spokane area. If the Senator wants to stay in the other Washington with his lick-spittle friends, he'll watch his backside, or we'll find someone honest to run against him in the next election."

"It's not wise to threaten me, little girl."

"I'm not a little girl anymore." Stiffening her spine, she adopted the stance she used at the Army base, allowing menace to edge her tone. "You ought to remember soldiers like me bring America's longest war home with them. Now, get out."

"You heard her." Frank jerked his head toward the door. "Go and don't come back."

Eli Roberts stood, glaring at them once more before he stalked to the door. "You haven't heard the last of this."

"What part of 'hell, no' don't you understand? I want to know what happened to Lucy and so does everyone else in town." Frank took a step forward and Eli scuttled away.

Ann stared after the man, wondering who he reminded her of, then decided it wasn't important. It'd come to her later. She focused on her father. "That was interesting. Why does it bother the Senator if Dick tries to find my mother?"

"I don't know." Frank crossed to the door, glancing into the wide aisleway obviously checking to see if the campaign manager was really gone. "I'll call Dick and see if he's made any progress, or if he needs something more from me. What's on your mind, honey?"

Ann took a deep breath, trying to appear totally calm. "Custody of Devon."

"What are you talking about?" Concern crept across his features, landing in the leaf-green eyes. "Annie, are you all right? Wars take their tolls and you've been in combat three times. Maybe you need to talk to someone."

"I did. Two lawyers and nobody's taking my daughter away from me."

"Is Will giving you grief?" Frank narrowed his eyes. "He'd better not be, not after walking away from Devon while you were in Afghanistan."

"Dad, stop it. Just stop." Ann took an angry step forward. "I know what you and Ginger are planning. You're not getting Devon. She's my daughter and I'm home now."

"Whoa. Hold up there." He raised his hand. "I don't know what you're talking about. Jack babbled some nonsense when he was here a few days ago and his mother set him straight. We're both glad you came home alive. We did what was needful when you were gone. We took care of Devon for you. We love the two of you very much. If you need a babysitter, we're here, but we're done raising kids."

"I don't get it." Ann lifted her chin, struggling not to cry. "Stop treating me like I've gone crazy. Barb and Chloe told me your plans to take Devon away from me."

"Oh, for God's sake."

When he strode to her and pulled her into a warm hug, Ann stiffened. "What's going on?"

"Your sisters are still jealous because you stayed with me and Ginger when they left home."

"What? Are you serious?" Ann pulled back to stare into his face. "I was eight when Chloe went off to college and Barb had left for the University of Washington two years earlier. Where did they expect me to go? Foster care?"

"I didn't say it was logical." Frank stroked her hair. "I said they're acting out as if they're teenagers, not 41 and 43 years old. I can't ground them or send them to their rooms until they grow up."

"And you and Ginger really aren't seeing a lawyer or suing to get custody of Devon?"

"We haven't and we're not planning on it. She's your kid and your problem. You can call or stop by if you and Harry want advice, but other than that, you're on your own."

Ann clung tightly to him, burying her face against the plaid material of his shirt and let the tears come. He rocked her as if she were still Devon's age, not a grown woman. Between sobs, she choked out the words, "I hate them."

"Honey, pity them. They're not worth the energy it takes to hate them."

"You're not firing either of them, are you? Barb will keep managing your real estate holdings and Chloe will continue being your accountant, won't she?"

"That's right."

"Why? I don't understand."

"They're my daughters too and I love them."

"And you're not angry with them?"

"I didn't say that."

"And you're also not telling the complete truth, Frank." Ginger spoke behind them. "It's a case of 'keep your friends close and your enemies closer.' Ann, you've seen the *Godfather* movies. You know that."

"I've never watched them." Ann turned her head and glanced at her stepmother. "I don't like movies where animals die."

"I should have remembered that. You were always the tenderhearted one." Ginger heaved a dramatic sigh and shook her head. "I also ought to have realized those two were out to make trouble, but I didn't think of it."

"I'm sorry I didn't come to you sooner."

"That's probably my fault." Ginger came across the room, all cool competence in ironed jeans and a crisp western blouse, lace-up riding boots shiny, her tone totally composed. "I'm not the touchy-feely type and it's hard for me to show my emotions. I'm crazy about you, Ann and I adore Devon. I'm sure I'll love Harry when I get to know him better."

Ann blinked, amazed. "It'd be easier to believe that if you didn't sound like one of those cops on an old black and white TV show. Just the facts, ma'am, just the facts."

"I already said I'm not sentimental."

"And you also always said you wanted to be paid for babysitting Devon when I was studying for my master's degree."

"I never gave you a printed bill, Ann, and that was to motivate Will to 'man up' and look out for his kid."

"Well, it didn't work."

"No. I should have let your father knock him into next week, but Will is such a whiner, I figured Frank would end up in jail."

Ann laughed, shaking her head. She hugged her father once more, then stepped back and hugged her stepmother. Ginger stood stiffly in the embrace before she finally patted Ann's shoulder. "You may as well get used to affection, Mother. It's time for both of us to act like functional adults."

"You never called me that before." Tears shimmered in Ginger's hazel eyes. "Why now?"

"You married Dad twenty-six years ago. It's about time, don't you think?"

"I suppose so."

Ann nearly told the older woman that her enthusiasm was

overwhelming and curbed the impulse. Ginger would need time to accept changes to the status quo. They all would. "So, do you want to bring Devon home tomorrow after church? She's attending school in Baker City now and if she stays overnight, you could drop her there on Monday morning."

"I'd like that," Ginger said. "Do you and Harry have plans for tomorrow afternoon?"

Ann shook her head. "We argued when my orders were cancelled. No orders, no money. I talked to Smitty O'Sullivan and I start teaching in Baker City on Monday."

"Sounds like you have everything under control." Frank crossed to the coffee station in the corner, filled three cups and placed the mugs on top of the desk. "What about Harry? What did he say when you found out about your orders?"

"That's over and done with, Dad. We're taking a break. I know you liked him. I'm sorry."

Her father and Ginger shared a look, before she said, "Ann, don't let your pride ruin a good relationship. Cut him some slack and he'll do the same for you."

"I would but this was his decision." Ann pretended adding cream to the coffee required all her attention. "I'm taking his grandmother to lunch tomorrow so we can talk about the puppy she wants to give Devon."

Frank chuckled. "We'll be hearing more about that when she's here."

"Indubitably," Ann agreed.

"And your sisters will have fits and fall in them when she brings it here to visit. They'll decide it's one more way we favor her over the rest of the grandkids." Ginger sounded utterly pleased by the idea. "What all will she need for it? Make a list and I'll take her shopping at one of those big discount pet stores in Everett."

"Seriously?" Ann eyed her stepmother. "I don't know about Devon, but I'd love it. I'm happy to chip in on the cost but those places still freak me out. Too many people, too much noise and definitely too much garbage that could be bombs."

Another long look and Ginger said gently, "Then leave the shopping to us, Angelica."

It took all Ann's strength to park in front of Janine O'Connell's house the next morning before church. Devon hurried up the brick walk ahead of Ann. "We'll see Harry, Mama, and I'll show you my puppy again."

Janine opened the door in time to hear the first comment. "I'm sorry, Devon. Harry's gone to the farm."

"Why didn't he take us?" Devon looked at Ann. "How come he's by himself?"

Ann dropped to one knee and cuddled her daughter. "I told you, honey. Mama has a new job. I'm teaching school for big kids and Harry's still working at the Army base."

"Is that what the two of you argued about?" Janine asked.

"No. It was something far more important. If an apology would solve it, believe me I'd offer him one, but he's really upset."

"I know and he needs to work through it on his own." Janine ushered Devon inside. "Go get Shadow, sweetie, and bring him here to see your mom." She waited till the child was out of earshot. "Devon might help resolve it. Sometimes children bridge distances. Harry really cares for her."

"I know." Ann tried to smile. "We're working out the puppy issue. We'll talk about it more at lunch, but do you know where she can learn to train Shadow?"

"Of course. I'll help you arrange for obedience classes. The last thing you need is a spoiled puppy that's going to grow into a sixty-pound dog. Don't worry. Harold never bears a grudge. He'll get over this."

"I hope you're right."

Sunday afternoon, Harry pulled into the driveway at Cedar Creek Guest Ranch, heading past the row of cabins where Ann and Margo lived. He drove toward the corral and the barn behind it. His grandmother allowed him to stay in her guestroom Friday night, but the constant banging of pots and pans in the kitchen, loud music pouring from the stereo, lights flashing on and off, Empress and her puppies barking for hours infuriated Janine and she told him to take his ghosts and go to the ranch. If he got tired of dealing with them, he should visit Cat O'Leary McTavish and her husband, Rob Hendrickson, and learn how to appease them.

Harry had followed his grandmother's orders, but there was even more racket in the two-story farmhouse. He constantly heard someone slamming doors and stomping around upstairs. When he checked, nobody was there. Yet, as soon as he went back to the main floor, noises recommenced on the second floor. Again, he didn't find anyone trespassing, but raucous rap music from the stereo in the living room interrupted the investigation.

When he went to bed shortly after midnight, someone turned the lights on, first in the master bedroom, then in the hall and throughout the entire downstairs. He spent most of the night dealing with them. He gave up the battle, dozing in the recliner in front of the TV until someone knocked on either the back or the front doors, banging until he went to answer discovering no one waited on the porches.

He parked in the lot in front of the barn, then sat in the driver's seat, debating the decision to talk to Rob Hendrickson. This ranked up there as one of the stupidest things he'd ever done, Harry thought, either that or it had to be one of the craziest. What was he supposed to say? *There's a dead person in my home making noise and I want him or her to stop.*

When he walked into the barn, he spotted a tall, dark-haired man about his own age pushing a wheelbarrow down the barn aisle and parceling out hay to the horses. "Hello, are you Rob? I'm Harry Colter. My grandmother, Janine O'Connell suggested I see you."

"About what?" Rob dropped a flake of hay into the next stall. "The soldier tailing you?" He glanced past Harry when grain buckets rattled, and one rolled down the aisle. "Fella, if you make a mess in my barn, you're damned well cleaning it up."

"You mean I am being haunted?"

"That's why you're here isn't it, Colter?"

"I guess so. Somebody is raising hell and putting props under it wherever I am. It gets old in a hurry."

"Okay, what does he want?"

"I have no idea. That's why I came here to see you or Cat O'Leary."

"My wife and daughters are napping and we're not waking them." Rob moved further down the barn aisle toward the rolling feed buckets. "Start talking, Sergeant Garvey. What's got you up in arms? What's Colter done?"

Her classes took up most of the next week and she didn't see Harry, although he was a constant topic in Devon's conversation whenever she wasn't playing with Aslan or looking after Shadow. To Ann's surprise, she didn't have as much trouble returning to teaching as much as she'd anticipated. True most of the kids called her Sarge or Sergeant Barrett, but they treated her with respect.

Thursday afternoon, Ann leaned back in her chair and studied the classroom. The students were working on their first extended response reading test and she had an odd feeling that things weren't progressing as well as she'd hoped. The bell rang and she stood. "Put your papers on my desk. Have a good night. I'll see you tomorrow."

The students were gone in short order and she reached for the tests, flipping through the pages as she scanned their written answers. No, she thought sickly. Harry couldn't have been right with his accusations, could he? Yet the proof was in these pages. So many of the middle-schoolers hadn't read all the questions and their responses didn't make much sense.

Maybe there hadn't been enough time. She'd provide them with an additional hour tomorrow during the time set aside for writing and have them take turns reading aloud as they started their new fiction project with *To Kill A Mockingbird* by Harper Lee. That would show if there was a problem.

By the middle of the next week, her hypothesis had been proven correct. Out of all her students, only a small percentage could read at their grade level. On Wednesday, Ann gathered up her notes and headed downstairs to the janitor's closet to find Smitty O'Sullivan. Something was going to change, and she wasn't the kind of person to say the kids would give up their extracurricular activities like sports until they could pass her class. That wasn't her style especially when it appeared to be the system's fault.

"Smitty, do you have a minute?" Ann asked from the doorway. "Make that several. I have to talk to you."

"If you're quitting, I don't want to hear it."

"Quitting?" Ann tossed her head. "Why would I do that? I'm enjoying being back in the classroom. We've got a serious problem. Most of my students have reading problems."

"So?" Smitty continued collecting cleaning products, flicking a sideways glance in her direction. "What else is new? That's a fact of life, Ann. It's not a surprise."

CHAPTER TWENTY-SEVEN

Ann stalked further into the supply closet, advancing on him. "I don't believe this. You mean you know these kids aren't making it and you're okay with it? They can barely read! How are they going to get jobs? How will they take care of themselves?"

"If you ask them, most aren't concerned with the future. Their brains won't be fully developed until they're in their twenties and nothing interferes with 'screen time', Ann. According to recent studies, the average teen spends more hours in front of the TV and with their electronic toys than on any other activity except sleep. That includes school. National statistics show 32 million Americans can't read and a recent survey revealed 25 percent of adults that can admitted they didn't read a book last year."

"Is that all?" Ann heaved a sigh, shaking her head. "I haven't stayed current with any of this. I was too busy staying alive the past few years."

"At least, the state is finally paying more per student than before and we're no longer in the bottom ten states in the country, but other states budget much more to educate their kids than we do here in Washington State. If you were willing to move to the East Coast, your salary would be a lot higher."

"Now, I feel really stupid. When I couldn't get a job, I blamed myself instead of looking at the bigger picture."

"Shall I keep going, Ann? I haven't even started on the standardized reading, writing and math test scores in Lake Maynard. Most of the middle and high school kids failed the assessments last year and graduation rates in the local area are far below the state average. That district is in academic jeopardy. It's no wonder so many parents want their kids in this school."

"You know the facts and figures, Smitty. What I want to know is what we're going to do about it. We're on the ground floor here. We can make a difference."

"And we will. What do you want to do? I'll back you and Margo a hundred percent."

"I need to go back to the basics and start by teaching reading strategies," Ann said slowly. "I've got a half-dozen eighth graders with problems. They're not going to make it next year at any high school, not just the one in Lake Maynard."

"Well, there is one good thing about being at war and having an all-volunteer military. The kids can enlist in four years."

"Not an option." Ann scowled at him, annoyed at the sarcasm. "My students go to college. They're improving their reading skills until they're at grade level."

"It isn't just the kids," Smitty said. "There's a large problem with illiterate adults in our community." He paused. "What if you volunteer to teach a class with the Community Education folks? The salary's minimal but it'd cover expenses. If the kids saw adults conquering their problems, they might try harder."

Ann remembered Harry. Would he come to reading classes? Probably not. He had far too much pride. "How do we know if we'd get any response?"

"We don't till we try." Smitty pulled out his cell phone. "Shall I make some calls? Ann, don't think this is just a Baker City problem. It's nationwide."

"Go for it. If we can even help one person, that'll be payment enough. You may hear some complaints, but I've also started assigning book reports and reading aloud in my class. We'll be acting out plays. Somewhere, I'll get job applications and teach the kids to fill them out."

"I'll get those," Smitty promised. "I'll also arrange for Herman MacGillicudy to come teach them about checking and saving accounts."

"Why him? He's not real popular in town now."

"He claims he wants to make amends. Let's have him here and he can put his mouth where he wants everyone's money."

Ann laughed, shaking her head. "You and Ginger have more in common than you think. She's always quoting that line about 'keep your friends close and your enemies closer.' Did Dad tell you about Eli Roberts and Senator Hawke threatening to shut down the school?"

"He did, but we're not worried. They'll be more concerned if we go to Eli's daughter."

"What does she have to do with anything?"

"Tiffany's an investigative TV reporter for a cable news show. Looking into a cold missing person case would boost her ratings."

"Isn't she loyal to her dad?"

"Not any more than the Senator's daughters are to him. No worries, Ann. We've always known the Senator's the kind of politician who doesn't stay bought, but he makes enemies wherever he goes. He can't even get along with Senator Killian from the east end of Liberty Valley and the two of them are from the same party."

"The enemy of my enemy is my friend."

"Exactly. There's a lot to be said for a classical education."

Ann nodded. "My students always learn that."

"Good." Smitty glanced past her at the sound of footsteps. "My crew is here, and I've got to get to work. Let me know what else you need. You're taking on more responsibilities with those evening classes."

"It'll work. I'll make sure of that."

On Wednesdays, she dropped Shadow at Janine's in the morning and Devon went there after school to take obedience classes with the puppy. So far, the training provided by a local teen proved successful. Ten-week-old Shadow had begun to learn how to heel on a leash, sit when Devon stopped and come when he was called.

Ann parked in front of the preschool, spotting Harry's pickup in the driveway. Did she want to see him? Of course, she did. She hadn't done anything wrong. He was the one who'd turned against her. She switched off the motor and headed up the walk to the front porch. She tapped on the door and entered the living-room.

"Mama, Mama!" Devon called, coming toward her, pulling him after her. "Harry's home. See."

Ann saw him, all right. She couldn't stop staring at him. His black hair was still perfectly trimmed. His camouflage fatigues looked sharp, but his face showed strain and his eyes were tired. "Hello, Harry."

He smiled, but there wasn't any warmth in his gaze. He gently freed his hand from the little girl's grip. "Go find your puppy, honey. Time to go home."

"You come too," Devon ordered. "We can get a pizza at the mercantile. I'll help Mama cook it."

"Not tonight, D.J."

"How come?" Devon demanded. "We want you."

"Get Shadow," Ann said. "Tell Janine goodbye. We have to go."

"Mama, I want Harry."

Ann sighed. "I'm sorry, Devon. He says he can't come tonight. There'll be another time."

"Really? Will he come next time?" Devon eyed both of them.

"Next time." Ann glared at him when he didn't speak. How could he be so cruel to her child? She waited till Devon left the room before she stalked toward him. "You have no business being mean to my kid. For some reason, she loves you even when you're acting like a complete and total jackass."

"I love her too," Harry said quietly. "Most people aren't like you, Barrett. They can't turn off their emotions like a water faucet."

For an instant, shock held Ann still. Was that what he thought? That because she didn't whine and cry, she didn't care? Her control snapped. She raised her hand and swung on him!

He caught her wrist before the slap connected. He yanked her against him. His mouth seized hers in a kiss that was as passionate as it was possessive. When he lifted his head, Ann glowered up at him. "What was that supposed to prove?"

"I still want you. No reason we can't have that affair you promised once."

Ann tore free. "Except I have too much pride for something so shoddy with a real asshat."

She spun away and went in search of Janine. There was no way that Devon would return to the preschool when he was here. The two of them were in the kitchen, Janine helping Devon buckle on Shadow's harness. Ann smoothed her daughter's dark curls. "Go tell Harry goodbye, sweetie. We have to go."

"I'll see you Friday after school." Devon hugged Janine and hurried from the room, leading her tri-colored collie puppy. "We're going, Harry."

Ann lifted her chin and deliberately met Janine's gaze. "Harry obviously needs space right now."

"He's in denial." Janine shook her head. "He saw Rob Hendrickson and learned that Zeke Garvey is here, but ghosts aren't easy for people to accept. I'm sure you're still adjusting to being at Mrs. O'Sullivan's school."

"I haven't seen anything strange in my room. Are you saying she'll be haunting me?"

"I don't think you'll be the one with problems with the local haunts." Faint amusement trickled into the older woman's gaze. "They're having too much fun harassing my grandson. When he comes to peace with them and you, he'll be able to get some sleep."

Once they were in the car and headed home, Ann asked, "How would you like to visit your daddy and your Gramma Vanessa and your Grampa Phil this weekend?"

"I want to see Harry."

"No, not anymore, Devon. He's too busy."

"No more Harry?"

"That's right, honey. No more Harry. Not for either one of us."

Devon's wail of hurt and rage brought tears to Ann's eyes. But it was better this way. Obviously, he didn't care about either one of them. It was pointless to hope for some sort of reconciliation.

The next week was all the evidence she needed of that. Harry made no attempt to contact her. Devon sulked all the way to Phil and Vanessa's on Saturday morning even when they let her bring Shadow on the visit. However, their spoiling and love seemed to be healing some of the child's hurt.

Ann sighed as she headed for the car on the warm May afternoon. She was tired but her hard work was beginning to make a difference.

She frowned as she spotted Derek Waller leaning against her car. "What are you doing here? Aren't you the guy in charge at Fort Bronson?"

"That's me, but I'm visiting to see how you're really doing. Colonel Williams said you'd called and told him you had a 'come to Jesus' meeting with your dad and stepmom and they backed off on the custody issue."

"It wasn't so much 'backing off' as clearing the air," Ann said. "My older sisters were playing 'let's you and him fight' games and we adults decided not to let them instigate trouble between us."

"Have you decided what you'll do to them?"

"At the moment, I'm ignoring the pair of them because kicking their fat butts is probably inappropriate and something a teacher shouldn't do when she ought to set a good example for her students."

"Yeah, well if you get sick of being perfect and need an alibi, let me know. I've got your back." He paused, then reached in his pocket and found a cigarette. "Colter is going through hell. He cares about you and Devon a lot. It really hurt him when you walked out of the office and taking the kid away from his grandmother's when he was there was the last straw, especially when she read him the riot act."

"It's what he wanted. He told me to get out of his life. I shouldn't have let Devon do puppy obedience when he was there, but I didn't realize his hatred would carry over to her."

"Damn it, Ann! Will you just listen? He doesn't hate you. He just has to step up and take a risk somewhere other than in combat."

Ann unlocked the car and dropped her school bag with the papers she needed to grade on the seat. She planted her hands on her hips. "I don't need to hear that from you, Waller. I need to hear it from him. Now, if you're going to do his talking, that's fine. But, don't expect me to be listening. I've got to go pick up Devon, take her and Shadow to my dad's and then I have an illiteracy class starting tonight. You'd better move, Derek. I'm leaving."

"Williams said something about that. He says Margo Endicott is after the business community to reopen the town library and she plans to start literature circles for the locals. Are you teaching the adult literacy class?"

"Of course. Giving back to the community is what teachers do along with paying for classroom supplies out of their wages." She slid into the driver's seat. Why couldn't Harry do his own courting? Why did he have to be so stubborn? Had Harry even known what Derek intended?

Anger still bubbled inside her when she arrived at Majestyk Morgan Farm, parking near the house. She helped Devon unfasten Shadow from his special car harness and take the puppy out of the car. The little girl immediately took him over to the grass to piddle so he wouldn't disgrace himself inside on the hardwood floors. Then, they headed for the back porch and the kitchen door.

Ginger hugged the child and petted the little collie mix who wagged his plumed tail and licked her hand. "Come in. I have cookies for both of you. Ann, your sisters are here and we're planning your wedding."

"What wedding?" Devon cocked her head to the side. "Mama, are we getting married?"

"Not today or tomorrow, but some day when Mr. Right comes along." Ann glared at her stepmother. "It'll be a while, honey."

"When it does, will I get to wear my frou-frou princess dress and throw rose petals like I'm going to do for Auntie Margo?"

"Sounds like a winner to me." Ann removed her daughter's backpack. "Be patient. It's going to take time."

"That's not what Ginger says." Barbara finished her coffee and stood, tall and professional in her navy blazer, pinstriped blouse and dark blue slacks. "She wanted to show us the invitations, so you don't need to keep your plans a secret from us. We don't care what you do this summer, but Reid and I are taking the boys to Hawaii to Chloe's timeshare when she has the condo in July."

"Really?" Ann shot another glare at her stepmother who bustled around the room, taking doggie cookies out of the special jar she kept for Shadow. "I hadn't even thought of how—"

"Oh, I broke the news to the girls, Angelica." With the puppy settled on his favorite rug, Ginger filled a glass with milk for Devon. "No more secrets in this family. I know you were concerned and didn't want hurt feelings because your big sisters won't be in the wedding party. I told you they'd understand perfectly that you want your friends who went to war with you to be your attendants. They kept you alive there so you could come home to us. The girls are just upset because your dad and I are paying for your wedding this time and we all know how they feel about money."

"What the hell?" Ann fisted her hands on her hips. "Mother, you know I've paid my way since I was a kid. When I get married—"

"Your dad and I paid for Barbie's and Chloe's weddings and it broke my heart when you eloped with Will and did me out of a party, Angelica." Ginger put the glass on the table in front of Devon, following up with three homemade chocolate chip cookies on a saucer. "Now, your big sisters can go to Hawaii, but I expect them home in time to attend the wedding in August and for them, their husbands and children to be dressed appropriately for the pictures."

"I haven't even had time to process this," Chloe said, narrowing blue eyes. A briefcase on the chair next to hers, she'd dressed for success like Barbara. "I need to talk to Kurt about his plans."

"Unless he intends to be the sole support of his family, he'll be here with you and your children and all of you will use your company manners and behave suitably, befitting the Madisons and your father's standing in Baker City."

Silence filled the room while Barbara and Chloe gaped at their stepmother, then looked at Ann before their attention reverted to Ginger again who just smiled sweetly at them. In less than five minutes, her sisters were out the door leaving Ann alone with her stepmom, Devon and the dog. "Do you want to tell me what you were thinking, Mother? You know full well that Harry and I argued, and we haven't reconciled."

"You have till August, Mama."

"Why do I think you two are in cahoots?"

"I don't know what 'cahoots' means, Mama, but me and Gramma decided you're too nice and you wouldn't yell at your sisters, so she'd do it, 'cause she isn't nice to mean people. I just didn't know it'd be about the wedding. Me, Gramma and Grandma Nessy are going shopping with Harry's gramma Janine to buy stuff for it. Sam and Sophie are coming with their grandma. Can they have princess dresses too?"

"I guess so, but I did have a plan." Ann snitched a cookie off Devon's plate. "I was never speaking to them again."

Devon and Ginger exchanged a look before the little girl heaved a huge sigh. "Mama, that doesn't work with bullies. Auntie Margo says you gotta kick their butts to the curb, so they go out with the trash."

"I'm going back to school."

"Not until you have cookies and coffee with us. If you leave now, your dad and brother will wipe out the rest of the box I bought, and you won't get any of Twila Garvey's goodies."

Ann drew out a chair and sat down at the kitchen table. "Okay, but you and my daughter are totally incorrigible and next time, I get to tell my sisters where to go and it won't be Hawaii."

"Where will it be?" Devon asked.

"Someplace hot that rhymes with swell and it's not Afghanistan." Ginger filled a mug with coffee and passed it to Ann. "Your mama may not be wearing her uniform, but she's still a brave soldier and talks like one."

"You'll be in big trouble with Harry's gramma again." Devon took a swallow of milk. "She'll make you pull weeds in the flowerbeds for saying bad words 'cause he already had to pick up all the cigarette butts in the parking lot."

"Thanks for the warning." Ann glanced around the kitchen, feeling more at home than ever before. She eyed Ginger. "I appreciate you standing up for me even if it's not the way I'd do it."

"It's what mothers do." Ginger sat down across from her. "Janine helped design the invitations. Do you want to see them?"

"Of course, I do."

When she arrived at the school, Ann unlocked the doors and headed upstairs to her classroom. She began to arrange books and paperwork on the center table. She turned as the door opened, ready to greet her first student. Her polite smile froze as Harry entered. "What are you doing here?"

He gently closed the door. "Is this the adult reading class?"

Unable to speak, she nodded. Was he serious? She eyed his broad shoulders revealed by the thin cotton shirt he wore and the faded jeans that encased his long legs. "Why are you here?"

"I came for class. That is if you'll teach somebody who's both bigger and dumber, Angel."

Ann choked back a sob. "There's nothing dumb about you, Colter."

She considered that for a moment, then added, "Well except your awful pride. At times, it totally pisses me off."

He started toward her and Ann met him halfway. His arms folded her close and he murmured apologies against her hair. "I do love you, Angel."

"I love you too," Ann pressed her cheek against his chest. "I didn't stop just because you act like an idiot sometimes."

"We're getting married, Angel. Are you going to make me wait till I can read the marriage license to you?"

"No, but you have to ask, not tell me even if your grandmother and my stepmother are already arranging the wedding." Ann pushed away from him and glared up into his chiseled features. "You're not learning to read here. If this is something you really want to do, I'll teach you in private, starting tonight."

He lowered his head and his mouth brushed hers. "Why don't you want me here? I gave you a lot of crap when you confronted me."

"You did, but reading is something you have to want, Harry. You don't have to do it for me. I love you just the way you are, a guy who can do everything else under the sun."

He framed her face with calloused hands. "I don't mind coming here."

"I mind." Ann locked her arms around his neck. "And sooner or later, you will. It's that pride of yours. You'll resent it if folks know your secret. Besides, I can't look at you without wanting to fall in your arms. This way it'll work for both of us."

"What about your other students? Are you considering their pride?"

"It's all set up. I phoned each of them when they registered and they get a half-hour of my time." She looked at the clock. "I'll walk you out to the parking lot. We can't embarrass them."

"Do I get to kiss you later?"

"You can even kiss me in the parking lot." Laughing, she headed outside with him to his truck. "So, are you scared of the ghosts in Baker City?"

"No, Zeke was a pain in the backside when he was alive. I shouldn't have expected him to change when he died."

Amused, she pressed close, sliding her arms around his neck. His fierce kiss robbed her of all rational thought, and she surrendered to the fiery claim. She leaned against his muscular body when he lifted his head. "I really love you, Harry Colter."

"I love you too, Angel." His mouth claimed hers in a kiss that set her emotions and nerves on fire.

"Everyone's going to say they told us so."

"Together, we can handle it."

He was right, Ann thought as his lips closed over hers again. Together, they could handle whatever the world threw at them and they would.

THE END

Coming Soon from Satin Romance!
A Man's World
Liberty Valley Series, Book 1

Don't miss out on your next favorite book!

Join the Satin Romance mailing list
www.satinromance.com/mail.html

THANK YOU FOR READING

Did you enjoy this book?

We invite you to leave a review at your favorite book site, such as Goodreads, Amazon, Barnes & Noble, etc.

DID YOU KNOW THAT LEAVING A REVIEW...

- Helps other readers find books they may enjoy.
- Gives you a chance to let your voice be heard.
- Gives authors recognition for their hard work.
- Doesn't have to be long. A sentence or two about why you liked the book will do.

ABOUT THE AUTHOR

Josie Malone lives and works at her family's riding stable in Washington State. She's taught children to ride and know about horses for so long that she often discovers she's taught three generations of their families. Her life experiences span adventures from dealing cards in a casino, attending graduate school to get her Master's in Teaching degree, being a substitute teacher, and serving in the Army Reserve all leading to her second career as a published author.

Contact Josie at:
josiemaloneauthor@outlook.com

Find her on Online at:
www.josiemalone.com
www.facebook.com/JosieMaloneAuthor

ALSO BY JOSIE MALONE

Baker City Hearts & Haunts

My Sweet Haunt

www.ingramcontent.com/pod-product-compliance
Lightning Source LLC
Chambersburg PA
CBHW031110030726
47496CB00002BA/481